A night in with
Grace Kelly
BY LUCY   HOLLIDAY

Lucy Holliday's first major work, a four-line poem called
'The Postman is Very Good', was completed shortly before
her fifth birthday. It was such an enjoyable experience that
she has wanted to be a writer ever since. *A Night in with
Audrey Hepburn* was her first novel.

Lucy is married with a daughter and she lives in Wimbledon.

Also by Lucy Holliday

A night in with Grace Kelly

BY LUCY HOLLIDAY

HARPER

Harper
An imprint of HarperCollins*Publishers,*
The News Building,
1 London Bridge Street,
London SE1 9GF

www.harpercollins.co.uk

A paperback original 2017

1

Copyright © Angela Woolfe writing as Lucy Holliday 2017

Lucy Holliday asserts the moral right to be identified as the author of this work

A catalogue record for this book is available from the British Library

ISBN: 978-0-00-758383-6

Typeset in Birka by Palimpsest Book Production Ltd, Falkirk, Stirlingshire

Printed and bound in the United States of America by LSC Communications

Find out more about HarperCollins and the environment at
www.harpercollins.co.uk/green

ACKNOWLEDGEMENTS

With colossal thanks to Kate Bradley, Charlotte Ledger, Charlotte Brabbin and all the fantastic team at HarperFiction. Thanks also to Clare Alexander, to my amazing husband, Josh, and my even more amazing daughter, Lara.

Chapter 1

Minimalism. That's the look I'll have to say I was going for.

Clean lines, a sense of space, the total absence of clutter.

All of which are actually perfectly sensible ways to keep your living space, especially if, like me, you're a designer by profession. It's just that in my particular case, the sense of space and total absence of clutter in this, my brand-new flat, are less to do with any creative sensibility and more because of the fact that my last flat was roughly the size of a broom cupboard. So I barely own any furniture. The handful of furnishings I *do* own, which used to make the old place feel over-stuffed and faintly claustrophobic, barely even make a dent here in the new one.

And, to be honest, it's not the worst thing in the world to pretend that all this empty space is a Design Statement rather than a mundane necessity. In half an hour's time my investor, Ben, who's just flown into London for a couple of days, is dropping round for a meeting. Bringing his BFF Elvira with him.

Elvira being Elvira Roberts-Hoare: ex-model, bohemian

aristocrat, Ben's chief talent scout and also, as of yesterday, my brand-new landlord.

I mean, her own flat, just a short distance away in South Kensington, is practically a museum to her incredible vintage fashion archive, with Ferragamo shoes displayed in a custom-made Perspex sideboard and Alexander McQueen scarves draped artfully over the soft furnishings. I know this not because I've ever been invited, obviously, but because I saw it in all its glory in a recent issue of *Elle Decor* magazine. My own attempts at turning this gorgeous flat into something worthy of *Elle Decor* are being seriously hampered by the fact that I don't have an incredible vintage fashion archive to display like artwork. And, even if I did, it would be let down by my crappy and – as I've already said – paltry furnishings: a futon, an IKEA wardrobe, a glass coffee table and – last but absolutely not least – a huge and ancient Chesterfield sofa upholstered in apricot-coloured rose fabric and smelling of damp dog.

Actually, now that I look at it, the mere presence of the Chesterfield, in all its chintzy, overblown glory, is a bit of a strike against my claims that I'm deliberately styling this place in a minimalist fashion.

Though I'm also being hamstrung by the fact that my sister Cass showed up ten minutes ago and is somehow, in her own inimitable way, cluttering up the place. Handbag slung on the floor, tea sloshing out of her mug, and just generally sort of filling the room up with *herself*.

'Oh, for *fuck's sake!*' she's shrieking now, peering down at her phone, and splashing yet more tea on the floor beside

2

her. 'Zoltan's ex has been speaking to the *Mirror*. It's all over their website.'

This, by the way, is the latest in the long-running series of Massive Dramas that make up Cass's life. A week ago, my little sister was outed for the three-month-long affair she's been having with a Premiership footballer. A *married* Premiership footballer, to be more precise. And while *I* may be wearily familiar with her nasty little habit of getting involved with married men, this particular married man's wife was not. The whole thing came as such a horrible shock to the poor woman, in fact, that she bodily threw her cheating scumbag of a husband out of their home and went on a rant on Mumsnet – a rant that was then picked up by the *Daily Mail* . . . The rest, as they say, is history.

It's even made its sordid way into this week's *OK!* magazine, a copy of which Cass brandished at me, with something disturbingly close to triumph, when she showed up at my door. Come to think of it, I'm pretty sure that triumphantly brandishing a copy of *OK!* was the reason she showed up at my door in the first place. It certainly wasn't to help me get my flat ready for my impending visitors.

'I don't know if it's all that fair, Cass,' I say, 'for you to be the one talking about having no shame.'

Though frankly I don't know why I bother continuing to express my disapproval over Cass's extramarital shenanigans. It's not like she's paid the slightest bit of attention to me at any other time in the last three years. Her relationship with Zoltan – a Charlton Athletic defender and member of Bulgaria's national team – is coming hot on the heels of her last married boyfriend, Vile Dave. (I called him Vile Dave, by the way, in my head; it wasn't like that was actually his name, or anything.)

And, as I expected, she ignores me.

'Isn't there anyone I can complain to?' she asks, dramatically. 'Some sort of – I don't know – union, or something?'

'A union for women who've been sleeping with other women's husbands?'

'No!' she says. 'I meant someone to complain to about the constant press intrusion!' Then she thinks about this for a moment. '*Is* there a union for women who've been sleeping with other women's husbands, though? Because even if my situation is a *bit* unusual, me being a celebrity, and all that . . . if there was somewhere I could get some expert advice . . .?'

My sister (half-sister, if we're being really specific, and on occasions like this, I have to say, I find myself emphasizing the *half* part) has her own reality TV show, *Considering Cassidy*. Hence her 'celebrity' status. Hence, I guess, the reason she's made it into a quarter-page snippet in the *OK!* that's now lying on my coffee table, with Prince Albert of Monaco and his lovely blonde wife Charlene smiling rather fixedly at me from the cover.

'I honestly don't think there's a union for that, Cass,' I say, firmly. 'Now, look, if you don't mind, lovely though it is for you to have dropped round to see my new flat . . .'

'Oh, well *done*, Libby,' she pouts, with a swish of her hair and another swill of her tea everywhere. 'Nice way to drop your swanky new Notting Hill pad into the conversation.'

'I wasn't doing anything of the sort! Besides, it's not *my swanky new Notting Hill pad.*' I feel the need to point this out to Cass, partly because it all still feels a bit surreal to me myself. 'I'm only living here because I'm renting the studio below.'

And because, despite the *extremely* hefty discount Elvira Roberts-Hoare is giving me on the rent of the ground-floor studio that Ben wanted me to start working out of – the posh address and upmarket surroundings making it ideal to use as a showroom – I still can't afford to pay that *and* to rent somewhere else to actually live in as well.

But still, Cass is right about one thing. This side street, a little to the north of Notting Hill, is a hell of a lot swankier than anywhere else I've ever lived. And this flat is a hell of a lot swankier, too: a bit jumbled-up, with the kitchen, bathroom and bedroom crammed up on the top floor and this, the living room, here in the middle, but I'm never going to complain about that. I'm living here, in a particularly gorgeous bit of Zone One, pretty much for free. Sure, I have no security on the place, and Elvira can throw me out tomorrow if she decides to find a new, proper tenant, but it's worth it for the sheer joy of living somewhere – anywhere – that doesn't rumble every time a tube train passes underneath it and doesn't have eye-wateringly pungent aromas wafting up from the takeaways below.

For the sheer joy of living and working somewhere this . . . *fabulous.*

'You know, I had a personal trainer that worked in a private gym on this same road a couple of years ago, when I was getting in shape for *Strictly.* Or rather,' Cass adds, bitterly, 'when Mum *led me to believe* that I was in with a shot of getting *Strictly*.' She's perched her perfectly plump posterior on the arm of my Chesterfield. 'I should probably go and start training there again and get in amazing shape, if I'm going to end up splashed all over the tabloids every five minutes.'

'I'm sure they'll lose interest soon,' I say.

'God, I hope so,' she says, unconvincingly. 'I mean, sure, in the olden days, I've never minded press intrusion. But this is different. My priorities are different now. I'm a *mother*.'

'Cass. You're not a mother.'

'I am! I mean, Zoltan has *two children*, you know! Daughters! And if I end up marrying him . . .'

'You've only been with him three months!'

'. . . I'll be their brand-new stepmother. Which, obviously, is going to be *amazing*. I mean, I've wanted to be a mother for, like, soooo long . . .'

I stop trying to arrange the sinfully expensive flowers I bought from a posh shop up the road, and stare at her. 'Really?'

'. . . but this way, I get to do the fun part without having to go through all the really shit stuff, too. You know, getting fat, and all that.'

'Pregnant, Cass. Not fat. Pregnant.'

'Well, you *say* that, Libby, but when I saw those christening photos of Nora, she looked absolutely massive! And that was, like, at least two months after she'd had the baby, right?'

'It was four months,' I say, defensively, because the Nora of whom Cass is speaking is my best friend of almost twenty years. I was the chief bridesmaid at her wedding last summer. I'm godmother to her eight-month-old daughter, Clara, for Christ's sake. 'And she didn't look fat, she looked amazing.'

'Yeah, well, either way, I'm not going to take the risk. Anyway, it's not just the getting-fat thing. Little children *cry*, and they make a *mess of stuff*, and you're really tired at night so you only get to have sex, like, three times a week and stuff . . . But then they get to, like, six, or nine or . . . well, whatever age Zoltan's kids are . . . well, they're just super-easy by then! You just hang out, and do really cute mother-daughter stuff like . . . talk about whatever boy bands they fancy, and . . .' Inspiration clearly runs dry for a moment. 'I don't know . . . go for spa days?'

'I don't think nine year olds are really into spa days, to be honest with you.'

'Well, *I* was. I had a lovely spa weekend with Mum for my ninth birthday!'

'When I was thirteen . . .? I don't remember us going to a spa with Mum that young.'

'Oh, it was probably a weekend when you were at your dad's, or something . . .Hey, I remember now! I think we told you she was taking me to an audition for *Doctor Who*.'

'I remember that!' Especially as I was no longer a regular weekend guest at my dad's by then, which still didn't stop him leaving me home alone with a box-set of Humphrey Bogart videos so that he could go out with some new girlfriend all afternoon on Saturday and most of Sunday. I made cheese sandwiches (partly because that was all I knew how to make and partly because cheese and bread was all there was in the flat) and fell asleep on the floor in front of the TV because there was a creepy old walk-in closet in the spare room and I was too scared to sleep there in case someone was hiding in it and crept out of it in the middle of the night. 'Anyway, look, Cass, can we talk about all this – your, er, new role as a stepmother – another time, please?'

'Why? You're not busy, are you?'

'Yes!' Has she completely missed everything I've been doing while she's been wittering on? 'I've told you! Ben and Elvira are getting here for a meeting any minute now!'

'Oh, yeah, right. Though you do know, don't you, that there's nothing you can really do, right now, to make the place look decent enough to impress Elvira Thingy-Doodah?' Cass casts a disparaging glance around the room, then wrinkles her nose as she peers down at the sofa. 'God, Libby, are you still so hard up that you can't afford something a bit better than this? You could get one for literally a hundred and fifty quid at IKEA!'

'I know. I like this one.'

She pulls a face. 'Then I can't help you. Anyway, you're the one who has to convince this Elvira woman that you're not about to infest her entire apartment with bedbugs, or whatever the hell is lurking in here.'

'Nothing's *lurking* in there,' I say. 'Bedbugs or . . . anyone else.'

'Any*thing*.'

'Right. Yes. Of course. But seriously, Cass, I do need to get ready . . .'

'Fine. I'll go.' She gets to her feet, tottering a bit on the five-inch heels that she considers mandatory for an average day out and about. 'I've got to get to the hospital to see Mum.'

Early this morning, Mum had her gallstones out at a private hospital near Harley Street. No, scratch that: she had *minor cosmetic surgery*. Or rather, this is what she's insisting on telling people, because gallstones are far too unglamorous a condition for my mother. She'd rather everyone thought she was having a face-lift or a nose job, evidently, than that they knew she had ugly old gallstones rattling around inside her.

As far as I knew, she'd banned me and Cass from visiting until tomorrow, when she'd be feeling sufficiently recovered to drape a bed jacket over her shoulders and hold court. But apparently Cass is exempt from this condition.

'You're seeing her *today?*' I ask.

'Yeah, she asked me to pop along if I was free. Why? Are you not going to make it today at all?'

'No! I thought she didn't want us there.'

'Oh. Well, maybe it was just you she didn't want there. Or,' Cass goes on, generously trying to find a way to make this sound less harsh, 'maybe it was just that she *does* want me rather than *not* wanting you, if you see what I mean.'

'Well, tell her I'll come along to visit tomorrow, as summonsed,' I say, pointedly. 'If she can find the time in her packed schedule to fit me in, that is.'

But Cass isn't paying that much attention. She's peering into the mirror by the door and getting her makeup bag out of her handbag to perfect her appearance – a few trowel-loads of blusher, an ocean of lipgloss and a small tidal wave of mascara – just in case she's papped en route to the hospital, I guess. Then she's off, with the briefest of waves in my direction, giving me a grand total of ten minutes to put my own makeup on, get into my chosen outfit, and head downstairs to the studio/showroom to assemble the pieces I want to show Ben and Elvira at our meeting.

I mean, it really does have to go well today. It *has to*.

The thing is that when Ben helicoptered in, this time last year, and put forty grand of his venture-capital firm's money into my jewellery business, Libby Goes To Hollywood, I couldn't believe my luck. His money, not to mention his bulging contacts book and business expertise, has turned LGTH from a teeny-tiny, financially strapped entity, with a handful of customers, into a proper little business with a glossy website, all kinds of terrific press, and – sorry, but this still excites me probably most of all – gorgeous swanky packaging, with eau-de-nil and dove-grey boxes stamped with silver lettering and filled with silver tissue paper. These days I can't keep up with demand for the cheaper pieces I sell on the website, so I've outsourced the manufacture of those to a fantastic little artisanal factory in Croatia instead, while I try to concentrate on the design side, and on the manufacture of some of my more intricate pieces. Six months ago I even ended up doing a brief collaboration with the jewellery department at Liberty (the glamorous department store after which, though she'll claim otherwise, I'm still pretty sure

Mum named me) as part of a New Designers' showcase. Recently there was an entire feature about me in *Brides* magazine, focusing on the vintage-style bespoke tiaras I've made for a few clients. I mean, I'm still small, but I'm growing, and none of it would ever have happened without Ben.

The flip-side of it all, however, is that it can occasionally be . . . well, a little bit of a fight to retain a hundred per cent of what I guess you might call 'creative control'. Or, more specifically, the direction the business is heading in. Twelve months ago, I might not have had a crystal-clear plan for it all. I just wanted to make quirky, Old-Hollywood-inspired costume jewellery, at an affordable price – but at least I was still happily meandering in that general direction. Ben, I'm slowly beginning to realize, has slightly different ideas and, in every conversation we've had over the last couple of months, he has been pushing me towards scaling back the cheaper end and concentrating on expensive, bespoke orders. Admittedly the margins are higher on these, but I have a suspicion that his reasoning is also motivated by the fact that he has other designers making more mass-market jewellery and accessories in his little 'stable' of companies, and – most of all – by the fact that Elvira Roberts-Hoare, his close advisor, is advising him to stick to the luxury end of the market where I'm concerned. I don't have all that much contact with her, but I know she's not all that sold on the Hollywood-inspired angle, for one thing – 'at the end of the day, darling, they're just dead celebrities. It's all a bit too *Sunset Boulevard*' – and, more to the point, she's even less sold on the whole 'affordable 'price' thing. *Her* vision for Libby Goes To Hollywood is, as far as I can tell, that I custom-make heinously expensive one-off pieces for a double-barrelled clientele – brides, mostly – who pop up on the society pages of *Tatler*.

I can only assume that this is because these things – double-barrelled clients, and the society pages of *Tatler* – are her particular area of expertise. And, I suspect, more to the point, because she's cheesed off that Ben was the one who brought me under his umbrella in the first place, without her being the one to scout me, as is their usual arrangement. And that she wants to stamp her authority and opinions on Libby Goes To Hollywood as a way of asserting her position.

But I can't complain. I mean that in its truest sense. I can't complain. Ben owns sixty-five per cent of my company, and has put tens of thousands of pounds into it. And Elvira is his right-hand woman, so he's always going to take her opinion over mine.

I'm just hoping that maybe, just maybe, today's meeting might swing things a little more in my favour. I've been working really hard on the designs for a new collection of chunky bronze cuffs, studded with semi-precious birth-stones, a few of which I've got to show Ben and Elvira today. I'm also armed with promising sales figures from the most recent collection that the factory in Croatia made for me, and . . .

I can hear that the front door is opening, and that Elvira and Ben are on their way in. Seeing as this means Elvira must have used her own door key, I'll have to have a little word with her about privacy as soon as . . . actually, let's be honest, I won't have a word with her about privacy at all. This is her place – well, her father's, but who's splitting hairs? – and I'm staying here as close to rent-free as makes no difference. She could tap-dance in unannounced, in the middle of the night, with a marching band playing loud *oom-pah-pahs* right behind her, and I'd still keep my mouth shut.

'Libby? You here?'

'I'm right here, Ben!' I reply, heading out of the back room and into the as-yet-empty showroom space at the front. 'Hi! Great to see you both.'

Ben, who I go up to kiss on both cheeks, is looking as immaculate as I've ever seen him: sharp suit, open-neck shirt, and a hot pink silk pocket square, just to give the nod to the fact he's the kind of multimillionaire venture capitalist who invests in fashion businesses rather than anything mundane like steel production or microchip technology. But Elvira . . . well, she looks positively extraordinary. She's rocking a tiny paisley kaftan that only just covers her practically non-existent buttocks, Grecian sandals that lace up as far as her equally nonexistent thighs, a Hermès Birkin bag in the crook of one emaciated arm; her silver-blonde hair, in milkmaid plaits, is pushed back from her face with a colossal pair of sunglasses.

'Elvira!' I contemplate giving her a kiss too, but her forbidding aura of haughtiness puts me off. 'Thanks so much, again, for all this.' I wave a hand around the showroom. 'Obviously I haven't really had a chance to think about how I'm going to fit it out, yet, but it's such a great space, I'm sure it's going to be—'

'I need water,' she says, abruptly, cutting me off and starting to head up the stairs without waiting for an invitation. 'Do you have flat mineral in the kitchen?'

'Mineral water? Er . . . no, only tap. I can pop up the road to the shop, if it would—'

'No time for that,' she throws over her shoulder, clearly a woman in the midst of a dehydration emergency. 'Tap will have to do.'

'So, Libby, good to see you settled here,' Ben says. His tone, as ever, is brusque, but I'm used to this by now and know that he (almost always) means kindly enough. 'It's a little fancier than . . . sorry, what's the name of the place you were living before?'

'Colliers Wood.'

'A little fancier than Colliers Wood, huh?'

'Yes, it's lovely.' I pick up my stack of bronze cuffs and the paperwork for my sales figures, and start to follow him up the stairs towards the living room. 'Thanks, Ben, for getting Elvira to let me have the place.'

'It's nothing. Besides, El's been talking about the idea of you working out of a showroom for months now, right?'

'Yes, she has. In fact, that was one thing I was really hoping we could speak about today, Ben.' We reach the living room; Elvira has gone on up to the next floor to source her urgent water from the kitchen. 'I mean, I love having the showroom too, obviously, and it's going to be fantastic for meetings with my bespoke clients and stuff . . .

but I suppose what I'm still really hoping for, one day soon, is to actually start up my own shop premises. And I guess I'd really just like to be sure that that's something you'd be supportive of, as well as the whole showroom thing, when the time—'

'I thought you'd moved in.'

'Sorry?'

'I thought you'd moved in.' Ben gestures around the living room. 'Where's all your stuff?'

'Oh, right! This is all my stuff!'

'You're kidding.'

'No, no, I like to live with . . . er . . . a very minimalist aesthetic . . .'

'You're kidding,' Ben repeats. He nods in the direction of the Chesterfield. 'I mean, is *that* old thing part of your minimalist aesthetic?'

'Well, no, but I like to mix minimalism with . . . vintage quirkiness.'

'That's vintage quirk, all right.' Ben wanders over and peers, gingerly, at the sofa. 'It doesn't have mice, or anything, does it?'

I'm offended, on behalf of the Chesterfield, that this is the second time today someone has implied there are things living in it.

Or, more accurately, offended that it's the second time someone has implied there are creepy-crawly, rodenty things living in it.

As opposed to the *actual* things living in it. Which are – and I'll keep this ever so brief, because it makes me sound nuts, no matter how I put it – Hollywood screen legends.

And, to be honest, I don't really think they *live in* the sofa, as such. It's more just that they *appear from* it. Because the sofa itself is . . . magical? I mean, this is the best – in fact, pretty much the only – explanation I've been able to come up with myself.

I said I'd sound nuts, OK? But there's honestly no other way for me to explain it.

'No, it doesn't have mice! Anyway, Ben, as I was saying, I'm really glad we've got this opportunity to have a bit of a chat about things, because—'

'What's going on down here?' Elvira demands, as she reappears at the bottom of the stairs, having come down from the kitchen. 'What are you two talking about?'

'Well, I was just saying—'

'I was asking Libby if she has mice in this old couch,' Ben says. 'I mean, did you ever see anything like it?'

'I didn't.' Elvira gazes at the Chesterfield. 'God, I kind of love it.'

I'm astonished by this. 'Really? Everybody else I know hates it.'

'Oh, well, nobody knows anything about vintage furniture, darling. Not unless they have an eye for this sort of thing.'

Her tone suggests that she herself *does* have an eye which, to be fair, she does, if that extraordinary feature in *Elle Decor* was anything to go by.

'It's an old film-set prop, actually,' I say, relieved to have found something to bond with Elvira over, after months of our uncomfortable alliance. 'From Pinewood Studios.'

'*No.*' Her eyebrows shoot upwards. 'How did you get hold of something like that?'

'I used to be an actress,' I say, before adding, swiftly, 'well, just an extra, really. But I was working on a show at Pinewood a couple of years ago when I first moved into my old flat, and a – uh – friend of mine who worked there too had an arrangement with the guy who ran the props warehouse. Anything they didn't really want any more was fair game to take away.'

'And nobody else wanted this?' Elvira puts her Birkin down on one of the sofa's cushions and runs a hand over the blowsy apricot-coloured fabric. 'God, people are such *idiots*. This is a stunning piece!'

'El, honey, you can't be serious.' Ben lets out a short bark of laughter. 'This old heap of junk?'

'Don't be such a philistine. This must have so much *history*, I'm sure, if it was at Pinewood all those years.'

I can feel myself redden. We may be getting along the best we've ever managed, me and Elvira – practically besties ourselves, now, in comparison to our usual strained relations – but I don't think we're anywhere close to a situation where I might confide in her the full extent of my Chesterfield's 'history'.

'Well,' I say, 'I don't know about that.'

'You know, darling, if you'd like to get it refurbished, I have some amazing furniture restorers on my speed-dial—'

'God, no!' I practically yelp. Because – and I'm very far

from an expert here, trust me – even though I may not have seen a Hollywood legend appear from the sofa since Marilyn Monroe, almost exactly a year ago last June, I have a gut feeling that it'll only ever work again if it stays exactly like this. So yes, it's a bit grubby, and yes, that smell of moist dog still never quite fades, no matter how many times I open a window and fan fresh air in its direction with a tea-towel. But for all I know, even the merest squirt of Febreze is going to take away its remarkable powers for ever. I'm not going to risk it. 'Thanks so much for the offer, Elvira,' I continue, 'but I kind of like it the way it is.'

'Oh! Well, that's up to you, I suppose.' But she's looking at me with a little more respect than usual. 'I can understand you don't want to take away from the soul of the piece.'

'That's exactly it.' I beam at her. 'And in fact,' I go on, hoping to use this unexpected moment of positivity between us as a springboard to more important things, 'talking of souls, I'd really love to have a conversation about the next phase of plans for Libby Goes To Hollywood.'

'That's exactly why we're here,' Elvira says. 'I mean, now that you've got the new studio, obviously it's time to start moving things forward.'

'Great!'

I feel a rush of relief at how well this is all going for a change. Our previous meetings have all been so awkward and stilted. I've been intimidated by her gawky beauty, her ineffable style and her screaming poshness, and she's probably been . . . well, not intimidated by a single thing about me. Visibly irritated, you'd probably have to say, by my all-too-apparent *lack* of screaming poshness. And now here we are, conversation (comparatively) flowing.

I take a deep breath, and begin the little pitch I've been practising in my head. 'Well, I've been looking at the sales figures from the website, and they're really on their way up over the last three months. So I've been thinking I'd like to—'

'Oh, yeah, that's what we wanted to speak about, too.' Ben sits down on the Chesterfield, either forgetting or ignoring his concern about rodent inhabitants. 'El and I were talking in the cab over here, and we both think it's really time to wind up that side of the business, and focus your energies more on the bespoke commissions.'

'Yeah,' says Elvira although, because she's so screamingly posh, this comes out as a *yah*. 'Specifically the bridal commissions. After all, I think we can all agree that's where your greatest talents lie, Libby.'

'What? No. I mean . . . I don't think we *can* agree that's where my greatest talents lie.' I stare at them both. 'That might be where my biggest margins have come from these last few months, but if you have a look at the website sales, the charm bracelets and opal rings have been doing really, really well. And,' I go on, remembering that I'm still holding a couple of my new bronze cuffs, 'I'm really hoping this sort of thing is going to be a big seller, too, when I launch them on the website.'

Elvira glances at the cuff I'm holding out for her to inspect. 'Pretty,' she says, with a dismissive shrug, not even bothering to look properly at it. 'But that's not really the direction we see the business heading in, is it, Ben, darling?'

19

'Nope, not really,' Ben says. He's taken out his phone, and is tapping away on the screen. 'Listen to El, Libby. She knows what she's talking about.'

'Right, I'm sure, but I know what I'm talking about, too.' I can't quite believe I'm actually saying this to the pair of them – the de facto owner of my business, and someone as scary as Elvira – but needs must. Besides, after our moment of bonding over the sofa, I think she'll respect me more if I stand my ground. 'Look, it's not that I don't enjoy bridal commissions—'

'Well, I'm glad to hear it.' Elvira bestows me with a rare smile. 'That piece in *Brides* has led to hundreds of enquiries, no? And – so far – dozens and dozens of actual orders.'

'Sure, and like I say, it's not that I don't enjoy it.' I take another deep breath. 'It's just that . . . well, the brides who've come to me after that article pretty much all want exactly the same thing.'

'You mean the vintage-style tiara they featured in the magazine article Elvira arranged for you?' Ben glances up from his phone. 'The one,' he adds, in a meaningful sort of way, 'with the *three hundred per cent* margin?'

'Yes, OK, I get that it's good for profit.' I stare, rather desperately, in Elvira's direction, wanting to appeal to her sense of creativity. 'I just really wanted to have a bit more say in the design process. Rather than just replicating the same thing over and over again.'

She looks back at me. 'Well, I do get that,' she says.

'I knew you would!' I can see a tiny little chink of light here, I really can. 'Look, Elvira, perhaps if you could have a closer look at some of the pieces I'm working on at the moment, not just the cuffs, but also *OH MY GOD, IT'S A RAT!'*

I wasn't planning on finishing the sentence this way, but then I wasn't expecting to see an *actual* rodent, just the sort that Ben has been suspicious about, scurrying out from the Chesterfield's squashy cushions.

I act, I think, with commendable speed under the circumstances – after all, it's my sofa, so therefore my rat, and I want to be clear I'm taking full responsibility for the horror – by pulling back my right arm and hurling both bronze cuffs towards the rat's head.

I mean, I'm an animal lover, so I'm not actually trying to kill the thing, just scare it off, or, I don't know, knock it out.

But Elvira, the moment she sees the cuffs go loose, screams as if I'm about to accidentally injure a newborn infant.

'Don't hurt my baby!' she screeches, diving into the cuffs' trajectory, but too late. One of them has actually made contact with the rat – its tail end, I think, and not its head – and it has let out a little squeal.

I'm confused, for a moment, as to why a rat would make a noise like that, and – much more importantly – why on earth Elvira is calling it her baby.

But then Ben is on his feet too, hurrying over to help Elvira tend to the creature.

'Is he all right?' he demands. 'Did it hit him?'

'I think so! Oh, my poor baby!' Elvira is *actually gathering the rat up*, into her arms, and raining kisses down on its head. 'I think it got him on the leg! At the very least,' she adds, turning to me with a look of murderous fury in her eyes, 'he's totally fucking *traumatized!*'

'I don't . . . sorry, but I honestly don't think rats can feel trauma, can they?'

'He's not a rat! He's a dog! *My dog!*'

My mouth falls open. 'Oh, God, Elvira, I didn't—'

'He's a Xoloitzcuintli,' Ben says, gruffly.

I blink at him.

'A miniature Mexican hairless!' Elvira spits. 'The Aztecs considered them *sacred!*'

All I can honestly think to this is: *more fool the Aztecs*. Because, seriously, this dog is a peculiar-looking beast. Well, obviously, given that I have just mistaken him for a large rat.

'He's only eight weeks old,' Elvira is going on, continuing to examine and kiss the dog/rat in equal proportion. 'He's just a puppy! How could you *attack* him like that, Libby?'

'Elvira, again, I'm so sorry. I didn't attack him . . . well, OK, I threw the cuffs, but only because I thought he was . . . er . . . well, you know . . . and Ben had been saying he thought there might be mice or something in the sofa . . .'

'He was in my bag!' Elvira points a shaking hand at her Birkin bag, still on the Chesterfield, that the dog must have just crept out of. 'And really, Libby, what did you *think* I wanted water for, when we got here?'

'I'm sorry, I just assumed . . . is he OK?' I add, taking a step closer, albeit a little bit gingerly, but Elvira jumps back as if I'm brandishing an entire arsenal of dog-injuring weaponry.

'You've done enough,' she snarls. 'Ben, darling, can you get a cab? I want to get Tino straight to the vet.'

'Of course, hon.' Ben shoots a rather weary look in my direction as he heads back to the sofa to pick up his phone. 'Jeez, Libby,' he says. 'What is it with you and other people's dogs?'

This is a rather unfair reference to the first time he met me – a time that, until now, both of us have chosen never to reference again – when I accidentally got myself stuck in a dog safety gate in my underwear.

'Honestly,' I say, as Elvira shoots me another evil look to end all evil looks, 'I'm an animal lover! I just thought—'

'Yes, we know. You thought he was a rat,' she spits. 'You've made that perfectly clear already, thank you, Libby.'

'But honestly, he looks OK,' I go on, looking at Tino in a manner that I hope appears concerned rather than (I have to be honest) ever-so-slightly revolted. And this is true, because his little rodenty face looks relaxed enough, and there are no visible injuries on his equally rodenty body. If anything, he's looking eager to leap out of Elvira's tight embrace, and head for . . . well, he's looking extremely longingly at the sofa, actually. He must be getting all those lovely doggy whiffs of canines past coming off it.

'Oh, what the fuck would you know? You're not a vet!'

'Cab here in three minutes, El,' Ben says, slipping his phone back into his pocket. 'We'll have to carry on this conversation another time, Libby, OK?'

'What? No! I mean,' I go on, trying to sound more calm and collected than I feel, 'I've been really looking forward to this meeting. There's so much to discuss, and we don't often get the opportunity to—'

'Come on. It's hardly the time.'

'It's certainly not.' Elvira is stalking over to the Chesterfield to pick up her Birkin, all ready to place Tino tenderly inside it. But he's evidently got other ideas, because he slips out of her grasp, and lurches down towards the sofa itself, where he starts to sort of . . . well, I don't know what the technical term would be, but it does look very much as if he's trying to pleasure himself against the chintzy, apricot-coloured fabric.

'Huh,' observes Ben, as we all gaze at Tino in a rather shocked silence for a moment. 'Guess there must be the scent of quite a few old mutts on this thing, right?'

But I don't think it's that. I don't think it's that at all. Yes, the Chesterfield does have an aroma of dog – always has – but from the transfixed expression on Tino's face, I think he's picking up on something more than mere waft of long-gone Labrador, or past poodle.

I mean, animals have sixth senses, don't they? Especially so, probably, if they're the kind of animals that the Aztecs considered sacred.

'Oh, for God's sake!' Elvira, puce in the face now with embarrassment as well as anger, grabs Tino mid-rut and holds him firmly under her arm as she heads for the stairs. 'We'll discuss this *incident* another time, Libby,' she tells me. 'But suffice it to say I am Not Happy. Not Happy At All.'

Which is, to be fair, pretty much the impression I've got

every other time I've met her. That she's Not Happy about anything I have to offer. It's just that there were those few minutes where we seemed to bond, ever so slightly, over the vintage sofa. And now it's all gone backwards again. Actually, worse than backwards, because even if she has not been that impressed with me before now, at least I'd never tried, in her eyes, to assassinate her precious Mexican hairless dog.

'Yeah,' says Ben, already back on his phone again, as he follows her down the stairs towards their taxi. 'We'll be in touch, Libby. I'll try to set something up, the next time I'm over.'

'But Ben, I really—'

'Bye, Libby,' he says, with a wave of the hand, not even glancing back at me. 'Oh, and try to keep up the orders for that vintage tiara, yeah? That thing's your bread and butter. Your books are never gonna add up without it.'

The front door bangs shut behind them a couple of moments later, leaving me and my Chesterfield alone, together, in our accidentally minimalist new flat.

Chapter 2

It's truly excellent news, from the point of view of my morale, that I'm due to have dinner with my friend Olly tonight. After the disaster of a business meeting with Ben and Elvira (actually, even calling it a 'business meeting' is being generous, given the amount of time we spent discussing anything business-related), I might otherwise be tempted to retreat into my pyjamas and eat the contents of my biscuit stash in self-pity. But I've promised Olly that I'll meet him over at the restaurant, and we see each other so rarely these days that I don't want to go back on my promise.

The restaurant, by the way, being his own restaurant, over in Clapham.

Nibbles.

That's what the restaurant is called.

It's a bit unfortunate.

Not the name Nibbles itself, as such – although I still think it's a name better suited to a twee seaside tearoom, rather than a tapas-style restaurant successful enough to have been nominated for all kinds of Best Newcomer awards recently – but more what the choice of name represents. I mean, it was a pretty last-minute decision to call it that, and—

Talking of last-minute decisions, a text has just popped up on my phone from Olly, literally as I approach the restaurant's front door, asking if I can meet him two doors down in the little French bistro instead. *We've ended up needing all the tables tonight*, his text informs me, *and anyway it's been a knackering day and I just want to get out of the place!!! Will get bottle of red. See you there. O xxx*

Which actually suits me pretty well, too, because the slight issue of having a meal with Olly at Nibbles is, no matter how hard he tries to avoid it, the constant interruptions. Even on a night when he's not officially working, he's always working: there's an issue that needs to be sorted out in the kitchen, or two of the waiting staff are threatening to kill each other, or a customer can't live another moment without finding out the origin of his recipe for pea and mint arancini.

Peace and quiet and privacy over red wine at the bistro sound just about perfect right now. Especially since I can't actually remember the last time I had a quiet evening and a chat with Olly. Two months ago? Closer to three? Despite the fact we've been close friends ever since I was thirteen, and he was Nora's worldly wise fifteen-year-old brother; despite the fact we used to get together to set the world to rights over a bite to eat and more than a sip to drink at least twice a week, we've drifted a bit of late. Probably something to do with the fact that he's busy running his restaurant, and I'm busy running my business.

Oh, and probably quite a lot, too, to do with the fact that I'm a little bit in love with him.

Actually, I'll rephrase that, because *a little bit in love* sounds like I have some girlish crush, or something.

It's not a crush. I am passionately, desperately, fervently, and worst of all *secretly* in love with Olly. Who – worse even than that – just so happened to be secretly in love with me, too, for almost the entirety of our friendship, until a year ago when (not unreasonably, let's be honest) he finally gave up on me and started going out with Tash, his now-girlfriend, who works with Nora up at Glasgow Royal Infirmary.

I mean, he'd planned to name the restaurant after me, and everything. Libby's, it was meant to be called, not Nibbles. That was the last-minute decision I just told you about. I guess he'd always had this idea that he'd open a restaurant named after me one day, and that this would be the big declaration of love that he couldn't bring himself to say out loud, and that I'd finally realize the way he felt about me. But then I was messing around thinking I was in love with my ex, Dillon O'Hara, and Olly just got tired of waiting.

It was the biggest mistake I've ever made in my life. The biggest mistake I've ever made without knowing I was even making it.

It's why I end up avoiding him so much these days. (While still – illogically – at the same time, desperately wanting to find ways to spend time with him.) For one thing, it often just feels too painful to have to sit there and stare down the barrel of What Should Have Been. And, for another, I'm usually scared that I might not be able to disguise my own feelings. Might end up, horror to end all horrors, jumping the table and doing to him pretty much what Tino the Mexican hairless did to my Chesterfield earlier this afternoon.

Because just look at me now, coming to a wobbly-kneed standstill as soon as I enter the bistro and see him at a corner table. He's just so incredibly, heart-breakingly gorgeous, with his hair all mussed up from his habit of rubbing his hands through it when he's stressed, and his big brown eyes, so open and honest, and—

'Lib!'

Those big brown eyes have alighted on me now, and he's getting to his feet, a huge smile on his handsome face.

'You're a sight for sore eyes,' he says, coming over to put his arms around me in a huge bear hug. (I inhale, as surreptitiously as I can, his scent: the familiar, warm, kitcheny smell I've known inside out for the last couple of decades, coupled with something spicier and more masculine that I never used to notice, but must have always been there.) 'Come and sit down and have some wine with me. Well, actually, I decided on a bottle of champagne. Your favourite kind. I mean, we're celebrating your moving into the new flat, right?'

'Oh, Olly. That's . . . so nice of you.'

'Don't be silly. It's a big moment. You deserve to celebrate it!'

'Well, I don't know about that. I mean, I feel like I've already screwed things up with my new landlord.'

29

'You mean the scary fashion woman who keeps trying to tell you what to do with your own business?'

'I mean the scary fashion woman who keeps trying to tell me what to do with my own business.' I smile up at him. 'Wow. That was well remembered, Ol. I only told you about her in passing when I last saw you.'

'I always remember the important stuff.' He ushers me towards the table. 'Now, I've ordered us a plate of charcuterie and a plate of cheese, but if there's anything else you'd prefer, I can get them to give us a menu . . .'

'No, no, I'm fine. I mean, that sounds perfect.' I slide into the seat opposite him, and do my best to slow down my hammering heart. 'Hi,' I add, with a nervous laugh, that I immediately try to turn into a cough. 'God, Olly, it's been ages.'

'Way too long. Here.' He pours champagne into my glass. Quite a lot of champagne, and then the same sort of amount for himself. His hand is a bit shaky – exhaustion, I should think, given the hours he works – which is probably why it slips a bit and why he's poured such big glasses. 'You look like you need this. What happened with the scary fashion woman?'

'Oh, you know, the usual . . . I mistook her beloved puppy for a rat and threw a large piece of solid metal at its head—'

'Ah. Of course. The usual.' He grins at me and lifts his glass. 'Cheers, Lib. And congratulations. On the exciting new move, that is. Not the puppy-maiming. I need to be absolutely clear that, despite our long and

30

happy friendship together, I can in no way condone that.'

'And I'd never expect you to.'

I chink my glass against his and grin back.

After a moment, it feels like a rather rictus grin and, to be perfectly honest, he looks pretty frozen too – probably wondering what the hell I'm still grinning about myself – so I take a long drink.

He does the same.

'So!' I say, brightly, when we both put our glasses down. 'That's honestly quite enough about me—'

'Oh, come on, Lib, I want to hear all about the new place!'

'Well, then you'll have to come over some time. With Tash!' I add, just in case he thinks I'm suggesting some cosy soirée, just the two of us. 'But until then, there's really not much to tell, Olly, honestly.'

I mean, in the past, I'd have bored his pants off, wittering on about my hopes and fears for the business, getting him to join me in over-analysing every word spoken by Elvira and Ben. But now that I fancy him so much – now that I can think of other, far less noble things I'd like to do to get his pants off, quite frankly – I'm suddenly a lot less keen to bore him. Not to mention the fact that there's the permanent wedge of Tash between us. It just feels wrong to seek that type of support from a man who's – very much – spoken for.

'Anyway,' I go on, 'you look like you've had a tough day, too.'

'I do?'

'Well, you look tired,' I say, after studying him for a moment without quite meeting his eye.

'Oh, that's just life in the restaurant business,' he says. He looks even wearier, for a moment. 'Things are always so busy, and I just never seem to have enough *time*. I mean, when was the last time you and I actually managed to do this, Lib?'

'This?'

'Yes, sit with a bottle of wine and catch up. It feels like for ever.'

'Well, no, I mean, it is a long time,' I say, not wanting to remind him that I've cancelled two of our most recent planned meet-ups at short notice (just couldn't face going through with it) and that he's cancelled three himself (last-minute restaurant emergencies). 'But you're right, life is busy. And, of course, you have Tash to prioritize, too.' I take another large gulp from my glass. 'How is she, by the way?'

'Tash? Oh, she's great. She's always great.' He picks up his own glass. 'I mean, obviously, there's always the issue of—'

He stops because, almost as if it's been eavesdropping on us or something (I mean, it couldn't have, could it?), his phone starts to ring.

'Oh!' he says. 'It's Tash! Sorry, Lib, would you mind if I . . .?'

'Not at all!'

'I mean, I usually call her around this time every evening, when she gets off her shift at the hospital . . .'

32

'Olly, I don't mind! Honestly! Answer it.'

'Thank, Libs.' He picks up the ringing phone. 'Hey,' he murmurs into it. 'You OK?'

That murmur – low, intimate, the tone of voice you only ever use with your Significant Other – makes me want to cry.

But, thank God, it's right at this moment that a waiter appears bearing two large platters of food, which he places on the table in front of me. I mean very specifically in front of me, in fact, with a somewhat lascivious smile and an assurance that if there's anything, anything *at all*, that I'd like his help with, I only need to—

'Yeah, thanks, Didier,' Olly says, breaking off his phone call for a moment to speak, rather sharply, to the waiter. 'I'm sure she can manage to find her way round a plate of cheese on her own . . . Sorry, Tash,' he adds, into the phone again, 'just fending off an ardent Frenchman . . . no, no, not for me! I'm having a bite with Libby . . .' There's a short pause. 'Tash says hi,' he tells me.

Of course she does, because Tash – annoyingly – is nice and friendly and downright perfect.

'Hi, Tash!' I trill back, waving a hand, pointlessly, because it's not like they're on a FaceTime call or anything.

And then I make a gesture at Olly, which is supposed to indicate that he should just carry on with the phone call, that I'm perfectly fine – delighted in fact – to be sitting here tucking into plates of delicious cold meat and cheese, and that everything is just so fine and dandy in the world that I'm only inches away from leaping up on to the table and kicking off a rousing chorus of 'Oh Happy Day'.

Because I think I might need to go way over the top just to avoid giving the slightest hint that I'd actually rather crawl *under* the table and miserably hiccup my way through 'Where Do Broken Hearts Go?'

This is why I should never have come this evening; why I should just have made up some spurious excuse and cancelled again.

The thing is, it's not like I'm not well used to sitting across a table from someone I'm in love with who isn't in love with me back. Dillon O'Hara, for example, whom I remained convinced I was in love with despite the fact that our relationship was a car crash, with him in the driving seat. And not even just Dillon: as an incurable romantic, especially one who spent most of my life convinced I was an unattractive frump compared to my stunning little sister, I've enjoyed a long and fruitless history of falling in love with men who wouldn't have noticed me if I'd been standing in front of them stark naked with a sign hanging around my neck reading *Available and Desperate: Please Apply Within.*

The difference – the colossal, heart-shattering difference – this time, with Olly, is the knowledge that this isn't how it should have been. That thanks to a disastrous combination of cruel fate and my own stupidity, he and I have passed each other by like ships in the night.

In fact, it hurts so much to dwell, even for a moment, on the role played by my own stupidity that I think I need to shift as much of the blame as possible on to the Cruel Fate part. Because otherwise it's just too sickening to endure. Like Juliet would have felt if she'd woken up beside a lifeless Romeo in the tomb and realized that she'd absent-mindedly put a poison bottle next to the orange juice in the fridge. Bad enough her soulmate is doomed to be lost to her for ever; soul-destroying to confront the fact she just should have been paying more attention.

'No, of course,' Olly is saying, into the phone. 'And I meant to . . . well, what time will you be home? . . . no, I imagine I'll head straight back after I'm finished here . . . OK, I'll Skype you then . . . no, of course . . . of course . . . of course . . . OK, bye,' he adds, finishing up with a swift, ever-so-slightly guilty-sounding, 'Love you,' before putting the phone down. His gaze remains fixed on the tabletop for a moment, almost as if he's avoiding making eye contact.

I swallow, hard. 'Everything OK?'

'No, of course,' he says, echoing exactly what he's just said repeatedly to Tash. (It's an odd phrase, actually, now I come to think of it. I mean, isn't *yes* the more usual companion to an *of course?* Still, it's not for me to analyse it. It's between them.) 'Tash is just . . . well, she's a little bit fed up with us never seeing each other, that's all.'

'Oh, Olly, I'm really sorry. Look, you should go home right now and Skype her—'

'Don't be ridiculous,' he says, rather sharply. Then he inhales, as if to reset himself, and picks up his champagne glass again, gripping the stem. 'Sorry, Lib. I just mean that me going home and Skyping her isn't really going to address the issue. It's much more about the fact that we live three hundred and fifty miles away from each other and we both work all the hours God sends.'

'No,' I say. 'Of course.'

'I mean, she's worked weekends the last three weeks in a row, and obviously I'm always busy too . . .'

'Sorry, Ol. Long-distance is hard, I know.'

'It is. But it shouldn't feel this . . .' He thinks about this for a moment, sadness passing over his face. 'Impossible.'

He looks so wretched that, even though the cause of it is his missing Tash, I shunt my own pain to the side for a moment.

'I think you probably just need to find a way to *make* more time, Ol, to be honest with you. I mean, I know how busy you are, but is there any way you can take a Saturday night off and go up to Glasgow? If you left straight after the lunch service, you'd only miss dinner, and then you're closed on Monday night and Tuesday lunchtime, so you wouldn't even have to come back until early afternoon on Tuesday—'

'Woah.' Olly holds up a hand, looking slightly surprised. 'Have you been thinking about this already, or something?'

'No, it just seems kind of obvious, doesn't it?'

'Not really. It's not just that I need to be at the restaurant for actual service, Lib. There's quite a lot more to it than that! I have the accounts to keep on top of, and all the staff paperwork, and you know I always prefer to supervise the deep clean after Saturday dinner, and then I have all my supplier meetings, and visits from the wine merchants . . .

and all that's even without adding in the fact that I do like to actually come up with new menu items occasionally!'

'OK, well, you'll have to persuade Tash to come down here more often.'

'She's a junior hospital doctor, Libby. It's not really that simple.'

'Then the two of you have to make it that simple.' I feel a bit like a bulldozer on full power, but now that I've gone down this route, I can't seem to stop. The only good news, I guess, is that maybe the effort I've been putting in to disguise my desire to cover every inch of Olly's body in kisses is actually paying off. I've faked it and now, apparently, I've made it. And hopefully he won't actually notice how massively I'm overcompensating for something. 'I mean,' I go on, heartily, 'you love her and she loves you, right?'

Olly has reached for the champagne bottle and is topping up both glasses, which is why he takes a moment to reply.

'No, of course.'

That bizarre (and bizarrely infectious) phrase again.

'So put yourself on the line. Tell her how much you want to see her. Ask her if there's any way she can get a couple of days off work. Or, I don't know, meet halfway. That might actually be really romantic. You could book a lovely hotel, somewhere you can have drinks at the bar beside a roaring fire, and amazing room service so you don't even have to get dressed to go for dinner, and—'

'Libby.'

Olly, thank heavens, has stopped me before I can divulge

any more of this detailed hotel-trip fantasy that's really one I've often played out in my head for the two of us, on the long nights this past year when the alternative has been crying into my pillow.

'Sorry, sorry, that was probably a bit too specific—'

'Is that the mystery cheese?'

This is why he's stopped me. He's staring at the cheese plate that's been sitting between us for the last few minutes.

'That one, right there,' he's going on. He points at the plate. 'I think it is. I honestly think it might be.'

If this sounds a slightly intense tone to take about cheese, I should probably just fill you in on exactly why this is.

Years ago – when I was eighteen and Olly was turning twenty-one – he and I took a trip over to Paris on the Eurostar for a hedonistic day of drinking, eating, and (this being Olly, a foodie to end all foodies) trudging round various destinations in search of highly specific types of Mirabelle jam, or spiced sausage, or *premier cru* chocolate. And cheese. So much cheese, in fact, that we ended up digging into it on the Eurostar home, whereupon we discovered that one particular cheese – a creamy white goat's cheese, rolled in ash, and tart and lemony to the taste – was in fact the exact definition of ambrosia. (This might have had something to do with the amount of *vin* we'd imbibed on the day's trek; also, possibly, something to do with the fact that we were deliberately trying to divert attention from the unexpected snog we'd found ourselves having in a bar on the Left Bank at some point in the afternoon, and waxing absurdly lyrical about a cheese seemed, at the time, as good a way as any of achieving this.) We didn't know the name and – despite many years of searching, or more to the point, Keeping An Eye Out – neither of us ever found that Mystery Cheese again.

'Well, you'll have to taste it,' I say, in an equally intense tone. 'We won't know until you try.'

'*We* have to taste it,' he corrects me, picking up his knife and dividing the portion of white, ash-flecked cheese into two with a chef's deft movement. 'Come on, Libby. Close your eyes. This could be the moment.'

We both fall into a reverential hush as we each take a half of the cheese, close our eyes, and put it in our mouths.

'What do you think?' Olly asks, in a hushed voice, after a moment.

'I don't know . . .'

'First impressions?'

'First impression was that it's definitely *not* the one . . . but second impression . . . I'm not sure. It might be?'

'The texture doesn't seem *quite* right.'

'I agree. But the taste was pretty much bang-on.'

'Do you think? I thought the Mystery Cheese had a bit more pepper to it.'

'Wasn't it ash?'

'No, no, I don't mean pepper *in* the actual cheese, I mean a peppery *taste*.'

'Oh. Right. No, I think you're right. I mean, you're the expert.'

'I'm not the expert!' He looks faintly annoyed. 'We were both there!'

'Yes, OK, but you're the one who takes this kind of thing that seriously.'

He looks, for a moment, wounded to the core. 'I thought *you* took the Mystery Cheese seriously, too.'

'I do!'

'I mean, I know it's only a silly thing, obviously. I'm not that stupid! It was always just . . . our thing. Wasn't it?'

'Yes.' My voice has got stuck in my throat. I reach for my champagne glass. 'I'm not saying I never took it seriously, Ol,' I say, after a long drink. 'I'm saying you're the cheffy, experty, foodie person. You're the one who remembers the precise taste of a Sangiovese wine you drank in Italy three years ago versus a Sangiovese wine you drank at your parents' house three weekends ago. I could barely tell you, most days, if I was eating a tuna mayo sandwich for lunch or a chicken mayo sandwich.'

'Then you need to start buying your lunchtime sandwiches elsewhere,' Olly says, faintly irritable. 'There's absolutely no excuse for tuna to ever taste anything like chicken.'

'It's not a big deal. It's only a sandwich.'

'And the Mystery Cheese was only a cheese. I get it. It doesn't matter.'

'Olly, no, it does matter! Come on.' I reach across the table, surprising myself even as I do so, and put my hand on his.

I'm seriously hoping he can't feel the faint throb of my pulse, quickening as my skin meets his skin.

But I don't think he can, because if he did, he'd react in

40

some way, wouldn't he? Pull his hand back, or give me a funny look, or ask me if I was about to expire, or something? And he doesn't do any of those things. He just leaves his own hand exactly where it is, under mine, and says absolutely nothing for a moment.

Then he says, 'I really don't think it's the cheese, anyway.'

'No. Neither do I.' I move my hand back to my side of the table. 'But that's a good thing, I guess. Because we can keep looking.'

'Yeah. That's true. I mean, it's always been a source of comfort to me,' he adds, meeting my eyes again and pulling a cheeky grin, 'knowing that it's out there.'

We're piss-taking again. This is a good thing.

'Just waiting for us to happen upon it,' I say.

'Biding its time.'

'Hiding its light under a bushel.'

'Waiting in the wings.'

'And I'm not even sure,' I say, 'that I even liked this one that much anyway.'

'Me neither.' Olly peers at the cheese plate, his handsome face looking more noble than ever in the bistro's candle-light. 'That Comté looks good, though. You have a bit of that, and I'll try some of the Camembert.'

We fall into a companionable silence as we find our way around the cheese platter together for the next few minutes.

Well, as companionable a silence as it's ever going to be between us any more, given that I can't even look at him without feeling lust and misery wash over me in equal measure.

41

Then, breaking the silence, he says, 'You're probably right about Tash, though, Lib. We do need to make more effort to spend time together. I mean, that's what grown-up relationships are about, right? Compromising. Going the extra mile.'

I'm about to quip that I wouldn't know, having never been in a grown-up relationship.

But, somehow, my heart isn't in it.

So I just nod, as enthusiastically as I know how, and reach out a hand to cut myself a sliver of Roquefort.

*

It's almost midnight by the time I get home.

Actually, make that 'home'.

Because grotty and minuscule though it undeniably was, my flat back in Colliers Wood was home. This new place, in posher-than-posh Notting Hill, doesn't feel like home to me yet. And if my relations with Elvira Roberts-Hoare get any frostier, I don't imagine I'll start to really relax here any time soon.

But perhaps it's just all that champagne making me a bit maudlin and self-pitying. All that champagne in the company of my lost soulmate. We ended up drinking two bottles before we parted ways, Olly back home to Skype Tash, and me back here to . . .

. . . well, what *is* my current plan? A pint of water, take my makeup off and get into bed for a restorative night's sleep?

Or, instead, how about I crack open the bottle of white wine that I know is nestling in the upstairs fridge, accompany it with the large bag of Frazzles stashed in one of the kitchenette cupboards, slump on the Chesterfield with the remote control and flick through late-night rubbish on the TV to distract myself from dwelling on my evening out with Olly?

Yes. The latter, I think. Temporary painkilling that's only going to make me feel even worse in the morning. A sensible decision, as ever.

I haul my weary body up the stairs to the kitchen, grab the wine and the Frazzles, and head back down the stairs again to locate the remote control.

'*Excusez-moi?*' says a voice from the Chesterfield sofa.

Oh, my dear God almighty.

It's Grace Kelly.

And not just any old Grace Kelly: Grace Kelly *in full wedding attire*. The iconic dress, with its 125-year-old lace bodice and its full silk skirt. The veil, with what must be a hundred yards of tulle suddenly taking up most of the available floor-space in my new living room. The beaded Juliet cap framing, perfectly, her serene face.

Except that she isn't looking that serene at the moment, it has to be said. Not that I can possibly comment, because I'm probably staring at her like a goldfish who's just been slapped in the face with a wet kipper. But she's looking, if it were possible, even more startled to see me than I am to see her.

There's silence for a moment.

'*Je suis desolée*,' she goes on, in a rather more wobbly voice than I'm used to hearing in her films, though the cut-glass diction remains largely in place. She gets to her feet; she's taller than I imagined she'd be, or perhaps this is just because she holds herself so well, her broad shoulders pulled back and her neck nothing short of swan-like. '*Mais je suis un peu . . . je ne sais pas le mot en français . . .* uh . . . *Parlez-vous anglais?*'

'I AM *anglaise*,' I croak.

'Oh!' Her elegant eyebrows lift upwards. 'I'm sorry. I had absolutely no idea there *was* anyone English working here.'

'Here . . .?'

'The palace. You'll forgive me, I hope,' she goes on, her voice more perfectly clipped, now that she's recovered herself, 'if I haven't the faintest idea who you are or what it is you do. It's been the most impossibly hectic few days since I first arrived, and obviously with the wedding tomorrow morning . . .'

'Right,' I say, faintly. 'The wedding.'

I mean, you'd think I might be somewhat inured to this by now. You'd think I might even be a bit blasé about what is starting, frankly, to look like an *infestation* of Hollywood legends, popping out of my magical sofa.

But this is *Grace Kelly*. Quite literally, Hollywood royalty.

I mean, if it was . . . I don't know, Ava Gardner, or Betty Grable, or even Lauren Bacall, I think I'd be a bit more able to take it in my stride.

I can't take Grace Kelly in my stride.

Yes, Audrey Hepburn was exquisite, and yes, Marilyn Monroe was a knockout. But Grace Kelly, if it were possible, knocks the pair of them into a cocked hat.

Her serene beauty, as she stands here five feet away from me in her wedding dress, is astonishing. She might literally have the most perfect face I've ever seen. Which obviously I already knew – it's not like I haven't watched and rewatched her movies throughout my life – but seeing it here, in the (sort-of) flesh, it's . . . astounding. Not that she looks as if she *is* made of flesh, to be honest. Her peachy-pale skin is so flawless that it looks as if it might actually be made of pearl nacre and slivers of Grade-A diamond. It's the same glow that Audrey and Marilyn both seemed to have, in fact, and one that probably owes more to the fact that they're magical manifestations from down the back of an enchanted Chesterfield rather than a one hundred per cent real deal. Her hair, swept back with its rather touching widow's peak, is baby-blonde, and her eyes as piercingly blue as they've ever been when I've seen them on screen. And, just like Audrey and Marilyn, she's wafting a very real-smelling scent of perfume – something sumptuously floral, in her case, that smells of violets and roses and irises. Fleurissimo by Creed, I suddenly remember, in the way random facts suddenly appear, popping up into your head when you didn't even know they were there in the first place. The scent made especially for Grace Kelly to wear on her wedding day.

'Are you one of the girls they assigned to unpack my things?'

'Huh?'

'Are you one of the girls,' she repeats, with that unmistakable New England inflection, all over-emphasized vowels and crisp plosives, 'they assigned to unpack my things?' Her manner, now that she's got over the surprise at seeing me, is polite, but distinctly distant. 'I don't know if you're all maids, or secretaries . . . really, there are *so* many staff here, it's a little overwhelming at present.'

'I'm . . . I'm not . . . staff.'

'Anyway, I wondered if, by any chance, you'd happened to unpack a prayer book?' She's ignored what I've just said, and is casting her penetrating gaze around the flat, before it alights on one of my as-yet-unpacked boxes. She glides towards it, the train of her dress swishing across the wooden floor, to peer inside. 'It's particularly important to me, you see, and . . . well, obviously the religious ceremony is in the morning. This is my trial run in the dress, if you like. I never do anything without a proper dress rehearsal!'

'No. I'm quite sure you don't.'

She looks up, this time fixing that penetrating gaze on to me. 'Perhaps it would be better if you looked, rather than me? I don't want to risk damaging the dress.'

'God, no . . . I mean, it's priceless. Iconic.'

'What do you mean by that?'

'Just that,' I swallow, hard, 'generations of women use it as a kind of Holy Grail of wedding dresses. The acme. The zenith. The . . . er . . .'

'Well, I haven't even worn it out in public yet!' She gives

a brisk but rather nervous laugh. 'I know there's been all kinds of fevered speculation, but I rather think all those generations of women had better reserve judgement until they actually set eyes on it. Don't you?'

'Yes, but—'

'Golly,' she goes on, with a little shiver, 'it's chilly up here! I shouldn't have come in here at all, really, but I just wanted to know what it feels like to move around in the dress, and the palace is so huge, I took at least two wrong turns . . . I didn't exactly plan to end up in an attic store-room, I can tell you that. But while I'm here, I'd very much like to find that prayer book.'

'But this isn't . . . it's not an attic storeroom. And it's not the, er, palace in Monaco, either.'

A perfect eyebrow arches. She looks distinctly unimpressed. 'I beg your pardon?'

'It isn't a storeroom,' I say, firmly. 'You're not in Monaco.'

Because this is what I vowed I'd do, the very next time this happened: cut to the chase and try to find out what the hell it *is* with this sofa. I never had the chance with Audrey – and, to be fair, I spent most of the times I saw *her* convinced I was talking to my very own brain tumour – and when I broached the subject with Marilyn Monroe she just thought I was telling her I was some kind of psychic . . . but now that it's Grace Kelly I'm face to face with, my golden opportunity to dig deeper into this mystery has surely arrived. She's cool, calm and collected, where Marilyn was daffy, breathless and – mostly – slightly squiffy. Admittedly Grace does seem a *bit* skittish beneath

47

her ice-princess aura, probably down to the fact that, in her world at least, she's about to become an *actual* princess tomorrow, marrying a man – in front of billions – that she doesn't even know that well. But still. She's *Grace Kelly*. She's smart, astute, and Teflon-strong. If I don't seize this chance, I know I'll regret it.

She blinks. 'I'm sorry . . . you did say you were English?'

'Why do you ask?'

'Well, because you're just not making an awful lot of sense. But it can't be a language barrier . . . I'll tell you what: I'll just try to make my own way back to my room, and call for someone else on the prince's staff. Then they can find my prayer book, and I can leave you to get on with . . . well, whatever it is you do here.' She takes a step towards the door, as if she's actually going to be able to get out that way. 'Very pleasant passing the time with you, Miss . . . I didn't get your name?'

'Lomax. Libby Lomax. Look, Gra . . .' I stop myself, just in time. 'Miss Kelly,' I go on. 'There's something you need to understand. Or, more to the point, I suppose, there's something *I* need to understand . . .' I point a finger towards the Chesterfield. 'OK, you see that sofa? It's magical, all right? Now, I know it doesn't make a lot of sense, but people – Hollywood stars, to be more accurate – appear out of it. Audrey Hepburn. Marilyn Monroe. And now you.'

Her blue eyes, the colour of the sky on a sunny midwinter day, rest on me. She doesn't blink.

There's a rather long silence.

'I beg your pardon?' Her crisp plosives are crisper than ever. 'You are aware,' she goes on, 'of what you just said?'

'I know it sounds . . . well, absolutely impossible. Crazy. But it isn't. I promise you. Well, it isn't impossible. It *is* pretty crazy. But the sofa *is* enchanted. I got it from Pinewood film studios, and—'

'Pinewood?' Her gaze softens, just for a moment. 'Is this . . . some joke of Hitch's?'

'Hitch's?'

'Alfred Hitchcock. Are you playing out some joke of his? It's just like him to concoct some bizarre pre-wedding jape, now I come to think of it . . .'

'No, no! Nothing of the sort.'

' . . . and besides, I know he's against this marriage in principle. Thinks I'll never come back to work in Hollywood, now I'm a princess of the realm. Which he's quite mistaken about,' she folds her gloved arms across her slender body, 'by the way. And you can tell him, the next time you see him . . .'

'I won't see him. I don't know him. Honestly. This isn't a joke. Everything I'm telling you is real.'

Grace Kelly frowns at me, her smooth forehead creasing. 'You honestly expect me to believe in an enchanted sofa in the attic?'

'Again, it isn't an attic. I live here.'

'You live *in an attic?*' She looks rather alarmed, all of a sudden; her steely composure momentarily fractured. 'I'm sorry to be so blunt, but . . . you're not . . . some sort of palace lunatic, are you?'

'No! Of course I'm not.'

'It's only that, well, I don't actually know the prince all that well yet . . . I mean, obviously we're very much in love – I'd hardly have agreed to marry him if we weren't, not even to keep my parents happy . . .' She clears her throat before continuing. 'But one never knows, until one actually starts living with someone, exactly what sort of skeletons they have in their closet. Or in this case, I guess, what sort of lunatics they have in their attic.' Something else suddenly seems to occur to her, and her bright blue eyes narrow. 'If you're making all this up to throw me off the scent because you're Rainier's *mistress* . . .'

'Christ, no!'

'Well, there's no need to sound so appalled, dear.' Grace Kelly looks, suddenly, more human than I've seen her look thus far. Just for a moment, her shoulders drift from ramrod-straight, and that crease in her forehead deepens. 'He's an extremely attractive man! And a prince, of course. I wouldn't be marrying him otherwise . . .' Then she stops. 'Not that I mean . . . I'm not marrying him *because* he's a prince, of course. I'm marrying him because I love him.'

'Of course, of course . . .'

'It's just as easy to fall in love with a prince,' she goes on, somewhat defensively, 'as it is to love a more ordinary man. Not to mention the fact that . . . well, it's all very well everyone thinking I have men falling at my feet, but what use is that when all the good ones are already married?'

'Yes, it's OK, you don't have to explain anything to me.

50

I mean, I've never been in love with a prince, and the guy I'm in love with *is* just an ordinary man . . . but that's all getting off the subject.' I take a deep breath and step closer to where she's standing, slightly less regally than before, in her princess-perfect dress. 'Look, I can prove it to you, OK? I can prove that what I'm saying is true. You think you're in the palace in Monaco, right? The pink palace, up on a cliff, overlooking the sparkling waters of the Mediterranean Sea . . .'

'Overlooking the marina, actually,' she says, sharply, 'and I don't see what the view has to do with—'

I take one step closer to the window and pull up the blind.

'Look out there,' I say. 'Look out of the window and tell me what you see.'

She opens her mouth – I can tell – to object to my instruction.

'Just one glance,' I plead. 'Look out there and tell me if you can see a marina, filled with bobbing yachts, the moonlight dancing on the water. Or – ' I peek out of the window for a moment myself – 'tell me if what you can actually see is an ordinary street, a load of parked cars, the rubbish bins all put out for the bin-men tomorrow morning and . . . oh, I think that's a fox rifling through one of the bins over there.' The streetlight is bright enough for me to see the scrawny, bushy-tailed animal wrestling with what looks, at least from this distance, like a Domino's pizza box and a Tropicana juice carton. 'Please, Miss Kelly,' I say. 'Just look.'

For a moment, I think she's not going to move.

51

Then, with a well-disguised air of curiosity, she takes one step closer to the window so she can peep out.

Her eyebrows shoot immediately upwards, in absolute astonishment.

'I don't understand!' She glances over her shoulder to look at me. 'Where has the marina gone?'

'Exactly! That's what I'm saying!' I perch on the window-ledge and look right at her. This close up, the scent of her perfume is stronger than ever, and I can see the faintest lines around her eyes that make her – oddly enough – seem more real, somehow. Well, if not real, then more down-to-earth. More vulnerable, perhaps. 'You're magical!' I continue. 'Not just Hollywood magic, but *real* magic. You pop up out of the sofa and into my world and then . . . well, actu-ally I have absolutely no idea where you go when you go back into the sofa.' I think about this for a moment. 'I mean, I have no idea whether you go back into your own world, or whether you just cease to exist for a bit . . . the only thing I *am* certain of – at least, I think I'm certain of it – is that it's not a two-way thing. I don't get to go into *your* world, as far as I know. This is more like . . . *Alice in Wonderland*, I suppose . . .'

'I see. I see.' Her voice is low, and she's talking to herself more than to me. 'I . . . I think I get it.'

'Oh, thank God! OK, so as far as I can tell, from what's happened before . . .'

'It's a dream. That explains it. It's not a joke. It's a dream. A very vivid dream, but only a dream.'

'What? No, no, that's not it at all!'

'Don't be absurd, dear.' She stares down at me, with a thrilling return to her regal *froideur*. 'Quite apart from the fact that what you're saying cannot *possibly* be true – I mean, a *magical sofa?* – it simply cannot be the case that *I'm* the one who's come into *your* real-life existence.' She lifts her rather strong chin. 'I'm Grace Kelly. Magic may happen *around me* – movie stardom, an Oscar win, marrying a prince and becoming a princess – but *I* am real.'

'Yes, OK, I can see why you think that, but—'

'I don't *think that*. I *know* that. I am not some bit-player in your life! Some magical being in a world where you're the real one . . .? No. It's simply not possible. Things happen to me, after all. *I do not happen to other people.*'

I blink at her. 'So . . . you're telling me *I'm* the magical one?'

She lets out a rather delighted, excitable tinkle of laughter. It sounds like musical notes on a scale, and would probably be enchanting if she weren't trying to tell me I don't exist.

'Oh, no, no, I'm not telling you you're magical! Isn't it obvious? You're in *my* dream!'

'No, I—'

'It's perfectly apparent to me, now.' She paces, in a very dynamic way for someone wearing yards and yards of lace, over to the Chesterfield, and sits down. She seems to be thinking aloud. 'I've been under a good deal of stress, the last few days have been frankly exhausting . . . I'm sleeping in a strange place, and I really *shouldn't* have tried that rather pungent French cheese at supper this evening . . . so although I'll admit this does all seem remarkably vivid, it's obviously a dream. Now, if I were in psychoanalysis, the way everyone else I know is – in fact, I probably *should* have been in psychoanalysis, back home, but Mother and Father have always made it so clear they think it's nothing but snake oil and codswallop – well, then I'd probably be able to glean all sorts of things from this dream that might help me in my real life.' She looks up at me, fixing me with that penetrating, blue-eyed gaze for a moment. 'Perhaps you're supposed to represent some other version of me? Ooooh,' she suddenly breathes, 'are you my alter ego? The person I'd be if I didn't look the way I do? If I *hadn't* made it in the movies and met the prince? After all, you do look so terribly downtrodden and, well, ordinary.'

'Hey! I've just had a bad night, that's all.' I give her a pretty penetrating gaze of my own. 'You try looking anything other than downtrodden when the man you love doesn't love you back.'

'Aha!' She seems to seize on this, actually clapping her hands together as if to capture the thought before it dares to sidle away again. 'This is the *second time* you've mentioned this man you're in love with! What message are you trying to convey? What inner truth are you trying to wheedle out of my subconscious?'

'No message! No inner truth!'

'Because obviously, I've had my share of love affairs . . .' Quite suddenly, she lowers that cut-glass New England voice, worried that somebody in the 'palace' might overhear her, I suppose. 'What I mean to say,' she goes on, 'is that perhaps I might, in the past, have fallen in love with a man who didn't feel the same way as I did. And obviously, the night of one's wedding, one's thoughts start to turn to all that sort of thing . . . I won't say I was *deliberately* thinking about Clark earlier today, when I was getting ready for the civil ceremony, but I certainly did find him popping into my mind—'

'Clark Gable?' I can't help blurting. 'You were in love with Clark Gable?'

Her pearlescent skin colours, ever so slightly. 'Well! If you're the manifestation of my subconscious, I'd think you ought to know about something like that!'

'But I'm *not* the manifestation of—'

'Anyhow, I don't know if I was any *more* in love with him than I've ever been with a man. He was just the one that kept popping into my head earlier. And I suppose Rainier does look a *little* like him, with his moustache . . . I say: this fellow you're talking about, the one you say you're in love with, does he have a moustache? Because it would make a lot of sense if you said he did.'

'No. He doesn't have a moustache.' I feel giddy with frustration though, to be fair, that could also be down to a combination of the lateness of the hour and the quantity of champagne I've drunk this evening. 'Look,' I try one more time, rather desperately, 'I don't know if you ever met Audrey Hepburn or Marilyn Monroe . . .'

'Well, of course I have. They're sweet girls . . . Oh!' Grace gasps. 'Is this *another* message? Because they do say that the prince was interested in meeting Marilyn Monroe, as a prospective bride, before he met me. Not that anything of that sort would have stood a chance of success, of course. Nothing against Marilyn, but I don't think the people of Monaco would have stood for that.'

And then, quite abruptly, she stops talking.

She's staring down at my coffee table.

More accurately, she's staring down at the *OK!* magazine that Cass dumped on my coffee table when she was round earlier this afternoon. The one with Prince Albert of Monaco, his wife Charlene and their children on the cover.

'Who is that woman?' Grace asks, pointing a rather shaky finger at the magazine's cover. 'And why is she wearing my earrings?'

A terrible feeling of dread pulses through me.

I can't tell Grace Kelly – even a magical Grace Kelly – that this is her adult son, a son who, as far as she's concerned, hasn't even been conceived yet. *Can* I? Even if she believes I'm a dream, some harbinger of her future, it's just too close to her tragic reality, too uncomfortable for me to voice . . .

'And who,' she asks, in a much smaller, fainter voice, all trace of regal grandiosity completely disappeared, 'is that man she's with?'

I open my mouth to tell her . . . what?

I mean, really, what? Because it says, quite plainly, in the magazine's block-lettered headline, that this is *ALBERT OF MONACO AND HIS BEAUTIFUL FAMILY ON THE EVE*

56

OF PUBLICATION OF NEW OFFICIAL BIOGRAPHY OF
HIS BELOVED MOTHER, PRINCESS GRACE.

'Miss Kelly,' I begin. I take a very deep breath. 'Grace . . .'

But she's gone. Disappeared. Vanished.

Where she was sitting, just three seconds ago, is now nothing but thin air.

Thin air wafting, of course, with the rose- and violet-tinged scent of her Fleurissimo perfume.

Chapter 3

Hangover or no hangover, I've tidied the entire flat this morning – and hidden the offending copy of *OK!* safely at the bottom of the magazine pile – ready for Bogdan's arrival at ten a.m.

Bogdan (Son of Bogdan) is – as the name might suggest – the son of my former landlord, Bogdan Senior, and now one of my greatest friends. He's a part-time handyman and a part-time hairdresser (secretly, because his Moldovan crime-lord father would have a thing or two to say about the hairdressing if he knew about it), and both those skills have come in very handy to me since I got to know him. This morning, he's popping over to help me put up a little flat-pack IKEA desk in the studio, so that I can work properly out of there until I decide exactly what to do with the space.

And, although he doesn't know it yet, to discuss last night's mystical arrival on the sofa. Because Bogdan is the only person in my life who's undergone the full magical Chesterfield experience. My memory is forever imprinted, in fact, with the image of him sitting on the sofa, chattering away nineteen to the dozen with Marilyn Monroe, and – always the hairdresser – attempting to persuade her to ditch her trademark blonde ('too much cliché, Miss Marilyn') and become a brunette. Bogdan's sang-froid in the face of the mind-boggling was nothing less than astounding and, though we've rarely spoken about it since, it's been a huge relief to know that he's in on the whole bizarre situation too.

I've just put the kettle on for one of Bogdan's strong cups of black tea when there's a knock all the way downstairs and I head down to let him in.

When I open the front door, he's standing on the pavement outside wearing his usual air of mild-to-moderate tragedy, along with a pair of (extremely brave) rainbow-striped cargo trousers, and a T-shirt that informs me that *Harry Styles Is Cute . . . But His Boyfriend Is Cuter.*

I still can't *quite* believe that his father hasn't noticed anything about Bogdan yet. Though I suppose it's possible that Bogdan leaves the family house in the morning wearing traditional Moldovan dress, or whatever else his scary dad would approve of, and then puts on his rainbow-themed, Harry-Styles-appreciating garb when he's at a safe distance.

'Good morning,' Bogdan informs me now, in his usual lugubrious manner. 'This is most exciting occasion.'

'It is?'

'New flat,' he reminds me. He uses a huge hand to wave at the street. 'In tiptop surroundings. Are you meeting celebrity neighbours?'

'I don't think I *have* celebrity neighbours.'

Bogdan makes a *tsk* noise before heading through the door and closing it behind him. 'Of course you are having the celebrity neighbours. Is Notting Hill, Libby. Am thinking you will be bumping into Claudia Schiffer when you are popping to Whole Foods for guarana smoothies and cashew nuts. Am thinking you will be exchanging the nod with Elle Macpherson when you are going for early morning run. Am thinking . . .'

'Hang on,' I say, leading the way up the stairs. 'What makes you think that now that I live in Notting Hill I'm automatically going to become some sort of healthy-living obsessive?'

'But this is exactly what you must be doing!' He sounds appalled that I've not considered this. 'You are very pretty girl, Libby, but I cannot be making words into mince-meat.'

'You're not going to mince your words, you mean?'

'Yes. Am saying that if you are successful jewellery designer living in Notting Hill, you are needing to be looking part.' He gives my outfit – jeans and a grey hoodie, which to be fair to me I only slung on because I was tidying up this morning – a disapproving once-over. 'Come to be thinking of it, guarana smoothie and early morning jog may be too advanced for now. Perhaps we are needing to be focusing on grooming basics before we are worrying about this.'

'Thanks, Bogdan, but I don't actually need your help with grooming basics . . .'

'Am begging to be different. You are being in very urgent

need of help with hair, for starters, Libby.' He stares, in a woebegone fashion, at my straggly mouse-brown ponytail. 'Am not able to be punching the pulls . . .'

'Pulling punches,' I correct him, and then, because I can't deal with too many more incidents of Bogdan mangling his English idioms this morning, I go on, 'Look, we can discuss my hair later. Right now, I need to talk to you about something more important.'

'More important than hair?'

'More important than hair, Bogdan, yes.' I go over to the sofa and put a hand on the over-stuffed back. 'It's happened again.'

'What is happening again?'

'The sofa. You know. The . . . *thing* it does.'

His impassive face barely registers this, but then to Bogdan a magical sofa isn't anything earth-shattering. He takes these things in his rainbow-coloured stride.

'Someone new is appearing?'

'Yes.'

He gazes down at the sofa. 'Is Elizabeth Taylor?'

'No.'

'Is Jean Harlow?'

'No.'

'Is Ava Gardner?'

'No.' I lower my voice, though I couldn't really tell you why. 'It was . . . Grace Kelly.'

Just for a moment, Bogdan looks impressed. 'I am loving her.'

'Right, well . . .'

'Seriously. Am being in love with her. She is my . . . how are you saying? Perfect woman.'

I glance at his *Harry Styles Is Cute* T-shirt. 'Er . . . are you quite sure you *have* a perfect woman?'

'There is no need for the being snarky. Am I ever asking you the personal questions about *your* specific sexual persuasions?'

'Well, OK, no, you don't ask me questions about my sexual persuasion, as such, Bogdan, no. But you've never exactly been shy about digging for details on my sex life with Dillon.'

My ex-boyfriend Dillon is – along with Harry Styles, Harry Styles's 'boyfriend' and now, apparently, Grace Kelly – another person Bogdan has a heartfelt crush on.

'Am falling in love with her,' he goes on, lyrically, 'from the moment am first seeing her in *Mogambo*. Was even trying to be growing moustache like Clark Gable, but is difficult as was only eleven at time.'

'I wouldn't have thought growing a Clark Gable moustache was *difficult* at age eleven. I'd have thought it was *impossible*.'

'No, no. For me, this is perfectly possible. Is simply difficult as world is not ready for eleven-year-old boy with Clark Gable moustache. Am being on receiving end of the terrible mocking in streets of Chişinău. Perhaps would have been different in London.'

'I highly doubt that, to be honest with you.'

'But Grace Kelly . . .' Bogdan heaves a sigh. 'Has ever there been such classical beauty? And such style! When am thinking of her in that wedding dress, am feeling—'

'Yes, well, that wedding dress is what she popped up in last night,' I say, hastily, before Bogdan can go any further down the route of the way Grace Kelly in her wedding dress makes him feel. 'Right here on the Chesterfield.'

'Right *here?*' Bogdan murmurs, sitting down on the sofa and caressing, with one of his huge hands, the cushion beside him. 'This is very exciting news, Libby. Very exciting indeed.'

'Yes, I suppose it is exciting, kind of . . . I mean, she was a little bit bossy, to be honest with you. And she's adamant that she's the real one and I'm just popping up in a dream. As the manifestation of her subconscious.'

'Is honour indeed,' Bogdan says, 'to be subconscious of Grace Kelly.'

'Bogdan! I'm not her subconscious! Obviously.'

'Of course. Am forgetting.'

'*And* I don't even know if she's going to come back again, because she accidentally saw a magazine cover with her son on it and – well, I don't know why, exactly – that made her vanish in a puff of smoke . . .'

'Ah,' says Bogdan, wisely. 'This is very interesting Chicken McNugget of information.'

'So, do you agree with me that we ought to try to find out a bit more? I wanted to ask you about that aunt you told me about the last time.'

'Aunt?'

'You told me once that you had an aunt who's some sort of . . . I don't know . . . mystic, or something.' I feel foolish, to be honest, even saying the word. 'And that she's experienced this kind of thing before.'

'The enchantment of the soft furnishings?'

OK, now I feel even more foolish.

'Yes, Bogdan, the enchantment of the soft furnishings,' I say, glad that it's only me and him (and, possibly, the faint stirrings of Grace Kelly) in the room right now.

'Ah, you are speaking of my Aunt Vanya. The sister of my father's cousin's second wife.'

This doesn't sound much like an aunt to me, but I'm absolutely not about to get into a discussion of Moldovan cultural practices with Bogdan.

'I was wondering if you could call her – this Aunt Vanya – and ask if she'd mind having a chat to me about it. Through you, obviously, so you can . . . er . . . translate.'

'There is no need for making the call.'

'Oh, OK, well, Skype, or something, then. I mean, whatever's easiest, what with her being in Moldova.'

'But Aunt Vanya is not living in Moldova. She is living in London. She is married to leading member of Haringey Council.'

'Oh! That's . . . I didn't expect that.' I'm really curious now. 'And her husband – the Haringey Council man – he doesn't mind that she's a . . . a mystic? With a specialist knowledge of enchanted furniture?'

Bogdan shrugs. 'He is man of world. Besides, he is experiencing some pretty strange things himself, in the cut-throat world of the politics of Haringey.'

'Right. Well, I'd really appreciate it, Bogdan, if you could let me meet her some time soon?'

'Will be getting in touch with her,' he says, in a mysterious tone that makes me wonder if he's planning to contact her by smoke signal, or Ouija board, or something, and then leaves me surprised when he simply pulls out his mobile phone. 'The text message is probably the safest way. Last time I am speaking to her she is convinced her phone is being monitored by husband's greatest rival, head of North London Waste Authority.'

'OK, well, I'll just nip up the road and get some milk for our tea, and maybe you could start taking a look at the flat-pack stuff while I'm gone?'

'Yes, can be doing this. And after, we can be taking serious look at your hair.'

'I'm fine with my hair, Bogdan.'

'This is what is worrying me,' he sighs. 'Am sympathizing, Libby, that you are losing your soulmate. But this is no reason to be letting self go.'

'I haven't let myself go!'

'Is important to be looking good for yourself, Libby, not just for man.'

'I don't have a man!'

He arches an eyebrow. 'And you are never wondering why?'

OK, I'm not quite sure how I've ended up backed into this corner, but it's a unique genius of Bogdan's: to somehow bring us on to the topic of Men. More specifically, why I don't have a Man. More specifically even than that, why I'm not, in the absence of anyone else in my life, going at it like a rabbit with my ex, Dillon O'Hara.

'Am sorry for you,' he's going on, 'that you are doomed never to be with your one true love . . .'

'OK, I think *doomed* is a pretty strong way to put it. It's just . . . the way the cookie has crumbled.'

'. . . but this is no reason to hide away from the romance for the rest of life.'

'I'm not *hiding away from romance*, Bogdan. And if you're about to suggest that I'm doing anything of the sort, just because I'm not picking up the phone for a booty call with Dillon every night . . .'

'Am not suggesting this. Well, am not saying this is *bad* idea . . .' He looks serious – well, more serious than ever – for a moment. 'But is time for you to be taking control of your own destiny. Am not saying has to be Dillon. But you are too young, Libby, to be coconut-shying away from men for ever. Too young and too pretty. And too nice.'

'Oh, Bogdan.' I feel a lump in my throat. 'That's the nicest thing you've ever said to me.'

'Is nothing.' His eyes narrow, for a moment. 'Do not be thinking that this means am forgetting about catastrophe in hair department.'

'Heaven forfend.' I pick up my bag. 'And I promise you, Bogdan, just for saying all that, the very next time I meet a tall, handsome stranger – because they're just crawling out of the woodwork, obviously – I'll let him sweep me off my feet and give me the full fairy-tale ending I so richly deserve, OK? Just for you.'

'This,' says Bogdan, evidently not picking up on my attempt at irony, 'is what am wanting to be hearing.'

Then he goes back to texting Aunt Vanya while I head

down the stairs, out of the front door, and towards the main road to buy the milk.

I pull my phone out of my pocket as I go, so I can take the opportunity to FaceTime Nora back. She's heading down to London later this week – a rare enough occurrence, unfortunately – to drop her daughter Clara off with her parents so that she and Mark can have a weekend away for their first wedding anniversary. We need to speak, even if only briefly (which, what with work and baby-feeding and what seems like *endless* hours trying to convince Clara that she actually wants to go to sleep, our calls always are, anyway) to arrange how and where we're going to meet each other for the couple of hours that she's here. A hasty coffee, a cheeky glass of wine . . .

'Nora!' I say, already feeling approximately six thousand per cent more cheerful as her face pops up on my phone. 'I've caught you!'

'Hi!' she says – or rather, mouths at me. Her eyes are rather wide and she's looking slightly terrified. 'Hang on a sec . . .' she adds, still mouthing, before vanishing from the screen for a moment. Everything goes rather wobbly, and then black, before she reappears a couple of moments later, still looking faintly terrified but talking normally. Well, in a loud whisper. 'Sorry! I've literally only just got her down for a nap! In five minutes' time a bomb could go off in her room and it wouldn't wake her, but right now a pin might drop in the street outside and she'll bloody wake up again. I'm just going,' she adds, 'up to the top-floor bathroom. It's the opposite side of the house, so if I lean out of the skylight there, she won't hear me talking.'

'Lean out of the skylight?' I'm slightly alarmed; I've only been to Nora's new house up in Glasgow once, but it's a four-storey townhouse with a paving-slab patio for a garden. 'You'll be careful, won't you?'

'Oh, yes, yes, I do it all the time! And frankly, Lib, I'd rather risk plummeting to my death on the patio below than risk waking her up!' Nora adds, cheerfully. 'How's everything down there?' she asks. 'I gather you had an evening out with Olly last night?'

'Yes. Um, did he tell you that, or did—'

And suddenly, I'm taking off.

Literally, I mean: into the air. My feet are leaving the pavement, and I fly up, up, sideways and up . . . before landing – *ow* – on my backside on another bit of the pavement about five feet away.

I sprawl there for a moment, too dazed to really understand what's happened, until I see a man's face hovering over me.

'Oh, my God! Are you all right?'

'Hnh?'

'Can you move? Can you talk? Do you think anything's broken? Did you hit your head?'

I don't know how to respond to any of these questions. So I just say, again, gormlessly, 'Hnh?'

'Oh, God, you *can't* talk . . . I'm calling an ambulance . . . Esti, call an ambulance!' he says, over his shoulder, to whoever it is who's with him.

'No, no, don't do that!' I sit bolt upright, and it's only thanks to his sharp reactions that we don't end up cracking our foreheads together.

He is, I notice the moment I sit up, incredibly handsome. I mean, incredibly.

He's dark-haired, blue-eyed and long-lashed, with skin the colour of vanilla fudge. It's quite an astonishing combination.

I'm interrupted, though, in my reverie by the sudden appearance of the Esti he just called out to.

'Everything OK here?' she asks, sticking her head over the man's shoulder. 'What can I do?'

'Don't call an ambulance. I can talk! Fine I am. I mean,' I say, correcting myself from talking like Yoda, or one of the characters from a Dr Seuss book, 'really, I'm absolutely fine.'

'But you went right over.'

His accent, like his delicious skin colour, is also hard to place. It's a little bit American, a little bit British, a little bit . . . Dutch? Scandinavian? As he starts to help me to my feet, I can feel some impressive muscles in his arms and back. Which makes sense, because he's wearing running gear and a jacket that says *FitRox Training*. He must be one of the trainers from the gym just along the road, the one Cass mentioned she'd trained at. And this Esti woman is, presumably, one of his clients – or, more likely, even another trainer, because she's super-fit-looking, too, with Madonna-esque arms and Ninja Turtle abs visible under the edge of her cropped running top.

'And you look a bit . . . pale.' The personal trainer guy looks worried. 'I think you should have a hot drink, something with sugar in . . .'

'Oh, that's OK, I was actually just on my way to get milk for tea.'

'I'll get you a cup of tea.'

'That's all right, honestly.'

'Don't be silly. I'm buying you a cup of tea. It's the least I can do.' He turns to point up to the main road. 'Starbucks OK?'

'Yes, sure, but really—'

'Esti, maybe you could pop up and get some tea?' he suggests, to super-fit Esti, who is still jogging, slightly annoyingly, on the spot. 'I'll wait here with . . . sorry, I didn't even get your name before I knocked you into next Tuesday.'

'Libby.'

'I'll wait here with Libby,' he adds, 'so she can have a bit of a sit-down for a moment. Here,' he suggests, guiding me to a low wall outside one of the houses on the street. 'We'll just sit here for a moment, and my very kind – er – friend Esti will go and get you something to drink.'

'Sure,' says Esti.

Although, come to think of it, it was probably more of a *sure?* As in *are you sure?* Because the personal trainer guy gives a little nod of the head, and it's only then that she jogs off in the direction of Starbucks.

I'm still a bit dazed, as I watch her pert, Lycra-clad buttocks round the corner and disappear.

'Can we chat a little bit?' the personal trainer asks. 'Just so I can reassure myself you don't have a terrible concussion, or anything equally alarming.'

'Oh, yes, right.' I glance at him. *Wow.* He's even better-looking, now that I'm upright and a bit more sentient, than I realized. Once you can see past those incredibly bright-blue eyes and that vanilla-fudge skin, you get to see that he's also got a handsome jawline, and full, soft lips, and . . . bloody hell, even his *ears* are attractive. 'Are you supposed to ask me who the prime minister is, and stuff?'

'Yeah, that's the sort of thing. Days of the week might do, too.'

'Ah. Trouble is, I'm never that good on days of the week even under normal circumstances. I had a head injury about a year ago, and even then I was never sure if I couldn't name the day of the week because I was concussed, or because I honestly for the life of me can never remember if it's a Tuesday or a Thursday.'

'Oh, God, you've already had a recent head injury?' He looks appalled. 'Are you sure we shouldn't be getting a cab to the hospital?'

'I'm honestly fine. Besides, it was a year ago. And it's Wednesday today. See?'

'Impressive.' He smiles at me, looking a little bit less stressed.

I smile back. 'So, you work on this street, right?'

'Sorry?'

'The jacket. You're a personal trainer, obviously. At FitRox.'

71

He glances down at his jacket and touches the logo for a moment. 'That's . . . well-spotted.'

'My sister trained there a while ago, when she thought she might get a spot on *Strictly Come Dancing*.'

'How . . . er . . . extraordinary.'

'That she thought she might get a spot on *Strictly Come Dancing*? Well, in a way, yes, because she can't really dance for toffee. But she is reasonably well known, so it wasn't a total shot in the dark, I guess. I mean, she wasn't just some random fan of the show, thinking she might get given a chance to go on it, or something . . .' I'm blithering, I know. It's the effect very handsome men have on me. 'So, what's your name?' I add, because if I can get him talking, that ought to stop me.

'Joel. My name's Joel. I . . .' He stops. He's staring at me. 'You know, Libby,' he says, after a moment, 'I'd really appreciate it if you'd do one thing for me.'

'Sure. Anything.'

Though I'm not a hundred per cent certain that promising a strange man, even one as apparently nice as this one, that you'll do *anything* is necessarily the most sensible idea I've ever had.

'I mean, within reason, of course,' I add, hastily.

'God, yes, yes, of course.' He fixes his blue eyes on to mine; they're incredibly earnest and seem to be looking deep into me. 'The question is, do you think it would be within reason for you to come out to dinner with me tonight?'

This is absolutely not what I was expecting.

'I mean, you may not be free . . .' he adds. 'In fact, you may not even be single . . .?'

'Oh, I'm single. And I'm free,' I go on. 'This evening. But . . . look, there's really no need to take me out to dinner to apologize again.'

'Then I won't apologize again. For the entirety of our dinner, not a single word of regret or remorse shall pass my lips.'

I smile. 'I'll hold you to that.'

'Good. It's settled, then. What works for you? I could come and pick you up from . . . sorry, do you live around here, or something?'

'Yes, I live on this street. I've just moved in. Well, I'm living above my new studio, really – I'm a jewellery designer – and I don't own it, or anything, it's just . . .' I stop myself blithering again. 'Yes, you could pick me up here. I guess it'll be convenient for you, too, after you've finished work?'

'Yes, it will. So . . . eight-thirty?'

'Yes. That would be lovely.'

'Terrific. Shall we go for a drink first and then we can decide what we fancy. To eat, I mean,' he adds, quickly. 'Sound good?'

'Sounds great.'

'Great. Ah, here comes Esti, with the tea . . .'

And here, too, at the same moment, comes Bogdan, who must have glanced out of the window and seen me sitting on the wall over the road.

And who, I'll wager, also spotted the incredibly handsome man sitting next to me.

'Libby?' He breaks into a little jog himself as he crosses the road. 'What is surpassing?'

'Nothing. Just a very small accident. This is a friend of mine,' I say, hastily, to Joel, just in case he hasn't noticed the rainbow trousers and the Harry Styles T-shirt, and thinks Bogdan is my boyfriend, or something. 'And I should really let you get on with your run.'

'I just got you an English Breakfast,' Esti is saying, in a pretty indefinable accent of her own, as she reaches us. She hands over a large Starbucks cup. 'Is that all right?'

'It's great, thank you, it's really kind of you.'

'OK, well, if you're sure you're OK,' Joel says, getting to his feet, 'we'll leave you in the capable hands of . . . er . . .'

'Bogdan,' Bogdan intones, gazing at Joel with a similar expression on his face to the one he had when he was mooning about Grace Kelly earlier. 'Am extra-delighted to be making the acquainting of you.'

'Please,' I say, rather desperately, 'continue your run. I'll see you this evening.'

'Eight-thirty,' Joel reconfirms. 'Looking forward to it. See you later, Libby.'

Bogdan and I stand and watch as Joel and Esti jog away in the general direction of the park.

'Am never knowing,' Bogdan says, in a marvelling whisper, 'how you are doing it.'

'How I'm doing what?'

'Having the super-hot men fall before you like the dead moths in the flame.'

'He didn't fall before me. He's invited me out to dinner because he felt bad about knocking me over.'

Bogdan snorts. 'This is your biggest problem, Libby. That you are naïve. That you are not seeing the thing that is staring in your face.'

'Hang on, I thought my biggest problem was that I won't let you give me a proper fringe.'

'You are having,' he clarifies, 'many problems. But biggest problem of all is that you are never paying attention to the Destiny. Are you not just saying that you are waiting for dark, handsome stranger to sweep you off the feet?'

Oh.

I suppose I did say that.

But . . . you know. In jest.

I wasn't actually expecting a dark, handsome stranger to . . . well, quite literally sweep me off my feet.

Before I can think about this too long or hard, my phone starts to ring. It's ringing, in fact, from somewhere in the nearby gutter, where it must have been knocked when I went flying.

'It's Nora,' I tell Bogdan. 'I'd better get it. She'll be wondering why I vanished so suddenly.'

'All right. But do not be taking too long. Will be finishing the flat-pack furniture in half-hour and then we can be sorting out hair before tonight's hot date.'

I answer the phone to Nora's worried face, and begin the explanation about where I suddenly disappeared to as I follow Bogdan, feeling rather sore as I do so, back towards my front door.

75

Chapter 4

Being a dutiful daughter, I'm obviously still planning to stick to the agreement to go and see Mum at the hospital this evening, even though (as Bogdan has helpfully pointed out) I could really, *really* use the time to get ready for my evening out with Joel the personal trainer.

Because, despite Bogdan's hovering around with a pair of scissors and a hopeful expression most of the afternoon, I didn't end up agreeing to a full makeover (plus fringe sculpt). In amongst all this craziness – Grace Kelly showing up, handsome strangers appearing out of nowhere – I do still have a business to run. This afternoon I spent two solid hours catching up on (mostly bridal) emails before popping up the road again to Starbucks to meet a new (bridal) client face to face to discuss the eight matching pendants she wants to give to her small army of brides-maids to wear on her wedding day and, of course, the vintage-style bridal tiara she's really hoping I can make for her in time for her wedding next month.

Oh, and then just as I was hoping I might get the chance to jump in the shower, shave all the relevant bits that I prefer to shave before I go out for the evening with a man as gorgeous as Joel, then pick out something über-flattering to wear and trowel on a shedload of subtle, natural-looking makeup, Elvira called.

So obviously I had to answer.

It wasn't great, incidentally. Any progress I thought we might have made on the getting-along front yesterday has, obviously, been shattered into pieces. I got a blow-by-blow update on Tino's appointment at the vet's (no broken bones or internal damage, apparently, but this hasn't stopped the vet charging her two hundred quid for the appointment, nor did it stop her announcing that she'll be sending me the bill) and then she finished up the call with what she called an Official Warning. I must have been feeling emboldened by something, or imbued with some of Grace Kelly's Teflon exterior, perhaps, because I did ask if it was actually fair to give me an 'official warning' when I'm still – nominally, if nothing else – working for myself, in charge of my own company. Which didn't go down well with Elvira, obviously, and simply led to another ten minutes of her ranting on about how I need to be careful about biting the hand that feeds me, and The Importance Of Trust, and Taking Responsibility for my mistakes.

So although I did get to shower, thank heavens, it was a hasty jobbie, and there was no time to linger in front of my wardrobe and pick out something heart-stoppingly fabulous, and there was certainly no time to apply quite as much makeup as I'd have liked. But still, despite the fact I've played it a bit safe in skinny jeans, vest top and blazer, and ended up doing most of my makeup at the back of the bus on the way to Harley Street to visit Mum, I feel – possibly mistakenly – as if I'll pass muster.

Not because I'm expecting anything to come of the evening. But still, it's a night out with an extremely handsome man, so I don't want to turn up looking like something the cat dragged in.

Talking of something the cat dragged in, though . . . I've just made my way to Mum's room, up on the third floor of the hospital, and a truly astonishing sight greets my eyes.

Not Mum, prone from her surgery. Mum, in fact, is nowhere to be seen. I mean, her bed is actually empty.

It's Cass.

At least, I *think* it's Cass.

She – the possible-Cass – is sitting next to an open window, smoking a cigarette and blowing the smoke out into the street below. Her hair is scraped into a ratty ponytail and she's wearing – bloody hell – not a single scrap of makeup. I mean, not even concealer. Not even *eyebrow pencil*. She's wearing leggings, and a baggy jumper, and the sort of papery flip-flops you sometimes get given after a posh pedicure.

She looks so different from the usual Cass – Cass of the five-inch heels, and the tight skirts, and the bouncy blow-dry; the Cass that I just saw the day before yesterday, in fact – that my heart skips a beat.

'Oh, my God, Cass . . . is it Mum? Has something happened to her?'

'What?' she snaps. 'No! She's in the bathroom – ' she indicates the closed door on the opposite wall, from which I can now hear a shower running – 'getting herself freshened up.'

'Then what . . . Cass, what's wrong with *you*?'

'I'll tell you what's wrong! Zoltan's fucking *kids*, that's what's wrong!'

Ah.

So the whole stepmothering thing isn't going quite as well as she imagined.

'Cass.' I go over to the window, take her cigarette from her hand, and stub it out in a tea mug beside Mum's bed before the smoke sets off any alarms and we get thrown out of the hospital. 'What's happened?'

'They've only bloody come to *live* with us, the little fuckers!'

'OK, you can't call a six year old and a nine year old *little fuckers* . . .'

'You can,' she says, savagely, 'if they *are* little fuckers.'

'. . . but what on earth do you mean, they've come to live with you?'

'It's her. The ex-wife. Her revenge on me. She drove them round last night, just when Zoltan and I were about to go to bed with a bottle of champagne. Dumped them on the doorstep and said she's going away to stay with a friend in New York for a few weeks, and they can stay with their father. Thanks to that, I've not had a single minute of Me Time all day! I haven't so much as had a shower, or done my makeup, or my hair . . . and they went into my room, without asking, and started playing Shoe Shops with all my shoes! Sticky fingers *all over my Louboutins*! And snot – actual snot, Libby! – on my new Kurt Geiger sandals! I mean, they *said* it was an accident, but I don't believe that for a minute, the horrible little vandals . . .'

'OK, Cass, calm down. They're just children. And come on, they've only been living with you for one day!'

'Yeah, and it's one day too fucking many, I'll tell you that . . . anyway, what would you know? Little Miss Footloose and Fancy-Free.' She scowls at me. 'Why are you so glammed up this evening?'

'I'm going out.'

'Huh! Must be nice.'

'Well, you know, Cass,' I say, 'if you hadn't got involved with a married man with kids . . .'

She sulks, but doesn't say anything.

"Look, can't you and Zoltan have a proper talk? See if there's a dignified way out of this mess?'

Cass crumples up her pretty, unpowdered nose for a moment, as she thinks about this.

'You mean, tell him we need a full-time nanny?'

'No!'

'*Two* full-time nannies?'

'Cass . . .'

'Or are you thinking boarding school?'

I stare at her. 'For a six and a nine year old?'

'Yeah. You can get boarding schools for kids that age, can't you?'

'I'm sure you can. But why not just send them to the workhouse and be done with it?'

'Ooooh, I haven't heard of the workhouse,' Cass says, leaning forward, eagerly. 'Is it far away? Do they let them out for half-term?'

My reply to this – which contains more swearing than I'm normally comfortable with – will have to wait, because the bathroom door is opening and Mum is on her way out.

She doesn't look too bad for a woman in her early sixties who's just had her gallstones out – sorry, sorry, *minor cosmetic surgery*. In fact, in her silk kimono and what look an awful lot like cashmere slippers, she's actually terribly glamorous. For a moment, and it's a rare moment, I feel rather proud of her. There's a certain kind of chutzpah, a certain kind of bloody-minded grit, behind the ability to look fabulous only forty-eight hours after invasive surgery, and Mum has it in spades.

'Oh,' she says, puncturing the moment with the sheer amount of dissatisfaction she can pack into one single syllable. 'Libby. You're here.'

It's not that my own mother *dislikes* me, or anything – though it does occasionally feel that way. It's more that she and I have literally nothing in common. And that Mum isn't very good at feigning interest in people she has nothing in common with. Mum isn't very good at feigning interest in people she *does* have things in common with. There are two things that matter to Mum: herself, and Cass. All right, maybe I'm being unfair: three things.

Herself, Cass, and Michael Ball's performance as Marius in the original London production of *Les Mis* in 1985.

There are then approximately two hundred things that intermittently matter to her a very little bit – depending on what else is going on with the three really significant things in her life – before you scrape right down to the bottom-ish of the barrel and find her elder daughter. Me.

'How are you feeling, Mum?' I ask.

'Oh, well, you know, I'm a fighter,' she says, in her best Bravery In The Face Of Adversity voice. 'It'll take more than being cut open on the surgeon's table to get the better of me!'

'Well, that's good, then. You look really well,' I add, in *my* best You Can't Have It Both Ways voice. 'Really glamorous and zingy, for someone who's just had an op.'

She glares at me. 'I'm trying to keep on keeping on for your sister's sake, actually. Do you have any idea what a terrible time she's been having? Stalked by paparazzi. Hounded by a vicious ex-wife. And now terrorized by these little horrors!'

'Actually, Libby's come up with a really good suggestion,' Cass says, reaching for the contraband cigarettes on the windowsill beside her. 'Have you ever heard of somewhere called The Workhouse, Mum?'

'That wasn't what I was trying to suggest, actually, Cass,' I say, as Mum's eyebrows shoot upwards. 'I'm really trying to suggest that maybe it would be best for you to call it quits with Zoltan. I mean, it's all very complicated, and it hardly seems fair to—'

'Oh, well, I'm not sure that would be very sensible,' Mum says, in the sort of disapproving tone most mothers reserve for stuff like going outside in the winter with damp hair, or forgetting to take a good multivitamin in the middle of cough and cold season. 'Are you aware, Libby, that he's a *footballer?*'

'I am aware, Mum, yes. Does that mean there's some sort of law that says she can't break up with him?'

'Of course there isn't. But it would be plain silly to give up on him this early!'

'Oh, come on. So Cass is meant to stay with this guy, with all the obvious problems, purely because he's a footballer?'

Cass shakes her head, her ratty ponytail wobbling as she does so. 'It's got nothing to do with the fact he's a footballer!'

'Exactly,' Mum agrees. 'Well said, Cassidy, darling!'

'I mean,' Cass goes on, 'why on earth would I want to be with someone just because they're good at kicking a ball around on a field? The *main* thing is that *because of the fact* he's good at kicking a ball around a field, he's *really loaded.*'

Even Mum has the grace to look a bit sheepish.

'*And,*' Cass goes on, 'being with Zoltan makes me an actual WAG! Which is all I've ever wanted,' she breathes, 'since I was, like, *thirteen years old.* I mean, I've never forgotten the image of the original WAGS walking around Boden-Boden . . .'

'I think you mean Baden-Baden,' I say.

'. . . their clothes, their shoes, their *hair* . . .' Cass clasps a hand to her chest. 'That's the kind of thing that *stays with you.*'

'The main thing,' Mum says, hastily, 'is that Zoltan seems like such a wonderful young man.'

'You've never met him,' I point out.

'I can *tell* he seems like such a wonderful young man.' Mum glares at me. 'I've been reading a lot about him these past couple of days, in the magazines. He does all sorts of wonderful charity work – hospital visits for sick children, that kind of thing . . .'

'Wow,' I say. 'That's great. Though, I mean, it might not be a bad idea for him to think about his *own* children, when he has a minute . . .'

'. . . and he's obviously a great family man, because he has the most wonderful house in Surrey,' Mum goes on. 'Doesn't he, darling? I saw it in *Hello!*'

'Yeah,' Cass grumbles, 'but the ex-wife will get that in the divorce.'

'Not if he plays hardball. After all, if you have the children living with you even *some* of the week, darling, you're going to have to move somewhere bigger and better yourselves. And in Surrey, obviously, because those poor wee mites can't be uprooted from their schools and their friends.'

Only three minutes ago, they were *little horrors*. But that was before they'd become quite useful pawns for Mum to justify why Cass needs a WAG-tastic mansion in Surrey.

'In fact, while I've been resting today, I've been looking

on Rightmove, darling,' Mum goes on, pottering over to the bedside table and picking up her iPad. 'There are some *lovely* places up for sale at the moment in the Cobham area . . . look,' she goes on, getting out her phone. 'This one even has stables!'

'Oooooh, I've always wanted to get back to horse-riding,' breathes Cass, peering into Mum's iPad with a fraction of her old get-up-and-go. 'This one's gorgeous. Is it anywhere near that workhouse place Libby was telling me about?'

I think this is my cue to leave them to it.

'OK, well, if you're OK, Mum, and if you're all set here for the night, I'll head off.'

'Libby's got a *date*,' Cass sighs, bitterly.

'Oh! With Dillon?'

This perks Mum up slightly; me going out with Dillon O'Hara was the Best Thing I Ever Did, in her eyes, and she can't really forgive me for the fact I don't seem to have any intention of doing it again.

'No, Mum. Not with Dillon.'

'Who, then?'

'No one. Just a guy I met in the street.'

'Oh, Libby. I know you're almost thirty-five—'

'I'm thirty!'

'. . . but I still think you ought to be setting your sights a little bit higher than some random man from the streets.'

'He's not *from the streets*! I met him *on* the street, right near my flat. He's a personal trainer, actually, and he's absolutely gorgeous.'

'Oooooh, is he one of the trainers from FitRox?' Cass

breathes. 'You jammy cow! They were all massively hot. Is it Nathan? Or Kyan? Or Sabrina?'

'Sabrina's a girl's name.'

'Yeah but, seriously, she was so hot, I'd have done her, too. *God*. Why does Libby get to go out with a gorgeous personal trainer while I'm stuck at home being Mum to my stupid boyfriend's kids?'

'I know. I know. It's very insensitive of her to point it out,' Mum says, soothingly. 'But look, darling: if you talk Zoltan into *this* place, near Walton-on-Thames, you could even think about putting the kids in the annexe . . .'

I leave them poring over the iPad, and head out of the room, somehow managing to refrain from banging the door behind me as I go.

*

I reach my flat at eight twenty-seven exactly, let myself in the front door, and just have time to hurtle upstairs to zhuzz my hair and bung on a coat of lipstick before, on the dot of eight-thirty, there's a knock.

Joel is waiting politely outside when I answer it, and is holding a bunch of extremely lovely dusty-pink roses.

'If those are apology flowers . . .' I begin.

'Nothing of the sort,' he says, with a grin. 'For an apology, you're really looking at a hyacinth, an iris, or a nice calla lily. These are Looking Forward To A Nice Evening Out flowers. I'd have thought that was obvious.'

'You're quite right. I don't know what I was thinking.' I

smile at him. 'They're really gorgeous, Joel, thank you. Oh!' I add, as I take them from him and notice the branded tissue paper they're wrapped in, inside the layer of cellophane. 'And you got them from that place up past the tube! For God's sake, they must have cost you an arm and a leg up there! You honestly shouldn't have.' .

'It was worth it. Besides, I'd never have been able to drop the words hyacinth, iris or calla lily so expertly into the conversation if it hadn't been for the woman who sold them to me. Were you impressed?'

'Ever so. I'll just dash up and put these in some water, and then we can get going.'

I should probably, for politeness's sake, if nothing else, invite Joel up while I bung the gorgeous roses in a sink-full of water, but we're not quite on that level of intimacy yet, I don't think. Besides, after Marilyn Monroe, I'm once bitten, twice shy. Even though there's been no further sighting of Grace Kelly since last night, I'm wary of the worst-case scenario, which is that she's materialized up there right now and is stretched out on the sofa in full wedding dress, still going on about me being her alter ego, or whatever the hell it was she had me pegged as.

She's not, as I can see pretty quickly as soon as I get up there. But still. Better to be safe than sorry. I'm pretty inexperienced at this whole dating thing at the best of times; no need to add to my awkwardness by introducing my magical sofa before we've even cracked open the first bottle of Pinot Grigio.

'Shall we start out at that nice pub on the corner of the

next street,' Joel asks, as I re-emerge and lock up the front door behind me, 'and then we can negotiate what sort of thing we'd like, eating-wise?'

'Perfect.'

I try not to make it too obvious, as we set off, that I'm looking at him. But he does look *good*. He's only wearing jeans, a plain white shirt and dark-brown desert boots, but the combination of these, plus his wonderfully fit body and that chiselled, handsome face . . . well, it's a winner, let's leave it at that.

'So, what do you like?' he asks, glancing down at me.

'Sorry?'

'To eat. Just so we can get some irons in the fire, dinner-wise.'

'Oh, right . . . I'm easy. About food, that is!'

'That's good. So you're not one of those gluten-intolerant, raw-food, permanent health-kick types?'

'No. But – er – aren't you one of those?'

'Should I be?' He sounds faintly astonished.

'Well, I just thought, with you being a personal trainer, you might be into the latest health fads and stuff.'

'Oh . . . well, up to a point, I eat pretty healthily, I guess. But I'm not one for . . . sorry, what did you call them? The latest health fads?'

'That might not be the technical term,' I say, feeling a bit silly. 'I'm a bit clueless about all that kind of thing, sorry. And just so I can get this out of the way at the start of the evening, before you make me feel a bit crap about the number of miles you run a week, or anything, I should probably just let you know that I've not set foot in a gym in about five years!'

'I would never make you feel crap about anything,' he says, in a slightly dismayed tone, as if I'm wildly under-estimating him. 'Least of all your record at the gym. Besides, it doesn't show. You look, if I may say so, amazing.'

This is generous, because although I've done my best, and I think I've scrubbed up reasonably well this evening, I think *amazing* is pushing it.

But fortunately, we've just reached the pub, and he's holding open the door for me, and we're heading in, which brings to an end this slightly awkward line of conversation.

We find a table, a surprisingly nice corner one given that it's already pretty packed in here, and then I hang on to it while he goes and gets a bottle of wine from the bar.

'Red?' he asks, a couple of minutes later, as he reappears with a bottle and two large glasses. 'I realized when I got there that I hadn't actually asked you what you prefer. It's just a Merlot. Is that OK?'

'Joel, honestly, it's fine. Please don't worry! I'm not fussy.' Though it has to make you wonder a little bit about the sort of woman he's used to dating, I suppose: the precise punctuality, the flowers, the checking about my happiness and preferences at every turn. Not that I'm complaining, because obviously his manners are pretty much as exqui-site as that flawless skin of his. I just hope he relaxes a little as the evening goes on.

I'm not used to being the chilled-out one, that's for sure.

'Good.' He sits down opposite me and pours us each a

well-judged glass: not so big that it looks as if he's trying to get me drunk, but not so small that it looks miserly. 'Cheers. And I know I *said* I wouldn't apologize again—'

'Then don't,' I say, firmly, 'because I'm absolutely fine. I mean, I'm pretty well padded.'

The image of me and my well-padded body linger, mortifyingly, in the air for a moment.

Then he chinks his glass to mine again. 'Bottoms up, I suppose?'

The ice, thank God, has been broken.

I laugh, he smiles, and then he takes a drink from his glass and starts looking – thankfully – a little more relaxed.

'So,' he says, 'tell me a bit more about yourself. I mean, all I have so far is that your name is Libby, and you're a jewellery designer. A *well-padded* jewellery designer.'

'Well, for starters, I don't think anyone wants to know more about my well-padded body.'

'Oh, I wouldn't be too sure about that,' he says lightly, and softly, into his wine glass.

I won't deny, this gives me a bit of a thrill.

I mean, I got so accustomed to Dillon's barrage of seductive charm – full-on, no-holds-barred, innuendo-laden verbal foreplay – that I've forgotten what it's like to indulge in some proper, grown-up flirting. No, scratch that: I've *never actually known* what it's like to indulge in proper, grown-up flirting. Everything I know about proper grown-up flirting, I've gleaned from the movies. Gregory Peck, Cary Grant, Fred Astaire. To name just three of the men I'd have given my eye-teeth to be dating rather than the sorry assembly that makes up my past. I've never been wined and dined. I've never been wined *or* dined, come to think of it. All my past relationships have taken a direct path from 1) Drunken Snog At Party through 2) Vaguely Ending Up Sleeping Together to 3) Saying We're Going Out With Each Other Just To Avoid The Embarrassment Of Actually Having To Address The Fact We Only Have (Unsatisfactory) Sex Because We Don't Have Anything To Say To One Another. Followed by 4) Hasty (but never quite hasty enough) Break-Up.

Seriously, my 'love life' has pretty much looked like the icky, embarrassing bits Taylor Swift has never wanted to chronicle in one of her hits.

All of which makes it even more ironic that during all those years of relationship failure, I could – *should* – have been settled in blissful harmony with Olly.

And dammit, there I go.

I'm not thinking about Olly tonight. I'm not. In fact, I'm putting a total ban on it. A total ban I'm going to have to tighten up pretty quick-smart if I want to enjoy the evening.

'Libby?' Joel is looking at me across the table, and looking mildly concerned about the fact I'm (probably) gazing into space like an idiot and not giving him an answer to his perfectly polite question. 'Everything OK?'

'Yes! More than OK! Gosh,' I say, in a super-enthusiastic, jolly-hockey-sticks sort of style, to make up for drifting off, 'well, yes! What can I tell you about me? Er . . . well, I've been running my jewellery company for almost two years now. It only started out as a hobby, really – I mean, I was an actress before that, and a pretty unsuccessful one – but it's really taken off, way more than I ever dreamed it would, really. I'm working with some . . . um . . . really great people.' Best not to sit here and whinge about Elvira's Official Warning, I think; it might lend a bum note to the evening. 'And I'm just concentrating on building the brand at the moment,' I say, which I'm rather pleased with, as an off-the-top-of-my-head statement, because it makes me sound purposeful and dynamic, both of which are things I suspect Joel is impressed by.

'Amazing.' He nods. 'What's the name?'

'Libby Goes To Hollywood. I'm a huge fan of old movies, and my stuff is sort of inspired by Old Hollywood glamour . . . you know, Marilyn Monroe, Ava Gardner . . . er . . . Grace Kelly . . .'

'Oh, well, now you're talking . . .' He puts a hand to his chest. 'Grace Kelly was my first love. Not that she knew it, unfortunately. But still . . . what I wouldn't have given to have met her in her prime.'

'Yes. I, um, imagine that would have been something.' I take a large drink from my glass. 'Truly.'

'Hey, if you love the movies, we should go to the cinema for our next date. I mean, always assuming there *is* a next date,' he adds. 'You might decide against it.'

'*You* might decide against it.'

'I can safely say,' he says, 'on the basis of everything I've experienced so far this evening, Libby, that no, I won't be deciding against it.'

I smile at him. He smiles back. And we just sit there, for a couple of moments, beaming at each other like a couple of idiots.

'Anyway!' I say, breaking the spell, 'that's quite enough about me. Tell me about yourself. I mean, a surname would be nice!'

'Perreira,' he says. He turns ever so slightly pink. 'Sorry,' he blurts, inexplicably.

'Why on earth would you be sorry about your surname?'

'Just because . . . well, I know it's a bit of an odd one. Brazilian, as it happens.'

'Oh, you're Brazilian.'

'Half. My dad. My mum was born in Slovakia.'

'Wow, so you're . . . Brazilian-Slovakian.' His vanilla-fudge skin and mysterious accent are making a bit more sense. 'That's quite a mixture.'

'Yeah, I'm just an old mongrel,' he says, with a short laugh. 'Well, maybe not that old, thirty-nine next birthday. And you're . . . what? Twenty-eight? Twenty-nine?'

'Nice try,' I say, wryly. 'I'm thirty.'

'Never!'

'Again, nice try,' I say. 'But yes. Thirty.'

He grins back. 'Thirty is good. In fact, thirty is terrific. You know, I accomplished more from the age of thirty onwards than at any other time in my life.'

'Good to hear.' I sip my wine. 'So. You're thirty-eight. And you're a personal trainer. Do you enjoy it?'

'Yes, I do enjoy my work.' He sounds oddly stilted, but after another sip of wine, he goes on, a little less awkwardly,

93

'I mean, I have some really great clients. And some good people working for me.'

'Oh, wow, so you actually *own* FitRox, then? I thought you were just one of the trainers who worked there.'

'No, no, I'm not one of the trainers.'

'That's amazing. Running the place, I mean. But is it ever difficult, owning your own business like that? Because I suppose I always thought it would be the most incredible fun – and it is, don't get me wrong – but are there ever times when you feel like it's not turning out quite how you wanted it to?'

'Oh, God, yeah. All the time. I mean, when I first started out, I had all kinds of visions and dreams for how my business was going to look. It was going to be this shining beacon, of course, the gold standard. But then, along the way, you end up making compromises, and having to live in the real world . . .' He shrugs. 'It is, in what I think is the technical term for this sort of thing, a real bummer.'

'It is that.'

'The only thing you can do – and having been doing this for almost twenty years, now, Libby, this would be my biggest piece of advice to you – is never to make the compromise that feels *too* much. If you feel like you're selling yourself down the river, or losing any of your integrity, or just not doing it the way you want to do it any more, then you should probably listen to your gut and hold firm.'

'Right. That's . . . that's good advice. I mean, not exactly what I want to hear, to be honest with you. I'm having – well, a few issues with the people I work for. *With*!' I correct myself, hastily, trying to ignore the sinking feeling as I realize the all-too-apt Freudian slip I've just made. 'I have one vision of the way I want the company to go, and my investors have another . . . but I won't bore you with any of that, sorry.'

'Don't be silly! If there's anything at all I can do to help . . . You know, I do have some clients,' he goes on, after another sip of wine, 'who might be able to give you a bit more advice. Lawyers, and management consultants, that sort of thing. People who sometimes give me business advice too, in fact. I could always ask one of them if they'd be able to have a chat?'

'Thanks, Joel. But I'll work it all out somehow. Your clients must like you a hell of a lot,' I add, 'if they're prepared to give you free legal advice while you're making them do sit-ups! Oh, though sit-ups are completely out of fashion these days, aren't they? Aren't we all meant to be doing that thing called the plank instead?'

'That's the one.' He pours a slightly larger glass for each of us. 'But enough about me. Tell me more about your jewellery. Do you have a website? Somewhere I could go and order something? My mum's birthday is coming up, and she always loves a good pair of earrings . . .'

'Oh, God, Joel, don't worry about that! You don't have to start ordering stuff from me just to be nice!' I'm appalled. 'I appreciate the gesture, and all that, but it's not necessary.'

'That's not why I'm doing it! My mum *does* like a good pair of earrings, and nice ones are surprisingly hard to find.'

'OK, but please, please don't go and spend two hundred quid on my website! My stuff is expensive. A lot more expensive than I want it to be . . . Look, I tell you what, I'll find something I think you might like, and let you have it for an absolutely massive discount. Is that OK? Just, like, a tenner or something.' I can feel myself turning pink, and wishing he'd never taken us down this uncomfortable avenue in the first place. 'I mean, I'd happily give you something for free, but the people I work with—'

'Libby, Libby.' He reaches across the table and puts a hand on top of mine. He looks almost as mortified as I feel. 'God, no, no, don't be ridiculous. What on earth makes you think I wouldn't want to spend two hundred quid on my mum's birthday present? Trust me, she's quite comfortable with me spending even more than that!' He smiles. 'Please, don't go giving me a pair of your gorgeous earrings for a tenner! How about if I promise you that I'll only order something – and pay the full price, mind – if I actually like it? Is that a deal?'

'That's a deal.'

God, I like this man.

And honestly, part of me is even starting to wonder if there's any chance *he's* just as magical as Grace Kelly and the other Hollywood icons who've popped out of my sofa. I mean, is it really possible to meet a man this nice, and sexy, too? In real life, I mean, not in a fairy tale. If it weren't for the fact that it would make me sound very, very strange indeed, I'd lean over and ask the woman at the next table if she can actually see a real-live man sitting opposite me, or if I'm just imagining it, and freaking everyone else out by having an animated conversation with thin air.

'And I promise you, Libby, if I like your stuff as much as I think I will, I'll end up being a really good customer. I have a mum, a grandmother, an ex-wife I like to keep on the right side of . . .'

I smile at him. 'Ah. Did you just want to drop that into the conversation?'

'The ex-wife?'

'Yes.'

'Busted.' He grins, sheepishly. 'I don't know the etiquette on these things, but . . . well, I thought it's the kind of thing you ought to fess up to early on in the first date, right? If you're really hoping there's going to be a second date, that is.'

Like I probably ought to be fessing up to the fact that I'm still getting over the fact I've lost my soulmate?

Except. . . . I don't know. That might be something more appropriate for Date Number Two. *Former* marriage: not that big a deal. *Still* getting over loss of soulmate: probably best to bring that up a little further down the line.

Or, ideally, getting on with getting over Olly, and then never even needing to mention it to Joel at all.

'Maybe. A lot of people have baggage, though, Joel,' I say, carefully. 'I honestly don't think an ex-wife is anything you exactly need to be self-conscious about.'

'I appreciate that, Libby. Oh, and I have a daughter, too, by the way. *Not* something I'm self-conscious about. That, I'm perfectly happy shouting from the rooftops.'

He starts to fish in his pocket for his phone. 'She's only five, though, so I don't know if I'll look on your website for anything for her. Disney Princess plastic tat is more her bag.'

'Ah. Well, I have toyed with bringing out a range of plastic tat,' I say. 'I don't know if it's necessarily the direction I ought to be taking, but right now I'm open to most suggestions.'

He smiles. 'Well, in that case all I can advise you is that the more glittery, the better. They don't tend to care for the understated look, these five year olds.'

'I'll take that into account.'

'Glad to hear it.' He holds out his phone, with a picture of himself, looking just as luscious on an iPhone as in the flesh, with his arms wrapped around an equally luscious little girl – white-blonde, but with the same vanilla-fudge-coloured skin and blue eyes as Joel. 'My baby. Julia.'

'Oh, Joel. She's gorgeous. Do you at least get plenty of time with her?'

'Not as much as I'd like. She lives in Sydney.'

'*Australia?*'

'Yep.' He puts his phone back in his pocket. 'It's where my ex-wife is from.'

'Wow. You must really miss her.'

'I do. I try to get over there as often as I possibly can. Every month, if I can swing it.'

'God.' I stare at him. 'That must be expensive.'

'More to the point, it's never enough. But you know, I

travel a lot, even when I'm based in the UK, so even if she was living right here, I'd probably struggle to see her as much as I'd like.'

'You could probably do with winning the lottery or something,' I say.

'Er . . .?'

'Well, then you could buy a private jet, and fly to see her as often as you like . . .' I tail off, because this sounds really stupid, now it's out of my mouth: the fantasy of a little girl more like Julia's age than my own. 'Sorry. That probably wasn't helpful.'

'No, no, I appreciate the thinking!' His face softens as he looks down at her picture again. 'I can show you about three thousand more photos of her if you like . . . but maybe not on the first date, hey?' He grins at me. 'An ex-wife and a daughter may already be more skeletons in the closet than you can cope with!'

'Not at all,' I say. 'We all have skeletons, Joel.'

He nods, and takes a sip of his wine.

'So,' he asks, 'what's yours?'

'Sorry?'

'Your skeleton.' He settles back in his chair. 'Ex-husband? Children?'

'God, no!' I actually laugh, then realize that this makes me sound an utter failure in the romance department. 'I mean, no. No ex-husbands. No children.'

'Then what's the skeleton? I mean, you said we all have them, right?'

'Oh, you know. I . . . er . . . oh, I have a problematic

family!' I say, clutching at this truth. 'Two skeletons, right there! Mum and sister.'

'Ah. Family skeletons. Yeah, I guess I have those, too. I mean, nothing major. The usual, really. Absent dad who never wanted to really get to know me.' He pulls a wry face. 'That's my sob story.'

'No, I get that. My dad is rubbish, too. I don't really see him these days.'

'Sorry to hear that. I don't see mine any more, either. I mean, the matter's not helped by the fact that he's dead, of course.'

'Oh, God . . . Joel, I'm so sorry . . .'

'Don't be! Before he died, our relationship *was* bloody difficult. Not to mention the fact he lived in São Paulo, and me and my mum were always moving around, so it was difficult to keep up much of a relationship at all. Difficult or otherwise. I mean, especially when you factor in the issue of him being an utter narcissist and a waste of perfectly good oxygen.'

It's pretty nice, I have to be honest, to connect with somebody who knows what it's like to deal with a compli- cated family set-up. I mean, absolutely no offence to Olly whatsoever but, with the best will in the world, with his lovely, happy, *nuclear* family, he can't ever *really* understand what it's like to have a dad who couldn't really care less if you were dead or alive. Nor can Nora, for that matter. And even Bogdan, who admittedly has one of the most compli- cated family set-ups I've ever witnessed, does at least have a father who cares about him, and demands his presence at the table for family dinner every Saturday night, even if I accept that there are obviously certain stressors in the fact that Bogdan can't tell his dad he's gay, and his dad can't openly acknowledge that he's a criminal.

'And . . .your mum?' I ask, tentatively, just wondering if Joel is going to complete the package by wearily admitting that his mum's a rampant drama queen who plays major favourites with his younger half-sister.

'Oh, my mum's *amazing*,' he says, fervently. 'She's an aid worker. You know, properly hands-on stuff – digging through collapsed schools in earthquake zones, flying into places that have been hit by drought and famine . . . She's a real-life heroine, to be honest with you.'

Right.

I see.

Well, we still have absent fathers in common, at least.

'Still,' he says, after a moment, 'I suppose I can't deny that there have been a lot of times when I'd have rather she were just a normal mum. At home with me, instead of out saving the world.'

If you take away the *out saving the world* part, this brings us back to having more in common again.

'So, tell me about your mum.'

I take a long drink. 'Well, she certainly wouldn't be much use in an earthquake zone. Unless the traumatized, starving, homeless survivors suddenly decided that what they really needed wasn't shelter and clean water but a good old tap-dance and a communal sing-song to a selection of Andrew Lloyd Webber.'

He laughs. I mean, he really laughs.

'You're great, Libby,' he says, when he stops. 'Do you know that?'

'You're pretty great, too.'

'Shall we go and get some food?' he asks. 'And carry on this conversation elsewhere?'

'And drink slightly too much wine and compare notes about our mothers? Absolutely! Let's go!'

But first, we finish off the bottle of wine that's still sitting between us. Because we're having a great time – a really, really great time – and it would be pretty rude not to.

Chapter 5

We ended up getting fish and chips, as it happened, though obviously – this being Notting Hill – at a pretty posh fish-and-chip place with actual tablecloths, and knives and forks and plates rather than plastic sporks and greaseproof paper. And we drank the entirety of another bottle of wine, and – best of all – the conversation literally hasn't stopped the whole evening.

And now we're walking back along the quiet streets to my flat, so that he can drop me off before heading home to where he lives himself – near Shepherd's Bush, I think he mentioned, though I'm a bit giddy with all the booze and can't quite remember for certain – and he's just taken my hand. Which is the big development of the last couple of minutes. And which feels . . . lovely.

'This has been a really terrific night, Libby,' he's saying, now, as we turn off the main road into my street. 'I've had a great time. The best I've had in ages.'

'Me too.'

'Really?' He glances down. 'I was a bit worried, a couple of times, that you're . . . how do I put this? . . . not quite *here*.'

I blink up at him. 'Are you saying I'm not all there?'

His face breaks into another of those smiles. 'Heaven forfend.'

'Joel, honestly, I've had a wonderful time.' We come to a stop, right outside my flat. 'And I'm sorry if I've seemed a bit distant at times. I have . . . a lot on my plate at the moment.'

'Ah. So, is there room for me? On your plate, I mean.'

To answer this, and without any forward planning in the slightest, I suddenly find myself going up on tiptoe to place a kiss on Joel's smooth, perfect lips.

After a little start of surprise, he kisses me back.

It's extremely nice.

I mean, *extremely*. Especially when he slides both arms around my waist, and pulls me a little nearer, so that I can get the full benefit of that pleasing personal-trainer body up close.

When we break apart, a few moments later, he smiles down at me.

'That was a nice surprise.'

'Well, I wanted you to know just how much I've enjoyed myself.'

'And there were no words to convey that?'

'There were no words.'

'Wow. I've rendered you speechless. I must be doing well!' He clears his throat. 'So, there *is* room on your plate for me, then? In amongst the meat and the potatoes and the—'

He can't finish the sentence before there's a sudden, blood-curdling yowl from somewhere behind us, and a dark figure looms out of the darkness, fists raised, in Joel's direction.

I have a split second to realize that the dark figure is, in fact, Dillon O'Hara.

But only another split second later, Dillon is lying, flat on his back, on the pavement, where Joel has just expertly deposited him with some kind of *extremely* impressive martial-art flip.

'What the fuck?' Dillon gasps up at me, while Joel, keeping his forearm on top of Dillon's chest to hold him firmly down, reaches into his pocket for his phone and tosses it towards me.

'Call 999,' he instructs. 'Tell them it's a mugging.'

'It's not a fucking mugging!' Dillon croaks.

'It's not!' I say. 'It's really, really not! I know this man! Although I've no idea what the hell he was doing coming at us out of the darkness like that . . .'

'All I heard was this dickhead talking at you about his meat!' Dillon wheezes. 'What the fuck else was I supposed to do?'

'He wasn't talking at me about his meat,' I say, more irritated with Dillon than I've ever been before in my life (which is really saying something, trust me). 'We're on a date. Can you let him up?' I ask Joel, who's glancing back and forth between us in a confused sort of a way. 'He's a friend of mine.'

'Ex-boyfriend, actually,' Dillon says, as Joel moves his arm and lets him scramble to his feet.

'Oh, *please*,' I begin.

And then I stop, as Dillon staggers, ever so slightly sideways, and I realize that he's drunk.

Which, for a recovered alcoholic, is a Very Very Bad Thing indeed.

Oh, no. Oh, *Dillon*.

'Hey!' Dillon suddenly declares, peering more closely at Joel from where he's standing, swaying a little. 'This isn't Olly!'

I'll kill him. Relapsed or not, I'll kill him.

'You said you were on a date,' he goes on, before I can stop him, 'but this isn't Olly! Not that I'm *objecting*, mind. I'd be perfectly happy if I never had the misfortune of running into old Turd-Brain ever again . . . I'm Dillon, by the way,' he says, sticking out a hand in Joel's bemused direction. 'Allow me to congratulate you, my fine fellow, on being the lucky man who has won Libby's heart.'

'Well, I wouldn't go that far,' Joel says. 'I don't think I've won anything yet.'

'Hey!' Dillon glares at him. 'It's not a *contest*, you know.'

'No, I know, I was just responding to your . . . look, would you like us to help you get a cab, or something?' Joel puts a concerned hand on Dillon's shoulder, though I think this is partly just to hold him up. 'You seem a bit . . . uh . . . well, if I can be honest, you seem . . .'

It's right at this moment that Dillon pitches forwards at a 180-degree angle, throws up all over Joel's shoes, and then slumps to his knees to rest his forehead on the pavement, two (rather expertly judged) millimetres *outside* the huge pool of vomit.

'Oh, God . . .' I'm utterly aghast. 'Joel . . . I'm so sorry . . .'

But Joel, with the same unhurried, *incredibly sexy* sang-froid he showed when performing his nifty judo move on Dillon a couple of minutes ago, simply steps out of the puddle, shakes the worst of it off his shoes, then leans down to scoop Dillon up into a fireman's lift over one broad shoulder.

'Shall I get him upstairs?' he asks me, and – mute with embarrassment – I nod, fumble for my keys, and unlock the door.

This isn't the time for thinking such thoughts, but I have to say, if Joel hadn't already been very, very attractive to me earlier this evening, it's just been multiplied by the fact that I now know he can carry a reasonably heavy man up a steep flight of stairs without so much as a huff, a puff or a grunt of exertion.

I follow, watching Dillon's head, his eyes closed, swinging along near the small of Joel's back, until – as Joel rounds the slight corner at the top of the stairs into the living room – he stops still.

I can see why, the moment I get up there too and squeeze through the doorway past him.

Grace Kelly's wedding dress is laid out on the Chesterfield.

The drunken ex didn't seem to put him off. The vomity shoes didn't seem to put him off. But the exquisite lace wedding dress – oh, and veil, by the way – all laid out waiting for me seems to be the straw that breaks the camel's back.

'Er . . .' he says, after a moment. His voice sounds quite

different: strangulated instead of smooth and confident. 'Should I . . . I mean, if you need that, uh, dress to stay there on the sofa, I can always put him on the floor . . .'

'No, no, I'll move it!' I can feel my face flaming as I lift the dress and veil off the sofa and drape them, with not even a moment's thought for their preciousness and rarity, over the heap of packing boxes nearby. 'Joel, it's . . . I mean, it isn't my dress. I'm not getting married, or anything!'

But, if anything, this just makes the whole situation worse, because now I just sound like some kind of desperately embarrassing Miss Havisham, all geared up to slip into a wedding gown the moment I get home from my date.

'Libby, it's fine. There's no need to explain anything.'

'But that's just it! There isn't anything *to* explain . . .'

'Bucket,' Dillon mumbles, from where Joel has just deposited him on the sofa. 'Sick.'

'You know what,' I say to Joel, as I leap to grab a bucket from the cupboard near the top of the stairs where I'm keeping my Henry hoover and all my limited cleaning equipment, 'just go. Please. I think it would be best.'

'But are you sure you can handle this?' Joel points at Dillon. 'Handle *him*?'

'Yes, I can handle it. It'll be better if you leave, in fact.'

'Well, all right, if you say so, but—'

'I say so.' This came out a bit more snappishly than I intended. 'Sorry, Joel, I just . . . look, it was a lovely evening. Thank you.' I shove the bucket under Dillon's head just in time for him to start throwing up again, noisily, into it. 'But honestly. Go now. Oh!' I suddenly remember something he said, as we left the restaurant, about not having an Oyster Card on him. 'Do you want to borrow my Oyster Card? For the bus home?'

'What?' He looks quite startled now, as well he might, given that him borrowing my Oyster Card would mean he had to see me again to give it back. 'God, no, no. I don't need . . . Look, I'll call you,' he adds, rather feebly. 'OK?'

'OK,' I say, in as bright a tone as possible so he doesn't have to feel embarrassed about the obvious lie. 'Thank you again!'

The door couldn't shut more swiftly behind him.

And then it's just me and a semi-conscious Dillon and Grace Kelly's wedding dress, all by ourselves in my flat.

*

I've just come down from emptying the bucket into the loo when I hear the unmistakable sound of Grace Kelly's voice coming from the Chesterfield.

'Oh, how thrilling! I was hoping this dream would last a little longer!'

She's sitting on the arm of the Chesterfield, wearing nothing but an ivory silk slip and an excited expression on her beautiful face. Her figure, beneath the slip, is taut and angular and very, very slim; the skin on her bare arms and legs glows in just the same shimmering, light-reflecting way that her face does.

I'm momentarily alarmed that she's popped up while Dillon is right here – slumped on the Chesterfield, in fact

– but he's pretty much unconscious now, so it hardly matters. And I'm actually a little relieved that the sofa still seems to be, you know, *working*. That I haven't screwed it all up by accidentally allowing Grace Kelly to lay eyes on a photograph of her real-life son and the daughter-in-law and grandchildren she sadly never met. Which, fingers crossed, looks like either something she's wilfully forgotten about or just isn't going to mention.

'I think I must have started dreaming about something else for a little while,' she goes on, getting to her feet, 'but I'm back now. Or rather, *you're* back. So perhaps we can get back to what we were discussing earlier in the night?'

I lift the bucket up.

'Does it look,' I ask, 'like I have the time to sit around discussing anything?'

'Oh, but you must! We were making such excellent progress earlier!' She doesn't seem to have noticed Dillon, slumped only a couple of feet away from her along the Chesterfield. 'Now, this man you were talking about. Your Clark Gable . . .'

'I don't have a Clark Gable.'

'Obviously you don't have a Clark Gable! You're not real! I'm talking about the man you mentioned, your true love. The one who *represents* Clark Gable, the same way you represent me . . . I need you to tell me exactly what you think it was about you that made him cool off.'

'Well, the fact that he got tired of waiting for me and fell in love with somebody else probably contributed quite a lot to it. But honestly, Grace, this really isn't—'

'No, no. That can't possibly be it.' Grace's patrician voice is even brisker and more clipped than usual; in fact, she sounds rather cross. 'Clark didn't tire of waiting for me! If anything, I've always thought that I was the one pushing him too hard for some sort of commitment. And then, of course, there was my mother's meddling in the whole business, which I still think put the tin lid on it . . . I don't suppose your mother has been meddling in your romantic affairs, has she? Anything to divulge on that front?'

'No,' I say, almost as briskly as Grace. 'My mother couldn't give two hoots about my romantic affairs. At least, not unless I happen to be involved with the crumpled heap of a man you see on the couch beside you. Who, by the way,' I add, as Grace glances sideways, looking startled to see him, 'I really need to get cleaned up, if you don't mind? I mean, can't we talk about all this stuff another time?'

'Oh!' She gazes at Dillon in horror for a moment – which I can't blame her for, because he's passed out and smelling unappealing – before looking back at me. 'Is *this* the man you've been talking about? Your true love?'

'Christ, no!' I dart forward with the bucket when it looks as though Dillon is stirring to – most likely – throw up again, but it's a false alarm. For now, at least. 'No, he's not my true love.'

'Then who is he?' Grace peers back at Dillon, studying him intently to try to work out, I guess, what sort of significance *he* represents in her Freudian dreamscape. 'Some sort of hobo?'

I have to laugh, albeit hollowly. 'No. He's an actor. Just a very drunk one, right now.'

'A *drunk actor?*' Grace gasps. 'Oh, my goodness! Then he *must* represent Clark in some way . . . do you think this is my subconscious hoping that Clark was totally broken by ending his affair with me? That he ended up sprawled on some sordid old couch, night after night, drinking to forget the woman he'd allowed to slip through his fingers?'

'Well,' I say, because I'm too tired to argue with any of this now, 'I don't know about that. But look, Grace, if you're still this hung up on a man you used to be in love with, are you sure you're doing the right thing marrying the prince? I mean, don't get me wrong, I totally understand the idea of trying to move on, but to actually go as far as *marriage* . . . and, let's face it, you're not even just marrying a man, you're inheriting an entire kingdom to go along with him . . .'

'But don't you think that's precisely what one *ought* to do? When one has been disappointed in love?'

'Er – marry a monarch and become the head of state of a small Mediterranean principality? I don't know that it's necessary to go *quite* that far.'

'That's not at all what I mean!' she snaps. 'I mean that quite obviously it's just plain good sense, when one has had one's heart broken, to get right back on the horse. If that isn't too much a mixing of metaphors . . .' She passes a rather tired-looking hand over her face all of a sudden. 'My parents,' she goes on, 'have always taught me that life is for Doers. Not for those who sit by on the sidelines, watching their lives pass by. I suppose what truly frightened me, after it all ended with Clark, was the possibility that I might never feel that way about someone again. Never have what I dreamed about having with him. A great marriage. A home. A family.'

'So you decided to fall in love with the prince, just so you couldn't be accused of sitting on the sidelines?' I ask.

'Oh, heavens, no, there have been dozens of men since Clark! Or rather, what I mean to say,' she says, turning rather pink in the cheeks, 'is that I didn't decide to fall in love with *the prince*. I decided not to just meekly accept what I thought Fate had decided for me, and remain alone for ever. After all, isn't life far too short to squander one's best years bemoaning the loss of one's soulmate? . . . Why are you looking at me like that?'

I realize that I probably am staring at her in a slightly too intense fashion. 'Sorry . . . it's just, what you said about Fate. I've been doing a lot of thinking about Fate myself, lately, and how it's screwed up everything I've ever wanted. And I don't seem to be doing quite as good a job as you on the whole meek acceptance front. Or rather, I'd *like* to be able to just forge on ahead, never casting a single glance backwards, I'm just finding it more difficult than that. I mean, I was out with Joel tonight, and I couldn't stop Olly from popping into my—'

'All right, all right, let's just hold on a moment.' Grace raises an impressively imperious hand. 'This is all about me, let's not forget. Before we go much further, I'd really like to try to be clear on who everybody represents. Now, this *Joel* fellow you say you were out with tonight – you're really talking about Rainier, right? The man you're forging ahead with? And then *Olly*, I suppose, is the representation of . . . Clark? Or is he just an amalgamation of all the men I've ever felt strongly about . . .?'

There's a sudden knock on my front door that makes both of us jump.

'That'll be Bogdan,' I say, because I called Bogdan right after Joel left and asked him to come round to help with Dillon. (After all, if I'm going to get the constant refrain from Bogdan that I ought to be sleeping with Dillon, he can bloody well come over and see first hand why that would be a disastrous idea.)

'Bogdan?' Grace's left eyebrow lifts upwards. 'Don't tell me there's *another* man lurking around the fringes of my subconscious? Golly, I'm glad my mother can't see inside my head right now! Or Rainier, for that matter.'

'Oh, I don't think either your mother or Rainier need have any worries about Bogdan. Anyway, he's just a friend. I'm sure he doesn't . . . *represent* anything at all.' I start to head for the stairs. 'I'll just nip down and let him in.'

Answering the door to Bogdan is a bit of a shock.

Somehow – since I last saw him almost ten hours ago – he's managed to grow a moustache.

An *entire* moustache: not fulsome and luxuriant, perhaps, but far from sparse and rather beautifully groomed.

'Bogdan, how . . . is that *stick-on?*'

'Is no such thing!' He looks offended. 'Why on earth would I be going about with stick-on moustache?'

'Why on earth would you be going about with a *real* moustache?'

'Because conversation earlier is reminding me that am always wanting to experiment with Clark Gable look. And if am going to be meeting Grace Kelly any time soon, what is wrong with wanting to look little bit like Clark Gable? Will be making her feel at home.'

'But how did you even . . . did you just grow that this afternoon?'

He shrugs. 'Am usually needing to be shaving two times per day. Sometimes even three. So this afternoon am just skipping usual four o'clock shave.'

'Bloody hell.'

'Do not be making me feel bad about this, Libby,' he tells me, primly. 'Or you will be no better than school bullies back home in Chişinău.'

'All right, all right, I'm sorry . . .'

'She is here right now?'

'Yes, as a matter of fact, she is here right now, but that's not why I called you over. Dillon's had a relapse, he—'

But Bogdan isn't listening. Instead, he's hurtling up the stairs, taking them two at a time like some sort of matinee-idol-impersonating homing pigeon.

'Oh!' Grace's gasp is audible even halfway down the stairs. 'Good *heavens!* But you said,' she goes on, as I reach the top of the stairs, 'that this new fellow didn't represent anyone!'

'Yes, look, he's not Clark Gable, I absolutely promise you that . . .'

Grace is clasping her hands to her swan-like throat. 'But he looks . . . so very like him!'

'You are thinking I am looking like Clark Gable?' Bogdan looks dazed for a moment. 'This is true, true compliment for me, Miss Kelly. Am whelmed over. Am smacked in gob.'

'Oh, my, your accent . . . it's just so *wonderful*,' breathes Grace. She's changed, before my very eyes, from majestic ice princess to smouldering sex kitten: to be fair, the very thing that, according to Hitchcock, made her so appealing on the silver screen. 'Is it Russian? Yugoslavian? Greek?'

'Am from Moldova.'

Grace Kelly lets out one of her peals of crystalline laughter. 'A made-up country! How amusing! You're reminding me that I thought Monaco was a made-up country when I first heard of it!'

'Moldova is not made-up country.' Bogdan takes a few steps closer to Grace Kelly, and I can see – for heaven's *sake* – that she actually goes a little bit weak at the knees for a moment. 'Is actual place. Is bordered in west by Romania and in east, north and south by Ukraine.'

'Oh, please,' Grace shudders with pleasure, 'keep *talking*. I could listen to your accent for ever and never, *ever* want to wake up.'

'We are fortunate enough to be enjoying presence of two major rivers,' Bogdan croons on, clearly recognizing that, with his expert knowledge of Moldovan topography, he seems to have Grace Kelly in the palm of his hand.

116

'Dniester in east and Prut in west. Climate is warm in summer, cold in winter. Major exports are—'

'Bogdan!' I interrupt. 'I actually called you over here because I need your help with *this*.'

Bogdan gazes over at Dillon, still prone on the sofa.

'Dillon,' I say, pointedly. 'One of your closest friends. I don't know if you've noticed the scent of vodka in the air . . .?'

'But am assuming this is because of you, Libby. Dillon is no longer drinking.'

'Yes, that's what I thought too until twenty minutes ago, when he turned up pissed outside my flat and threw up on Joel's shoes.'

'But this is great tragedy.'

'Well, it's not great, no, but can we try to keep a little bit of perspective, just for the moment, and concentrate on getting him cleaned up? Can you maybe get him up the stairs to the bathroom so I can . . . I don't know, hose him down with the shower?'

'This is true.' Bogdan turns back to Grace Kelly. 'Will you be excusing me for a moment, Miss Kelly?'

'Oh, but of course!' As he leans down and scoops Dillon up with even more ease than Joel managed it earlier, Grace sidles over to me and grabs my hand. 'Look,' she hisses at me, back to her single-minded self, after all the doe-eyed looks and the tinkling laughter, 'I've no idea how this all works – I mean, obviously you're my alter ego, and all that, so it might not even be viable – but is there any way you could sort of . . . get out of the way for a while?'

'Get out of the way?'

'Yes. Give me a few minutes to be alone with this . . . magnificent creature.'

'Oh, well, I think *magnificent* is pushing it . . .'

'I mean, as of tomorrow, I'll be a married woman . . . in fact, legally I'm already married! Can't I at least enjoy one last sensuous dream before I commit myself to my husband in the eyes of God?'

'Libby?' Bogdan suddenly calls down the stairs. 'Can you be upcoming? Dillon is awoken and is requesting for you. Also,' he adds, 'is looking as if he is going to be sicking all over place again . . .'

'Oh, God . . .'

I abandon Grace to her naughty thoughts about Bogdan and hurry up the stairs to the bathroom, where Dillon – propped up, in his underpants, with a spray of water coming down on his head from the shower over the bath – is indeed awake.

Well, *awake* is pushing it a bit, probably: his eyes are open and words are coming out of his mouth, but whether he's necessarily a hundred per cent sentient . . . or even fifty per cent sentient . . . actually, hang on, giving him a closer look I'd be surprised if he's even twenty-five per cent sentient.

'Libby, my darling girl,' he slurs, as soon as he sees me through the plastic shower door. 'And Boggy, my good fellow. Two of my favourite people in the same room at the same time. How often does that happen, eh? How often do I get to just hang out with two of my very best buds?'

'I'll keep showering him,' I tell Bogdan. 'Can you pop into the kitchen and make a strong cup of tea?'

'Of course, but am thinking that Miss Kelly is preferring, perhaps, the champagne—'

'For Dillon!'

'Ah. Then yes. Without question, I can be doing this.'

As he lumbers off, I continue hosing Dillon down for a moment or two. He's got his head leaning against the tiled wall, and barely seems to be noticing the warm water splashing down on him. In just his underpants, his body is as impressively muscled as it ever was: all man, the way Dillon has always been all man. But his face is slack, and his eyes have no light, and – most of all – his expression is that of a very lost, very little boy.

I can't carry on being angry with him for something so small, in the grand scheme, as ruining my date. Dillon is a friend, and it's just awful to see him messing up like this.

'Who's Miss Kelly?' he suddenly asks, his words a bit less slurred now that the shower is helping to sober him up a little.

'Sorry?'

'Bogdan wanted to give champagne to a Miss Kelly . . . was that the blonde I saw in your living room?'

'Oh, God. You *saw her?*'

'Well, you were chatting to someone down there, right? I don't know. I was snoozing, mostly . . . maybe I was dreaming.'

'Aren't you – er – always dreaming about blonde girls?' I suggest, hopefully.

'Hey, sweetheart, I don't have to *dream* about them.' The effort of engaging in his usual banter is evidently too much for him. He puts a hand to the side of his head. 'Fuck me. I feel atrocious.'

'Good,' I say, but kindly, as I reach in and switch off the tap before grabbing a towel and holding it out for him to wrap around himself. 'Hopefully you'll feel even worse in the morning, too.'

'Hey! I came here tonight – oh, thanks for the new address update, by the way – because I thought you were my friend!'

'And as your friend, I hope you'll feel even worse in the morning. Because we need to get you back to rehab, Dillon,' I say, gently. 'You know that, don't you? I mean, I'm assuming that's really why you came here. Because you knew that's what I'd say and, deep down, you want to help yourself.'

He steps, shakily, out of the bath and on to the bath-mat. Wrapped in his towel, he looks even more like a little-boy-lost. Seriously, I'm fighting the urge to give him a big cuddle, brush his teeth, and put some Spiderman pyjamas on him before tucking him into bed with a story and a cuddle.

'Ah,' he says, not quite meeting my eye. 'The psycho-babble begins.'

'It's not psychobabble. And honestly, Dillon, what do you expect me to say? You turn up outside my front door, throw up all over my date's shoes . . .'

'Yeah. Sorry about that.' He sits down on the side of the

bath. 'So, tell me about that! I mean, I know I've been rubbish about keeping in touch for the past few months, but this guy is a new development, right? I mean, what's happened to you and Olly Walker?'

'Nothing's happened to me and Olly Walker. Nothing *will*. He's with somebody else, remember? Anyway, we're not talking about me. We're talking about you. Like, when did all this happen? The falling off the wagon, I mean. And, more to the point – *why?*'

'Oh, you know.' He shrugs. 'Things have gone a bit shit for me since I last saw you, Lib. I've . . . sort of been kicked off *Sodom and Gomorrah*.'

This may sound like a description of one of Dillon's average weekends but is, in fact, the name of the new TV show he's been filming for the last few months, over in Belfast.

'Kicked off? What on earth for?'

'The usual stuff.' He waves a hand. 'Shagging the makeup artist. Calling the first assistant director something unrepeatable. Shagging the makeup artist's assistant. Who turned out to be the first assistant director's girlfriend . . .'

'That's not *the usual stuff!*'

'Yeah, well, it is for me.' He laughs. 'Oh, come on. Don't I even get a giggle?'

'You do not.'

'A chuckle?'

'No.'

'Then how about a mirthless chortle?'

'Not even that.'

'Then that proves it. This really isn't funny.'

'It's not, Dillon. It's really not. But, look, if we get you back to rehab first thing . . .'

'So you're just, what? Giving up on true love?'

I give him a look. 'Don't change the subject.'

'Hey, I'm just asking! Because you're surprised that I've started drinking again since the last time you saw me. And I'm just surprised you seem to have moved on from Olly so fast.'

'It's not *so fast!* He's been with Tash for a bloody year! And,' I go on, suddenly feeling a hint of Grace Kelly's single-minded steel in my veins, 'I'm not going to sit around bemoaning the hand dealt me by Fate any longer, if that's all right with you?'

'Well, I don't know about that. Who *is* this new guy, anyway? I mean, he could be *anyone*.'

'He's not *anyone*. He's a personal trainer. And a really lovely guy.'

'Jack the Ripper was a really lovely guy.'

'I don't think he was, actually.'

'Well, he probably *seemed* like a really lovely guy, right up to the point that he asphyxiated you.'

'I think he cut their throats. And I honestly don't think he did seem like a really lovely guy, Dillon.'

'Well, all right, maybe he didn't seem *quite* such a lovely guy as this Joel character . . .'

'He carried you all the way upstairs. Even after you were sick on his shoes.'

'Well, all that proves is that he's good at carting lifeless bodies about. And there we are, back to Jack the Ripper all over again.'

'Look. He isn't Jack the bloody Ripper. And we're not discussing my love life, Dillon, we're discussing you, and your relapse, so if you could just stop—'

But Dillon has turned faintly green again and is suddenly lurching towards the loo.

I pat his back for a moment or two and then, when I get the sense he'd just rather be left alone with his embarrassment for a minute, I get to my feet.

'I'll go and check on the whereabouts of that cup of tea,' I say, gently. 'Back in a minute.'

'You're an angel,' Dillon croaks, his voice echoing a bit from the fact his head is still stuck in the toilet bowl. 'You deserve the best, you know? You deserve a prince.'

I leave him in privacy, and head next door to the kitchen to see what's going on with this cup of tea.

But Bogdan, predictably enough, isn't in there. In fact, the kettle isn't even warm.

From the living room downstairs, however, I can hear the distinct sound of Grace Kelly's laughter.

'So tell me more,' she's saying, in a throaty purr that owes more to Mae West than the East Coast, 'about this funny little made-up country you say you hail from . . . if this were real life, and not simply a dream, would you take me back there with you and make me its princess?'

'This is interesting question,' Bogdan replies, earnestly. 'History of royalty in Moldova is not being very happy one. And of course, you are knowing what is happening

123

to nearby Russian royal family, all violently murdered in cellar by Bolsheviks who are not even sparing family dog . . . but is possible that in your case, Miss Kelly, even most ardent of republicans would be dialling back instinct to shut you in cellar and bayonet you to death . . .'

It's a good thing Bogdan *is* (mostly) gay, if this is his best effort at chatting up a woman.

Despite this, I can't actually bring myself to interrupt them. After all, there's pitifully little-enough romance in the world, so why should I begrudge either of them this rather sweet, admittedly peculiar flirtation.

So I leave Bogdan to Grace's charm offensive, and I leave Grace to Bogdan's . . . well, weirdly detailed descriptions of the massacre of the Romanovs. They're obviously making a connection, unfettered by the fact that she's not real and that he's not usually heterosexual. I, of all people, am never going to lay down laws about this sort of thing.

I turn, as silently as I can, and head back up to the top floor to put the kettle on for Dillon.

Chapter 6

So, last night ended up being the weirdest sleepover that's ever happened in the entire history of the planet.

Dillon passed out in my bed next to his undrunk cup of tea, wearing nothing but his underpants and one of the baggier of my trusty grey hoodies as a not-that-flattering crop top. Bogdan and Grace Kelly stayed chatting (thank God, *just* chatting) on the Chesterfield until the wee-est of wee small hours, when she suddenly pulled that familiar vanishing trick, leaving Bogdan to fall asleep (with a dreamy smile beneath his ever-sprouting moustache) on the sofa. And I, with neither a bed nor a sofa to sleep on, eventually curled up beneath a blanket on the bedroom floor, as far out of Dillon's vomiting reach as possible, to get a few hours of shut-eye before my phone rang a little after six a.m.: a call-back from Grove House, Dillon's old rehab clinic, where I left a voicemail very late last night asking them to call first thing in the morning.

I should have realized that for a clinic that offers sunrise yoga and Reiki at dawn, *first thing in the morning* really does mean *first thing in the morning*.

Anyway, once I'd recovered from the horror of speaking with one of the Grove House's abnormally perky receptionists at that hour of the morning, it was probably a good thing that the day started so early. Because it took a good hour to properly rouse Dillon, then another couple of hours for me and Bogdan to persuade him that last night's bender wasn't a mere 'stumble' on the 'road to sobriety' (he really does talk shit at times) and that he really, really needs to get back into rehab as fast as you can say *Jack Daniels*. By the time he and Bogdan set off for Barnes, where the Grove House clinic is located, it was already close to ten a.m., when I was due for a Skype call with one of my only non-bridal clients, a very nice fashion PR who often gets me to make bits and bobs to send out to stylists on magazine shoots.

She wanted the call, in fact, to tell me that she's just got engaged, and that she'd love me to make her a vintage-style tiara, just like the one she saw in the piece about me in *Brides* magazine, to go with her original 1930s dress for her wedding.

I've just finished the call, in fact, and I'm just about to call Bogdan to find out how things are going with depositing a reluctant Dillon at rehab, when I notice that a new email has just popped up at the top of my inbox.

It's from someone called Celeste Browne, and the subject is *Trying to schedule a meeting?*

It's probably just yet another bride-to-be, wanting me to create a replica of the vintage-style tiara in *Brides* magazine, but I need to keep on top of my emails (or they tend to get on top of me), so I give it a quick click before I give Bogdan that call.

Dear Libby, says the email, *Could you possibly let me know when might be a suitable time to come into our offices for a meeting with Caroline and Annika? They're big fans of your work and would really like to speak with you about the possibility of a Pressley/Waters collaboration with your brand. Please email me back with your availability, or give me a call when you have the chance. Kind regards, Celeste.*

It takes me a moment or two of rather stunned staring to get to grips with precisely what this email is about.

This is Pressley/Waters the vastly successful jewellery website, right?

And Caroline (Pressley) and Annika (Waters) want to meet me for a chat about . . . working together?

This sort of fashion-hotshots set-up has to have come through Elvira, right?

But why on earth would Elvira, who has wanted me to go smaller, more expensive and more 'niche' ever since we've started working together, want me to have this kind of conversation with a mass-market (albeit high-end) online jewellery boutique? And shouldn't she have mentioned it to me before I got the out-of-the-blue email, if she did?

It's too strange – not to mention enticing – a situation to simply email this Celeste back and arrange a far-off date. So I scroll down to find her direct line, then press on the screen to dial it.

'Pressley/Waters, Celeste speaking, how may I help you?'

'Oh, hi! Celeste . . . um . . . my name's Libby Lomax. You've literally just emailed me . . .'

'Libby, hi!' She sounds young, and very friendly. 'Thanks for calling me back so quickly. I should have said, actually, in my email, that Caroline and Annika are both travelling a *lot* as of the middle of next week. So if you did happen to have any time available before then – even just a half-hour – I know they'd try to make that work if they could.'

'Er . . . yes. Yes, I have time available. I mean, I'll make time, obviously! This is . . . sorry, did you get my details from Elvira?'

'Elvira?'

'Elvira Roberts-Hoare.'

'Oh . . . I have no idea about that, Libby, sorry. Caroline just asked me to contact you when she came into the office this morning. I mean . . . I *doubt* it was anything to do with Elvira Roberts-Hoare, though. You're talking about the model, right?'

'Yes, that's the one.'

'Oh, no, then I highly doubt it would be anything to do with her. She and Caroline don't get along. At all.'

This is, if I needed it, another huge plus in favour of Caroline Pressley.

The other one being, of course, that she's the brains behind the most successful jewellery website in the country: the net-à-porter of bling. I love almost everything on the site – and it's a pretty extensive, though carefully curated, collection – from totally affordable friendship bracelets to

128

drool-worthy £10k pearl earrings. They sell rhinestone cocktail rings just as enthusiastically as they do great hunks of real diamond, and though I expect they sell far more silver initial pendants than they do rose-gold and pink-sapphire chokers, it's just as gratifying, as a customer, to order the former as it is the latter. I sent Nora, in fact, a lovely simple necklace with N (Nora), M (Mark) and C silver charms on it when Clara was born, partly because I don't make initial pendants myself, and partly just because I know the arrival of a gorgeous Pressley/Waters package, Special Delivery and all boxed up in covetable black and gold packaging, is just the thing you might appreciate after you've been through a two-day labour and an emergency C-section.

'So, might you be able to come in a couple of days from now? They do have a little bit of time on Thursday morning, if there's any way you could make it?'

'Yes. Yes, I can make it.'

'Great! Can we say ten thirty? At our offices in Paddington?'

'Ten thirty is perfect. I'll be there. Thank you, Celeste.'

'Oh, you're really welcome, Libby. I'll ping you through a confirmation by text, OK?'

'Thanks, that's great.'

As I put the phone down, I allow myself a little celebratory whoop.

I mean, this may all come to nothing, but even just getting the opportunity to meet Caroline Pressley and Annika Waters is so exciting.

Especially at a time when I'm feeling so thoroughly sick

to the back teeth of my job, to be honest. Knowing that these particular two women have spotted my stuff, and like it enough to want to meet for a chat – it's a huge fillip.

Of course, there exists the perfectly real possibility that they're thinking of establishing their very own vintage-inspired bridal line. Which would obviously be a teeny-tiny bit of a disappointment, creatively speaking . . .

But what am I saying? If Caroline Pressley and Annika Waters wanted *any* work from me at all, I'd do it like a shot. I'd agree to make nothing *but* vintage-inspired bridal tiaras for the rest of my entire career . . . Well, OK, I might baulk at that when it actually came to it, but still, I'd be honoured to be asked. And it would be pretty impossible to turn it down.

Anyway, I'll cross all those kinds of bridges if I'm lucky enough to get to them.

For now, the main thing to focus on, I guess, is putting together an up-to-date portfolio of my stuff, and working out – vitally important, obviously – what to wear for the meeting on Thursday, and—

There's a brisk knocking at the front door, which I go to open.

Seeing Joel outside is enough, after the exciting call I've just had, to knock me down with a feather.

'Joel!'

He's in his workout gear, obviously, and looks, in the bright sunlight, even more bright-eyed and bushy-tailed than he did last night. Though perhaps that's just because the last two men I've seen this morning were Dillon and

Bogdan: the former bleary-eyed and painfully hung-over, the latter sleep-deprived from his late-night fawning all over Grace Kelly, and – after so many hours without shaving – almost completely covered in a thick foliage of facial hair.

'Libby. Hey.'

'Hey.'

My first thought is that he must have dropped something when he shot out of here like a bat out of hell last night.

'Sorry, did you forget something yesterday?'

'Yeah. My manners.'

'I don't understand.'

'I know you said you wanted privacy, Libby, but I shouldn't have just left like that. It was wrong of me. Did you manage OK?'

'With Dillon? Yes, Joel, it was fine. I mean,' I add, suddenly noticing Dillon's vomit on the street behind him (I *must* dig out a bucket and sluice that down), 'it was manageable. I won't say it was the most fun night I've ever had. But there's absolutely no reason for you to feel bad about that. It was much better that you left.'

'Even so. I thought about it all the way home – I thought about *you* all the way home.' He takes a deep breath. 'I wish you'd just told me you were getting married, Libby. Then I wouldn't have let myself enjoy the evening as much as I did.'

'I'm . . . I'm not . . .'

'And what I came here to say this morning was . . . well, I know all too well how these things can end up taking on a life of their own, but if you are having doubts about going through with it – and you must be having doubts,

131

surely, if you were out on a date with me – then my advice would be to just hold off. I know it seems impossible, when the dress has been bought and, I don't know, the cake has been ordered. But—'

'Joel. Listen to me. I'm not getting married.' I put a hand on his arm. 'I'm really, really not. That dress was . . . it belongs to a friend.'

'Oh!'

'I'm just looking after it for her. I mean, I design wedding jewellery,' I go on, which isn't fibbing, at least, 'and often I have to take into account the design of a dress when I'm working on the accessories . . . honestly, if you'd looked more closely, you'd have seen that I'd never fit into a dress that size! You need a twenty-two-inch waist to get into something like that. And I don't know if you've noticed, but I certainly don't have a twenty-two-inch waist measurement. I barely have a twenty-two-inch *thigh* measurement,' I add, so desperate am I to convince him that I'm not the owner of the dress he saw last night.

'Right. Well, in that case, I'm really sorry.' Joel is turning slightly – attractively – pink. 'I just thought, after you were a bit detached over dinner . . . the wedding dress actually made a lot of sense, to be honest with you.'

'Trust me, the wedding dress doesn't make any sense.'

'Well, OK, then. If there's really no murkiness your end about secret weddings, or problematic ex-boyfriends . . .'

'There's really no murkiness about weddings or problematic ex-boyfriends.'

'. . . then will you still go out with me again?'

132

'I'd love to,' I say, trying not to sound too astonished that he's asked. 'I really would, Joel.'

'Great! I'm . . . I'm really chuffed about that, Libby.'

Really chuffed, in his oddly accented English, sounds heart-meltingly attractive, I have to say.

'I'm away for work later today and tomorrow, but if you're free Thursday night . . .?'

'Yes, I'm free.' This is perfect, because it gives me the whole of today and tomorrow to focus on preparation for the meeting with Pressley/Waters, and then I can relax and enjoy myself that evening with Joel. 'And I promise, there'll be no drunken exes turning up and ruining it this time. On my side, at least.'

'Hey, he didn't ruin it.'

'He didn't *improve* it.'

'Oh, I don't know. Having a hostile ex-boyfriend show up in the middle of a date is something I've never actually experienced before . . . I won't say it warrants inclusion in any of those *Fifty Things To Do Before You Die* lists, but it's always nice to try something new. Besides, it gave me the chance to try out one of my much-practised Krav Maga moves, at least.'

'Oh, that's what that was. I thought it was judo.'

'Oh, no, no, it's far more impressive than judo.' He grins. 'Esti was pretty proud of me when I told her, actually. She's normally the one chucking me to the floor. Gratifying though it always is, obviously, to get your arse handed to you by a girl, it was nice to be the one handing out the arses for a change. If that makes any sense.'

'Oh, so Esti is . . . your trainer?' Now I'm confused. 'I thought you were training her.'

'Er, no,' he says. 'She . . . um . . . she's not my trainer, but she does teach me Krav Maga. I think she learnt it in the Israeli army. Either way, she's lethal . . . Anyway,' he goes on, 'it's the sort of skill I always hoped might come in handy some day. I just hope Dillon doesn't feel as sore as I always do afterwards. From the Krav Maga, that is. I expect there was nothing he could do about feeling sore for other reasons.'

'Yes, true. He has . . .' I stop, because it's not fair to out Dillon as a lapsed addict to someone who doesn't know him. '. . . he just can't handle his drink, that's all.'

'Hey, don't worry about that. I've had a couple of friends with . . . that kind of problem as well.' He puts a hand on my shoulder. 'It's never easy.'

Dear God, he really is the perfect man, isn't he? Discreet, understanding, devastatingly sexy . . .

. . . and leaning down, as I look up into his eyes, to place a soft kiss on my lips.

It's heavenly.

And it goes on.

And on.

And on a bit longer.

OK, quite a lot longer.

When we both eventually pull away to catch our breath, he smiles down at me, his eyes crinkling at the sides.

'I'm so glad I met you, Libby.'

'Me too.'

'You're a breath of fresh air, you know? I mean, it's so nice to meet someone I can talk to. Someone who's not just . . . out for whatever they can get.'

Which is a strange thing to say.

Except it isn't, I guess, because I can well imagine that there are lots of women who are attracted to Joel merely by the pretty package on the outside. Those eyes. That skin. The sexy accent. The body . . .

I mean, obviously never having been in the (ever-so-slightly enviable) position of people fancying me for nothing but my looks, I can't imagine how that must feel. But it could make it hard, I do understand, for him to trust that he's met someone who likes him for more than that.

'So, shall we do something different on Thursday evening? A movie, perhaps? I haven't been to the cinema in ages, and I know you said you like it . . .'

'A movie would be wonderful, Joel,' I say, pathetically hoping he suggests something I'm not all that bothered about seeing so we can justifiably spend most of the time snogging on the back row like a pair of randy teenagers. 'I look forward to it.'

'Me too. I'll drop you a text tomorrow, shall I, to arrange a time?'

'That would be great, but don't stress about it if you're busy . . . where are you going, anyway? For work, I mean.'

'Barbados.'

'Wow, that doesn't sound . . . er . . . like work.'

'Oh, yeah.' He looks embarrassed. 'It is, though. I mean,

I have a client who is based out of there, so . . . yeah. I go there if I'm needed.'

'That sounds amazing! I need more clients like that!'

'Well, you know . . . Barbados isn't all it's cracked up to be.'

'I'll take your word for it.'

'You should!' He glances down at his watch. 'Anyway, I really should get going now, but I'll see you on Thursday, OK?'

'OK. Looking forward to it!'

'Me too.' He blows a little kiss with the tips of his fingers as he turns away and starts to jog along the street towards FitRox's studios. 'Have a great day, Libby. And take care.'

I've barely had time to turn back into the house before I hear my name called from the other direction.

'Libby?'

It's Elvira, marching down the pavement towards me in cobalt-blue over-the-knee boots, a fringed suede miniskirt and, of all things, a rather incongruous navy-blue sou'wester. Throw in her customary Hermès Birkin bag and the Alexander McQueen skull-print scarf slung round her neck, and it's certainly an unusual look, though one – I have to admit – she somehow manages to pull off in the way that only a bohemian aristocratic ex-model can.

From the sound of her heels stomping along the pavement, she's not happy about something. I mean, not happy about something *specific*; obviously by now I'm quite accustomed to Elvira's general air of irritation and misery.

'Hi! Tino's looking really well,' I begin, as she reaches me, Tino clutched as usual under her non-Birkin-carrying arm. 'Can I get him a—'

'Can I just ask,' she interrupts, in a tone that suggests she's not actually *asking* anything at all, 'why I've been getting calls this morning from the Willington-Joneses asking why there was *fighting* and *vomiting* going on in the street outside last night?'

Shit. Shit, shit, shit.

'And don't tell me it was nothing to do with you,' she goes on, actually wagging a finger in my face, 'because they saw you coming in here after . . . well, whatever street-brawl you were participating in.'

'OK, first off, it wasn't a street brawl,' I say, evenly. 'It was a . . . misunderstanding. And honestly, there wasn't any fighting. There might have been one judo move – well, actually, Krav Maga – but it was all very swift and very silent. As I think Krav Maga is meant to be.'

'Libby—'

'And as for the vomit,' I say, 'I'm really, really sorry about that. I'm about to wash it away, but I'll certainly pop next door and apologize to the Willington-Joneses.'

'Too little, too late,' she says, sweeping through the front door without asking if it's OK to go in. 'Tino needs water,' she adds. 'Can you go up and get some?'

'Of course . . .' I hurry the two floors up to the kitchen for the water, and then back down again. When I get back to the ground floor, Elvira has made herself comfortable at my trestle table, while Tino snuffles around, getting his nose into my piles of packaging supplies and starting to play, with numerous yappy barks, with a pile of my brand-new and very expensive eau-de-nil-coloured tissue paper. 'Here's his water!'

'Water, Tino, darling,' Elvira says, but – having sent me all the way up to get it – she doesn't seem all that interested in Tino actually getting his required daily amount of hydration. She. is, I think, much more keen on accomplishing her true purpose here this morning: to give me a proper bollocking. 'I don't really know where to begin, Libby,' she goes on. 'Street fights, vomiting in the gutter . . . I mean, I know you're not accustomed to living anywhere as select as this, but I certainly didn't expect you to start turning the place into your own personal *ghetto*.'

'I've not! Look, Elvira, like I said, I'm really sorry about—'

There's another knock at the door, on the other side of the studio.

Honestly, this place is like Piccadilly bloody Circus this morning.

'Sorry, Elvira, I just need to go and get that. It's probably just my DHL delivery, I'll only be a sec.'

But it isn't – as I see the moment I open the door – a delivery, from DHL or otherwise.

'Libby Lomax?' asks the middle-aged woman at the door. She's dark haired and fully made-up, with a thick slick of fuchsia on her lips that matches, rather perfectly, the pink scarf over the shoulders of her black suit jacket. Her handbag is fuchsia too – an over-brimming affair that's weighing down her broad shoulder – and she's also carrying a big Tesco's reusable shopping bag that's almost as stuffed full.

'Yes, I'm Libby, how can I—'

'Where is sofa?' she asks in heavily accented English before barging in past me. 'Bogdan is here also?'

'Oh! You must be Aunt Vanya, Bogdan's aunt, that is: the Moldovan mystic married to the Haringey councillor. 'Look,' I go on rather desperately, because I can see Elvira, in the back room, craning her neck to see who it is I'm talking to, 'it's not actually the best time for me right now. And Bogdan isn't here. I don't know if you could come back a bit later?'

'Is not possible. Am having the time available *now*. Who is knowing,' Aunt Vanya adds, darkly, peering around the studio and running her hands, in an exploratory fashion, over the walls, 'when am being able to come here again?'

'Well, sure, but there really isn't any urgency, as such—'

'Sofa is upstairs, yes?'

'Yes, but—'

'Then this is where I am needed.' She hoicks her pink handbag up on to her shoulder. 'Please be showing me?'

'Honestly, I . . . no, no, I'll show you!' I yelp, as Aunt Vanya takes it upon herself to head for the stairs and starts to go up them. 'Really, I think it would be better to wait until Bogdan gets back. I mean, he'll be able to explain to you all about what's been happening in, well, in Moldovan.'

'Am speaking the perfect English,' she states, confidently,

walking straight to the Chesterfield and starting to run her hands along the length of it. 'Do not be getting your pants in a pickle. Please, you are having the matches?'

'Matches? Oh, no, no, I don't think there's any need to set light to anything!'

'Is for the candles,' she says, reaching down into her Tesco's bag and pulling out a handful of tea-lights. 'Is important for the setting of the mood. The dead,' she adds, matter-of-factly, 'are not being happy to be appearing in the bright daylight.'

'Right . . . er . . . I don't know what Bogdan told you, but I don't think the people that appear on my sofa are *dead*, per se—'

'Libby?' This is Elvira, calling irritably up the stairs. 'What are you doing up there? Weren't we just in the middle of a conversation?'

'Yes, yes, on my way!' I call back. 'I don't think I have any matches, Aunt Vanya,' I tell her, in a quieter voice, 'but really, I'd much prefer it if you waited until Bogdan gets back, and until I've finished my meeting downstairs.'

'Will just be getting set up, then,' she says, with a shrug. 'Please, be going about your business.'

I can't do anything but leave her to it, as I really don't want Elvira popping up to investigate what's going on. After all, if she's already annoyed with me about the street-fighting and the vomit, she's going to be incandescent with the idea of a strange Moldovan woman using her flat to host what looks like . . . well, possibly some sort of séance, if I'm honest.

I hurry back down the stairs and into the studio, where Elvira, her arms folded in irritation, is waiting for me.

'Who was that?'

'Oh, that's just . . . a new cleaner I'm trying out. I struggle to keep on top of it all, having a bigger flat than I'm used to.'

'Well, maybe this whole arrangement was a mistake after all, then.'

'What? Oh, no, no, Elvira, it's not a mistake!'

'Really? Because I just wonder, Libby, if I was right about you in the first place.' The rather pinched, sour expression on her admittedly beautiful face is getting more pinched and more sour. 'I know Ben has rated you highly in the past, but – and I think it's time you actually began to take this on board, Libby – he has plenty of other businesses he could just as easily invest in, with a lot less of the trouble that you seem intent on causing.'

'Sorry – are you saying that Ben would pull his investment?'

Because this is even more serious news than the suggestion that Elvira might kick me out of her flat.

'I'm saying that neither he nor – more importantly – I have the time or inclination to work with people who end up creating more trouble than they're worth. There are *reputational* implications, Libby, if it hadn't occurred to you yet. It's not merely a matter of upsetting my family's neighbours, or even the terrible trauma you were responsible for inflicting on my dog.'

'But with the greatest respect, Elvira,' I say, with a slightly

141

shaking voice, because I don't enjoy confrontation at the best of times, and certainly not with an upper-class brat like Elvira who holds a lot of the cards in this situation, 'it seems *precisely* as if it's a matter of upsetting your family's neighbours and the trauma inflicted on your dog. Because, honestly, I don't think I've done much else wrong, have I? I mean, I'm keeping my costs down, I'm following the business plan you and Ben's team devised for me; I'm even – ' my voice has stopped shaking and has risen slightly – 'going along with exactly what you think should be the creative direction for the business. Even though I never actually intended to specialize quite so heavily in vintage-inspired bridal tiaras as I am doing . . .'

I break off, as from above us on the first floor comes the sound of what can only be described as caterwauling.

'What the fuck?' snaps Elvira.

'Oh, that's just . . . um . . . I think it might be "Whistle While You Work" in Moldovan, actually.'

'I don't care if it's "Some Day My Prince Will Come" in bloody Cantonese! Go and tell her it's a godawful racket and it needs to stop.' Elvira's eyes blaze at me. 'Do you think the Willington-Joneses want to put up with that din coming through the walls after you already woke them in the small hours last night? Do you want to end up getting slapped with some sort of *ASBO?* Or, more likely, given that I own this place, I'd be the one getting the ASBO!'

'No, no, Elvira, of course I don't want that,' I say, hastily. 'I'll go and stop her.'

I hurry back up the stairs to the living room, where – to

my real alarm – Aunt Vanya, singing her lungs out, has now lit a good dozen or so candles and placed them, in an ominous-looking pentacle shape, on the floor around the sofa.

'Aunt Vanya,' I hiss at her. 'What are you doing?'

She stops singing. 'Oh, hello, darling. Am finding the matches in bottom of own bag. This is good news, no? Is not possible to be setting the mood for the summoning of the spirits otherwise.'

'But they don't need to be summoned! And anyway, it's not a *spirit*, Aunt Vanya! I don't know what Bogdan told you, but I'm pretty sure the sofa is magical in some way—'

'You are calling it magical,' she says, with a shrug. 'I am calling it possessed. Potato, po-tah-to.'

'But *possessed* implies . . . look, it's not a demon in there, or anything!'

'Demon,' she intones, in the manner of a high priestess, 'is able to be disguising itself with many faces.'

'Maybe, but not with the faces of Audrey Hepburn, Marilyn Monroe and Grace Kelly.'

'Ahhhh, Grace Kelly.' Aunt Vanya gazes into the middle distance for a moment. 'This is most beautiful woman who is ever existing.'

'Yes, I'm aware of that, I've recently met her. And I promise you, she's not a devil in disguise.'

'But this is precisely what devil is wanting you to think. What – you are thinking all devils are turning up looking like Halloween night costume, with horns and pitchfork? Is pretty unsubtle approach.' She reaches into her capacious

Tesco bag again and pulls out a large plastic spritz bottle, the sort you might use to mist plants with water in a greenhouse. 'And one thing demons are not is unsubtle.'

I'm getting more alarmed by the minute.

'What's in that bottle?' I ask, as she starts to spritz the contents, in a methodical way, all over the sofa.

'Am not able to be telling you precise components. Is proprietary recipe. But is containing the deionized water, the surgical spirit, and – obviously – the holy water . . .'

'Holy water? Aunt Vanya, sorry, I really am not in the market for . . . well, whatever it is you're planning on doing.'

'You are *not* wanting me to be ridding you of demon spirit?'

'No!' I gaze at her. 'Sorry, Aunt Vanya, but I thought – Bogdan *told me* – that you were a mystic.'

'Ah. This is misunderstanding on the part of Bogdan.' She shakes her head, clucking affectionately. 'Am seeing where he is getting the wires in a cross. Word for mystic, in my language, is same as word for exorcist.'

'Oh, God, I don't want . . .' I lower my voice, conscious that Elvira is still downstairs. 'I don't want an exorcism!' I hiss.

'You are wanting to *keep* evil spirit?' She looks surprised. 'As some kind of *pet*? Am counselling most strongly against this, darling. You are biting off more than you are able to be chewing.'

'No, look, it isn't an evil spirit at all. Look, can we just—'

'While am on subject,' she goes on, using a far more matter-of-fact tone for a moment, 'can I just be checking if you are having any *actual* pets? Pet is very soft target for demon to take possession of, which is why am including exorcism of one pet in whole Cleansing Package. More than one pet – or particularly complicated pet – is costing the extra. But for you, as you are coming to me on Friends and Family recommendation, am only charging you the extra if is very unusual pet. One time, am having to be performing the exorcism on capybara.' She pulls a face. 'You are ever seeing this thing? Is like giant guinea pig but without sweet and gentle temperament of guinea pig. This is why am having to charge extra for anything that is not—'

'*Libby?*' This is Elvira, yelling up the stairs. 'Can you just get down here, please?'

'Coming . . .' I turn to Aunt Vanya. 'Look, there's obviously been a communication error, but I don't want any sort of Cleansing Package, OK?'

She stops spritzing her holy water spray and folds her arms. 'Am getting it. You are wanting to be haggling.'

'No! Nothing of the sort—'

'Libby!'

'I'll be back in a sec,' I say, hurrying down the stairs, where – oh, dear God – Elvira is also standing with her arms folded in the archway that separates the studio from the showroom.

'Can I ask,' she says, icily, 'why you're getting iCal updates through on your phone for meetings at Pressley/Waters?'

I stare at her.

'You looked at my phone?'

'It was right there on the table. The message popped

145

up.' She doesn't sound in the least concerned about this invasion of my privacy. '*Are you aware,*' she goes on, more icily than ever, 'that the terms of Ben's investment *specifically forbid* that you take on any work for anybody else?'

'I'm aware of that,' I say, evenly. 'But this is just one meeting.'

'One *clandestine* meeting!'

'It's not clandestine! I only spoke to them five minutes before you got here! I haven't even had time to mention it to you.'

'I'm going to have to speak to Ben about this,' she says, stalking back into the studio and picking up her Hermès Birkin bag. 'But I can assure you, Libby, that he is *not* going to be impressed. At all.'

'Look, I'll speak to him. I'm perfectly happy to explain—'

'Where's Tino?' Elvira interrupts me, looking around the studio. 'Tino, darling? Mummy's ready to leave, now!'

I'm expecting Tino to appear from underneath the new IKEA table, where he was last seen destroying large wads of expensive tissue paper, but he doesn't.

'Tino?' Elvira makes her usual clicking sound to summon him. 'Darling? Mummy needs you!'

There's still no sign of him.

'Where is he?' Elvira peers down underneath the table, but comes up empty. 'Tino?'

Up above us, Aunt Vanya suddenly starts singing again.

Actually, it sounds less like a song and more like an incantation.

146

A handful of notes in and there's a sharp, rather worried-sounding, bark.

'Tino!' Elvira shrieks.

I'm hot on her cobalt-blue-booted heels as she races up the stairs, my own heart hammering as Tino's single bark turns into a volley of them.

'Aunt Vanya!' I call out. 'Whatever you're doing . . .'

What Aunt Vanya is doing, as Elvira and I reach the top of the stairs, is holding Tino aloft, with one arm, in what can only be described as a sort of sacrificial manner, and spritzing holy water all over him with the other.

'Put my baby down!' Elvira leaps forward, only to be met by a puff of holy water right in her eyes. 'What the fuck?' she screams, sinking to the floor as if she's been Maced.

'Aunt Vanya, no!' I say, trying to seize a frantic, scrabbling Tino from her hand. 'Put the dog down.'

'Is not dog.'

'No, I know he looks exactly like a large rat, but—'

'Or rather, is not *currently* dog. Is body of dog but is possessed by evil spirit. Is exactly what we are just discussing,' Aunt Vanya goes on, giving Tino another couple of puffs with her spritz bottle. 'Household pets are very often easy targets for the demons to be slipping inside.'

'Who's slipped inside my baby?' Elvira gasps, staggering to her feet. 'Did she just say *demon?*'

'You are owner?' Aunt Vanya asks. 'Am sorry to be breaking this news to you. But yes, am as certain as can be that this dog is possessed by same demon that Libby is hosting in her sofa. Am getting very bad vibe off this animal. Is having most unpleasant look in its eye, for one thing. And for another, am not sure is natural to be having so little of the body hair—'

'No, no, it's a Mexican hairless,' I tell her, but can say no more before Elvira rounds on me.

'You brought a fucking *exorcist* into my flat?'

'No! Of course n—'

'To be fair,' Aunt Vanya interrupts me, 'is only sensible course of action for Libby to be taking. Seeing as she is bringing demonically possessed sofa into flat in first place.'

'*Give me back my dog!*' Elvira roars, heroically managing to snatch Tino out of Aunt Vanya's vice-like grip, bundling him under her own arm and staggering towards the stairs like someone fleeing a natural disaster. Which, to be fair to her, Aunt Vanya and her demon-baiting certainly feels like. 'You,' she chokes, turning back to point an accusing finger at me, 'pack your things and get out of my flat.'

'Elvira, please, this is all just—'

'If you use the word *misunderstanding*,' she snarls, 'I swear to God, Libby, I will call the police and get you evicted.'

'But you can't—'

'Of course I fucking can! This is my flat!'

She turns and clatters down the stairs with Tino, and slams the door – a noise that's only going to further inflame the Willington-Joneses – behind her.

Chapter 7

Stevenage. That's where I think I'm going to end up living.

Because, seriously, I've spent several hours this afternoon frantically trawling through Rightmove, and Stevenage is the only place I can find, within striking distance of London, that's remotely affordable.

And it really is going to have to be affordable, if – as I strongly suspect – Elvira talks Ben into pulling his financial support. Since she stormed out of my holy-water-drenched living room earlier this morning, I've received a brief, curt text message from her informing me, as per her screamed instructions, that she wishes me to vacate the building by the end of the week, and that she will be speaking to Ben *to discover if he wishes to continue working in partnership with a person who has no qualms about plying her trade with another investor.*

Oh, and in a follow-up text, which I suspect is the one that really gets to the heart of the issue, *And, as Tino's godfather, I can't imagine he'll be too impressed by you trying to get him EXORCIZED, either.*

I mean, I'm a bit screwed, aren't I?

Because I know how much Ben listens to Elvira (the fact that he's agreed to be her *dog's godfather* should indicate just how much) and I also know that he has enough competing demands on his time to be perfectly happy to drop me like a hot brick if I'm looking to be more trouble than I'm worth.

It's never felt like a better time to be seeing Nora this afternoon, I can tell you.

This is why I'm waiting outside Olly's right now, in fact; sitting on the outside front doorstep, poring over Rightmove on my iPhone. I'm assuming they've just been a bit delayed on the tube journey from King's Cross, where I know Olly was meeting them about an hour ago, because nobody answered my knocks at the door, and I can't get hold of any of them on their phones.

So, Stevenage.

I've already spoken to a couple of estate agents there, in fact, with a view to going tomorrow and taking a look at some of the places I've seen on Rightmove. There's a cheap-enough unit in a light industrial estate near the mainline station that I could use as a studio, and I might be able to rent a little flat to live in not too far away . . . And, I mean, it'll be all right, won't it? I can join a couple of things – a book group, maybe? A running club? – and make some new friends. The estate agent (who didn't sound *that* desperate. Did he?) told me there are some really nice pubs, and a small cinema, and . . . I think he might have mentioned a Nando's . . .

Not that I'll be in the market for piri-piri chicken and chips, if I'm trying to keep fit for a running club, of course!

Who knows: maybe getting kicked out of my new flat, ditched by my investor and moving to Stevenage might just be the best thing that ever happened to me. That book group, the running club, clear water between me and Mum, some healthy distance from Olly . . .

I'm just trying to envisage my New Life in Stevenage – leaner; healthier; better versed in the classics – when my phone rings.

Bogdan.

I answer, immediately.

'Bogdan.'

'Libby. Am getting your message about what is happening with Aunt Vanya . . .'

'Wait, before we get into that. Did it all go OK with Dillon this morning?'

'At rehabilitation centre? Yes, is fine. He is being most grateful to you for encouraging him to return there, Libby. He is saying what fine human being you are. How thoughtful. How caring. What good friend—'

'There's no need to overdo it.'

'All right. But am just wanting to be saying that am happy to be paying Aunt Vanya myself, Libby, as sign of remorse and regret for mistake.'

'Wait. You actually think she's still going to charge me?'

'Be fair, Libby. She is trying to make a living. Is not easy being wife of senior council member for Haringey.

Standards are having to be maintained. There are being official dinners, garden parties, all this sort of thing.'

'She's married to a councillor! She's not the bloody queen of England! Nor is she a mystic, just FYI. She's a bloody exorcist.'

'This is being clear to me now. Am thinking that maybe am getting her muddled with family member who has similar talents. Now that am thinking of it, perhaps is Aunt *Anya* who is being the mystic. She is sister of *mother's* cousin's second wife. Completely different branch of family. And am pretty sure she is also living in London—'

'No! No, Bogdan, I don't want any more of your spurious relatives coming over to do anything with my sofa.' Not that they would, probably, if it involved them getting a train all the way to Stevenage and back. 'Mystics, or exorcists, or necromancers . . . none of them, OK?'

'OK. Again, am so very, very sorry, Libby. Am hoping there is way you can be making this right with Elvira.'

'I think that ship has sailed, actually, Bogdan,' I say, with a sigh. 'I've got to leave her flat, as a matter of fact, so I'd really appreciate your help getting everything—'

I suddenly tip backwards as the door opens up behind me.

For a moment, I lie there on the floor, gazing up at the lean, slender, golden thighs that are standing over me. Thighs that belong to . . .

'Libby!'

It's Tash.

She's answered Olly's door, wearing nothing but a short

towelling dressing gown, fluffy slippers and a towel wrapped around her head.

'Oh, my God, were you knocking? I've been in the shower . . .' She leans down and puts her hands under my armpits to haul me to my feet. 'I'm so sorry! Come on in, and don't sit there freezing on the step, for heaven's sake!'

'I wasn't freezing, honestly, it was quite pleasant . . . oh, I'll call you later, Bogdan,' I add into my phone, which I'm still holding.

'Hi, Bogdan!' Tash calls, in the direction of the phone. 'Aw. He's always such a sweetheart. It's so good to see you, Libby,' she goes on. 'How have you been? What's been going on?'

'Oh, er, you know. The usual . . . sorry, Tash, I had no idea you were coming down today . . .'

'Oh, well, I have you to thank for that, actually!'

'You do?'

'Absolutely.' She leads me towards the kitchen, settles me in her rather no-arguments manner at the kitchen table, then goes to pop the kettle on. 'Olly Skyped me the other night and told me you'd been telling him to get his act together. You know, about not spending enough time with me.'

'Er, I don't think I put it *exactly* like that . . .'

'So after that, I just decided I'd surprise him and head down here with Nora and Mark this afternoon to stay for the weekend! It was win-win for everyone, really, because Nora and Mark got some help with Clara on the flight, too . . . they've all just popped over to see Jack and his

153

family in Stockwell for a quick cuppa, actually, let the cousins meet the baby for the first time. Lovely children, Jack's are, but they were ever so raucous at Nora's wedding, so I thought I'd keep the numbers down and stay well away! Do you know them at all?'

'Jack's children?' Jack is Nora and Olly's older brother; I've known him, therefore, since I was thirteen. 'Yes, I know them. They always seem like really nice kids.'

'Oh, absolutely! I think maybe we just have different parenting styles.'

'But . . . er . . . you're not a parent.'

'*Yet!*' she says, with a wink and a smile. 'How do you like your tea, Libby?'

'Oh . . . actually, Tash, you know what? I'd really like a glass of wine.'

She glances, just for a moment, at the bright yellow clock on the kitchen wall.

'I've had,' I explain, 'a really, really shit day.'

'Oh, then of course.'

My heart breaks a little as I watch her bustling proprietorially around Olly's kitchen, getting wine glasses and a bottle.

Even in her dressing gown, with her wet hair now tumbling over her shoulders, she looks gorgeous. Clear-eyed and dewy-skinned and – despite having just got off an EasyJet flight from Glasgow – a little bit like she's just stepped off the kind of mountain you might find Heidi and her goats living on.

'Well,' she says, sitting down at the table opposite me,

putting the glasses down on the wooden top, and pouring us each a glass of wine, 'if you've had a bad day, then seeing Clara is going to be *such* a tonic!'

'Yes, I can't wait.'

'I mean, you've no idea how heavenly she is at the moment, Libby! She's started laughing, and she's found her toes . . . honestly, you just want to eat her up with a spoon. I mean, you'll notice the difference from the last time you saw her, because it's been . . . how long?'

'Three months.'

'Oh, my goodness, she's a completely different creature! Of course, I get to see her almost every day, so I don't notice the changes all that much, but you'll be blown away by it!'

Is it just me, or does this sound like Tash is trying to rub in the fact that she gets to spend so much time with Nora and the baby?

No. It's probably just me. After all, I'm the one with the jealousy problem here. She's not jealous of me. Why would she be, when she's got everything I could possibly want in life?

'And of course, Nora's such a natural mother,' Tash is going on. 'I tell her, every day, how important I think it is that she has another one sooner rather than later. After all, she and Olly are so close, wouldn't it be lovely for Clara to have a wonderful brother, too? And we all have to keep our eyes on the ball on that front, don't we?'

'Sorry – on what front?'

'Babies, Libby! I mean, these things don't just happen.

They have to be planned, strategized, thought through. What are you doing about all that, by the way?'

'Er . . . what am I doing about having a baby?'

She nods. 'Please don't become one of those women who hit thirty-five, Libby, and then *suddenly* realize time is running out! It's so much better to stay on the ball about this stuff. Are you seeing anyone?'

I'm so confused: is she asking if I'm going out with anyone, or if I'm booked in with a fertility specialist? I mean, two minutes ago, I was lying flat on my back accidentally looking up Tash's dressing gown, and now I'm here being given what feels like a lecture about my declining fertility levels and my upcoming descent into menopause. I mean, I know she's a doctor, and this sort of brisk, unsentimental talk about the human body and its limitations is the way she earns her living . . . but it's yet another thing that makes it hard to gel with her.

'I mean,' she's going on, 'I know that Nora's always desperate for you to find the right man and settle down.'

'Hey, I was going out with Dillon O'Hara for months!' I say, defensively. 'It's not like I'm some permanently single saddo.'

'Oh, well, yes, but he wasn't at all the kind of guy you'd have settled down with, was he?'

'He might have been,' I mutter, conveniently ignoring the fact that less than twenty-four hours ago, Dillon was throwing up in my toilet, and that he's now cosily ensconced in rehab for the second time in a year. 'You never know. And anyway, I *am* seeing . . . someone. As it happens.'

'Good!' Tash reacts to this with her usual no-nonsense lack of romance. 'Name?'

'Joel.'

'Age?'

'Thirty-eight. But you know what, Tash,' I add, 'it's really early days, and I'd rather not—'

'That's an OK age gap. I mean, he'll be wanting to have children before he's too far into his forties. And you'll be needing to get on with all that side of things, as we've already agreed.'

'Um, no, we didn't, actually!'

'And obviously, as things go further with him, you'll really need to clarify your plan.'

'Plan?'

'Plan.' She nods. 'You must have a plan. Like, I want two children, and obviously it'll be best for me to squeeze them in as close together as possible – I mean, twins would be really ideal, if there was any way I could legislate for that – so that I can keep the hit to my career to an absolute minimum. And you know, there's an awful lot you can do even before you have the children – even before you conceive them – to make things go more smoothly when you actually have them. I mean, my cousin planned out all her children's first five birthday parties before they were born. She's a lawyer, so it really made sense.'

'How could that . . . *possibly* make sense?'

'Are you kidding me?' Tash stares at me, as though I'm the one saying bonkers-sounding things rather than – surely? – the other way around. 'Do you have any idea the length of time it takes to properly organize a child's birthday party? *Huge* amounts of it can be done well in advance, if you're on the ball. Ordering the supplies – balloons, banners, napkins, whatnot – and doing your research on a good local baker to make the cake . . .'

'Wow.' I swallow, hard. 'You could save yourself . . . literally an hour for each birthday.'

Her eyes narrow, just for a moment. 'Do you not agree with me,' she asks, rather sharply, in a voice quite unlike her usual hearty tone, 'or something?'

'I just . . . it all seems . . . is Olly on board with all this sort of stuff?'

'Why do you ask?'

'I don't know.' I can feel myself getting rather warm, and I wish I'd just kept my opinions to myself. 'I mean, it does all sound quite mapped-out.'

She puts down her glass. 'You're saying Olly prefers to be a slacker?'

'What? No! No, I'm not saying that for a minute. I was just wondering whether he's – uh – aware that you're thinking this way. All the specifics, I mean, about when you want to have children, and—'

'Yes, Libby. He's aware. I mean, you may find it hard to believe, seeing as you obviously think you know Olly better than I do, but—'

Thank God – thank *God* – there's a noise from the front door as it opens, in the hallway, and Olly and Mark and Nora and, of course, Clara, arrive home.

I say *of course*, partly because Clara's obviously the main attraction, but also because as they all head inside, she's screaming fit to burst a lung or two. I mean, seriously, you've never heard a racket like the one coming out of this child right now. She's purple-faced with fury and scrabbling at Nora's chest like exactly the sort of demonic creature Aunt Vanya was trying to exorcize out of my sofa earlier this morning. Nora is the eye of the storm, all serenity and calm – while around her Mark flaps and Olly stresses out – and gestures for me to come upstairs with her to the spare bedroom as she carries the flailing bundle of rage that is my beloved (and, right now, pretty terrifying) goddaughter with her.

It takes about five seconds, once in the bedroom, for Nora to expertly unbutton her top, clamp Clara on to her boob, and the screaming stops.

My ears are still ringing, to be honest with you, but Nora just beams at me, beatifically, pats the little double bed she's sitting on with her free hand, and says, 'God, it's so great to see you, Libby.'

'You too! And Clara—'

'Oh, don't lie. That screaming fit horrified you just now, Lib, I can see it!'

'Don't be si . . . well, OK. That was a tiny bit horrifying. But I'm sure she was just hungry.'

'You're right. At all other hours of the day – and night – she's nothing but a ray of sunshine.'

'Really?'

'No, not really. She's been in a bloody awful grump the entire journey. I think her first teeth are starting to make their way through. Either that or she was just pissed off that we flew crappy old Ryanair when she thinks of herself as more of a private jet passenger.' Nora grins down at Clara's little bald, gently bobbing head, and kisses it. 'You OK there, old buddy?'

'Well, not entirely . . . oh.' I stop. 'You were talking to Clara.'

'I was.' Nora transfers her smile to me. 'But I'll probably get better conversation out of you, for now. What's up? You look a bit shell-shocked. It's not still the racket she was making, is it?'

'Oh, God, no. It's just been a weird day. Profoundly weird. You don't want to hear about it.'

'Trust me, Libby, when your usual day is filled with wheels on buses going round and round, bobbins being wound up, and asking inane questions of talking black sheep, I most certainly do want to hear about it . . . oh, but before you start, can you just reach into my bag –' she indicates her shoulder-bag, dropped by the door – 'get the KitKat from the zip pocket and break a bit of it off for me? Breast-feeding makes me *starving*. But please,' she adds, in a bit of a whisper, as I do as she asks, 'don't mention this to Tash. I'll only get a bit of a lecture about how I should be eating nothing but green veg and Brazil nuts, or something. And honestly, I don't have the energy for her right now. I mean, for *that*,' she corrects herself. Because Nora is never unkind about anyone. Ever. It's one of the things I love most about her. 'She means really well, obviously, and I know she only has Clara's best interests at heart! But still. I'd rather avoid the issue altogether, and just, you know, enjoy the KitKat.'

'No arguments from me,' I say, handing her a bite-sized piece of KitKat to eat.

'So really. What's up?' Nora eats the KitKat, then holds out her hand for more. 'Is it work or – um – love life?'

I know why she's hesitating before the words *love life*. Olly. It's supremely awkward for us to talk about, mostly because of how horrendously guilty she feels, now, for never mentioning anything to me about his feelings.

'Work,' I say, firmly, before adding, 'I mean, I am seeing a guy, as it happens—'

'Lib!' Happiness and something else – relief? – flood over her face. 'That's terrific!'

'Yes, though why does everyone have to act as though I'm announcing that I'm Lazarus arising from the dead, or something?'

'Sorry. I'm just pleased. So pleased. You have to tell me more about him!'

'Well, I don't know all that much about him yet, except that he's a personal trainer, and he's half-Brazilian, half-Slovakian . . .'

'Wow.'

'. . . and we're going out on our second date on Thursday night. Although, come to think of it,' I go on, this only just occurring to me myself, 'it's going to put a real spanner in the works if I have to end up moving to Stevenage.'

'Why on earth,' Nora asks, staring at me, 'would you have to move to Stevenage?'

161

'It's a long story.' I lean, wearily, against the pillows. 'But if you want the short version – the version that doesn't involve street fights, exorcisms and the false accusation of industrial espionage—'

'Libby, what the actual fuck . . .?'

'. . . then the bottom line is, I probably don't have a financier any more. And I certainly don't have a place to live any more.'

'Oh, God. Oh, *Libby*.'

'Nor?' There's a light knock at the door; it's Olly, who opens it a fraction but doesn't actually put his head round. 'Sorry to interrupt, but Tash is making some snacks, and she wondered if you'd like her to bring up some Brazil nuts?'

'It's OK, Ol, you can come in.' Nora somehow produces a huge muslin from somewhere – like all nursing mothers I've ever seen, she seems to have an inexhaustible supply of them, stashed in pockets and thrown over shoulders – and drapes it around herself so Olly can join us without older-brotherly embarrassment. 'Tell Tash that's sweet of her, but I'm fine. More importantly, tell Libby she can't move to Stevenage!'

Olly sticks his head properly round the door now.

His cheeks are faintly pink, probably from a combination of the warmth in the kitchen below, and residual discomfort about the breast-feeding thing. It makes him look very young – rather like the fifteen-year-old Olly I first met, in fact – and my heart aches for him.

'Why is Libby moving to Stevenage?' he asks, with genuine bewilderment.

'Oh, well, things haven't worked out too well with Elvira Roberts-Hoare,' I say, shooting Nora a look, 'so she's asked me to leave her flat . . .'

'And insisted that you move to *Stevenage*?'

'Olly, come on, there's no need to look so horrified.' I try to sound cheerful. 'There's absolutely nothing wrong with Stevenage! It has – er – pubs. A Nando's. It's jolly convenient for the M11.'

'Do you *need* to be convenient for the M11?' Olly asks.

'Well, not the M11, specifically, no, but obviously the location is a major factor in selecting Stevenage,' I say, trying to sound as if I've spent ages debating the pros and cons of various commuting towns before plumping for Stevenage, rather than the fact that it's pretty much the only place within striking distance of London where I can afford to rent both work and living space.

'Besides, plenty of people move out of London! It's not the hub of the universe, you know!'

'No, but it's the hub of *your* universe. I mean, your family's here.' His cheeks grow even more pink, with indignation. 'Your friends.'

'Not all my friends! Nora isn't in London.'

'Yeah, because Stevenage is really convenient for Glasgow!'

'It's close to Luton Airport,' I say. 'Only half an hour, in fact.'

'Has it occurred to you,' Olly asks, heatedly, 'that the real reason Stevenage is so well connected is because everyone else is doing their best to get out of it?'

'Well, what do you suggest, then?' I glare at him,

completely forgetting that we really ought to be keeping the atmosphere in this room nice and peaceful and quiet, so that Clara can enjoy her feed. 'I don't know if I have anyone backing my business any more, Olly, and if that's the case, I'm going to have to plough every penny I've got into fulfilling the orders I've got on my books. So am I supposed to rig the National Lottery? Dig around and find a spare ten grand in an old coat pocket that I can use to cover the next six months' rent somewhere big enough in London?'

Olly actually seems to be giving this some thought for a moment, then he takes a deep breath and says, 'No, but you could come and stay here while you at least try to find a better option than Stevenage.'

'*Here?*'

'Yes. Here. In this spare room. Which, obviously, I won't charge you a penny to do.' He's talking rather fast, presumably because he's thinking this through even as he says it aloud. 'And then you could afford to rent somewhere else as studio space, right? Oh! Actually, there's a converted warehouse I just saw the other day on the way to work, right on Kennington Road, that's definitely got studio spaces to rent. Probably big enough to use for storing your furniture, too. You could give them a call and see what their rates are . . .'

I'm staring at him.

Nora is staring at him.

'Olly,' she says, after a moment, 'are you sure it's . . . I mean, I'm not saying it *isn't* a good idea. But . . . the, er, the two of you haven't flat-shared since that month or two when Libby first left drama school.'

'It isn't flat-sharing,' Olly says. 'It's just a temporary solution. Just for a few weeks, Lib, or a couple of months, until some other solution presents itself. And what the hell has happened with Ben, by the way? Can he just pull his investment, just like that?'

'I don't know,' I begin, just as Tash appears in the doorway.

She's holding a tray with a glass of water and a dish of Brazil nuts.

'Hey, guys, I just thought Nora might have wanted these . . . what's going on?'

There's a very brief silence, which is filled, after a slight cough, by Olly.

'I'm just suggesting that Libby come and stay with me for a while,' he explains. 'She's being kicked out of her flat, and it makes sense to save the money.' He clears his throat again. 'Don't you think it's a good idea, Tash?'

I'm unsure as to what Tash's reaction is going to be, to be honest. Because even though she's always the very epitome of jolly-hockey-sticks mucking-in, I was getting a distinctly chilly vibe from her just before Nora and the others got home earlier. Not, that is, the vibe of the sort of person who's going to be all that thrilled about someone else – a specifically *me* someone else? – moving into her boyfriend's flat while she's hundreds of miles away in Glasgow.

'And *I* was just saying—' Nora begins, only to be interrupted by Tash.

'That's a really great idea! Spot on, Olly.'

The pangs of guilt I always feel about having the slightest hint of a negative thought about Tash are turning, rapidly, from pangs into actual stabs.

'You'll be so comfortable here, Libby.' She strides into the bedroom, a dressing-gown-wearing Julie Andrews in *The Sound of Music* all of a sudden, seizing the curtain fabric in her hands and assessing it, expertly. 'These are decent enough, and the walls will be fine once they've had a lick of paint . . .'

'Tash, no, I'd only be staying for a few weeks!' I say. 'There's absolutely no need whatsoever to start redecorating!'

'. . . and there's a double bed, so you could even have – sorry, what's your new boyfriend's name again?'

'You have . . . a new boyfriend?' Olly asks me, looking even more startled than he did by the Stevenage suggestion. He meets my eye properly again. 'You didn't mention anyone to me the other night!'

'He's not my new boyfriend,' I say, firmly, giving Tash a . . . no, actually, I don't give her any kind of a look. She's scaring me a little, for all her chirpy Maria von Trapp demeanour. 'Nothing of the sort. He's just . . . he's just a guy I'm seeing. There's no need,' I add, 'for anyone to be buying hats just yet. OK?'

Nobody joins me in my (admittedly awkward) laughter.

'You know. For weddings. People buy hats.'

'Hang on: there's going to be a *wedding?*' Olly asks.

'No.' Tash sounds ever-so-slightly snappish with him, in stark contrast to the cloud of sheer fluffy loveliness she's wafting over me. 'Libby said there was *no* need for anyone to be buying a hat.'

'Exactly,' I say, firmly. 'It's only a second date.'

'Only a second date,' Tash repeats, before adding, equally firmly, 'but still, we're all crossing everything that it does work out for you, Libby! Aren't we, guys?'

Nora mumbles her assent. Olly opens his mouth as if he's about to say something, but then closes it again just as Tash carries on.

'And we can make this room a really nice place to bring him back to. Oh! I could even go shopping tomorrow, while Ol's doing the lunch service at the restaurant, and get some lovely new fresh guest towels, maybe a new bedside lamp . . . or would it be more useful for me to come over to your flat and help you pack, Libby?'

'That's . . . that's really nice of you, Tash.' I glance over at Olly, who's looking as if he might be regretting his offer of help, all of a sudden. 'Look, Ol, *if* you're honestly sure it's OK, then it would actually be a massive help to stay here for a bit. Just while the dust settles, and I know what's going to be happening with work. I mean, I do have a meeting with another jewellery company on Thursday, as it happens, so if the worst comes to the worst, maybe I'll get a job there, or something—'

'Libby, don't stress.' He reaches out a hand and puts it on one of my shoulders. I can feel my skin tingling, even though his touch is through a layer of T-shirt and another layer of cardigan. 'It'll all work out. And you know you can stay here—'

'. . . as long as you like!' finishes Tash, putting a matey arm around my other shoulder and giving me a squeeze. 'Tell her, Olly! What's that phrase – *mi casa e su casa?* Well, your *casa* is Libby's *casa*, isn't that right?'

'Honestly, there's no need to go that far,' I begin, rather awkwardly. 'I'm not going to claim squatter's rights, or anything!'

'Oh, we wouldn't even mind that, would we, Olly?' Tash sings. 'Libby squatting, that is.'

'Well, I'm sure it won't come to that.' Olly is turning rather pink. 'But my place is always open to . . . to my friends.'

At this moment, Clara, from somewhere beneath the giant muslin, lets out a loud and very satisfied burp.

'That's her last word on the subject, then,' Nora says, with a grin.

'Then it really is settled!' Tash heads for the door. 'I'd better go and get dressed. Drinks in the kitchen in ten minutes, everyone!'

'Yeah, I'm going to go and make a few bruschetta-ish bits and bobs.' Olly turns back, for a moment, after Tash has left the room and headed for his bedroom to get dressed. 'I'm really glad you're doing this, Lib. I mean, I'm glad I can help out.'

'Me too. Thanks so much, Olly. I can't tell you how much I appreciate it.'

His eyes fix, briefly, onto mine. 'Anything for you,' he says. 'I mean, you do know that. Don't you?'

'I do.' Then, because this all sounds oddly intense (and,

168

therefore, a little bit like the kind of "I do" I might have said if we were standing at an altar right now instead of in Olly's spare bedroom) I add, perkily, 'A friend in need is a friend indeed, right?'

Olly pulls a strange kind of smile and then rather quickly pulls the door shut behind him.

When I glance round, Nora is pulling silly faces at Clara before holding her out in my direction.

'Can you take her for a sec, Lib?' she asks.

'Are you sure?'

'Yes, Libby, I'm sure. She won't freak out or anything.'

'No, but I might.' But I'm still eager to take the warm little bundle that Nora hands over to me, even if I'm terrified I might drop her, or squash her, or otherwise alienate her in some way. 'Hello, gorgeous,' I say to her, while she gazes in a curious manner up at my face. 'Remember me? I'm your Auntie Libby.'

'So, are you going to be OK with this arrangement?' Nora asks, as she gets off the bed and starts buttoning up her top. 'Staying here, I mean.'

'Of course I'm OK with it.' I tap the tip of my little finger on Clara's nose, to see if I can make her laugh, but she stays resolutely serious – almost ministerial, in fact. 'It's a hell of a lot more enticing than moving to Stevenage.'

'No, I agree. Obviously it makes sense. I mean, Olly's almost never home, anyway, so you won't find it . . . you know . . . uncomfortable.'

'Nora!' I lower my voice to a hiss. 'Bloody hell! I am able to control myself around him, you know. I'm not going to be sneaking into the bathroom while he has his shower in the morning and pulling back the curtain.'

'Please, Lib. That's such a gross image,' Nora says, queasily. 'This is my brother we're talking about.'

'So don't bring up . . . that old stuff in the first place! Besides, I'm moving on, can't you tell?'

'With hot personal trainer guy?'

'Yes. I mean, for the time being. I'm not saying he's . . . well, he's not some replacement soulmate, or anything . . .'

'Oh, Libby.'

'But honestly, who even needs that? I mean, you know what they say. Life is far too short to squander one's best years bemoaning the loss of one's soulmate.'

'*One's?*' Nora looks a bit confused. 'Are you OK, Lib? You're talking weirdly.'

'I'm fine. I'm just,' I go on, trying to summon up a bit of Grace Kelly's steely determination, even if I don't really feel it, 'trying to explain that it's going to be perfectly fine for me to stay here – with Olly – for a bit. Because . . . well, I'm moving on. Getting right back on the horse. I thought,' I add, rather desperately, 'that you'd be pleased to hear that?'

'Oh, I am. I am, Libby. I mean, it's great. You sound like a new person.'

'Well. You know. I've been doing some thinking about it.'

'Then good for you!'

But she still sounds, however hard she's trying to disguise this, incredibly sad.

Which, I have to say, isn't a huge help. I know she

170

probably has secret yearnings that I might still get together with Olly, and that I'd get my big happy ending the way she has. But if I'm managing – just – to move on, then she's going to have to as well.

'Let me take her back,' she goes on, as Clara suddenly wriggles and pretty much jack-knifes herself out of my grasp, as soon as Nora's within clutching distance. 'Come here, Mummy's girl,' she tells Clara. 'Come back for a cuddle.'

Clara reaches up one of her soft, pudgy, squishy little hands, places it square on Nora's cheek, and lets out the most perfect peal of delighted laughter you've ever heard in your life.

I feel as if someone has just snuck into the bedroom and punched me, hard, right in the gut.

I actually have to sit down, quite suddenly, on the edge of the bed.

'Lib? Are you all right?'

'I'm fine,' I croak, thankful that Nora is indeed an A&E doctor, just in case I start finding myself actually unable to breathe in the next couple of minutes, or anything. 'Just . . . you're really lucky, Nora,' I go on, in a big rush. 'She's so wonderful. She loves you so much.'

'I know.' Nora's voice softens to the consistency of whipped double cream as she gazes back at Clara. For a moment, I can tell, it's just the two of them in the room. 'I'm luckier than anyone deserves to be.'

I don't say anything. I watch them as they exist in their glorious little bubble for a moment or two.

'Sorry,' Nora says, tearing her eyes off Clara, and back to me. 'We were just talking about—'

'You know what, Nor? Let's have this conversation another time.' I get to my feet and slip an arm round her narrow shoulders. 'I only have one night of you and Clara, and the last thing I want to do is waste it wittering on about this old stuff. Now, tell me more about where you're going with Mark. It's the South of France, right? A hotel by the sea . . .?'

We head for the kitchen, from where familiar Olly-led scents of warm toast and frying garlic are emanating.

Chapter 8

Pressley/Waters' offices are a little north of Paddington Station, in a swanky (albeit rather soulless) new development that overlooks the Regent's Canal. It's only about a fifteen-minute walk from where Cass lives, in Maida Vale, which is why I suggested – when she called me first thing this morning for a long, Zoltan-related moan – that she head here for a coffee after my meeting, so she can moan at me in person instead.

Though actually, seeing as Bogdan has unexpectedly accompanied me to Paddington, I might just suggest that he meets up with Cass while I'm in with Pressley/Waters, and then – you never know – the two of them might be having such a good bitch about their mutual loathing for Bulgarians that they don't even need me around afterwards, and I can head back to Notting Hill to make a proper start on my packing instead.

Which I really need to do, because Elvira texted, not long after I left Olly's last night, reminding me once more that she wants me out of her flat by the end of this week. So, in not-very-surprising news, she's sticking to her guns.

She obviously hasn't discovered an inner fluffy bunny since I last saw her.

Oh, and that Ben is 'currently travelling' but that he'll be in touch 'to discuss how best to proceed' when he gets back.

Which sounds, let's face it, ominous.

It's why I've been really glad of Bogdan's presence this morning, even if I know the main reason he's here is because he's feeling so guilty about the whole Aunt Vanya thing that right now he'd accompany me to the moon and back if I said I was popping up there to get a few lunar bits and bobs. He's actually managed to keep me pretty calm. And, more to the point, distracted, because when he's not giving me a blow-by-blow account of everything that happened when he dropped Dillon off at the Grove House clinic yesterday morning (and I mean *everything*, from the forms they had to fill in at reception to the colour of the bedroom walls), he's been constantly restyling me so that I look my best for 'big make-break interview.'

This being Bogdan, of course, he hasn't managed a *completely* perfect record in keeping me calm.

'For the third time,' I say, as we get off the Tube and walk in the direction of the Regent's Canal development, 'this isn't a make-or-break meeting! And, even if it is, it really doesn't help for you to call it that!'

'Am apologies. Am all confidence though, Libby. Am being certain that you will knock them out in the park.'

'Knock *it* out of the park,' I correct him, although – let's be honest here – with all the disasters that keep befalling

174

me, lately, it's very far from impossible that I somehow *would* end up knocking out either Caroline Pressley or Annika Waters in a park somewhere. 'But thank you, Bogdan. And thanks for coming with me. I really appreciate it.'

'Is no problem. Am glad to be doing this. And am glad that am able to be improving look of your hair. If nothing else,' he adds, tweaking a couple of strands of my fringe in the manner that he's been doing every two minutes since he got on the tube with me, 'at least you are knowing that you are going into this make-break interview looking your most best.'

This is reassuring to hear, especially from Bogdan, who doesn't stint with his criticisms. Clothes-wise, I've gone for as simple a look as possible – just skinny black trousers, a pale grey top and a black blazer – so as to keep the focus on the jewellery I'm modelling for the purposes of the meeting. I've pulled out all the stops and gone for my favourite pieces I've made over the last few months: a monochrome necklace of onyx and opal beads, some rather extravagant onyx-and-silver chandelier earrings, and a simple silver bangle with a single grey cultured pearl dangling off it as a charm. Not a vintage-style bridal tiara in sight.

'Thank you, Bogdan,' I say. 'You're looking pretty good today too, actually. The moustache works on you.'

His reply is to stroke, in a gratified manner, the moustache he's still sporting, which has grown even more luxuriant since I last saw him.

'Now, look, keep my phone in case Cass calls, so you can tell her exactly where you are. But if I were you, I'd head for that Starbucks over there,' I point to the little Starbucks right next to the canal. 'And I'll come and meet you both in there straight after my meeting, OK?'

'This is OK.' Bogdan takes my phone. 'Oh, and before I am forgetting, Libby, Aunt Vanya is calling me last night to ask where she should be sending invoice. Am able to be giving her the address of Olly?'

'Invoice?' I stare at him. 'So she is actually charging me?'

'Yes. But good news, Libby. As kind gesture, and in recognition of any pain and suffering, she is offering you the half price.'

'I'm not paying her half of anything!'

'Is generous discount.'

'Bogdan, she got me kicked out of my flat! And, more to the point, she might have broken my magic sofa!'

A smartly dressed woman, passing by with her dog, gives me an extremely funny look, so I lower my voice as I go on.

'What I mean is that there was absolutely no sign of Grace Kelly last night, so for all I know right now, whatever weird exorcizing crap she did to my sofa might mean nothing ever appears out of it any more.'

It's Bogdan's turn to stare at me in just the same appalled fashion as I've been staring at him. 'So you are saying am never able to be seeing Miss Kelly again?'

'I don't know! Perhaps she's just drenched in holy water, wherever the hell she is, and she'll be back when she's dried out. Or perhaps not. I'm not sure that having half an exorcism has done the Chesterfield much good, either way.'

His brow darkens. 'Then am thinking you should definitely not be paying Aunt Vanya. No discount is worth this disastrous outcome.'

'Well, can you tell her that, please? Anyway, I have to go into my meeting now.'

He performs one last fringe-tweak, then lumbers off in the direction of Starbucks while I take a deep breath and go in through the large plate-glass doors that lead into Pressley/Waters' office building.

A chirpy security man directs me towards the lift, with instructions to take it to the fourth floor where, as the lift doors open, a pretty blonde girl steps forward.

'Hi, Libby?' She extends a hand. 'I'm Celeste. We spoke on the phone.'

'Hi! Great to meet you.'

'You too.' She peers at me. 'Ooooh, I really like your earrings.'

'You do?' I touch them, anxiously. 'I wasn't sure what to wear.'

'Oh, you don't need to worry about Caroline and Annika. They're lovely, honestly. Come this way, and I'll take you straight to Caroline's office.'

Lovely or otherwise, my heart is still hammering as I follow her through the big, open-plan office towards a set of glass doors at the far end. Now that I'm actually here, in this hive of activity, I feel like a total imposter. And my carefully picked-out jewellery doesn't even feel that special any more, despite Celeste's kind compliment, because every single person in this office is wearing absolutely stunning accessories, from armfuls of bangles to huge hoop earrings, and a particularly stunning gold torque necklace on the woman who's just coming out of the glass doors to greet us . . .

'Hello,' she says. 'You must be Libby. I'm Annika.'

I have an enormous girl-crush on Annika Waters two seconds after meeting her, I have to admit. She has terrific hair (Bogdan would weep at the perfection of that pixie cut), a stunning, slightly wonky smile, and she's wearing precisely the kind of outfit I've tried to emulate myself this morning, except that her own skinny trousers, plain tee and blazer all look, somehow, a hundred per cent more chic.

'It's great to meet you,' she goes on. 'Will you come on through to meet Caroline, and we can all have a coffee?'

'I'll bring a fresh cafetière,' Celeste says.

'Thanks, Celeste. Oh, and could you bring the press clippings folder when you come back? Caroline wants to file everything we've just been reviewing from this month. It's actually one of our favourite jobs,' Annika adds, to me, as she leads me through the door, 'going through all the press we've received in the past month. It's always pretty gratifying to read what people are saying about us! So long as it's nice, of course! But you've had some good press yourself, since starting out, right?'

'Oh, um, yes, I've had a bit. I mean, I've been really lucky.'

'Luck has nothing to do with it! I was just glancing over a nice piece about you in *Vogue* yesterday.'

178

'Well, that only came about because . . .'

I stop myself just in time. Because I'm not going to screw up this – whatever it is – by doing myself down. The time for all that has passed. If ever I needed a bit of Grace Kelly self-belief, now is the time.

'Yes,' I say, instead, in a voice that I hope is imbued with some Kelly confidence. 'It was a great piece in *Vogue*. I was really pleased with it.'

'Caroline!' Annika says, as a slightly older woman, sitting on a sofa in the corner of the office, gets to her feet. 'This is Libby Lomax, of course. Celeste is bringing coffee.'

Caroline Pressley, auburn-haired and wearing a pencil skirt and cashmere combo that makes her look uncannily like Joan from *Mad Men*, shakes my hand and smiles.

'Thanks so much for coming in. Come and have a seat . . .' She leans down and starts to tidy the magazine print-outs that are spread all over the glass coffee table into a neater pile. 'Sorry. We're always in chaos here. Too much work and not enough time to do it in.'

'It doesn't look like chaos,' I say, honestly 'And thanks so much for having me. I know you're busy.'

'No, thank *you* for coming to meet us!' Caroline sits back down on the low leather sofa, and I sit next to her, while Annika flops down in the armchair opposite. 'We're both massive fans of your work. Your charm necklaces, your birthstone earrings. . . wasn't Emilia Clarke wearing those earrings promoting *Game of Thrones* at Comic-Con?'

'She was!' I beam at them. 'That was a bit of a coup. I think her stylist must have just ordered them through my

179

website, though, because I didn't know until someone told me. If she'd asked, I'd have given her them for free! I mean, who says no to Daenerys Stormborn, right?'

For a horrible moment, I think I've blurted out too much and sounded like a complete idiot. But – thank God – Caroline and Annika are both beaming back at me.

'Well, it's why we asked you here,' Caroline says. 'For a discussion about how we might be able to help you get that sort of exposure on a more consistent basis. About what we can do for each other, in fact. I mean, I don't know how you see your career developing, and I don't know if you're absolutely wedded to going it alone, but we have a terrific history of collaborating with talented young designers.'

'Oh, no, I'm not absolutely wedded to going it alone! Far from it . . .' This might sound a little bit too much like I'm clinging to their life-raft here, so I add, 'I mean, it's definitely something I'm keen to talk about.'

'Well, we could talk about a one-off collection, exclusive to Pressley/Waters . . . or if you wanted to keep your work entirely on your own site, we might be able to discuss you coming to work with us a couple of days a week on a consultancy basis, bringing some fresh ideas to our in-house brand.'

'Wow. That's . . .'

'Annika, tell her about the recent hires we've just made,' Caroline adds, 'so Libby can get a feel for the different ways we make things work around here.'

'Well, for example, we've just brought in a terrific young

designer to work full time on the Pressley/Waters own-brand collection,' Annika says. 'She's been building up her own business for the last few years, but then she had twins a year ago and she's decided she needs something more structured while her children are small. So she's put her own brand on hold for a while to come and work with us.'

'And that's the kind of thing we're very supportive of, by the way,' Caroline interrupts. 'Working women with young families. We like to be very flexible when it comes to attracting the best talent.'

'Or,' Annika goes on, 'as Caroline said, if you were wedded to the idea of continuing your own business, we could discuss the possibility of some consultancy work. I can put you in touch with a couple of lovely women who do exactly that for us . . . I don't know if you've come across Jess Fredricks, or Polly McAuliffe, but . . . ah, Celeste, perfect timing.'

It is indeed perfect timing for Celeste to appear with a large cafetière and three mugs on a tray, because it gives me a moment to gather myself and not – as I think I am doing, at the moment – continue to sit here staring dumbly at Annika and Caroline with my mouth wide open.

Because this is just . . . nuts.

Are they really offering me the chance to work with them in whatever capacity I deem fit for my – according to them – staggering talents? I mean, I know I'm doing my best to channel Grace's self-assurance, and obviously I don't think I'm just a total dud when it comes to creative jewellery design (I wouldn't be so desperate to branch out of vintage-look bridal tiaras if I did), but the best, the *very* best I was seriously hoping for this morning was that they might offer me a job on their own-brand label. But now they're bandying around words like *consultancy* and *exclusive collection* . . .

I'm going to have to really get with the programme here, and fast, otherwise they might change their minds about me and back away. After all, confidence inspires confidence, right?

'I guess,' I say, sitting forward on the sofa, 'that my gut reaction is that I'd really like to look at the possibility of some sort of collaboration with you. I mean, I've worked so hard on building up my own brand that – even if I'm having one or two issues with it – I don't think I could bring myself to wind it up. And I still feel like I have a lot more I can do with Libby Goes To Hollywood. Actually, if you guys really like the stuff I was doing until quite recently – the charm necklaces and the Emilia Clarke earrings – it might even help me convince my backers that I don't need to keep re-making the same vintage bridal tiara for the rest of my career.'

'Ah. Tell us more about these backers. Thanks, Celeste,' Caroline adds, reaching for the cafetière as Celeste puts it down in front of her. 'And you've brought the press clippings file,' she goes on, 'thank you. Can you just pop this little lot into there and file it with last month's?'

She passes the sheaf of magazine print-outs towards Celeste and, because Celeste is still holding the tray with coffee mugs on it, I helpfully take the papers for a second, until she's popped the tray down on the coffee table.

It's a bit of a shock, on the top sheet of paper, to see Joel's face smiling out at me.

He's standing in between Caroline and Annika, in fact, with another couple of women I don't recognize. He's wearing a smart tuxedo, and all the women are in gorgeous long gowns, and it looks like . . . is it an awards do, or a fund-raiser of some sort? There's a big round table in the background right behind them, with a big floral arrangement and champagne glasses . . .

I don't have time to notice anything else before Celeste takes the sheaf of print-outs from my hand, slides them into her file and, coffee safely delivered, heads out of the office.

'Libby?'

'Huh?'

'Black or white?'

'Sorry?'

'Coffee. Black or with milk?' Caroline is poised with the cafetière.

'Oh, right . . .' Having tried to channel Grace Kelly for the duration of this meeting so far, I'm pretty sure I'm now doing an exact impression of her when she clocked that magazine picture herself, on my coffee table. Except I don't feel I can ask Caroline or Annika what on earth the picture is all about, because I don't want to seem . . . paranoid?

'Oh! Right. Um . . .' All my carefully collected poise is gone. 'Just black, please.'

'Sure.' Caroline pours the coffee, and then hands me a mug. 'Now, obviously you might want to take time to think about the sort of working arrangement you're most keen on. I mean, if it's some kind of collaboration – a Libby Goes To Hollywood capsule collection, perhaps – that would be fantastic. But why don't you come back to the office again, perhaps for a day or two, to get a feel for us, and what we're about?'

'That would be great,' I say, instead of what I really want to say, which is: *Excuse me, but was that a photo of Joel Perreira? And how do you know him?*

And is this meeting, and all the incredibly generous options you're offering, anything to do with that?

I mean, I'll sound totally weird. And the last thing I want, in this all-important meeting, is to sound weird.

'Terrific! So look, why don't you take a few days to mull it all over, and get back to Celeste as soon as you know when you'd like to come back in? We're pretty chock-full for the next week or so, aren't we, Annika, but we'd love to see you again as soon as possible after that.'

'Absolutely,' says Annika. 'And if you've got a few minutes now, I can take you for a quick chat with Jules – she's the mum of twins I was just telling you about – and she can give you a quick run-down of how it all works for her.'

'Right,' I say. 'Jules. I'd like that.'

'Fab! Let's have a little wander with our coffee, then,' Annika suggests, getting up from her armchair, 'and see if she's free for a few minutes.'

'But don't you want to see any of my new stuff?' I ask.

'I mean, I brought in sketches of all the latest things I'm working on, and—'

'We love what we've already seen,' Caroline says, getting up, too. 'And really, Libby, it's mostly about us all trying to find the right fit. We work with people we really like. That's just as important to us as anything else.'

Which does absolutely nothing to reassure me that this whole meeting is a hundred per cent genuine.

'Come and meet Jules,' says Annika, leading me out through the glass doors into the open-plan office, 'and you can ask her any questions that you might have. Anything at all!'

But the only question I want to ask this Jules is: *Do you know Joel Perreira as well and, if so, do you have any kind of sneaking suspicion that this is what got you an interview with the exalted Caroline Pressley and Annika Waters in the first place?* And obviously I'm not going to be able to ask anything of the sort.

I'm just going to have to keep a lid on my unease, aren't I, until I can head out of here and speak to Joel in person? And, I guess, try to enjoy some of this extremely unusual experience of being quite so fêted and fawned-over while it lasts.

*

Immensely frustratingly, going down in the lift at Pressley/ Waters knocks the signal out of my phone, and I don't get so much as a single bar until I'm on my way through the doors of the small Starbucks, where I can see that Bogdan and Cass have occupied a corner booth.

Cass is still in full-on Put-Upon Stepmother mode, I can also see, with her hair scraped into another ponytail and wearing deliberately downtrodden leggings and a hoodie again, although she has managed at least half a face of her usual full makeup, and she's sporting distinctly WAG-like diamond stud earrings that I've never seen before.

'How is big make-break meeting going?' Bogdan is the first to ask, shuffling up to make (not much) space beside him in the booth.

'Oh, it was good . . . great, in fact.'

'Nice to see you, too, Libby,' Cass says, sarcastically, because it's taken me too long to acknowledge her. 'Aren't you even going to ask me how I'm doing? Why I look this shit?'

'You are not looking shit,' Bogdan croons, pushing her cup of tea in her direction. 'You are looking tired. You are looking in need of good break.'

'Exactly. But when am I going to get one?' She glares at me. 'Libby, for fuck's sake, can't you put your phone down for a single fucking minute? I mean, we all know you're the hotshot businesswoman nowadays, but you don't have to literally ignore us.'

'Sorry, I'm just . . . ah. Got it.' My signal is back up to an acceptable number of bars, so I should be able to drop Joel a quick message and ask him . . . what? How he knows Caroline and Annika? If this had anything to do with the astonishingly positive tone of the meeting I've just attended?

It's the uncertainty of exactly what to write that leads me, while I hesitate, to try a second option.

I type *Joel Perreira* into Google, just to see if anything comes up.

And something does come up.

Eighteen million, four hundred and thirty thousand somethings, actually.

Joel Perreira to donate $20m to disaster relief for Bangladesh, declares the first Google headline, updated thirty-six minutes ago on Reuters.

Perreira opening chequebook for flood victims, The Times Online informs me, going on to add, *making a substantial private donation in addition to the £15 million also pledged by the Perreira Foundation.*

'What in God's name . . .?' I murmur.

The *Daily Mail*, the next one on the list, has posted only twenty-one minutes ago that *Heart-throb billionaire Joel Perreira digs deep for Bangladesh: unknown amount donated to tragic flood victims from 'personal funds'.*

'Libby?' Bogdan is staring at me. 'You are looking as if you are about to be vomiting. Shall I be getting you cup of tea?'

When I don't reply, he gets up and heads over to the counter as fast as his legs will carry him, possibly to avoid any chance that, if I am going to be sick for some reason, I'll do it over him.

'Joel's a . . .billionaire.'

At the word *billionaire*, Cass's eyes sharpen and she lunges forward in her seat.

187

'What?' she demands. 'Who?'

'Joel . . . the guy I went out with the other night . . . Joel Perreira . . .'

'Joel Perreira?' Cass echoes.

'Yes.'

'*You're going out with Joel fucking Perreira?*'

'Yes.'

'The *billionaire* Joel Perreira?'

'Apparently.' I stare at the iPhone screen. 'He told me he was a personal trainer.'

Unless . . . *is* it possible to make billions from personal training? I mean, I know Davina's made a fair few bob from her workout DVDs, and then there's that 30 Day Shred woman who's earned a small fortune from her commodification of off-putting abdominal exercises . . .

But no. I don't think it's possible to make *billions* from that. I don't think it's possible at all.

Cass snatches my phone from my hand. 'This is him, right?' She stabs a finger at the picture that's come up on screen in the Reuters link. 'The guy you're dating?'

'Yes.' I stare at the photo. It's him, all right, although he's looking smarter – positively dapper, in fact – in an exquisitely cut suit and a rather gorgeous pale blue silk tie that brings out the colour of his eyes. 'That's him.'

'Well, that's Joel Perreira.'

'But there must be some mistake . . .'

'So if there's been a mistake, Libby, why do you think it says right here . . .' Cass flicks down the screen with a finger until she alights on a link to an article in the *Daily*

Mail, 'that he's worth two point six billion pounds? That his divorce a couple of years ago cost him six hundred million quid? *That he owns homes in Holland Park, West Sussex, Manhattan, Sydney, the Gold Coast, St Lucia and—* ' she chokes, ever so slightly, on reading the last one, '*Beverly Hills?*'

'No. *No.* He lives in Shepherd's Bush. Ish.'

'Shepherd's Bush-ish *is* bloody Holland Park!' she shrieks at me, displaying, suddenly, more knowledge of London metropolitan geography than she ever has of anything else in her entire life. 'For fuck's *sake*, Libby! How the fuck are you shagging a drop-dead gorgeous *billionaire*?'

The middle-aged couple at the next table glance over at us, though whether in disapproval at Cass's appalling language, or out of interest (to see whether or not I look as unlikely a candidate for gorgeous billionaire-shagging as has been explicitly stated), I don't know. Or, right now, much care.

'But I . . .' I croak. 'I mean, we haven't . . .'

I'm staring at the words on the *Mail* Online page, and trying to make them make sense.

It may only be a couple of years since Joel Perreira was named the second richest Under-40 in the United Kingdom, but he's not a man to sit around resting on his laurels. This week the self-made billionaire has pledged $50 million from his eponymous children's aid foundation to be put towards the construction of at least four maternity and paediatric medicine clinics and half a dozen schools in the Central African Republic and Liberia. The foundation's director and

Perreira's mother, Barbara Reitman, made the announcement
at the glittering annual fund-raiser for the Perreira Foundation,
held this year in . . .

But I don't care where the glittering annual fund-raiser for the Perreira Foundation was held. Even though, it seems pretty obvious now, this must have been where the photograph in Caroline and Annika's press pile was taken.

'I don't understand.' I feel the most horrible, sick sensation in my stomach. 'I don't understand why he lied to me.'

'Because men *are* a bunch of fucking liars, that's why.'

'Yes, but usually they're exaggerating the other way, aren't they? Trying to talk themselves up, make themselves sound better or more important or . . . or richer than they really are . . .'

'Well, maybe he had a bet with some friends to see if he could find literally the only woman on the entire fucking planet who didn't know who he was!' Cass spits.

'How the hell was I supposed to know who he was?' I'm stung. 'I don't spend my life reading . . . I don't know . . . *Billionaire's Gazette.*'

'Nor does anyone, Libby!' Cass shrieks. 'There is such a thing as bloody Google, though. Didn't you even *think* to do that *before* you went on this date?'

'No. I didn't.'

'Then you're a moron,' she shoots back. 'If you don't Google the hell out of someone before you go out with them, how are you supposed to know *who* they are? They could be a *serial killer* for all you know!'

'If they were a serial killer,' I say, rather faintly, because

190

I'm still trying to take in what Cass is telling me about Joel, 'I think it's unlikely it would be plastered all over Google.'

'You don't know that! What if they *used* to be a serial killer in the past, and then they went to prison for all the serial killing, and now they're out, and claiming they've turned over a new leaf . . . anyway, none of this is the point!' Cass wails. 'Why are you dating a billionaire when I'm stuck with bloody Zoltan and his horrible sprogs for the rest of my life?' She reaches over the table and grabs my hand. 'I've always been a good sister to you, Lib, haven't I?' she goes on, desperately. 'You won't forget me? You'll see if you might be able to funnel a bit of cash my way, you know, for the bare essentials? A full-time nanny? Those boarding-school fees – or maybe the fees for that workhouse place you were talking about—'

'What is trouble?' This is Bogdan, returning with my cup of tea. 'What is going on?'

'Libby's only gone and snagged herself a bloody billionaire,' Cass says. Her tone is half-bitter, half-triumphant.

Bogdan stares at me. 'Gorgeous man who you are meeting in street? How is this possible?'

'Ha! I'm asking myself the same bloody question,' says Cass, 'trust me. I mean, first Dillon O'Hara, and now Joel Perreira . . .'

'Wait – I am knowing this name.' Bogdan frowns, thinking about it. 'Joel Perreira is social media entrepreneur, no? He is guy who is investing in early days of Tumblr?'

'And Instagram. And Snapchat. And about a million mega-successful apps. Yeah,' says Cass. 'That's him.'

I feel as if the floor has been pulled away from beneath me. I don't know, now, if anything Joel told me on our date was actually real.

Apart from the fact that his name is Joel Perreira, that is.

And it's obvious, now, why he looked so anxious when he blurted out his surname like that.

I mean, was the whole thing just a big joke to him? Going out with the one woman on the planet who didn't realize who he was?

'He just sat there and lied to my face,' I mumble. 'He said he was a personal trainer. He said . . .'

I have to think about this for a moment.

Because if I think about it, I'm not actually sure that Joel *did* say he was a personal trainer.

I think *I* said he was a personal trainer and he . . . didn't deny it.

Which is a pattern that he stuck to throughout the evening, come to think of it, whenever I asked a question about any of that stuff. He said he has great clients. He said he travels a lot for work. He said he was going to Barbados to meet a client out there, and obviously I just assumed it was a personal training client. Whereas it was probably something, instead, to do with all his money . . .

So it wasn't even outright lying, it was more the kind of clever sort of half-truths that make you feel oh-so-hilariously superior to the person you're telling them to. Sitting there all poker-faced, paddling madly like a duck beneath the surface to think about the clever way you'll avoid their next probing question.

'I just don't get it,' Cass is saying, to Bogdan. 'I mean, she's my sister, and I love her and all of that crap, but I mean, seriously – how the fuck is she doing it?'

'Perhaps,' Bogdan muses, 'she is capable of the amazing feats of stamina and/or acrobatics in the sex department—'

'Guys! Please! Can you have a bit of bloody compassion? I've made an absolute fool of myself with . . . Oh, God,' I suddenly groan, loudly, as I remember some more of the things I was saying. 'I told him not to order off my website because the jewellery on it was too expensive for him! I offered him my Oyster card to get home on the bus!'

'This is mortifying for you,' Bogdan agrees. 'Is begging question of why you are not Googling him before you are going on date?'

'Exactly!' says Cass.

'Or, once on date, while you are going to bathroom? Or while *he* is going to bathroom? There are plenty of oppor-tunities,' Bogdan continues, 'for the Googling that you are not taking, Libby. This is why I am finding it hard to have the sympathy with your predicament. This, plus the fact that you have just been on date with hottest richest man am ever seeing in my life.'

'Why didn't I Google him?' I ask, in astonishment. 'Because I was having a great time! Because I was too busy enjoying getting to know him – or rather, who I *thought* he was – to think about getting out my phone and doing my due diligence! But mostly because I think it's plain depressing to do due diligence on a first date. I mean, where's the romance in that? Where's the mystery?'

'Who the fuck cares about romance or mystery,' Cass asks, 'when you're all set to marry a billionaire?'

'I'm not marrying him! For fuck's sake, Cass! I'm not even going to go on the second date.'

Cass and Bogdan stare at me.

Then they turn and stare at each other.

'Is clear to me now,' Bogdan tells Cass. 'Your sister is mislaying the marbles.'

'Mislaying them? Bogdan, honey, I'm starting to doubt she ever had them in the first place!'

'Look,' I say, furiously, 'I'm not going to go out on a date with someone who's just sat across the table from me and lied their socks off all night!'

'Libby. I don't think you're quite getting it.' Cass takes a deep breath, places both palms on the tabletop and gazes across it at me. 'He's. A. *Billionaire*. That means he has *billions* of pounds in the bank. Not millions. Not squillions. Not . . . hang on, there is such a thing as gazillions, right? Or is that more than billions?'

'Am thinking that gazillions may be highest possible denomination.'

'So, more than billions, then?'

'Am thinking so. But am not sure.'

'Oh, *I* know. We can look it up *on Google*,' Cass says, pointedly, getting out her own phone as I pick up mine again.

I'm going to send a message to Joel right this minute.

Hi. Just to let you know I won't be able to make it tonight. It was nice to meet you and . . .

Good luck with all your future money-making endeavours? Good luck counting your billions? Good luck donating millions to a raft of impossibly good causes?

I can't think of anything to say that doesn't sound snippy or defensive.

'Ah,' Bogdan is saying, as he and Cass peer at her phone together. 'Is looking as if there is in fact no such thing as actual gazillions.'

'Well, that just doesn't make any sense . . . I'm absolutely certain there's such a thing as gazillions, or it wouldn't be a *word* . . .'

I put my own phone down again. I'm not going to send a message. A message is the coward's way out.

What, is the question, would Grace Kelly do in this situation? I may not be able to ask her, after she was (possibly) accidentally exorcized from the mystical depths of the Chesterfield, but I think I already know.

I am going to go and meet Joel tonight, and I'm going to confront him about this – with a dignity and class that belie the mortification and hurt I actually feel – and then I'm going to sweep out of his life and never see him again.

Because, even though I never intended anything serious to develop with him, I *am* hurt. Surprisingly hurt. I've never been all that good at trusting men at the best of times, and for Joel to act the good guy while secretly making a fool of me behind my back – setting up, as he must have done, that little love-fest at Pressley/Waters just now . . .

Letting me get my hopes up about a way out of the mess my career is fast becoming.

Letting me take a sneaky peek at a world where I'm no longer agonizingly in love with Olly, but can move on with someone else instead.

I take a large gulp of burning-hot tea, and shrink back as far into the booth as I possibly can, listening to Cass and Bogdan squabble about whether billions are more than gazillions, or the other way around.

Chapter 9

An hour before the appointed time of our date this evening, I'm here in Hanover Square, standing right outside the London offices of Jansen-Perreira Ltd, Joel's multibillion-dollar tech company.

I mean, I can't even comfort myself with the fact that he's some evil exploiter of precious natural resources, or an arms manufacturer, or something.

His company, as far as I've gathered from my belated Google research this afternoon – all afternoon – is green. Clean. Family-friendly They consistently top the rankings for employee satisfaction, thanks to all kinds of wonderful workers' provisions, from heavily subsidized crèches to amazing cafeterias, plus everyone getting their birthday off work and a discretionary number of 'duvet days' per year, when they're allowed to just recharge their batteries without having to make up some spurious fib about food poisoning.

So he's practically a saint, in the world of big business.

A saint who also happens to be, in his private life, an out-and-out liar.

Which I'm going to tell him to his face. And which is

probably a huge mistake, but now I've decided to do it, I don't think I can turn back. It'll feel like I've backed down from something important. Something I really need to do.

And OK, I'll admit it: there's a (much) less impressive part of me that just wants to see Joel's face in the instant that he realizes that *I know*.

I'm ever-so-slightly losing my nerve, now that I'm actually here, however, outside this impressive building in Hanover Square.

But I can't go back now. I won't go back now.

Trying to adopt the sort of chilly, don't-fuck-with-me air that Grace Kelly has down pat, I head through the revolving doors, stride towards the little seating area near a bank of lifts, and sit down on a white leather sofa that probably costs more than the entire property market of Stevenage put together.

There are enough people – Joel's grateful, well-subsidized employees – heading in and out of this huge lobby that I don't think anyone is going to question why I'm here. Still, I pick up a copy of the *FT* that's folded, neatly, on the coffee table in front of me, and pretend to read it while I wait, and watch the lifts, and the revolving doors, for any sign of Joel.

I'm actually a little bit relieved, though, when my phone suddenly rings, because having a conversation is going to make me look more convincingly busy, and – I can but hope – less ambush-y.

It's Mum.

Mum calls me so rarely that I assume, for a moment, that she must need help in some way. She's still at the hospital, taking full advantage of her insurance-covered stay for as long as she can but, knowing her, she's remembered some vital possession she needs to be brought to her from her flat, or she's decided that one of the nurses has (surprise, surprise) Got It In For Her and just wants a good old bitch. Either way, I'll answer, because it's better than skulking behind a copy of the *Financial Times*.

'Libby! Darling!' Her voice, as I answer the call, is syrupy-sweet. 'Do you have a minute? Have I caught you at a bad time?'

'No, I have a couple of minutes, Mum. What's up?'

'Oh, darling, can't I ever just phone for a little chat?'

This is when I know, immediately, the real reason she's called.

Joel. Cass has told her about Joel.

'I mean, here I am in hospital with all this time on my hands all of a sudden . . . I mean, that's the main reason I don't usually get the chance to call up for a good old gossip, Libby. I'm so busy, and you're so busy . . . this just seems like a golden opportunity to make up for lost time!'

'*I'm* still busy, actually, Mum.'

'Of course. Well, I wouldn't want to interrupt you. I tell you what, why don't we plan a nice evening out somewhere really soon, when I'm out of the hospital? Give ourselves the opportunity to catch up on . . . everything that's going on in our lives.'

I don't know whether to laugh or cry.

On the one hand, her shamelessness is sort of funny. On the other hand, it's incredibly depressing that after all these years of disinterest, all it takes to get her champing at the bit to be my BFF is the news that I'm involved with a billionaire.

Correction: *was* involved.

'Well, that would be nice, Mum,' I say. 'Let me know when's good.'

'Oh, darling, *any* time!' She clears her throat, almost inaudibly. 'I mean, obviously you must have quite a bit of your time taken up with this . . . new man Cass has told me about.'

'Not really.'

'Then you must!' The syrupy-sweet tone transforms into a panicked-sounding shriek. 'Libby, it's vitally important that you make him your top priority! Where would Kate Middleton be now, darling, if she hadn't dropped everything else in her life to make sure she was there when William needed her? And what sort of mother would I be,' she goes on, images of herself as a sort of doppelgänger for Carole Middleton, all skirt suits, coat dresses and discreet diamonds, clearly popping into her mind, 'if I counselled any differently?'

'Mum, I have to go now, actually,' I say, and then I lower my voice. 'But just to keep you completely in the loop, I'm not actually going to go out with Joel Perreira again.'

Mum lets out a little peal of laughter.

'I'm serious,' I say.

There's a deathly silence at the other end of the phone.

'Liberty Alexandra Lomax,' she croaks, after a moment, 'if you think that's funny—'

'My middle name isn't Alexandra! For Christ's sake!' I'm too exasperated to carry on this conversation any more. 'Look, I'll call you tomorrow, Mum, OK?'

'Libby, wait—'

But I do, actually, hang up on her.

It's perfect timing, in fact. Because the doors of one of the lifts nearby have just opened, and Joel is heading out, towards the revolving doors.

He's deep in conversation with a rather beautiful and serious-looking woman who's taking notes on an iPad as she goes, so who – I assume – must be some sort of personal assistant. And he's being followed by a tall, muscular man and the short, almost as muscular woman I recognize as Esti, who I thought was his Krav Maga coach but who, from the looks of this set-up, is in fact some sort of . . . bodyguard?

I get to my feet and – taking the probably insane gamble that I'm about to be Krav Maga'd to the ground by one of the bodyguards simply for stepping into Joel's path – step into their path.

Joel stops.

So they all, obviously, stop.

There's a brief, extremely tense moment where it looks as if I might *actually* be Krav Maga'd to the ground by one of the bodyguards.

And where Joel, gratifyingly, drains of all colour and looks as if he's about to pass out on the spot.

And then he opens his mouth.

'Libby.'

'Joel,' I say.

'Can we . . . talk?'

'Sure.' I glance around the busy lobby. 'Here? Or—'

'Would you come up to my office?'

'No. I don't want to do that.' Because I just have a feeling that, on his own turf, Joel is going to find a way to explain away everything.

'All right. Here, then.'

He glances over his shoulder to the beautiful PA and the bodyguards.

'Give me a few minutes, guys?'

'But, Joel—'

'I know, I know, I was going to call Palo Alto from the car. Just call ahead for me, Sav,' he instructs the PA, 'and tell them something important has come up and I'll call them in a few minutes.'

'Wow,' I say, as the PA turns and heads back towards the lifts, already on her mobile, and the bodyguards . . . woah. They've just melted into the background in a way that's as impressive as it is scary. 'You have a whole few minutes for me. I'm flattered.'

Annoyingly, I can't help but notice as he sits down on the white leather sofa, he looks good. Incredibly good. In fact, now that he's not pretending to be a personal trainer, and is instead looking the very epitome of what you'd expect a tech billionaire in his late thirties to look, after a day in the office – gorgeous suit, white open-neck shirt – he looks better than ever.

He takes a deep breath. 'So. You know.'

'Yes. I know.'

We stare at each other for a moment.

Then he says, 'I didn't actually lie, you know.'

My jaw drops. 'Are you *kidding* me?'

'No. Nothing I told you was an untruth. I promise you, Libby. I might just have . . . been careful with my answers.'

I snort. 'Did you take advice from your crack team of lawyers before we went out that night, or something?'

'No.' He shakes his head. 'Not my crack team. Just the second-tier ones.'

'Hilarious.'

'I'm trying to lighten the mood.'

'Joel, seriously. I didn't come here for any more jokes and japes.'

'It wasn't a joke. None of this was a joke.'

'You could have fooled me.'

He looks a bit desperate. 'Look, will you come out to dinner like we planned and we can talk about this?'

'I can't.' I stare at the ground, feeling more miserable than angry, all of a sudden. 'My plan was to go out to dinner with a personal trainer named Joel. Not a tech billionaire named Joel Perreira.'

'Libby . . . I'm the same person.'

'You're really, really not.'

The expression on his face is hard to read; in fact it strikes me that he's probably an exceptionally talented poker player. But it looks like a mixture of despair, mild irritation and – somewhere in the mix – weary amusement.

203

'I just have one question for you, Joel.'

'Only one?' he asks, looking more weary than ever.

'Was it you who set up the meeting with Pressley/ Waters?'

He hesitates, which is enough for me.

'Right.' My stomach wrenches. I get to my feet. 'I see.'

'No, no, Libby, you're getting this all wrong! Look, OK, I did happen to mention you to Caroline Pressley when I spoke to her the other day . . .'

'Why did you speak to her the other day?'

'Because we've worked together for years. I was one of the first people to invest in her website.'

'You're her *investor?*' This is worse than I thought. 'Bloody hell, Joel! No wonder she agreed to meet me! No wonder they were all so *nice* to me!'

'She was nice to you because she's a nice person! And because she really likes your stuff. Look, all I did was ask her if she knew you, and—'

'Just forget it.' I start to walk towards the revolving door. 'You've done enough.'

Joel gets up and follows. 'Libby, please. Stop.'

He puts a hand on my shoulder, but evidently thinks twice when I wrench it away. After all, we're in a busy place, a place full of his employees, and he obviously doesn't want to look as if he's assaulting a lone female, or anything. With this in mind – all the employees around, that is – I do actually stop and turn back to look at him, because I don't want to embarrass him, or anything. Well, obviously I *do* want to embarrass him, because otherwise I wouldn't have come here in the first place. But I don't want an actual *scene*, with passers-by staring, and taking surreptitious footage on their iPhones and stuff. It's enough for Joel to realize he's behaved badly; I don't need his entire staff to realize this as well.

'It was like a fairy tale,' he says.

'What?'

'Meeting you. You not knowing who – what – I am. It was like a fairy tale. You know . . . the kind where the prince disguises himself as a swineherd, and—'

'Hold up, hold up.' I lift a hand to stop him. 'If you're the prince disguised as the swineherd – in whatever bonkers scenario you seem to have playing in your head – then what does that make me? Some sort of unusually credulous peasant?'

'No! Well, OK, I get that it looks like that, but—'

'Thanks, Joel. Have a nice life.'

'Libby, come on. Is your life really so full of enchantment and magic that you can afford to ignore the moments when Fate really does present you with something fantastical?'

I turn away again, because I can feel my resolve wavering.

'Bye, Joel,' I say. 'I'll let you make your call to Palo Alto now.'

'Libby—'

'Please don't call me again.' I step into the revolving door.

And then I misjudge the exit, and have to go all the way back round the wretched thing again, while Joel stands there staring at me.

I get it right the second time, thank God, and finally step out into the street.

He doesn't try to follow.

*

I avoid going home for as long as I realistically can.

It just feels so miserable there, now that I'm starting to get things all packed up, and now that everything's gone so badly wrong, both with Ben and Elvira, and – after such hope – with Pressley/Waters.

And with Joel. Who, I realize now, I was probably far more keen on than I let myself admit.

Besides, I'm slightly avoiding going back there because I don't particularly want to be confronted by the Chesterfield: I don't want to have to acknowledge, for real, that it might not be working any more.

Especially when, of all the occasions where Grace Kelly's opinion might be a bit suspect, the time you really might want her input – if you were able to stop her wittering on about herself long enough to get it – is the time when you learn the man you like is actually a billionaire.

I mean, to all intents and purposes, in this day and age, that pretty much makes him a prince, right? Forget the fact he doesn't have an actual title. He has a charitable foundation, dispensing largesse, in the form of huge cash donations, to the poor and needy and natural-disaster-stricken. Forget the fact he doesn't have a castle. He has homes all over the world, some of which (if I had the brass neck to search for this on Google; I'm assuming this is exactly the sort of thing my mother is doing even as I speak) are probably castle-*sized*.

Anyway, he said it himself. He was the prince disguised as the swineherd. Modern-day royalty, slumming it with a commoner.

I kill time by trailing round the Marks & Spencer's food hall near Notting Hill tube, picking out a depressing pasta salad and an even more depressing single bread roll for me to eat for supper. Then I cave, just as I approach the check-outs, and go back to add a bottle of red wine, a packet of iced mini yum-yums and a bucket of chocolate cornflake crunchy things to my basket.

Slightly buoyed by these junk-food-and-booze purchases, I have the stomach (no pun intended) to head back down the side streets to my – to Elvira's – flat.

Oh, dear God, there's *another* shadowy figure lurking on my doorstep.

Has Dillon escaped from rehab as fast as all that? Or is it not him at all . . .?

'Tash?' I say, incredulously, as I get close enough to see who it actually is.

'Libby, hi.' She's wearing a warm jacket, but it's chilly for a June evening and she looks cold. 'Thank goodness you're finally home.'

'Sorry . . . have you been waiting long?'

'Only a few minutes. I didn't know how long you'd be, though. I looked up your address on your website. I hope you don't mind.'

'Oh, no . . . No, I don't mind.' Though it reminds me, I think, randomly, that I'd better update my website, as soon as possible, and take this address off it. 'You must be freezing . . . um . . . do you want to come in?'

'If that's OK?'

'It's more than OK.' I fumble in my pocket for my keys. 'Sorry, Tash,' I go on, as we head through the front door, 'but was there something . . . particular? That you wanted to talk to me about, I mean?'

'Not really. I just thought you might want some help packing, like I said yesterday.'

'Right.' I try not to look too astounded, and then blurt, 'It is nine o'clock at night, Tash. I mean, don't get me wrong, I'm grateful for the offer of help, but surely you have better places to be! You're only in London for a few days – don't you want to be with Olly?'

'He's at the restaurant until ten thirty. The perils of surprising a restaurateur with an unannounced visit, I guess.'

I lead the way up the stairs to my darkened living room and switch on a light . . .

. . . There's no Grace Kelly. Which is actually a huge relief, under the circumstances, because I didn't actually think about this possibility before I brought Tash up here.

'And look,' I say, 'as you can see, I really don't have very much to do. Packing-wise, that is. I mean, now that you're here, you're more than welcome to stay and have a glass of wine.'

I regret, more than ever, my M&S bagful of Single Saddo's

208

Night In food and drink, because no doubt when Tash is home alone up in Glasgow, she prepares herself edifying and health-giving meals from scratch, featuring green vegetables and quinoa. Fortunately, though, she doesn't seem that interested in the contents of my bag, as I pop it down on the floor near the sofa.

'I'm OK without wine, actually,' she says. 'I drank last night, and I try not to drink more than one night in the week. Have you ever tried that?'

'No. Never.' I answer the question at face-value, and only immediately afterwards wonder: was that a dig?

'Oh, well, you should really try it too, Libby. Olly's doing the same as me – avoiding alcohol six nights a week – so now that you're going to be living with him—'

'Staying with him!'

'. . . it'll be an opportunity for you to do the same. And it'll just give you so much more energy, and shift that annoying half-stone you never seem to be able to shift.'

OK, that definitely sounded like a dig.

'In fact,' she goes on, before I can say anything, 'I'd actually really appreciate it if you *didn't* entice him into drinking while you're living at his flat, Libby. I'm sure you understand where I'm coming from.'

I freeze, for a moment.

I mean, is that the reason she's come over here tonight, with spurious explanations about helping me pack?

'So, tell me,' she adds – again before I can actually speak. She perches on the arm of the Chesterfield; she isn't taking off her coat, or doing anything that might make the tension in this room any less palpable. 'How did it go on your date tonight?'

'My date?'

'Yes. You said you were going out with this . . . Joel, is it?'

'Oh, yes. It went . . .' I don't have the energy to lie. More to the point, I'm too uneasy to lie. Tash is staring right at me with the sort of searching expression that I imagine usually precedes a formal caution in a police station, followed by a few hours of aggressive questioning. 'I'm home at nine p.m.,' I say, 'with a bottle of wine and a family-pack of iced yum-yums. How do you think it went?'

'Oh. That's a shame.'

'Well, you know,' I say, warily, 'dating is difficult.'

'God, yes, I know. But you shouldn't give up that easily, Libby. I mean, maybe it hasn't worked out with this Joel guy, but that doesn't mean you should stop looking for . . . someone else.'

I know, without her having to make it explicit, that she isn't saying I should find someone else that isn't Joel.

She's telling me I should stay away from Olly.

For all my attempts to disguise the way I still feel about him, she's still managed to cotton on, hasn't she?

'In fact,' Tash goes on, 'if you're going to be gadding about on dates, and stuff, perhaps you'd be more comfortable living in a flat on your own. And perhaps you should tell Olly you won't go and live with him.'

'I . . . er . . .'

'I mean, I know he's keen to ride to your aid on a white

charger, and all that. But that's just Olly. He likes to help people. Needy people. It doesn't mean it's always a good idea to take advantage of it.'

OK, this has gone far enough. I understand why she's come here tonight – to give me a heads-up that she knows about my inadequately buried feelings for Olly – but now she's calling me *needy* and saying I'm taking advantage of Olly, and I'm not going to have that. Not to mention the fact that if we're going to have this conversation, I think we should Have This Conversation, and not skirt around the elephant in the room, poking it with a small, sharp stick in a threatening sort of manner.

'Tash.' I look her right in the eye. 'If you don't want me to go and stay with Olly, could you just say so?'

'Did I say that?'

'No. You very carefully didn't.' Which, presumably, is what all the over-the-top Julie Andrews jollity was about when Olly first suggested it. She doesn't want him to know how she really feels. 'Look, Tash, the last thing I want to do is piss you off . . .'

'Oh, Libby. I don't get pissed off by little things like this!' She smiles. 'Really, this is for your own benefit far more than mine or Olly's! I just think that if you're so determined to stand on your own two feet, you should really go the whole hog. Even if it does mean you have to move out of London for a bit. It can be a good thing, sometimes, to have a total change of scene. Make some new friends. Start afresh.'

OK, now this is just getting a little bit scary. I'm suddenly hoping that the Willington-Joneses, next door, are pressing glasses up against the wall in an attempt to catch me out making any suspicious noises unworthy of our salubrious address. Because at least that way, if this nasty conversation with Tash escalates any further, there'll be witnesses.

I try, just one last time, to acknowledge the elephant.

'Tash, come on. You don't have to worry, not for a single minute, that I'm ever going to act on—'

'I'm not worried, Libby. Trust me. There's nothing you could do or say that could possibly worry me.'

'But you still don't want me to move in,' I say, pointedly.

'Right.'

Her smile freezes, bringing the temperature in the room down by another few degrees as it does so.

'Well, it was just friendly advice, Libby, that's all. For you to take or leave.'

'It's OK. I'm taking it.' I swallow, hard. 'I'll find somewhere else to stay for a bit.'

'Oh, well, if there's anything I can do to—'

'It's fine,' I say. 'You've helped quite enough already, Tash. Thank you.'

She doesn't say anything else. She just gets to her feet and heads down the stairs.

The front door clicks shut, a moment later, behind her.

Chapter 10

Olly hasn't answered his phone all morning.

Nor, more worryingly, has he responded to two messages or a text asking him to call me back.

Which is why I'm here, now, on my way into his restaurant, to catch him just before he starts lunch service. I can't just leave a voicemail or a text to let him know I'm turning down his generous offer of accommodation. It'll set alarm bells off, if I seem to be avoiding him when passing on such important information, and the last thing I want is to set alarm bells off.

Mostly because I'm a tiny bit terrified of Iash, obviously.

But also because it might lead to a conversation with Olly that I'd rather stick red-hot needles into my eyes than initiate.

So I've come to Nibbles in the hope that he'll be too busy and too distracted by the restaurant opening in five minutes, and that therefore he will accept the explanation I'm offering, which is that I'm going to stay at Dillon's instead, so that I can be there for him as soon as he gets out of rehab.

This isn't, I should add, entirely untrue. I *am* going to stay at Dillon's instead. It's just that it's not specifically to 'be there' for him as soon as he gets out of rehab. If anything, I'll have to make sure I'm well clear of his place before he gets out of rehab, because I know it'll actually be really important for him to have his own space when he gets out, and not to have me there as some sort of co-dependent crutch to lean on. But this aside, it's actually a pretty good plan. Dillon called me early this morning – his daily permitted call from Grove House, which I'm very flattered that he made to me – and once he'd grunted a few reluctant replies to my questions about his welfare and swiftly moved the topic off himself again, I mentioned Tash's late-night visit.

'For fuck's sake, Lib,' he said, once he'd inveigled the rest of the story out of me (his appetite for Olly-related gossip being, apparently, limitless), 'just move into my flat for a bit instead. The place is going to be empty until I'm out of here. And I promise, I won't let any of *my* psycho girlfriends come round and threaten you into going elsewhere.'

'Look, I didn't say Tash was a psycho,' I said, firmly. 'I just don't feel right about moving in with Olly when . . . well, it probably wasn't the best idea in the first place.'

'Trust me, sweetheart, moving in with Olly Walker is *always* going to be a lousy idea. I'll bet he's the worst flat-mate alive, anyway. Leaves hair in the shower drain. Gets butter in the Marmite. Skidmarks on the—'

'It's all right, Dillon. You don't need to persuade me.'

'Not to mention the phwoar factor engendered by all that cosy domesticity,' he goes on, clearly feeling that, despite what I've just said, he *does* need to persuade me after all. 'I mean, there you'll be in the mornings, all fresh and damp out of the shower, seductively licking toast crumbs and jam off your lips, accidentally brushing past each other in your dressing gowns . . . poor bloke won't be able to contain himself.'

I glance, sharply, at him. 'What the hell are you talking about? He doesn't fancy me any more. He's with Tash, remember?'

'Oh, come on. You don't think the sight of you with the toast and the jam and the licking. . . you don't think that's going to take him right back to where he started?'

'OK, well, all I think right now is that you've obviously got some sort of toast/jam fetish going on yourself,' I say, hastily, because I'm finding this whole topic rather heart-hammeringly uncomfortable, and I'd rather not dwell on it. (I mean, you never know, with Dillon, if he really thinks what he's saying, or if it's all just a bit of a tease and a wind-up.) 'But if it's really all right with you, moving into your place for a few weeks would be brilliant. I promise, I'll have found somewhere else by the time you get out of Grove House.'

'Hey, there's no hurry. Anyway, there's a good chance I won't even be back at the flat for long when I do get out of here. My agent called yesterday with a potential offer of a new TV series, filming in Vancouver.'

'Wow, Dillon, that's terrific news!'

'Yeah, it was unexpected, that's for sure. I thought I might never work again, to be honest with you. But either way, you can stay as long as you need. And I promise you, if I do end up living with you, I'll be the world's best flatmate. A nice clean shower. Untainted Marmite jars. I can even provide an extra, fully complimentary service where I come and warm you up in bed at night . . .?'

Which is why, obviously, I need to be long gone by the time he's home.

Anyway, this is what I'm here to explain (a version of) to Olly, right now.

I push the door of the restaurant open and head inside.

I love this place.

The thing about it is that it's pretty much exactly the way I always imagined Olly's restaurant would look, long before the idea became reality. It's cosy without being twee, cool without being try-hard. There are comfortable booths for couples to snuggle up in, and a couple of big tables for groups, or for communal seating. There's a tiny bar area that I know Olly would love to expand, by knocking through into the vacant property next door, as soon as he can comfortably afford to do so. The room is light-filled, and somehow sunny, even on this rather grey June day, and there's all kinds of hustle and bustle from the waiting staff setting the tables as I walk in.

'Hi,' I say, with a smile, as one of the waiters approaches me with a *sorry, we're not quite open yet* forming on his lips. 'I'm a friend of Olly's. Is he around?'

'Oh, sorry, yes, he's in the kitchen.' He smiles back. 'I'll pop back and tell him you're here, shall I? Sorry, can I get your name?'

'Libby.'

'Oh! Libby! I've heard so much about you.'

I blink at him. 'You have?'

'Yeah, you're like Olly's best friend, right?'

'Yes, I suppose . . . I mean we don't hang out as much as we used to, unfortunately, but—'

'Oh, well, he still talks about you all the time. You're the one he used to go travelling with and stuff, aren't you?'

'Um, well, yes, we Inter-railed around southern Europe a couple of summers in a row.'

'Yeah, that's what he told me. You went to some tapas bar in Madrid that he modelled the look of this place on, he said.'

'Oh, yes, I remember that place . . .' I swallow down the lump that's suddenly arisen in my throat. 'God. That was so long ago.'

'Well, he obviously remembered it. Anyway, I'll go and get him, shall I? Unless you'd prefer to pop back there yourself?'

'Oh, yes, if that's OK, I'll do that,' I say, and then am already halfway to the kitchen before I remember that some of Olly's chefs tend to be a bit on the leery side, behaving as if they're recently released convicts who haven't seen a woman since they were sent down for aggravated assault five years ago. Still, it's too late to do anything about this now, because I've told the waiter I'll find Olly in there, so I push open the door and peer inside.

As ever, it's hot back here, and full of steam, and frying pans spitting and hissing, and people in chef's whites talking loudly to each other in mingled Italian and Spanish (Italish?) . . . and I can see Olly, all the way at the back near the walk-in refrigerator, holding a list in his hand and looking faintly stressed.

'All right, Jorge,' he's telling one of the chefs. 'If we're this overrun by rhubarb, then I agree with you, we need to find some other way to get it on to the menu today. Is there any way you could make some ice-cream from it this afternoon, and we could serve that with the almond tart on the dinner set menu instead of the plain vanilla . . . Libby!' he says, in a startled voice, as he sees me hovering. 'What are you . . . sorry, Jorge, can we finish this later?'

'No, no, don't worry, I'm only here for two minutes,' I say, hastily. 'If you're dealing with a rhubarb emergency, that's far more important.'

'Oh, it's just that the supplier delivered about four tonnes of the stuff this morning instead of what we ordered. We'll make it work, won't we, Jorge?'

Jorge doesn't respond to this, but simply stares at me for a long moment before raising a hand in greeting.

'*Hola*, Libby,' he says. 'We have all heard so much—'

'Let me go and make you a quick coffee,' Olly says, swiftly, coming over and holding the swinging door open for me to head back out towards the bar area. 'It's really great to see you,' he goes on, 'and it's been ages since you came to the restaurant!'

'I know. It's looking terrific, Ol.'

'Well, it'll be even better if we can get the licence to extend into next door . . . create a proper bar, more tables for eating, even expand the kitchen if it doesn't look like it'll blow the entire budget . . . I must show you the plans, actually, Lib. One morning after you've moved in, we'll have a leisurely breakfast together, and you can have a proper look while I ply you with hash browns and bacon—'

'Actually, that's what I'm here to let you know,' I interrupt. I keep my tone casual. Which is easier said than done, frankly, given that he's just brought to mind precisely that toast-and-jam-licking breakfast Dillon was teasing me about. 'Just to say, Ol, that I'm ever so grateful for the offer, but I've made other plans instead.'

He turns round from the coffee machine. 'Sorry?'

'Other plans for somewhere to stay. So that I won't put you out, I mean.'

'But I already told you, it wouldn't be putting me out.' His forehead is creased in confusion. 'Honestly, Lib, it's absolutely no trouble whatsoever.'

'That's so nice of you, Ol, but actually, I'm going to go and stay in Dillon's flat for a while. I mean, it's empty right now, which is good, because I can spread out all my work without having to worry ab—'

'Dillon?'

'Yes.' I clear my throat. 'He's, um, sorting out a couple of problems at the moment, but it'll be really good for him to have me around when he gets back home.'

'He's drying out in rehab again, you mean.' Olly's voice

is short. 'And he wants you there to cosset him and stoke his ego the minute he gets out.'

'No! That's not it at all.'

'Oh, so he *doesn't* like being worshipped morning, noon and night by a beautiful girl, then. My mistake.'

I'm all ready to announce, crossly, that I don't *worship* Dillon, as a matter of fact, but another part of what Olly's just said stops me in my tracks.

'Beautiful?' I croak, the word tumbling out before I can stop it.

Olly looks faintly horrified for a moment, then turns, sharply, back to the coffee machine. 'Well, obviously you're a very attractive girl, Libby. Woman. Person. Black?'

'What? No, I'm—'

'Coffee. Black coffee. Is what I'm asking,' he gabbles, not quite putting together a complete sentence. 'Or was a cappuccino it? God, hang on, that makes no sense. I mean, was it a cappuccino you wanted?'

'Oh! No, black is fine . . . in fact, I think I don't really have time for a coffee anyway, Ol.' I can feel my heart hammering; this conversation isn't going at all the way I wanted it to go. 'Look, I really just wanted to tell you how massively appreciative I was of your offer, it's just . . . better if I stay at Dillon's instead, that's all.'

'All right. If it's better for you.' Olly doesn't turn round. 'That's all I wanted,' he goes on, 'just somewhere for you to stay. If it's better for you to stay at . . . *his* . . . then that's obviously no problem. Whatever suits. Here's your coffee.'

'Oh, but I should let you get on with—'

'Please,' he says, turning round, 'have a coffee.' He's got a slightly strained smile fixed on his face. 'Please, Libby. Just while I . . . well, while I say this.'

'Say what?'

"This . . . thing I have to say.' He holds up a hand, opens his mouth, closes it again, and then opens it a second time. 'I've just got to tell you something. All right?'

'Yes, Olly, of course, you can say . . . anything. You know that.'

'Good. Because I . . .' He stops. 'I . . . I've got a new coffee supplier.'

'Huh?'

'I've got a new coffee supplier,' he repeats.

I don't know what I was expecting – something a bit more momentous, perhaps, given his tone of voice – and I'm obviously pleased to hear he's found a new coffee supplier, given how important coffee is to Olly. But I wasn't expecting it to be about a coffee supplier.

'That's, er, good to hear,' I say, rather hoarsely.

'Yes. It's been a struggle. Finding the one. The right one, I mean.'

'I can imagine.'

'They're based in Verona,' he goes on, suddenly fussing and faffing with getting me a spoon I don't need, and a little almondy biscuit from a large jar beside the machine. 'And it's really small batches so it's pretty pricey, but I think it's worth it. I'd love your opinion.'

'Um, right . . .' I take a sip of the coffee. 'Delicious!' I fib. (I mean, it's probably *not* a fib; it almost certainly *is* delicious, but I'm too wound up to be able to taste anything just now.) 'Really . . . er . . . coffee-flavoured.'

'Well, yes. I mean, I'd hope.' Olly lets out a rather mirthless (as Dillon might call it) laugh. 'But do you find it too bitter? Too strong?'

'Oh, I don't know, Olly! It's exactly what I said about the cheese thing: I don't know about all this stuff!'

He doesn't reply for a moment. Then he says, 'You know more than you think you do, Lib. About coffee, I mean. And cheese. And . . .' He stops. In fact, he sort of freezes, before saying, stiffly, a couple of moments later, 'Actually, I probably should really get back to Jorge in the kitchen.'

'Of course! I never meant to distract you!'

'No, Lib, it's fine. It's always fine. Stay, please, and enjoy your coffee. I'm really glad you came over.'

'Well, I just wanted to tell you in person.'

'I know. And thanks.' He comes out from behind the bar and takes a step towards me. For a very odd moment I think he's about to shake my hand, or – I don't know – give me a matey punch to the shoulder, or something. But I'm completely wrong, because what he's actually doing is leaning down to put both arms around me and envelop me in a huge, long hug.

And I mean long. Because I count a full ten seconds go by – counting the seconds is the only way I instinctively know how to prevent myself from nuzzling his warm, lemon-scented neck, you see – and then another ten seconds. . .

He doesn't say anything, but I can feel his heart thumping, noisily, in his chest.

Or maybe that's my heart. More likely, that's my heart.

Before I can work it out for certain one way or the other, he's pulling away from me.

'Let me know,' he mumbles, as he turns and heads towards the kitchen, 'if you still need any help moving stuff over to Dillon's.'

And then he's disappeared through the swing doors, back to his rhubarb crisis.

*

Packing up the flat has given me the best excuse ever to ignore my phone for the rest of the day.

Both incoming (Mum, Cass, Bogdan, Mum, Mum again) and outgoing. Which, all right, isn't the most sensible thing to do when I have clients to deal with. But they can all wait. Like I say, packing up for my second move within a month is a perfectly reasonable explanation.

And I'm taking solace, I'll be honest, from the silence. After all, I've had enough difficult, unpleasant and just plain crackers conversations these last few days that it's a plain relief just to switch off from it all for a bit.

Which is a bit of an effort, to be honest, when it comes to that conversation I had with Olly earlier this morning. In fact, I don't think I've so much *switched off* from that as *played it over and over again in my head, on permanent repeat, to try to work out if his anger really Meant Anything.*

Meant Anything beyond his age-old dislike of Dillon, that is. A dislike that was – as far as I know – rooted in

223

jealousy. A dislike that you'd think he might have moved past, now that he's moved past *me*.

And then there was that hug. That hug that – at the time – I was fairly sure *must* Mean Something but that ever since, over the course of the day, I've convinced myself was just his way of making it clear that he's always there for me. No more.

The trouble being that I can't possibly ask him, can I? I can't possibly try to have the kind of open and honest conversation I'm yearning for, not with someone who's so very definitely attached to someone else. It would make me just as bad as my man-eating sister, wouldn't it, if I started up a sneaky line of questioning with Olly to find out why he—

'Oh, so it's just you again, then, I see.'

The voice, coming from the Chesterfield, makes me jump.

I spin round from my packing case to see Grace Kelly, resplendently back in her wedding dress, sitting on the sofa.

'You're here!' I gasp.

'Yes. As are you.' She sighs, rather irritably. 'I must be honest, I really was hoping that marvellous Moldavian fellow would show up again. Things never really . . . *got* anywhere with him, earlier tonight. I mean, he was terribly doting, and it was all very sweet, but I was rather disappointed it didn't go any further than that. It's only a dream, after all. What are dreams for, if you can't be gloriously ravished by a dashing stranger?'

'No, well, I'm not really surprised things didn't end

up . . . going further with Bogdan.' I gaze at her. 'Wow,' I add. 'I mean, it's really good to see you. I didn't think you'd ever come back again.'

'Back? From where? Actually, never mind about that,' she adds, briskly, as I open my mouth to reply. 'Who knows how long we'll have before I wake up? I'd rather like to finish the conversation we were having earlier, if it's all the same to you. Well, of course it's going to be all the same to you, because you *are* me . . .' She stops, casting a rather beady eye over me. 'Though I must say, I'm a little surprised that my subconscious has chosen to represent me with someone quite so . . . scruffy.'

'Hey! I'm packing at the moment,' I say, indignantly. 'That's the only reason I'm wearing this.' I gesture down at my baggy shorts and T-shirt. 'Trust me, if I could swan about the place in a couture wedding gown, I would. Not that I'd look quite like you in it, I grant you . . .'

'That was rather my point. Still, perhaps you're just a salutary warning of what might happen to me if I let myself go.' She has a business-like air as she gets up from the Chesterfield and begins to pace up and down. 'Now, talking of salutary warnings,' she goes on, swishing the train of her wedding dress as she turns back on herself, 'the last conversation we had, you were telling me all about some fellow named . . . Joe, was it? John?'

'Joel.'

'That's right, Joel. Let's continue to call him that, shall we? Rather than . . . well, Rainier, obviously.'

'Yes, look, he didn't represent Rainier, I promise you.

And it hardly matters, anyway, because he's not in the picture any more.'

'What do you mean, he's not in the picture?'

'Just that. I'm not going to see him again. He lied to me, you see, about being a billionaire, and—'

'Hold on.' Her mid-Atlantic voice is imperious. 'He told you he was a billionaire, and he wasn't?'

'No, he told me he wasn't a billionaire, and he was. Or rather, to be more accurate, he didn't tell me he was a billionaire. It's not like he—'

'You're making absolutely no sense.' Now she sounds really cross. 'Why on earth would any girl in their right mind turn down a billionaire?'

'Oh, come on.' I sound rather cross myself, although I'm much less good at it than she is. I just sound petulant and grumpy rather than regally wrathful. 'That's the worst reason in the world to be with someone!'

'Is it?' she demands. 'Don't you think it's just as easy to fall in love with a billionaire as it is to fall in love with a man who doesn't have two cents to rub together?'

'It's not about whether or not he's a billionaire! It's about the fact that he lied.'

'So?' She raises an eyebrow. 'Men lie, darling. That's not enough to turn down a fellow if he has all kinds of other things going for him. Is he handsome? Funny? Kind?'

'Well, yes, OK, he is . . .'

'Lord above, then don't cut off your nose to spite your face! Snap him up! Tie him down! It's exactly what I did with the prince! I wasn't about to let some other girl come swanning along and nab him, not when I was in with a chance . . . Didn't I say exactly this to you earlier? That life is for doers?'

'Yes, you did. But I'm not cutting off my nose to spite my face. I'd rather be alone for the rest of my life than be with someone I couldn't trust wholeheartedly.'

'Oh, pish!' Grace whirls around, snapping the train of the dress behind her this time. She seems rather feverish, I have to say, perhaps because she thinks there's a ticking clock on our encounters, and that any minute now I'm going to vanish with the dawn and never communicate to her whatever messages she thinks I'm filtering from her subconscious. 'You're only saying that because you're still mooning over your other fellow. The one you really wanted to be with, before Fate . . . what did you say? Screwed it up for you?'

'Yes, that's what I said.' I'm suddenly feeling rather desperate, which is probably why I blurt out, 'I mean, I know you're impeccably clear-eyed and unsentimental about love, Grace—'

'Miss Kelly.'

'Miss Kelly . . . I know you're perfectly happy thinking of romance as some sort of business transaction, but not everyone can do that quite like you can.'

'Well, now! That's not entirely fair!' She glares at me. 'I've never said I think of romance as a business transaction. I've just said that I don't believe in leaving something as important as love in the hands of Fate. Frankly, I can't believe anyone ever does anything so foolish. Fate is fickle, and cruel, and stupid. If I'd just blindly accepted what Fate had in store for me, I'd still be scrawny little Gracie from Philadelphia, least successful of my vastly accomplished siblings and destined for a lifetime of disappointing my mother and father. If anyone's an advertisement for making their own luck, it's me. Now, are we going to agree that you're doing the right thing by getting involved with this billionaire, or not?'

'No! I'm not involved with him. I'm not going to be. And this isn't about you, justifying your choice to marry the prince! This is my life, OK?' Now that she's letting me get more than two words in edgeways, I don't seem to be able to stop myself. 'I'm not some cipher for all your own hopes and dreams. Which, by the way, I don't know if you're all that great an advocate for in the first place. I mean, for someone who's so sure they're doing the right thing by marrying their prince tomorrow, you've certainly spent a hell of a lot of time talking about the ones that got away!'

She looks, quite suddenly, as if I've just punched her rather hard in the stomach.

'I'm sorry,' I say. 'I . . . shouldn't have said that.'

'No. You shouldn't.' There's another of her rather beady-eyed stares, and then she seems to give up. She folds, somehow, in the middle, and ends up sitting back down on the Chesterfield. 'Golly,' she says, in a rather small voice, 'but I'm exhausted.'

'I know.' I go closer, think about sitting down right next to her, and then think again. She might seem suddenly vulnerable, but she's still Grace Kelly, after all. I pick a spot a respectful distance along the sofa, and sit down there instead. 'I can only imagine.'

'Thank you.' She remains silent for a moment, then she goes on. 'If it does seem as though I can't stop talking about . . . well, certain people from my past, it's only because you're the only person I can speak to about it.' She lets out a rather brittle laugh. 'Absurd, isn't it? That this is what it's come to. Only being able to have an honest conversation with the dream-girl inside my head.'

'I wouldn't feel too badly about that,' I say. 'I've had some of the best conversations of my life with people who aren't really there.'

'I see,' she says, although she isn't really paying attention. Her bright blue eyes are rather misty, and she looks just as exhausted as she says she feels. 'Of course I think about the men I've loved before,' she goes on, more to herself than to me. 'Tonight, more than ever. But if there's one thing I'm certain of, it's that moving on is the right thing to do. Why waste a single moment crying over a doomed love affair when the chance to forge a lasting one is staring you in the face?'

There's a sudden sharp knock at the front door downstairs.

And just like that, Grace Kelly vanishes.

I stay sitting on the Chesterfield, rather dazed, for a moment.

Then the knocking starts again, so I get to my feet to go and answer it.

'Libby?' I can hear, even as I approach the door, that it's

Cass on the other side. 'For fuck's sake, it's freezing out here!'

I open the door. 'Cass, hi, it's . . . not really a great time.'

'Yeah, all right, I probably should have called. But honestly, Lib, I was just so relieved to get out of there in one piece! Oh, do you have a couple of quid for the Uber guy,' she goes on, gesturing over her shoulder to where a man is hauling suitcases out of a slightly ropey-looking Prius just along the street. 'He's been such a sweetheart, fitting all my cases into his car and being a shoulder to cry on . . . I mean, this is the kind of situation that makes you *so* reassured about people's basic kindness. Plus, he's Romanian and so he's got *nothing* good to say about Bulgarians, trust me. Isn't that right, Corneliu?' she adds.

'Is right,' Corneliu the random Uber guy agrees, as he struggles along to the front door with a case in either hand and a huge holdall slung over each shoulder. 'She is lucky to be escaping from this man with life.'

I'm still too dazed by my encounter with Grace to do anything more than hand Corneliu a couple of quid I dredge up from my hoodie pocket, and then hoick Cass's bags through the door myself so that they don't stay there blocking the pavement outside and enraging the Willington-Joneses . . . It's only when the door shuts behind us, and I watch Cass heading up the stairs ahead of me, that I can form a coherent enough thought to ask a question.

'Sorry, Cass . . . what are you doing here? With all your bags?'

'Isn't it obvious, Libby? I'm escaping! Fleeing while my sanity and self-respect are still intact! While there's still just a little something left,' she pauses, dramatically, 'of *me*.'

'Wait: you've left Zoltan?'

'I have!'

'In *your* flat?'

'Yes.' Her forehead creases, just for a moment, as she realizes the folly of what she's just done. 'But,' she goes on, recovering fast, 'that's just the thing. After all that time feeling so beaten down about everything, I didn't even know it *was* my flat any more. And they've taken over the place, Libby. It doesn't *feel* like home any more.'

'Right . . . er . . . and so you've turned up here with your luggage because . . .?'

'Because I'm coming to stay with you!'

I stare at her. 'Cass, you have to be joking.'

'Why?'

'Because you know I have to move out, right? And that I currently don't really have anywhere else lined up to move *to?* I mean, I'm just going to bunk down at Dillon's for a couple of weeks, until—'

'But what about Joel Perreira?'

'What *about* Joel Perreira?'

'Well, he won't want you *out on the street*, will he? I mean, how would that look, if the *Daily Mail* got hold of it? A billionaire's girlfriend, homeless?'

'I'm not his girlfriend.'

'All right, all right, maybe not *yet*, but if you go on another couple of dates . . . and I don't know if you've had sex with him or not, Lib, but if you haven't, that might be a good way to really seal the deal—'

'Didn't you listen to me the other day?' I ask, pointlessly, because, let's face it, when did Cass last listen to me about anything at all? 'I'm not going out with him again. I've broken it off.'

'Libby Rose Lomax!'

'My middle name isn't—'

'Of all the stupid, selfish—'

'Oh, I'm sorry. Was I supposed to know you were going to walk out on your boyfriend and need somewhere to live?'

She glares at me. 'I actually really need you to be supportive right now. I've just escaped a very *abusive* situation . . .'

'Cass. Don't be ridiculous. It wasn't abusive.'

'I was *in fear for my shoe collection*! How much more,' she gasps, 'do you think I should have been willing to take? I mean, shoes is where it starts, isn't it?'

'Is it?'

'Yes! One day, they're getting snot on your new strappy Kurt Geiger sandals, and the next thing you know, you're scared to go to sleep every night in case they come into your room and attack you while you're lying there . . . it's called *escalation*, Libby. I'm surprised you haven't heard of it.'

We're not getting anywhere.

'OK,' I say, 'but Cass, honestly, you can't stay with me. I'm looking for a place to live myself. Possibly even Stevenage.'

'Where the fuck is Stevenage?'

'Does it matter?' I can hear myself snap, so I take a deep, calming breath. 'Look, you can stay the night, obviously, seeing as I'm still here, but after that, you're really going to have to find somewhere else to live. Or, alternatively, seeing as it's your name on the lease at your flat, get Zoltan to move himself and his kids out so that you can go home!'

'Yeah, like I say, I don't really feel as if I want to do that . . .' Cass parks herself on the Chesterfield, where Grace had just been sitting. 'You know, if you *were* going out with Joel Perreira, Lib, and if he *did* decide to put you up in a really lovely flat, I could come and be your flat-mate!'

The real reason for her sudden walkout is becoming depressingly clear.

'Think about it!' she goes on, her eyes shining. 'I mean, you and me have never shared a flat together. It could be a real bonding opportunity! Plus, obviously it would be somewhere really nice, so we'd be perfectly located for shopping trips, and girlie lunches, and spa days . . ooouh, is that him now?' she gasps, as my phone rings on the coffee table. She grabs it before I can. 'Oh.' She sounds disappointed. 'It's just Mum. Hi, Mum,' she answers, before I can stop her. 'No, it's me . . . no, I'm at Libby's . . . oh, right, that sounds good . . . she's at number thirty-two . . . yeah, see you in a minute.'

'She's on her way here?' I ask, aghast, as Cass tosses the phone back on to the coffee table.

'No, she's not on her way. She's right outside. Well, she

didn't know exactly which number you were . . . that'll be her now,' she adds, as there's a knock at the door. 'Better go and let her in, Lib. Oh, and I think she said she had wine, but if she hasn't, it might be worth sending her back out to get some?'

'You go and bloody answer it!' I say, furiously.

'Oh, *I* see.' Cass eyes me, narrowly. 'Too much of a diva to answer your own door, now you're all set with a billionaire?'

'No, it's not that, Cass. It's that Mum hasn't come to visit me one single time – not once – in any of the flats I've ever rented, and now, just because she thinks I'm going out with Joel Perreira, she suddenly turns up, out of the blue? With wine?'

'Oh. Right. Yeah, that's going to be a real pain for you now, Lib. People trying to leech off you because you're a billionaire's girlfriend. But you just relax,' she adds, in a bizarre croon that sounds nothing like her usual voice, as she gets to her feet, guides me to the sofa and pushes me down to sit on it, 'and *I'll* deal with Mum. I've got your back, Libby. Don't ever doubt that.'

I actually cover my face with my hands for a moment, wallowing in the darkness and wondering if the best bet right now is just to feign a sudden attack of food poisoning, or suspected Ebola, perhaps, and get the pair of them off my back so I can *think*.

'Libby,' comes Mum's voice, from somewhere on the other side of my cupped hands, as she sails into my living room. 'Oh, darling, has it all just got too much for you?

234

Packing up your flat, I mean. That's why I came! Straight from hospital, in fact. Well, I got out this morning, but still—'

'To help me pack?' I take my hands off my eyes. 'You didn't even know I was moving.'

'Well, all right, I just came round to offer *general* support. Because obviously you're going through a hard time at the moment, darling. Uncertain about how you feel about this . . . sorry,' she adds, unconvincingly casual, 'is his name Joel?'

'Yes, Mum,' Cass says, bossily, coming to sit beside me on the sofa, and putting an arm around my shoulders that I think is meant to feel supportive and sisterly but in fact feels more vice-like and proprietorial. 'And we really don't want any fuss made, do we, Lib, just because he's massively loaded and all that?'

'Fuss? I'm not making a fuss! I just know that when a girl is in the middle of relationship difficulties, the person that can really, truly help her is her mother. I mean, I still wish I'd had the benefit of a mother's advice when I was marrying your father, darling. But my own mother, as you know, was always a very selfish, self-interested individual, so I could never rely on her to just *listen*. To just *be a mum*.'

I get to my feet. 'I need a drink.'

'Ooooh, well, I've brought some wine, darling,' Mum says, reaching into her bag and pulling out a Waitrose bottle-bag with some red inside. 'What would a girls' night in be without wine?'

'I don't mean wine. I mean something stronger.' I grab

my own bag from where it's sitting, near the door. 'I'll be back in a bit.'

'Oh, if you're getting vodka, Lib, better get some tonic, too. The low-calorie one. Oh, and maybe some cranberry juice. I quite fancy a vodka and cranberry tonight – don't you, Mum?'

'Actually, now you mention it, I quite fancy a screwdriver. So if you could get some orange juice, darling, that would be perfect. Oh! And while you're at it, I'm trying to drink a lot more pomegranate juice since leaving the hospital . . . it's *so* healing and regenerative . . . even mixed with vodka,' she adds, slightly defensively.

'Fine. I'll go and find a wide selection of juices to suit every palate.' I stamp down the stairs. 'This might take me *quite a while*.'

Because I need some fresh air, away from all their stifling self-interest, and I'll happily walk all over west London until there's a chance they've exhausted all their Joel-related gossip on each other, and stuck the TV on instead.

Or, better yet, until they've gone back to Mum's and left me in peace.

I head up towards Notting Hill, walking as fast as I can in the chilly evening air. I've gone out in nothing but my hoodie and my baggy-and-comfortable-for-packing denim shorts, and I'm already regretting it by the time I reach the main road.

I'm just debating whether to turn back and run the gauntlet of Mum and Cass again, just so I can pull on a pair of jeans and a jacket and therefore stay out for longer without freezing half to death when, quite suddenly, a car pulls up alongside me.

It's Joel, in the driver's seat of an open-top . . . well, I'm no expert, but I think this is a Bentley.

'Libby!' He looks thrilled to see me. 'I was just driving round to your place!'

'But . . . I said I didn't want to see you.'

'Yes. You did. But will you just get in and talk to me?'

I stare at him.

'Take pity on me,' he adds, 'please. I'm stopped on a red route.'

'I wouldn't worry. I'm sure you can afford the fine.'

'Ah, but can I afford the blot on my sense of civic responsibility? I mean, I'll be holding up a bus any minute now, Libby. A bus with ordinary working folks on it, Libby. The kind of honest souls that capitalist bastards like me eat for breakfast. With a sprinkling of diamonds for added crunch.'

'Joel, I'm not quite sure where you got the idea that I'm some kind of rabid communist,' I say. 'My objections to your wealth relate solely to the fact you lied to me about it and made me look ridiculous. I couldn't care less if you eat honest working folks for breakfast. With diamonds or without.'

'Well, that's just uncharitable of you. Won't you think of The People?'

I refuse to be charmed.

'Actually, Joel, I don't think I do want to talk to you. I think you've said everything you needed to say.'

'Hey.' There's a spark – just a spark – of irritation in his voice. 'That's not fair. You can't presume to tell me what I needed to say, Libby. And won't you even let me explain? Don't you owe me that, at least?'

'I'm really not sure I do.'

'In which case, all I can do is appeal to your humanity. Please, Libby. If you hear me out, maybe what I say might actually make sense to you.'

I waver.

Grace – damn her – has got into my head.

And Joel – probably with the same instinct that's seen him make 2.6 billion dollars since dropping out of Harvard at the age of twenty to form his own software company – pounces on my moment of weakness.

'Maybe you don't owe it to me. But don't you owe it to *yourself?* To get an answer you deserve?'

He's good. Of course he's good.

And what he doesn't know, of course, is that on the other side of this particular equation, as I make the rapid calculation in my head, are Mum and Cass, ensconced in my flat, working out ways to egg me on and up the aisle with a man I barely know.

'All right,' I say. I open the car door, and get in. 'Fine. I'm listening.'

Chapter 11

Given that I have a feeling Joel's explanation is going to take a little while, I take the opportunity, while he waits to perform a U-turn in pretty heavy traffic on Bayswater Road, to send a quick WhatsApp to Cass.

Have run into friend and grabbing quick drink. Make yourselves at home.

Cass replies before Joel has even managed the turn.

Is it Joel?????

Followed, a few seconds later, by a new WhatsApp pinging in from Mum.

Don't worry about coming home tonight, darling, if you're having a good time with Joel. I'm sure Cass will be fine with you staying out overnight.

Am absolutely fine, a message from Cass confirms, almost simultaneously, *with you staying out all nite. If it turns into all-night sexathon, that is. Oh, and if it does turn into all-nite sexathon, then remember he's a BILLIONAIRE so is probably used to women offering everything under the sun. All am saying is, tonite is not nite to be shy.*

I'm just shoving my phone furiously back into my

bag when I see a final message appear from Mum.

Totally agree with Cass, darling. Don't know what sort of thing you're used to in bedroom department, but you might have to up your game with man of world like Joel Perreira (hope have spelt that right!).

I'm so bloody glad, now more than ever, that I've escaped my flat for a bit. I mean, all this scheming starts to make you realize why the Anne Boleyns of this world ended up with their heads hacked off, doesn't it? What with hustling family members trying to position themselves for what I believe, in the olden days, was called 'advantage'. Mum and Cass would have been the ones adorning themselves with rubies and diamonds, sitting pretty in their brand-new crenellated castles, while I was the poor sap pushed into marrying some syphilitic old king who kept eyeing up the ladies-in-waiting and keeping the local executioner on stand-by in case I looked at him the wrong way over the roasted swan one lunchtime.

Not that Joel is syphilitic, obviously. I mean, I assume.

And not that he has an executioner on stand-by. Again, I assume. Though I imagine if you're as rich as he is, you can get pretty much anything, for a price.

'Thanks, Libby.' Joel has managed his U-turn, and is now driving back in the direction of Holland Park. His right hand, loosely on the wheel, is very sexy; his left hand, loosely on the gear-stick, even sexier. 'I'm really glad you got in. So, do you like the car?'

Oh, *God*. Maybe I should have stuck out the evening with Mum and Cass, instead.

'Joel, for crying out loud! I'm not impressed by your bloody car!'

'Oh.' He looks disappointed. 'Not even if I've just bought it for you?'

'What do you mean?'

'Well, I bought this a couple of hours ago. For you. If you want it.'

I feel my stomach lurch in horror. 'You've bought *me* a Bentley?'

He nods.

'Joel . . .'

'Oh, and if you open the glove box, you'll see something else in there I picked up for you at the same time.'

With shaking hands, I open the glove compartment.

Inside is a flat, square, bright red Cartier necklace box.

'Joel . . .'

'Open it.'

'I'm not opening it.'

'Open it,' he says, 'go on.'

Out of morbid curiosity, more than anything else, I open the box.

And I'm nearly blinded, seriously, by the millions of watts' worth of diamonds that blink up at me: a double-strand necklace of perfect, round-brilliant-cut diamonds.

You wouldn't have to be any kind of a jewellery expert to know that this is over half a million quid's worth of stones here.

'You have to be fucking kidding me.' I stare at Joel. 'You think you can persuade me to forget about everything by buying me half a million pounds' worth of diamonds?'

'Over a million, actually. They're particularly perfect stones, as I think you'd be able to see in a better light.'

I feel too weak and sick to speak.

'But no, in answer to your question, Libby. I very much doubt that I can persuade you to forget about everything with a million pounds' worth of diamonds. I suppose, really, I'm just using the Bentley and the necklace as illustrations of what it's really like, being me.'

I don't follow.

'So you're saying that being a billionaire means you get to drive expensive cars and buy expensive jewellery? Do you think I'm an idiot, Joel? I'm aware that you can buy all this kind of stuff if you want to.'

Though I have to say, seeing it all in the flesh, as it were, brings it all home to me with a really alarming jolt.

'I'm not explaining myself very clearly. What I should probably say is that these things – this exact car, pretty much that exact necklace – are things I've been asked for recently. By women I was dating at the time.'

'Sorry – you've been out with women who've expressly asked you for luxury sports cars?'

'Yes.'

'And Cartier diamonds?'

'Yep.'

'I see.' I close the Cartier box, and shove it back in the glove compartment. 'Well, the first thing that springs to mind, Joel, is that you should probably try to find a way to meet a better class of woman.'

'I have. You. I mean, it's the reason why I carried on that silly pretence of being a personal trainer,' he goes on. 'And why I'd have carried it on for weeks, probably, if you hadn't caught me out.' He pauses for a moment, then lets out a long sigh. 'Every woman I meet, Libby, knows who I am. Or, if they don't right away, they do about five minutes later, when they Google me. And you . . . well, you were the first woman I've met in the last, oh, I don't know, the last decade or so who didn't.' He takes a deep breath, then speaks extra slowly and clearly, for emphasis. 'You. Have. *No. Idea.* How. Refreshing. That. Is. Seriously. It was like a drink of cold water after a decade in a desert.'

'If you hadn't drunk anything after ten years in a desert, you'd be dead.'

'Yeah, well, trust me, there are times when dead is exactly the way I feel. I mean, the sheer predictable misery of it: every woman I meet, doing The Face.'

'The face?'

He stops the car at a set of lights, and takes the opportunity to perform a pretty accurate impersonation of pretty much exactly what Cass's face looked like when I told her the name of the man I'd been dating: eyes wide, jaw slack, something slightly waxy about the cheeks.

'You know the way they say the queen thinks the entire world smells of fresh paint? Well, I've been starting to think women's faces all look like startled goldfish. And I'm under no illusions that it's my good looks or charming personality that's reducing them to piles of jelly.' He sounds deflated – sad, even – all of a sudden. 'It's the fact that they can't seem to look at me without seeing flipping great wads of dosh. The last woman to look at me properly was my ex-wife, and that's because we met fifteen years ago, before all this really took off.'

I don't want to give this sob story – however genuine it seems – too much opportunity to work its way under my skin, so I distract from it by saying, 'So the ex-wife in Australia is real, then?'

'OK, so this is why I knew I really had to talk to you! Everything I told you – all the information I volunteered myself, that is – is one hundred per cent real. I have an ex-wife, yes. She lives in Sydney, yes. We have a five-year-old daughter, yes.' He puts the car into first gear and we move off from the lights again. 'I really don't know my dad, who really is Brazilian. My mum really is an aid worker from Slovakia. Well, she's in charge of my foundation these days, but that's pretty much the same thing. Oh, and it really is her birthday soon. And I really do want to get her something from your website.'

I can feel my cheeks burn, remembering this.

'I honestly can't tell you,' he goes on, 'what a pure joy it was to have an evening off from all the *shit*. And I really liked you. Really fancied you. And I didn't want to mess that up by letting all the usual crap get in the way. Besides, what was I supposed to do? Wait until I'd poured the wine at the pub and then said, *Oh, by the way, just so you know, I happen to be a billionaire?* Wouldn't that have made me look like a prize numpty before we'd even started?'

'Yes. I suppose it would.'

244

'Then please. Give me one more chance. Let me prove to you,' he goes on, 'that I'm just . . . me. Who just happens to be worth a few bob.'

'Joel, you're not worth a *few bob* . . .'

'So? If the money doesn't matter to you, then don't let it matter to you.' He shrugs. 'If you're not impressed by it, don't be overwhelmed by it. Sure, I own expensive homes, and I wear expensive clothes, and I fly to places in my own helicopter—'

'You have a *helicopter?*'

'OK, OK, I get how that sounds, but in all honesty, Libby, it's just a practicality. I have a lot of people to oversee in a lot of different countries . . .'

'There is a thing called Skype, you know. There is a thing called video-conferencing.'

'Yeah, but neither of those is anywhere near as awesome as flying around the place in your own helicopter.'

I laugh, despite myself.

'Look,' I say, 'believe it or not, I do understand. I can imagine that it can't be all that nice to have everyone evaluating you on nothing but the size of your bank balance. Which, by the way, I'd have understood even if you hadn't just pulled this silly stunt with a Bentley and a million quid of diamonds.'

He winces. 'So you think this was silly?'

'Just a bit, Joel, yes.'

'No, you're right. I don't really know what I was thinking. Would I have been better off focusing on the whole *just a normal guy* angle?'

The very fact that he's just called this an *angle* is, if I had the time and space to think about it, probably evidence that he really isn't just a normal guy.

'Joel, honestly, it's not about being a normal guy, or an extraordinary guy . . . it's more that, either way, I don't really know you.'

'Sure, but that's just what a new relationship is all about, isn't it? Getting to know someone? I mean, ideally they'll be telling you the absolute truth . . . look, I've got a suggestion. Why don't you come back to my house with me, right now?'

'Oh, Joel, er, I don't know . . .'

'It won't just be you and a man you barely know in a big old house. There are staff there.'

'Wow. You have staff.'

'Well, it's the house I use for formal dinners, and stuff, for the foundation, so I really need to keep the place ticking over . . . I'm much more at home at my place in Sussex—'

'Joel. It's fine. There's no need to explain everything.'

'Thank you.' He reaches over and puts a hand on mine, and strokes my palm very, very gently with his thumb.

The impulse to hurl myself across the gearbox, into his lap, is – all of a sudden – completely overwhelming.

I blame Cass for this. And Mum. With the mere mention of the words *all-night sexathon*, they've set my mind venturing down the path of . . . possibilities. What, if Joel's hand feels this nice on my mere palm, would it feel like on other bits of my body . . . What that solid, Krav Maga-honed body looks like without a shirt on . . .

246

And then, of course, there's the fact that I haven't had sex since I broke up with Dillon, almost eighteen months ago.

I mean, let's call a spade a spade, here.

This isn't even anything to do with what Grace Kelly was saying to me earlier. Maybe her advice about moving on and forging ahead is sound, maybe it isn't . . . but right now, all I can think about is the fact that I fancy the pants off Joel Perreira, and I'd give my eye-teeth to be falling into bed with him right this very moment.

'So,' he asks, after a moment. 'Would you like to come to my place, or—'

'Yes.' My voice has gone pretty husky, with undisguised lust, and I know he can hear it. 'Yes, Joel, let's head to your place.'

'That's the best news I've heard,' he says, his own voice suddenly a bit thick with lust, too, 'since I floated my company on the stock market fifteen years ago and made my first hundred million.'

Hang on, is this all a big mistake . . .?

'I'm kidding,' he says, 'by the way.'

Then he puts his foot on the accelerator, just a little, to get us to his place faster.

*

Well, as far as getting to know him better goes, ending up in bed together three minutes after we'd arrived was possibly the most efficient way to accomplish this worthy goal.

And I can now report, with the new information I have to hand, that Joel's hands really *did* feel even nicer on other parts of my body, and that his Krav Maga-honed body really *was* very nice with his shirt off. A shirt that I'm now, incidentally, wearing, as I sit in the bed.

I mean, there's quite a lot else I could report, too – and all of it pretty spectacular – but, right now, I'd rather just wallow in the sheer deliciousness of it all.

Most delicious of all, to my shame, the excellent scrambled eggs on toast he's just whipped up in the kitchen, and brought to me in bed, for a late-night (and, I can't help hoping, energy-boosting-for-round-two) snack.

(I say *to my shame* not just because I'm so bloody starving that I'm genuinely enjoying the scrambled eggs almost as much as I did the fantastic sex, but also because the fact that Joel seems to be such a dab hand in the kitchen has just reminded me, uncomfortably, of Olly. Who, I've all-too-often imagined, would follow up a dreamy bedroom session by producing something scrumptious on a plate. Or, more likely, knowing Olly's preference for tapas-style food, several scrumptious things on several plates. And if there's anything more inappropriate than *still* letting Olly pop into my head after the amazing half-hour I've just spent in Joel's bed . . . well, I'd have to ask Cass, the Queen of the Inappropriate, for help with that.)

'More champagne?' he's asking me, now (because yes, of course, we really are drinking champagne with our midnight feast; the evening really is this much of a fairy tale), 'or if you prefer, I can call over to the main house and get someone to go to the cellar for something red?'

'No, champagne is wonderful, Joel, thank you.' I take a sip of the glass beside the bed. 'But you're going to have to explain all this stuff about the main house. And, to be fair, explain to me exactly where we are now.'

'Ah. Of course. It's a bit confusing, in the dark. And then there was the fact that you could barely restrain yourself from jumping on me the moment I stopped the car in the driveway . . .' Joel grins. He looks absurdly handsome, loosely wrapped in a bathrobe, as he gets to his feet and pads to the nearby window. 'OK, so over there,' he says, pulling up the blind, 'is my official London residence.'

Even though it's dark outside, I can see, across a half-acre or so of garden, a looming white mansion that I did vaguely clock once we'd pulled up on the driveway almost an hour ago.

And it really is looming: huge, at least four storeys tall, and sort of crenellated.

'Er . . . it's . . .'

The word *lovely* dies on my lips.

'Monstrous?' Joel asks. 'Obscene? Bordering on the offensive?'

'I . . . well, I mean, we're all keen on different things, obviously . . .'

He grins. 'Politeness itself. But, as it happens, I agree with you. I really only bought the house for formal functions. I mean, we can host all kinds of fund-raisers here, for the foundation, and it's big enough for a professional kitchen . . . but the main reason I chose this particular monstrosity – over any of the other monstrosities my accountants were keen for me to buy – was this place.' He gestures around the room we're currently in. 'I don't know if it was originally some sort of staff quarters, or what, but when I saw that the property included an entirely separate cottage on the grounds, I had to snap it up.'

I'm embarrassed to admit that, in my sheer lust to get out of the car and into Joel's pants earlier, I really *didn't* notice that we were in an entirely separate cottage.

Though looking around, now that I'm a little less dazed by desire, it makes a lot of sense. Because the bedroom, although beautifully decorated, and with some pretty fancy modern art on the walls, is, nevertheless, just a normal-sized bedroom. Just big enough for a king-size bed, a Scandi-style (though probably not IKEA) wardrobe and a couple of small armchairs.

'My daughter has a bedroom across the hall – don't worry, she's not here at the moment!' Joel says, 'and then downstairs there's just a kitchen and a little den. In fact, come down to the kitchen with me now,' he adds, coming over to my side of the bed and holding out a hand, 'while I get the champagne bottle from the fridge. Come and see where I spend most of my time.'

We leave the bedroom, go down a small, spiral flight of stairs, and cross the narrow entrance hallway to reach the kitchen.

Again, it's unassuming, in an expensive sort of way. I've never been in a billionaire's private kitchen before, obviously, so I've nothing to compare it to, but if I might have imagined solid-gold taps and priceless Picassos as splashbacks above the cooker, I couldn't have been more wrong. The units are Shaker-style and painted a soft dove grey, and the floor is slate, and warmed from underneath by some incredibly toasty under-floor heating. A big oak table stands in the middle of the room, with wide benches running either side. There's a big American-style fridge, covered with letter and number magnets and some primary-coloured artworks that I assume have been constructed, painstakingly, by Joel's daughter. And there are at least half a dozen photographs of his daughter standing on different shelves of the gorgeous Welsh dresser in the corner.

It looks, even the most raging anti-capitalist would have to admit, like nothing more or less than a much-loved home.

'Well?' Joel is taking the champagne bottle out of the big, American-style fridge. 'What do you think? Is there any chance I might actually be exactly the same normal guy you thought you'd met the other day?'

'Yes. OK. You win. You're normal.'

He bows. 'Thank you.'

'And, like I said in the car, I do understand that you were only spinning me a pack of lies—'

'Being economical with the truth,' he says, with the merest hint of an edge to his voice.

'. . . because you've been so horribly disillusioned by all those dreadful gold-diggers suddenly getting dollar signs in their eyes every time you bring out the titanium Amex to pay for a cup of coffee.'

Joel laughs. 'Ah. Maybe that was the problem. How different the last few years might have been for me if I'd only had the good sense to use cash.'

'But the thing is, Joel,' I go on, taking a seat, for a moment, on one of the oak benches next to the big table, 'I just get the impression that you're looking for a really serious relationship.'

'Yeah. I am.' He shrugs. 'I make no secret of that. I mean, trust me, I've had my share of casual hook-ups—'

'I'm sure you have,' I say, hastily, because I *really* don't want to hear about Joel's casual hook-ups (and, even if I did, for some masochistic reason, it's just a tad insensitive of him to bring the subject up only fifteen minutes after we've just enjoyed our own extended hook-up).

'. . . but can I just ask, Libby, if you believe in such a thing as a soulmate?'

'Soulmate?' I echo.

'Yes.' He sits down next to me, his body warm through his robe. 'I know some people think it's just a silly, romantic notion. That there are hundreds – thousands – of people in the world that any one of us could fall in love with. Not just one very special one.'

'No. I mean, I don't think it's a silly, romantic notion. I believe in soulmates. One hundred per cent.'

'You sound as if you think you have one.'

'Yes,' I blurt. 'Or rather, I did. It's . . . not an issue any more.'

'That's good. Because I think you might be *my* soulmate, Libby. Even though I only met you a few days ago.'

252

I blink at him. 'Really?'

'Yes. Really. Don't you think we have a connection? Something special? I don't just mean, by the way, that I fancy you rotten, and that – as I've very happily just discovered – you're absolutely incredible in bed. But I already told you that I thought there was something magical in the air when we met. And I'm a tech guy at heart, Libby. I don't use words like *magical* lightly. Not to mention that I know it makes me sound more than a little crazy.'

'It doesn't make you sound that crazy. Trust me.'

'Well, then. You'll understand why I think you're destined to be with me. Now, I don't know what your strategy was for persuading Dillon that he was supposed to be with you—'

'It wasn't Dillon!'

'No?'

'No! I already told you, he's just an ex. If that.' I move an inch or two away on the bench, so I can look at Joel more easily. 'Why are you fixing on Dillon?'

'I'm not. I just thought . . . look, all I'm saying, really, is that I'm not the sort of person to sit passively by and watch from the sidelines. If I see a chance of happiness, I grab it. Life is all about seizing the moment.'

'Yes . . . I've heard pretty similar advice from . . . a friend.' I swallow. 'It's good advice.'

'It's great advice. I'd never have had all the success I've had, in my professional life, if I didn't go after the things I really want. The things I really believe are right for me. So really, Libby, all you need to know is that I thoroughly intend to woo you with every fibre of my being.'

I can't help smiling. 'Woo me?'

'Woo you.' He looks, for a moment, slightly consternated. 'That's the word, right? I'm not suddenly making a mistake with my English?'

'No, Joel. You're not. It's just a funny word, that's all.' I reach out a hand to touch his face. 'You're so incredibly perfect,' I suddenly say. 'You really are, Joel.'

He drops his head down to place a soft kiss on my wrist. 'Not as perfect as you.'

My phone, somewhere outside in the hallway, where I dropped my bag as we came inside, has started ringing.

It's Nora's ringtone.

'Sorry, Joel, but I should get that.'

'Really?' He looks mildly irritated that he's being interrupted, mid-woo. 'It's urgent?'

'It's my best friend. She's on holiday in France, away from her baby for the first . . .' I stop, because obviously I don't have to justify to Joel why I'm answering my ringing phone. 'Yes, it's urgent!' I say. 'Or rather, it could be. I won't know unless I answer it.'

'Of course. You go ahead. I'll pour us some more champagne. And I've probably got strawberries somewhere in the fridge.' He gets to his feet. 'We could dip them in some fresh cream.'

This had better be bloody urgent from Nora, that's all I can say. Here I am, cosily drinking post-sex champagne with a handsome man, who had already proved himself to be dynamite in bed before strawberries and cream were brought into the equation . . .

I hurry to the hallway, grab my phone from my bag and answer.

'Nor?' I hiss. 'Sorry, but it's a bit of a bad time. Well, actually, it's a great time, but—'

'Libby? Are you with them?'

'With who?'

'Olly and Dad! At Central Middlesex!'

'The *hospital?*'

'Yes, the hospital.' She sounds absolutely frantic. 'Mark's trying to get us a flight, but there's nothing until five in the morning, and we're in this *fucking* village, miles from anywhere—'

'Nora, what's going on?'

'Clara. And Mum. Mum fell down the stairs taking her down for a bottle a couple of hours ago.'

'Oh, my God.' I feel the floor shift beneath me. 'Nora, I . . . Are they OK?'

'I don't fucking know, that's the whole point! Olly called me half an hour ago from A and E, and he said they'd taken Clara straight through to Paediatric Intensive Care . . . I don't even know about Mum, I didn't ask.' A sob escapes; cool, calm Nora is more panicked than I've ever heard her. 'But she's seventy-five, and it's a steep staircase . . . I just keep having visions of Clara's little head, slamming to the floor at the bottom . . . she'll have been so sleepy, and it'll have been such a horrible shock . . .'

'OK, don't panic,' I say, even though I'm feeling panicked enough myself, and it's not even my child we're talking about. 'Let's try to think clearly. Can you hire a car? Get an overnight train?'

'Nothing until tomorrow morning!' Nora is actually in tears, now; I can hardly understand her. 'I don't know what to do, I have to get back . . . if I'm not there . . .'

'Everything OK?'

This is Joel, coming out into the hallway, a dish of strawberries in one hand and a bowl of cream in the other. I just stare at him for a moment, my muddled brain unable to compute why, in the middle of a crisis, he's wandering around with soft fruits, until I remember that he doesn't actually know what's happened.

'Nora's baby,' I croak at him. 'She's fallen down the stairs . . . well, her mum fell down the stairs, holding the baby—'

'Oh, fuck.'

'Who's that?' Nora gasps. 'Is he a doctor? Does he think it sounds as bad as I do?'

'No, he's not a doctor, he's . . . please, Nora, try to just stay as calm as you can. She's stuck in the middle of nowhere in France,' I tell Joel, desperately. 'They can't get a flight for – ' I glance down at my watch – 'another six hours.'

'France? Where in France?' Joel is turning around and striding back into the kitchen. He puts the bowls down, and grabs a landline phone from the counter. 'I can send my helicopter.'

I stare at him.

'Helicopter?' Nora screams down the phone. 'Who the

hell is this guy you're with, Libby? Does he think that's funny?'

'No, no, he really does have . . . er . . . a helicopter.'

'I'll get Sav on it right away,' Joel is saying, dialling a number into the phone. 'Sav, hi, it's me,' he says, a moment later. 'I need to send the helicopter for an emergency pick-up. It's at Battersea Power Station, right?'

He doesn't, I somehow manage to notice, greet her with any kind of a *hello* or a *sorry it's the middle of the night*, but he's obviously aiming for speed. And also, I guess, if you work as a billionaire's personal assistant, late-night demanding phone calls are probably just part of the job.

'So can we get a pilot at this time of night?' he's asking. 'No, it's not a very long trip, just France . . .' He glances over at me. 'Where exactly is your friend right now, Libby?'

'The South,' Nora gulps, on the other end of my phone. 'Near Arles.'

'OK, so that's good news, there are a tonne of helipads round there,' Joel says, knowledgeably. 'What do you think, Sav, we can probably get someone out there about . . . ninety minutes from now?' He listens to the reply. 'OK, I'll do that . . . Yep . . . Thanks, Sav, I'll let you get on it.' He puts the phone down and comes over to me, then takes my iPhone from my hand. 'OK, Nora,' he tells her, 'I'm going to call my assistant Savannah back in five minutes, with your phone number. She'll have it all sorted by then, and she'll call you right back. Just stay by your phone. Oh, and pack whatever you need, because she'll probably have a car on its way to you any minute now. Is that OK?'

'It's more than OK.' I can just hear Nora's voice, on the other end of my phone. 'I . . . I have no idea who you are, but . . . this is . . . thank you. Thank you *so much*.'

'It's nothing, honestly . . . Look, you go and get yourselves sorted out, and then keep the line free for Sav to call, OK?'

'Yes. Yes, we'll do that. Libby, give him my number,' she calls, and then the phone goes dead.

With a shaking hand, I scribble Nora's number on the piece of paper Joel is holding out in front of me. If I weren't so horribly shocked by the awfulness of this entire situation, I have to say, I'd be even more agog at Joel's swift command of the situation. I mean, sure, it's easier to be in command of a situation like this when you happen to have a helicopter and a scarily efficient assistant at your disposal . . . but that's not really the point.

'So, do you want to go, too?'

'Sorry?'

'In the 'copter. To pick your friend up. In case she wants you? I mean, getting you to Battersea will slow take-off down by about half an hour, because otherwise I reckon they can get someone airborne in about fifteen minutes—'

'No, no, I don't want to slow anything down . . . but I would like to get to the hospital, actually. To be there when she gets there, and . . . well, her family are like family to me, too, Joel . . .'

'It's OK. It's no problem.' He puts a hand on my shoulder. 'We'll get you there by car. I'll drive you myself. I've only had half a glass of champagne. If that's OK with you?'

'It's fine. It's great.'

'Good. We'll take something a bit less draughty than that ridiculous Bentley. Come on,' he adds, drawing me towards the bedroom. 'Come and get dressed, and I'll call Sav with your friend's details. Then we can get going.'

'You're . . . this is so nice of you, Joel.'

'It's nothing.'

'It's not nothing.'

'It really is. I mean, the only real use of all this ridiculous money is if you can actually help people out when they need it. Oh, that'll be Sav,' he adds, as the landline rings. 'I'll give her Nora's number right now. You go and get dressed. And relax, Libby. I'm sure it'll all be OK. And nothing,' he says, before he picks the phone up, 'is going to be helped by panicking.'

Chapter 12

I've texted Olly, a few times, to let him know that I'm on my way to the hospital, but seeing as all I've had is a terse *OK* in reply, I don't expect to see the sight that greets me as I hurry towards the A&E building from the car park, with Joel at my side.

Olly is waiting outside, peering out into the darkness to look for me.

'Libby,' he says, hurrying towards us as we approach.

It's hard to tell in the darkness, and with the blindingly yellow lights around the entrance, but he looks about ten years older than he did the last time I saw him.

'Nora's just called.' He stares at me, and then at Joel, and then back at me again. 'She's on her way in . . . a *helicopter?*'

'Yes. It's Joel's. How's Clara? And your mum?'

'Clara's OK, we think. A lot of blood everywhere, and a few stitches, and they want to do a CT scan in the next few hours, just to be sure there's no bleeding inside her head. But she's pretty wide awake, and seems quite happy . . . Tash is in with her right now, actually . . . sorry,' he adds, peering more closely at Joel. 'You're . . . you have a *helicopter?*'

'Yeah.' Joel sticks out a hand for Olly to shake. 'I'm glad it can be of some use to you. Is your mum OK?'

'Broken wrist, dislocated shoulder, some cracked ribs . . . she must have contorted herself to take most of the impact of the fall, bless her.' Olly's voice wobbles, ever so slightly. 'They're scanning her right now, in fact. I've not seen her yet, but Dad's in with her. I've been manning the phone.' He waggles his phone at us. 'I'm almost out of power, actually.'

'Oh, I should have a portable charger in my car some-where,' Joel says. 'I can go and get it for you?'

'That would be amazing, actually, mate,' Olly says. 'If you don't mind?'

'No problem. Is there a coffee place open anywhere here at this time of night?'

'Yeah, just through the entrance of the main building.' Olly points. 'Right there.'

'OK, why don't you two go and get some coffee and I'll see you there with the charger in a few minutes?'

We watch him head back in the direction of the car park.

He's obviously giving us a few minutes together to regroup, which is lovely of him.

In fact, I'm still pretty astounded by Joel's general love-liness all night.

'Is he . . . some kind of super-hero?' Olly asks, in a dazed sort of manner, a moment after Joel's out of earshot.

'No. At least, I don't think so. Come on,' I add, taking him by the arm and leading him towards the main hospital building. 'He's right, you should get a coffee. Have you eaten anything since you got the call from your dad?'

'No . . . I'd taken the night off the restaurant, tonight, for me and Tash to get an evening together . . . I cooked us a tagine, but we got, well, a bit side-tracked . . . and then Dad called—'

'OK, so you definitely need to eat.' I try to whitewash from my brain the image of Olly and Tash getting *side-tracked* on their romantic, tagine-eating night in together, as I park Olly in a plastic chair beside a plastic bistro table, then head to the counter to get him a double espresso, a couple of sandwiches and a selection of those wafer biscuits with the cream fillings. My phone is ringing as I open my bag to pay, but a quick glance shows me that it's only Cass, so I (wisely, I think) ignore it. This is no time – if there ever *were* a time – for her to be asking me for status updates on the sexathon with Joel.

'Right, now, I know you're fussy about quality,' I tell Olly, as I return to the table with my tray. 'But you've got to have something from this little lot. And no complaints about the coffee, either. This is Central Middlesex Hospital at midnight, not Verona on a warm spring afternoon. You'll drink it as it comes.'

'Duly noted.' Olly does, in fact, down the double espresso in about two sips, without a single word of complaint, and then reaches for one of the wafer packs. 'Thanks so, so much, Libby.'

'For the wafers? Don't be ridiculous. They were seventy pence.'

'Not for the wafers. For coming. And for . . . Joel. The helicopter. I can't even tell you the state Nora was in when I first spoke to her . . .' He actually shudders. 'And now she's on her way, and she might even get here in time for the CAT scan . . . it's all just so, so much less horrific than it was an hour ago.'

'Don't thank me for that. I've done precisely nothing, Ol. It was just sheer dumb luck that I was . . . with Joel when Nora called.'

'Luck,' he repeats. 'That you were with Joel.'

'Yes. Don't you think?'

He doesn't say anything. His forehead creases with a deep, exhausted-looking frown.

'Olly?'

'Yes, sorry. You're right. It's. . . lucky you were with him.' He picks up his nearly empty espresso cup, and lifts it in a toast. 'Here's to sheer dumb luck. Or let's call it Fate. It sounds better, right?'

'Yes. Like the gods were on our side.'

'For once,' he says, softly.

Given that we're meant to be making a toast, we should probably both drink from our coffee cups right now. But we don't. We just look at each other, across the table, for a long moment.

'And what a good thing,' I force myself to say, before this moment goes on any longer and gets – I don't know – out of hand, or anything, 'Tash was with *you*. Having a doctor here, it must have made it a bit easier.'

'Yeah, she's been amazing, obviously.' Olly bites his lip.

'And Clara absolutely loves her, so it's great that she can hold the fort until Nora makes it. Plus the doctors are actually telling her stuff, you know, rather than just assuming they have to tell us *well, obviously the baby's had a nasty boo-boo . . .*'

'Of course. But what a horrible end to your romantic evening, nevertheless.'

'Oh, I think we'll survive. We'll have plenty more of them.' He takes a deep breath. 'In fact, about an hour before I got the call from my dad, we decided we're going to get married.'

It's a good thing I'm sitting down, because otherwise I'm pretty sure my legs would just have gone from under me.

I stare back at him.

'Married?'

'Yes.' He 's watching my face, intently 'Sorry, I realize this is probably the least appropriate time on the planet to be announcing this.'

'But . . . you mean . . . married, as in . . . walking down a church aisle?'

'Oh, no, no, not at all.'

A tidal wave of relief washes over me – even though I still don't actually understand what he's saying – until he speaks again.

'I mean, obviously we haven't talked about that sort of detail yet, but I don't think we'll be doing anything as formal as a church wedding. We'll keep it small and simple, I'd have thought. Tash will probably have a few ideas about exactly what she wants.' He breaks the intent gaze he's had fixed on me, and busies himself with his coffee cup instead. 'Well, I'm *sure* she'll have a few ideas about what she wants! You know Tash!'

I can't reply.

'But that's what's good about her, you know?' He's still busy with the cup. 'I mean, just one of the many things that's good about her. That she knows what she wants out of life, you know? She brings that out in me, you know?'

It's the third time he's asked me *you know*, so I feel obliged to actually put a response together.

'Olly, come on. You run an incredibly successful restaurant! You're not someone who needs help knowing what they want out of life!'

'Yeah, OK, professionally I have it all sorted.' He glances back at me for a fleeting moment. 'But, you know, in my private life I tend to . . . sit back. Let it all pass me by. Until it's too late.'

My heart is in my throat. 'Olly . . .'

'But not any more,' he adds, firmly. 'Tash needs a commitment from me – and I get that, you know? I understand why she wants that – and I'm not about to let things slip through my fingers just because . . .' He stops, swipes a hand over his eyes, and keeps it there. 'Shit, Libby. You know, I can't believe I'm even sitting here talking about any of this, when we nearly lost Mum and Clara tonight. The shock, I suppose. Will you keep it under wraps? Until we're sure everything's OK?'

'You mean . . .' My voice barely comes out; my throat

seems to have been lined, somehow, with sandpaper. 'You mean not mention that you're . . . engaged.'

'Yes. Though even *engaged* sounds a bit wrong.' He emits an awkward laugh. 'I mean, I didn't get down on one knee with a ring, or anything. . .'

'That sounds—'

'Romantic, right?' he says. 'I'm sort of regretting it already, if you must know.'

'Well, then, you can just back out!' Without thinking, I reach across the table, through the sandwiches and the wafers and the coffee cups, and put my hand on his. 'Seriously, Olly, there wouldn't be any shame in that. I mean, you said it yourself, it's not even really a proper engagement, as such, and it's only been a few hours . . . other people do way more embarrassing things all the time. I mean, Kim Kardashian got *married* for only seventy-two days, and Britney Spears—'

'Urrgh, no, Lib, hang on!' Olly looks more uncomfortable than ever. 'That's – oh, God – that's not what I was saying.'

'Oh!'

'No, I only meant I was regretting doing it in such an unromantic way! That's all.' He squeezes my hand, all of a sudden, but in an involuntary sort of way, almost like a spasm. 'Are you saying I shouldn't do this?'

'No, no.' I pull my hand away as if his has suddenly turned into molten lava. I'm beyond mortified, now. He's obviously furious with me – that sharp hand-squeeze he gave me just now is more than a hint of his anger – and I guess I can't blame him. He's just made his big announcement and here

I am suggesting he backs out before they've even started. 'I'm really, sorry, Ol. I shouldn't have said. . . any of that.'

'But do you think I'm making a *mistake*, or something?' he demands. His cheeks are turning very pink, the way they do when he's really annoyed about something. 'I mean, you seem pretty *anti*, Lib, if I'm honest, and. . .'

'No! Honestly, Olly, just forget I said any of that! You know, the Kim Kardashian crap, and everything. . .' My phone has just started ringing in my bag again, so I could always get out of this horrible conversational alleyway by answering it . . . oh, no, hang on, it's still just Cass. I'll leave it, actually. I take a deep breath. 'I'm just surprised, OK? It's a lot to take in, and . . . look, even without everything that's happened with Clara and your mum, it's been a very, *very* strange evening. And you've just sprung this on me . . . and it seems quite sudden.'

'*Sudden?* We've been together a year, Libby! I'm thirty-four. Tash is thirty-five. It's time to make a proper commitment to each other. I mean, what else are we supposed to do? Just bob along together in a kind of ho-hum way, while around us everyone else throws themselves into marriage and kids as if their lives depend on it?'

'No. . .'

'It's what people *do*, you know, Lib! Meet each other, fall in. . . in love. Spend the rest of their lives together.'

'Yes. I know. I know that, Olly. And I'm . . . look, I'm really, really happy for you. Just ignore all the stupid stuff I've just said. Please. *Please*.'

There's a short silence.

'So,' I go on, in a very small voice, trying to drag us back to something approaching companiability, 'where will you live?'

'Oh, God, Libby, I don't know.' He sounds irritable, now. He sighs. 'Sorry. I don't mean to snap. It's been a weird night, like you said. And trust me, where we'll live is honestly the least of my worries right now – you know, having nearly lost my mum and my niece, and all that – but I just feel bad for Tash that the night's been forever tarnished by this stuff. She's such a great person. She deserves more.'

'Oh, Olly.' I reach a hand, tentatively, back across the table, and touch his hand lightly again. 'You're right. She is a great person.'

Because she's in there with Clara now, running point between the doctors and Olly's family, in a way that I'd never manage to do. I can't even get Clara to smile at me, for Christ's sake. And she's the sort of grown-up, properly sorted individual who doesn't need any silly romance, any hearts and flowers, when she gets engaged to be married. That's rare. It's admirable.

And if you cancel out the slightly scary part of her that came round to my flat to warn me off Olly the other night – or even just reframe it as a strong woman staking her claim to her man – then I've got absolutely nothing I can possibly say against her. Nothing I can even *think* against her.

Besides, I think Fate has pretty much given me its absolutely final word on the subject right now, hasn't it?

'It's lovely news,' I say. 'And it doesn't matter how the evening went. You've got . . . well, a whole lifetime ahead together.' I take a burning sip of coffee. 'One evening is nothing.'

'I suppose so. And, uh, it looks like things are going pretty well for you, too! This Joel guy—'

'It's early days.'

'I mean, coming to the rescue with his helicopter, and all that . . . what an incredible bloke.' He reaches for the wafer packet and fiddles with the opening. 'Incredible.'

'Well, I mean, you've only just met him . . .'

'Yeah, but he's been a real hero tonight. And he seems pretty shit-hot in all other areas of his life, too. From what Tash has been reading about him on her phone tonight.'

'Oh. Of course. Google.'

'Sorry.' He looks embarrassed. 'It was a long wait, before they let us in to see Clara. And we were just a bit confused about exactly who it was that Nora claimed was sending a helicopter to get her . . . do you need to get that?'

It's my phone, ringing for a third time.

'No, it's just my sister . . .'

Anyway, Joel is making his way through the plastic tables to join us.

'Charger duly located,' he tells Olly, holding out a shiny portable charger. 'It should give you a full charge. Any news on the patients, by the way?'

'No, but I'd better get back and see what's going on . . . Lib, would you mind picking up a coffee for Tash and a

269

cup of tea for Dad? I'll see you back in A&E reception, if that's OK?'

'No problem, Ol.'

'Thanks. And thanks again, mate,' he tells Joel, giving him a handshake and a slightly awkward, overly blokey clap on the back. 'For everything.'

I watch him, for a moment, as he heads back towards the main doors that lead outside.

As he reaches the doors, he glances back towards us. I think he's about to wave, but he just sort of . . . stares in our direction.

Then he turns away again, pushes the doors open and vanishes through them.

Which is when I look back up at Joel, slide my arms around his waist and reach up to kiss him.

And kiss him. And kiss him some more.

I feel, quite a lot, like a drowned woman who's desperately trying to fight her way back to the land of the living, with the kiss of life.

My phone rings, again . . . Cass, *again*.

I don't want to get into any of this right now.

I reach down and turn the ringer on to silent.

'I know,' murmurs Joel, as we pull apart for a moment. 'I know. This has all been an awful shock for you . . .'

But he doesn't know, of course, that this isn't the real reason I'm holding on to him for dear life, and some sort of comfort.

And then I start kissing Joel again, as if my life depends on it.

*

It's only when I'm almost back at my flat, at almost six in the morning, that I remember that I switched my phone off at all.

But by the time Nora arrived, and then I spent a couple of hours with her while she waited for Clara's scan, and then I sat with her mum for a bit so that her dad could pop home for a shower and some fresh clothes, turning my ringer back on somehow got forgotten.

So I'm pretty alarmed, when I get my phone out of my bag, to see that there are a grand total of seventeen missed calls from Cass, between the hours of eleven-ish and three a.m., and almost as many WhatsApp messages.

And none of the WhatsApp messages are mindless snooping about last night's sexathon.

OK, well, the smoke smell is really vile so I'm going to sleep at Mum's.

This is the *last* of the messages that she sent me, at 3.07 a.m.

What smoke smell?

I scroll back to the start of the messages to see what the hell has been happening at my flat – Elvira's flat – in my absence,

Oh my God, Libby, what the hell have you been spilling on your sofa?????

Why aren't you answering your phone?????

Chucked a load of water over it but it's not going out

Am outside now, Mum knocking on next-door's door to see if they have fire extinguisher

Answer your fucking PHONE!!!!!!!!

Just so you know, it was Mum's idea to light the bloody candle in the first place. And it was one of the ones YOU had lying around the flat, so you have to take some responsibility for this too. And still have no idea what the fuck was on the sofa. It went up like a bloody rocket. I could have been HORRIBLY BURNED

My heart is turning to ice as I put my key in the door with a shaking hand.

The sofa went up like a rocket? Set alight by one of Aunt Vanya's candles?

Having been made extra-flammable, of course, by Aunt Vanya's alcohol-laden holy water . . .

Snooty next-door neighbours did have fire extinguisher, Cass's message from 11.32 p.m. reads. *So we've put it out without needing to call fire brigade. Sofa's pretty wrecked though. But probably done you a favour, right?*

I reach the top of the stairs.

There, in the middle of the living room, is nothing but a charred shell where my magical Chesterfield used to be.

Chapter 13

Six months later

Obviously, it's all going to be incredibly romantic by the time it actually happens.

I mean, a winter wedding – practically a Christmas wedding, in fact – in the tiny chapel tucked away in the grounds of Joel's stunning country house in Sussex . . . the forecast for the day after tomorrow, the Big Day, is for a cold, sunny day, with possibly even a light dusting of snow . . .

But right now, my stress levels are roughly at DEFCON 1. Or DEFCON 5. Whichever the really dangerous, scary DEFCON is, the one where the end of the world is quite literally nigh, that's the one I'm talking about. And I never saw myself as capable of being any kind of Bridezilla. One of the whole points of having such a small wedding – just our immediate families and our closest friends, a grand total of twenty-seven people – was to try to keep typical wedding-faff to a bare minimum.

But somehow today, two days before the main event, and it just feels as if everything that can go wrong *is* going wrong.

273

And it's all, of course, to do with my family. I currently have Mum raging at me on the landline, while Cass has been sending me one of her near-constant streams of WhatsApp messages since six thirty this morning.

'I mean, all right, *technically* he's your father, but I still don't see why you'd even *want* him there on your wedding day,' Mum is saying, for what feels like the millionth time in the course of this fifteen-minute phone call. 'And as for inviting The New Wife . . .'

'Mum, look, I'm just trying to do the right thing, OK? And you've been divorced for over twenty-five years. And remarried yourself since then! There's not really any need to direct any aggression towards Phoebe. She was perfectly pleasant when I met her at her and Dad's wedding, and she sends me friendly Christmas and birthday cards.' (Which is more, way more, incidentally, than my dad ever did.)

'Exactly!' Mum shrieks. 'Trying to wheedle her way into your affections, now that you're marrying a billionaire!'

'No,' I say, firmly, as words like *pot* and *kettle* spring into my mind. 'She's done it since they were first married. And come on, Mum, it's not like you're going to have to interact with her in any major way! It's going to be a brief ceremony, some photos with the drinks reception, and then dinner. I haven't sat you anywhere near each other on the seating plan, so—'

'I should hope not! I mean, what is she – thirty-five, thirty-six? She's going to make me look ancient! Completely upstage the mother of the bride!'

'She's in her late forties, Mum,' I say, firmly, momentarily distracted as a text from Cass pings up on my iPhone.

Look, I haven't spent the whole of the last month getting up at six fucking a.m. and hauling my arse to the gym just for you to say you'd rather I didn't wear hot pants to your rehearsal dinner.

I start messaging her back: *Cass, you can wear hot pants every single day for the rest of your life. Can you JUST PLEASE grant me this one request, the night before my wedding? Joel's grandmother is going to be there, she's ninety-one and survived Treblinka, so I don't think it's too much to ask that you—*

'Well, I think you're being very insensitive, Libby,' Mum says. 'Have you thought about how this makes me feel?'

'Look,' I say, making a great effort to keep my temper, 'has it occurred to you, Mum, that I thought long and hard before even inviting Dad in the first place, and—'

OK, comes a new message from Cass, before I've even sent my reply to her last one, *am trying to be reasonable here. IF you are 100% PROMISING ME that you're going to put me RIGHT NEXT to Joel's best man tomorrow night, I will rethink hot pants and go plunge-front instead. After all, it's a sit-down do, right?*

I'm just wondering if it would make a truly terrible mess of one of the pristine walls in this gorgeous sitting room if I threw both my mobile and the landline, one after the other, smack against it, when the door opens and Joel sticks his head around.

'Free?' he mouths at me.

I nod, and get to my feet.

'I have to go, Mum. Joel's just landed.'

'Oh!' Mum's tone changes, immediately, from the whine I was so familiar with for most of my life, to the bright, breezy, happy-to-accommodate voice she tends to use with me now, and *always* uses whenever Joel is present. Or mentioned. 'Then you must go and look after him! Practise your wifely duties! After all,' she trills, 'it's only forty-eight hours until it's all signed and sealed!'

At which point, presumably, she can properly relax, knowing that – since there isn't going to be any pre-nup – she's still in with a chance of having the world's most comfortable retirement. As long as, you know, I don't go and do anything she'd regard as certifiably nuts, like not asking Joel for a single penny of his money, or anything.

In the event of this not working out, of course. Which is a pretty depressing thought she's obviously having, only forty-eight hours before we plight our troth. But then, she's never made a marriage work herself, so it goes without saying that she has a pretty cynical view of the whole enterprise, even if she's gamely hiding it behind traditional mother-of-the-bride strops.

'Send him my love!' she adds, gushingly. 'Tell him I'm looking forward to seeing him for the rehearsal dinner tomorrow!'

Which reminds me, as I hang up, that I need to send a quick reply to Cass.

Cass for the last time Joel's best man is not I repeat not also a billionaire

'Hey!' I greet Joel with a hug and a big kiss (possibly not up to scratch in terms of the wifely duties Mum's thinking about; I imagine Mum would rather I greeted him with a freshly mixed cocktail in one hand and my knickers in the other) and inhale the slight aroma of helicopter fuel from his jacket.

Yes, this is how ludicrous my life has become since I accepted Joel's proposal two months ago: I can now correctly identify the smell of helicopter fuel.

Though I still don't see exactly why he has to take the helicopter *quite* as often as he does, to be perfectly honest – I know we joked about it once, just before we first got together, but seriously, I'm sure Skype or some sort of cutting-edge video-conferencing would more than meet some of his needs – but I'm not about to say anything of the sort. Joel is surprisingly defensive about the helicopter. Actually, he's surprisingly defensive about quite a few of the things he claimed to shrug off as the silly trappings of his fabulous wealth. My suspicions about this were cemented only a couple of weeks ago, when I caught sight of the eleven-thousand-pound invoice for a new suit he'd had made to wear to the annual Christmas party he throws for his UK staff's children. I was only teasing him about it at first (I mean, eleven *thousand* pounds. For a suit. How can anyone say that with a straight face?), but he got so irritable in defending himself that we ended up having a Proper Row about the whole thing. Ridiculous of him, really, to get quite so defensive, seeing as – as he reminded me repeatedly during the course of the row – it's not like he doesn't give thousands of times that amount to clothe destitute kids through his Foundation every year – but defensive he certainly got. And not just defensive, but aggressive, because he somehow segued on to a whole thing about how I should start giving more serious thought to my own wardrobe needs, 'because people will expect certain things from you, Libby, now that you're marrying a man like me.'

We made up later, and he assured me that he adores the way I look, and that he wasn't – as I think most right-thinking women would instantly assume – telling me I needed to get on with losing a stone. The trouble being that this came along with an assurance that he's quite happy for me to spend whatever I like 'when' I need to kit myself out with some sumptuous gowns for 'all the events we're going to have lined up, once we're married'.

(By *events*, by the way, he doesn't just mean parties. When Joel does *an event*, it's something far more akin to what a celebrity might call a Personal Appearance. There's a lot of glad-handing, a lot of back-slapping, and – more often than not – he's called upon to make a speech. I know this because I've been to a couple already, and was frankly wildly under-equipped from the moment I got there. I mean, if only Joel had *warned* me, in advance, that I'd be expected to make scintillating small talk about Anglo-US trade agreements, and be able to hold my own in a champagne-fuelled debate about Nicaraguan politics, I'd have holed myself up with Wikipedia for three days before the event and genned up as much as humanly possible.)

278

'Hey,' he replies, now, kissing me back. 'You look more stressed than I do, and I've just got back from a particularly shouty two-hour board meeting in Luxembourg.'

'You know, just family stuff. Weddings don't bring out the best in my mum or my sister.'

'Oh, I wouldn't worry about that. I don't think weddings bring out the best in women, full stop.'

'Hey!' I glance at him, sharply, as he sits down on the nearby leather sofa, pulling out his ever-present iPad to start checking his emails (a procedure he conducts roughly once every two minutes, annoyingly; but then, I suppose you don't have the luxury of a few consecutive minutes of downtime when you're responsible for the employment of seventeen thousand people worldwide, and for countless more shareholders). 'That's not fair! To me, or to women in general!'

'OK, OK, sorry. I just remember my ex getting really stressed out right before our wedding, too. And I've already had my own mother on the phone for most of the ride back from Luxembourg, asking all kinds of crazy questions about what your mum is wearing for the rehearsal dinner, and what colour she's wearing at the wedding itself . . . I mean, this is a woman who spends her days administering emergency tetanus vaccinations to children in disaster zones, or organizing the hand-out of food parcels to famine victims! And now here she is trying to find out if she'll clash with the bride's mother if they both wear purple!'

Fleetingly – unimpressively – I wish that Joel didn't have to mention his mother's saintliness every *single* time he mentions her at all. But this is probably mostly just my own acute nerves talking: tomorrow evening, after all, his mother is going to meet my mother for the first time, and the comparison between them is going to be odious. Joel's mum all good deeds and selfless devotion to the wellbeing of others and Mum all . . . not.

Frankly I'll be quite happy if the two of them *do* both wear purple, as it'll give them one teeny-tiny thing in common for the course of the day.

Not to mention the fact that *I* haven't actually met Joel's mother in person yet, so my nerves really are sky-high on that front.

'Well, I'm not stressing out,' I say (OK, I fib), 'so you can leave your sweeping generalizations at the door. I've missed you,' I add, sinking down to squidge in beside him on the (not all that squidgy) sofa. 'You're here now, right? Until the wedding, I mean?'

'I'm right here.' He slides an arm around me and kisses the top of my head. 'I just have a conference call this afternoon for a few hours, and then a meeting with my lawyers tomorrow morning. But that'll be right here – in fact, we'll probably keep that pretty casual and have a round of golf at the same time – so I really am absolutely here now, Lib. You don't have to worry that I'm going to abandon you to my family and friends and staff in the run-up to our day.'

I'm secretly relieved, because this is a little bit what I've been worried about. Not so much Joel's friends, because they're not arriving until tomorrow evening, and not even so much his family (although the saintly mother and the

Treblinka-surviving grandmother are a pretty intimidating prospect), but, if I'm honest, the staff.

He has a *lot* of . . . people.

Here at Aldingbourne Abbey, Joel's – soon, I guess, to be *our* – house in Sussex, for example, are twenty-two full-time staff. Gardeners, groundsmen (these are, apparently, two different things), a housekeeper, a small army of cleaners . . . Then, of course, wherever Joel goes also go one of his three personal assistants: Savannah, Rachael and Rebecca. I'm never sure exactly what the difference between their precise jobs is and, to my shame, I'm often confused about the *actual* difference between Rachael and Rebecca themselves. There are also, thankfully only occasionally, personal security guards like Esti, who pop up when one of the death threats that Joel receives, on Twitter, roughly a hundred times a week (some people *really* don't like billionaires, apparently, not even when they donate millions to charity and champion the rights of oppressed women and children across the world) sounds less like the rantings of a faraway nutter and more like an actual plan to do him in when he least expects it. There are the foundation staff, who often travel wherever Joel goes like some kind of medieval court with its king, and who number anywhere between five and fifteen, depending on what event is coming up. There's usually a lawyer or two in the background, and these are generally accompanied by an exhausted-looking accountant or two . . .

Is it any wonder, really, that we both wanted to keep the wedding as small and simple as humanly possible? The thought of some sort of wedding-planning team lurking about the fringes of our lives, on top of *all the others*, is just too horrifying to contemplate.

It does give me one of my frequent twinges of sadness, thinking about it, that I can't ask Grace Kelly how she planned to handle the invasion of her life by a phalanx of Staff. She, no doubt, did a way, way better job of it than I do. I mean, I just find the whole thing so horribly embarrassing, and live in such fear of accidentally saying something that could be interpreted as remotely rude or high-handed that I probably come across as the meekest of church mice ever to have existed.

'Actually, talking of staff,' Joel goes on, 'Savannah was with me just now on the way back from Lux and she was wondering if she could have a few minutes with you today. Just for a general discussion about the next couple of days, and who needs to be where, when, and how she can help you out with anything you need.'

'Oh, that's really nice of her. Do you think she's willing to take on the job of managing my mum and sister for the duration of the festivities?'

Joel grins at me. 'I don't think I pay her quite enough for that. But she likes you, so she might be willing to cut you some sort of deal.'

It's pretty surprising to hear that Savannah likes me, because she has such a stern and forbidding aura that I've never imagined she cares for me any more than she'd care for a bout of head lice.

'Actually, if you and her do get to know each other a bit

better over the next few days, Lib, you might like to think about taking her on yourself.'

'Taking her on?' This sounds faintly alarming. Is he talking about some sort of competition of strength? Speed? Endurance? It doesn't really matter: Savannah would quite blatantly beat me, hands down, at all of them. 'What do you mean?'

'As your assistant.'

'For work? Er, I don't know if you remember, Joel, but I don't really need an assistant at the moment.'

This, by the way, is because Libby Goes To Hollywood is, in name, at least, no more. After all that drama with Elvira, Ben and I (relatively amicably) agreed to part ways several months ago, but the fact that I'd once foolishly given Ben sixty-five per cent of the company in return for his investment means he's effectively walked away with what was left of it. I could – according to Joel, *should* – probably have used the expensive lawyers Joel was offering me, on tap, to fight and win, but using Joel's money to fund the battle was the last thing I was ever going to do. But needs must I mean, I want to relaunch the business one day, with my own money – so I've swallowed my pride and taken on the consultancy work with Pressley/Waters. Which, I have to admit, is actually turning out really well. Yes, Joel was the one who engineered our first meeting, but they absolutely love the stuff I'm designing for them, and they've just suggested renewing our consultancy agreement for another year beyond the original six months. I'm learning a lot from them, too, and it's been lovely to get to know everyone else in the office . . . and really, the fact that there's not been so much of a sniff of a vintage-style bridal tiara in my life for months now is just refreshing beyond belief.

'Not for work!' Joel takes his eyes off his iPad and tucks a stray strand of hair behind my ear. 'What are you doing with your hair for the wedding, by the way?'

I'm slightly taken aback by the non sequitur. 'Bogdan's coming down this afternoon — he should be here any minute now, in fact — to try out some different up-dos. That's why I've grown it a bit for the last couple of months. Why?' I put my hand to it. 'Don't you like it longer?'

He shrugs. 'I don't love it. I mean, it's a tiny bit more . . . unkempt than it used to be, don't you think?'

'Well, no, actually, I've been quite enjoying—'

'Anyway, an up-do will look gorgeous on you . . . look, obviously you don't need an assistant for work, Lib, but don't you think you might want someone to help out with everything else?'

I actually giggle. Because he's joking, right?

'Joel, I can't so much as put down an empty glass of water around here without someone materializing out of the woodwork and spiriting it away! How much more help do you think I need?'

'Yes, Libby, I know.' His voice tightens, ever so slightly. 'I know you don't like all that.'

'It's not that I don't like it,' I say, carefully, because this has been a sore point between us before. 'It's just that you said you liked to come down to Aldingbourne to get away from it all . . . and we seem to keep bringing It All with us.'

'Well, I don't know if you've noticed, Libby, but we are putting on a wedding here the day after tomorrow! Besides, part of the reason I *can* get away from it all here is because everyone keeps the place running so smoothly. I mean, you and I have had some fantastic times here, haven't we, without having to worry about boring day-to-day crap?'

'Yes,' I say, drily. 'It's like having your own personal luxury hotel. But what were you just saying about me needing more help?'

'Admin!' Joel says. 'And the social side of things! Isn't it going to be a big weight off your mind if Sav can take over most of that?'

'Oh, you mean . . . um, events and stuff?'

'Yeah, events and stuff . . .' He smiles at me, wryly. 'And obviously you'll be wanting to take on a much bigger role within the foundation itself, Lib. That's going to take up an awful lot of your time.'

'Er . . . sorry, *am* I going to want to take on a bigger role within the foundation?'

'Why wouldn't you? There are all kinds of projects within it that are right up your street. Sav is the one who'll be able to tell you much more about it all, but I know we've just started up a project in Madagascar to bring about decent working conditions for the sapphire mining industry. And for a long time we've run a campaign to end child exploitation in Indian diamond mines . . . actually, you can discuss that with my mother when you meet her tomorrow, because that's really been her baby for the last three or four years.'

'And that's all amazing, Joel.' I've learnt, with Joel, to choose my words quite carefully. When he's a little bit stressed, as he obviously is with the wedding approaching, and tired, as he obviously is when he's been up at four a.m. to fly to Luxembourg, having only got back from New York at eleven last night, he tends to get tetchy if he feels he's being misunderstood. 'But I don't know the first thing about international development or anything. I wouldn't even know where to begin on stuff like that. And it's all a bit too serious for someone like me to just blunder in and screw it up!'

'So, you'd learn. That's sort of the point,' he adds, 'of asking Sav to take on the job of helping you. She's worked on this kind of thing for a while now. And I'd have thought,' he says, tucking another strand of hair behind my ear, 'that you'd be really pleased with the prospect of being a part of it all.'

'Well, sure. And I'm glad you think I can contribute. But I don't want to drag Sav away from all the important stuff she does for you just to help me tinker about on the sidelines.'

'Lib, I don't want you to tinker about on the sidelines!' He slides his arm off my shoulders, so that he can look at me properly. 'I'd really love it if you were hands-on with some of these projects! I mean, you have no idea of the satisfaction of really getting to grips with this stuff on the ground. And it's so much more impressive, for the donors, if my wife is out there in the field sometimes, putting their money where our mouths are, if you like. I mean, I can just see you,' he goes on, nuzzling into my neck, 'looking all sexy and dynamic in some khaki cut-offs and a Panama hat, meeting and greeting the workers at the Madagascan sapphire mine . . .'

I pull away, because he is actually turning me on here, and I think this is a conversation I'd better have while in full command of all my faculties. 'And while I'm only too happy to try to fulfil as many aspects as possible of this, er, fantasy of yours, how am I supposed to fit in these far-flung field trips around my own work?'

He stops nuzzling. 'What work?'

'Pressley/Waters?' I'm a tiny bit worried that the late night and early morning have given him some sort of amnesia. 'I'm working full time for them, now, remember?'

And very happily so, I should add, especially now that I've relaxed about the whole Joel connection. Because, as Caroline Pressley has impressed upon me almost every time we've ever spoken about it, she really *did* know about me, and admire my work, before Joel ever mentioned my name to her. Joel's mentioning my name simply brought me to the forefront of her mind, she assures me – and, having got to know her a little better these last few months, and seen how passionate she is about seeking out new talent, I believe her.

'Oh, that! Oh, well, sure, but that can come secondary to the foundation work, Lib, I don't think anyone there would mind.'

'I would.'

'OK, so if you're worried about how you'll fit it all in, then you can just tell them you don't want to renew the consultancy arrangement at the end of the six months.'

'Joel, I already renewed for another year . . . I told you about this on our Skype call the other week, when you were in Tokyo.'

'Oh, yeah, that rings a bell. But again, Libby, I don't think that's a problem, honestly. I mean, even if you cut it back to a day a week with them, and the rest of the time you can give to the foundation—'

There's a knock at the door and, in response to Joel's brisk *Come in*, Rachael pops her head round. Or it might be Rebecca. Either way, I didn't know *all* the assistants were here now.

'A Mr Bogdanovich and a Mr O'Hara have just arrived from the station,' she says. 'I don't know if they're wedding guests, or some of Libby's staff . . .?'

'They're guests,' I say. 'At least, Bogdan is . . .'

I'm not entirely sure what Mr O'Hara (I mean, Dillon) is doing, showing up with Bogdan like this. It's not like he's been banned from the wedding for being an ex, or anything – even though Lillian, Joel's ex-wife, is obviously not attending for that very reason, despite the fact she's flying into London tonight with Julia, who's going to be my flower girl – but given that we're keeping it all so small, there just wasn't room for him on the guest list. Not to mention the fact that I barely see or hear from him from one month to the next . . . and then of course, like the proverbial bad penny, here he is showing up unannounced right before my wedding.

'You'd better go, then,' Joel says, rather brusquely. He turns back to his iPad. 'I'll be in here if you need me.'

'But don't you want to come and say hello—?'

'I'm busy.'

Great. So now he's sulking, though whether it's about Dillon's unexpected arrival (which would be odd, because Joel's never proved himself to be the jealous type before) or my reaction to the brand-new job he's just unilaterally given me with his Foundation, I don't know.

And I can't ask, because Rachael/Rebecca is still here, and is now heading over to Joel, in fact, with her own ever-present iPad aloft, asking him if he's got five minutes to talk over the itinerary for Geneva, whatever the hell that is.

So I just make a bit of a passive-aggressive show of closing the door rather sharply behind me, swallowing the discomfort that's crept up inside me, and head out on to the driveway to greet Bogdan and Dillon.

They're getting out of the black Land Rover that one of the (myriad) groundsmen uses to do pick-ups from the station. My heart swells with excitement, and I actually have to choke back a sudden, out-of-the-blue sob as I hurry towards them. I mean, I only saw Bogdan two days ago, for crying out loud, when he accompanied me to the final fitting of my dress. I've no idea why it should feel like it's been more like two lifetimes.

'Hey, there, sweetheart.' Dillon grabs me first, and puts

both arms around me for a huge, rib-crushing hug. 'How's this for a surprise?'

'You didn't say you were coming.'

'That's the definition of a surprise, Fire Girl. I was hanging out with Bogdan yesterday, and he mentioned he'd be heading down here today, so I thought I'd pop down with him before it all gets really serious tomorrow.' Dillon grins down at me. He looks, thankfully, about a million times better than he did before he went back to rehab six months ago: leaner and fitter and less saggy beneath the eyes. 'You look skinny.'

'Is that a compliment or a veiled criticism?'

'I don't know yet.' He scrutinizes me more carefully. 'That depends whether you've lost weight to fit into some stunning wedding dress or because Mr Hotshot Billionaire wanted you to.'

'Dillon! For Christ's sake!' I glare at him. 'Joel's right inside! Can you try and be a bit less rude, do you think?'

'And am being able to inform you that Libby is shedding the pounds to be looking good in wedding dress,' Bogdan adds, walking round from the other side of the Range Rover. 'Am telling you, Dillon, you are never seeing anything so stunning as this dress. Is the Jenny Packham, is the bias-cut, which obviously is already helping Libby out in the department of the figure—'

'She doesn't need any help in the department of the figure,' Dillon says, loyally (and inaccurately). 'But I bet she does look stunning in it.'

'Am helping her to be choosing it,' Bogdan says. 'If she

is being left to own devices, she is no doubt walking down aisle in grey hoodie and tracksuit bottoms.'

'Thanks, Bogdan.'

'You are being most welcome. Now, can you be telling me where am to be putting bags . . .?' He stops, as he suddenly clocks the house in front of us.

Well, house is putting it a bit mildly.

Aldingbourne Abbey, the house that I thought (that Joel led me to believe) was going to be just some simple, even tumbledown, country bolthole, is in fact almost as impressive as Joel's Holland Park mansion. Except that, unlike the Holland Park mansion, Aldingbourne is actually gorgeous. It's late Georgian (with Edwardian additions, as either Rachael or Rebecca told me when I first came here four months ago; I think she has her eye on writing the official history of the house, after all the endless information she gave me) and built from pale grey stone. It has fourteen bedrooms within the main house itself, and about a dozen others scattered in the little cottages around the rest of the estate. It has sixteen acres of formal landscaped grounds, forty acres of 'parkland' and its own wood. It has a lake, big enough to fish in, if you happened to be so inclined. It has incredible views over the South Downs.

It is, truly, exquisite.

'Well,' says Bogdan, after a long moment, during which he and Dillon gaze up at the house from the huge, sweeping driveway, 'am guessing that we are being in the Kansas no more.'

'Too flaming right,' says Dillon. He sounds edgy, deliberately unimpressed. 'So this is the house of which you are to be . . . whatsit . . . chatelaine?'

'Oh, I don't think there's any need for words like that,' I say.

'All right, then. Mistress. Of all you survey.'

'Or those,' I say, fixing him with a look. (Though he is, much as I hate to admit it, closer to the truth than I'll ever admit to him. Another discussion that Joel and I have had quite recently – another somewhat *heated* discussion, in fact – was around Aldingbourne, and how he'd really like me to oversee the plans for some renovation work starting next spring. Along with Nicaraguan politics and a passing knowledge of international trade agreements, I'm expected, apparently, to be confident about taking charge of the plan to repair some damaged masonry and fit out a brand-new professional-level kitchen in a Grade I-listed Georgian mansion. I know Joel was only being nice, in his way, because he wants this place to feel like home, and he wants me to feel I can put my own stamp on it, but still. I've never so much as successfully renovated a crappy one-bedroom flat, so this is a scary prospect.) 'In fact, if you just came here to be aggressive—'

'Nothing of the sort. I'm really happy for you, sweetheart. As long as you're happy.'

'Very.' I detach his arm from over my shoulder. 'Anyway, let's get you settled, Bogdan, and then we can maybe all have a bit of a walk or something . . . I think you've probably been allocated a room in one of the cottages, but I'll just check that with Rachael . . . or, er, Rebecca . . .'

'Is no problem. But are you minding if am just popping into main house for one moment, Libby? Am just wanting to be checking something.'

'Oh . . . er . . . no, I suppose that's fine. But what is it you want to . . .'

Too late, because he's already set off in search of whatever it is he wants to 'check'.

I'm about to head off at some speed after him – because honestly, he's a liability, wandering around the place without a clue where he's going – when Dillon stops me.

'Mind if I have a smoke out here?'

'Oh, Dillon. You're not smoking again?'

'Well, it's that or wake up in the morning and do a line of coke and knock back three shots of vodka before I even hit the shower, so—'

'All right, all right. Have a bloody cigarette.'

'Thanks. It'll kill me a bit less quickly than the booze and the drugs.'

'That's heartening to hear.'

He takes a cigarette from his pocket, lights it and then leans against the Land Rover, exhaling.

'So. You're actually doing it.'

'I'm actually doing it.'

'Marriage. To this Joel character.'

'Yes, Dillon. Marriage. To this Joel character. Whom I happen to be in love with, by the way. Just in case you were about to mention . . . anything else.'

293

'Hey, I wasn't about to mention anything else. Or anyone.'

'Good.' I watch him blowing out a cloud of smoke into the chilly air for a moment, and then, even though I'm not planning to say anything I go on, 'Olly's getting married himself, actually.'

'Yeah, I remember you said, when you picked me up from rehab back in July. So that's still going ahead, then, yeah?'

'Of course it is! I mean, they haven't set a date or anything yet, as far as I know . . . I haven't had much chance to see Olly in the last few months, obviously. He goes up and down to Glasgow a lot, and then there's work . . . In fact, I think the last time I actually saw him was just before we got engaged.'

'Right . . . how did that even happen, by the way? I mean, no judgement, but isn't it quite *quick?*'

'It's on the quick side, Dillon, yes. But you know: when you know, you know.'

'You've just used the words *you know* three times in the same sentence.'

I ignore this, and instead rub, gently, the tip of my thumb against my engagement ring. (It's a very beautiful, incredibly tasteful – obviously – brilliant-cut diamond on a white-gold band; Joel had it cut and designed in London but the stone is from one of his foundation projects in Central Africa.)

'And as for how the engagement actually happened,' I go on, 'it was right here, in fact.'

'On the driveway?' He raises an eyebrow. 'Romantic.'

'By the bloody lake!' I snap at him. 'At sunset. So yes, it was pretty fucking romantic, as it happens. And if you've only come here to have a good old snark . . .'

'Is that what it looks like?'

'Yes, Dillon, that's what it looks like. And, to be fair, it's not entirely unreasonable of me to assume that when, let's face it, you have *form* for this.'

'Oh, you mean me slagging off Olly because I was jealous of him?'

'Yes.'

'Well, that was different.'

'Was it, now?'

'Yeah. I'm not jealous of Joel. I just think you're making a massive mistake marrying him.'

'Thank you, Dillon,' I say, icily. 'If I didn't have enough to deal with already, with my mum flipping out about my dad being invited, and Cass pretty much wanting to perform a lap dance for the best man, and Joel going into a strop because he thinks I should start running his foundation the moment we're married—'

'You know he got me my job on *Kings and Legends?*'

I stop. 'What?'

'Joel. Your fiancé. He got me the job on *Kings and Legends*. The show I'm filming over in Vancouver.'

'I don't understand.'

'I only found out about it a couple of weeks ago. I was chatting to the first AD – *not* getting involved with any more AD's girlfriends these days, I hasten to add – and he let slip something about the casting director getting a call from the head of the production company about me when the role came up . . . It was a bit odd, so I went and looked into the production company. Stellar Media. And their main investor is Jansen-Perreira Limited.'

My head is spinning a bit here, with all the links and associations and, I have to be honest, the slight air of Conspiracy Theory that Dillon is exuding about the whole thing.

'Sorry, Dillon, you're saying that Joel must have . . . what? Called the head of the production company and told him to give you a job on their new show?'

'Yeah, that's what I'm saying.'

'And even if that's true . . . is there something so horribly *sinister* about that?'

'Well, I don't know. You tell me.'

'I'd love to, Dillon, but . . . honestly, I don't know what you're talking about.'

'All right. I'll say it.' His dark eyes fix themselves on to mine. 'I think he got me out of the way.'

I don't say anything for a moment. Then I say, in a quiet but firm voice, 'Dillon. As I so often say to my mother. Not everything is about you, you know.'

'That's not the way I mean it!' He looks frustrated, and takes a deep drag on his cigarette. 'It's the timing of it, Lib. He met me, in a bit of a state, outside your flat. Less than forty-eight hours later, my agent gets this totally out-of-the-blue call from the casting director saying she wants me to come to Canada to audition. This is a casting director who hates my guts, by the way, because I once kept her waiting two hours to audition me for another show after I missed my flight home from Ibiza—'

'Oh, for the love of God!' I actually shout. 'And you wonder why anybody might think, out of the goodness of their heart, that maybe giving you a bit of a helping hand might be an act of kindness? As opposed to the Crime of the Century . . .'

I stop talking, because a white van is suddenly pulling up on to the sweep of the gravelled driveway.

It's a particularly scruffy-looking white van, billowing a cloud of pewter-coloured smoke out of its exhaust pipe, which is probably why the front door of the house suddenly opens wide and – where the hell do they *come from?* – Esti and another of her lethal-looking security colleagues hurry out.

The van stops, a short distance away from the black Land Rover, and the passenger door opens, letting out a dark-haired man in an Adidas tracksuit and a faintly sinister pair of sunglasses.

I have to be honest, the oddness is obviously even getting to cynical Dillon, because he puts his arm over my shoulders again and draws me slightly backwards, behind the Land Rover, as Esti marches up to them.

'Can I help you?' she asks, in a tone of voice that suggests she's merely a split second away from hurling him to the ground and cutting off his air supply with one swift Krav Maga move.

'I am here for Bogdan.'

'Bogdan?'

'Yes. Bogdan, Son of Bogdan. He is arranging for us to make this delivery—'

'Delivery of?' Esti snaps, a little closer to that hurling manoeuvre.

'Of sofa.'

'Sofa?'

'Yes. Sofa. From Chester.'

Bogdan himself now appears from the house, with Joel – looking utterly bewildered – at a bit of a distance behind him. He heads down the steps and starts speaking in rapid-fire Moldovan to the Adidas guy, before the latter lumbers round to the rear of the van and starts to open the back doors.

'What's going on out here?' Joel asks, heading down the steps himself. 'Bogdan was just in the sitting room . . . er . . . measuring up . . .'

I can already see what Adidas guy is starting, with the help of another Moldovan who's just got out from the driver's side, to pull out of the back of the dodgy old van.

It's the Chesterfield.

'Is wedding present to you, Libby,' Bogdan says, his face breaking into a small, slightly nervous smile for pretty much the first time since I've known him. 'Am getting it fixed after fire. Some of frame is able to be saved. Some of padding also rest is new. Including upholstery. Is not quite same fabric as before,' he adds, as more of the Chesterfield emerges from the van, showing itself to be covered in chintzy *pink* roses rather than chintzy *apricot* ones. 'But is same sofa. In essence. If you are getting what am meaning.'

Wordlessly, I go to Bogdan. I lean my head on his chest. And I begin to cry.

'Hear, hear,' he says, softly, patting my back and meaning, I assume, *there, there*. 'Am glad this is making you happy.'

Because only someone with a soul like Bogdan's would realize that, despite my tears, I'm happy.

I mean, it's not *just* happiness, obviously. There are some nerves mingled in. A general sense of high emotion, what with the wedding, and Mum, and Cass, and Joel, and *Dillon* . . .

But I'm so, so happy to see the Chesterfield again – to even have the whisper of a glimmer of a hope that I might get its magic back – that this is mostly what my tears are about.

'Well, this is all very kind of you, Bogdan, but I honestly don't know where it's going to go in the main sitting room,' Joel is saying, sounding faintly alarmed, as the two random Moldovans start to lug the frankly atrocious-looking lump of furniture towards the house. 'Libby, darling, can you come and sort this out, please? It'll have to go in one of the cottages, or upstairs in the attic until we can decide a better place for it . . .'

'The attic is fine,' I say, firmly, wiping my tears away with the back of my sleeve, and heading for the house myself. 'Come on. I'll show you the way up. I'll be back out in a couple of minutes, Dillon,' I add. 'Unless you want to come in for a cup of tea?'

'No, no. I'm grand out here, sweetheart.' Dillon drops his cigarette to the gravel and stubs it out with his heel.

'Good to see you again, Joel,' he adds, pleasantly. 'And many congratulations on the upcoming nuptials.'

'Thanks, Dillon. And it's great to see you again, too.' Joel is still looking fairly pissed-off about, well, everything, but his excellent manners won't permit a hint of incivility. 'Won't you come in for a cup of tea?'

'I'm all right, mate, actually. Mind if I have a bit of a stroll about? This is a gorgeous place you've got here.'

Without waiting for an answer, he wanders off across the (very) well-tended lawn, towards the lake.

Chapter 14

Even though Rachael/Rebecca have both offered, very kindly, to arrange for my dress to be brought down to Aldingbourne for me, I've decided to go up to London this morning and collect it myself.

I mean, it's not like there's a huge amount I can actually be doing back at the house today. The assistants have it all well delegated and under control, from the big pre-wedding clean of the little chapel beside the lake, to the setting-up of the tables for the rehearsal dinner in the big dining room. Flowers were arriving for this evening's dinner as I set out for the station, and I could see some of the chefs who have been drafted in for the occasion heading out to the walled garden to pick some of the biodynamic vegetables and herbs that are grown there.

Honestly, it's better for me to be out of the way of all this fuss. And it'll keep my nerves in check, to actually go and Do Something today.

And anyway, it's not like there's any particularly good reason for me to stay at the house. Neither Mum nor Cass, who admittedly might need some policing, are arriving until late afternoon. Bogdan is happily ensconced in his little cottage on the estate, ordering, courtesy of Joel, old movies on iTunes to watch on the large TV in there (at least, I hope to God that's what he's ordering). In addition, I suspect, he's going to end up wandering up to the main house a little later on, to see if he can track down the hot pastry chef he spotted on the house tour I gave him yesterday. And, trust me, you never want to get in the way of Bogdan and a hot pastry chef.

And Joel . . . well, Joel has his lawyers' meeting-slash-golf-day today.

And he's still in a bit of a grump about the whole sofa thing, anyway.

Which, I should say, doesn't actually seem to be working in the way it used to. It doesn't change a thing about the loveliness of Bogdan getting it all done up for me. But sadly – though I haven't told him this yet – the refurb hasn't brought the magic back.

I went up to the attic as soon as I could, after supper last night, and just . . . sat there for a bit. More than a bit. I even dropped off up there, actually. The new stuffing in the sofa has made it much more comfortable, and the fact it no longer smells of damp dog (well, perhaps only a very little bit, from somewhere deep, deep down inside the original body) does make it easier to spend time close up to it. But even the fact that I was up there for a good couple of hours in the end didn't have any effect. There wasn't even a faint whiff of Grace's perfume.

There was nobody but me. And my thoughts.

Which are probably no more than the usual thoughts a bride-to-be has, the penultimate night before her wedding. Butterflies. Apprehension. A very, very occasional twinge of anxiety, even, that you're definitely, one hundred per cent, doing the right thing.

It would just have been nice to have had Grace there on the sofa with me. That's all.

I mean, she was the one who really spurred me on with Joel. She was the one who hammered home the point about Moving On and about Seizing The Day, and about the virtue of all that shoulders-back, nose-to-the-grindstone Kelly grit that had got her an entire kingdom at her feet.

It would have been really great, now I am where I am, to have the chance to tell her. Not that she'd have paid the slightest attention to the details, probably; only inasmuch as she decided to use it as yet another message from her subconscious. But still. It would have been nice to have her around to talk to.

But I can probably have a bit of a butterflies-calming talk with Nora today, to be fair, because she's meeting me in town to pick up my dress. It was her suggestion, because – according to her, not me – she's been a 'crap bridesmaid', what with being so far away in Glasgow all the time, and having work, and Clara, and – a fabulous surprise, the last time we spoke – another baby, already ten weeks in, cooking away nicely inside her.

I can't wait to see her. I literally can't wait. It will probably kick off the really exciting feeling, that my wedding is happening tomorrow, rather than all the nerve-wracking, stress-inducing stuff. We're meeting at The Wolseley on Piccadilly for a late brunch and mimosas – well, orange juice for Nora, obviously – before we head up to Jenny Packham, on super-posh Mount Street, for my dress.

I'm just getting off the tube at Green Park when my phone rings.

Oh, dear God. Mum, again.

I answer, because the knowledge that five minutes from now, I'll be sipping (or possibly downing) my first mimosa, in Nora's soothing company, makes the prospect of Mum's latest whinge-fest more bearable.

'Mum, hi.'

'Darling! Great news!'

'Oh!' I'm pleasantly surprised to hear this; no whinge-fest, it appears. 'What?'

'I've decided to have a complete makeover before tomorrow!'

'Er . . . when you say *complete* . . .?'

'Well, for starters, I totally rethought the frumpy old Jacques Vert thing I was planning to wear. So I popped to Selfridges as soon as they opened this morning, and treated myself to this *fabulous* little Oscar de la Renta number instead . . .'

'Wow. Mum, that's got to have been expensive.'

'Darling, how often does a daughter of mine get married? Oh, that reminds me, can you *please* do your best to introduce Cass to all Joel's friends this weekend? Honestly, if I have to listen to her moan, one more time, about the fact that she'll probably never have a billionaire of her own to keep her warm at night—'

'She's already got me on the case, Mum. But really—'

'Anyway, I got this lovely blush-pink dress, and fabulous jacket, and then obviously I had to get some new shoes to go with them – nude L.K.Bennett pumps, because the sales-girl reminded me that they're the kind all the Middleton women wear – and now I'm literally right here in a chair at Nicky Clarke! They've given me a fabulous colour, and now they're just finishing up my cut. They squeezed me in at the last minute, darling, wasn't that nice of them? Of course, it probably helped that I just *happened* to drop Joel's name when I called—'

'Mum,' I say, sharply. 'Please. Don't do that.'

'Of course, darling,' she says, solemnly, though I'm not in the least convinced that this is the last time she'll pull this schtick. 'Anyway, I just wanted to let you know, because I know you're collecting your dress just round the corner from the salon some time today . . .'

'Yes. I'll drop by if I have the time, Mum. But otherwise, you and Cass will be on the five o'clock train from St Pancras, right?'

'I will. Looking like a new woman! This is going to give that Phoebe a run for her money!'

'Mum . . .'

'Only joking, darling!' she trills, unconvincingly. 'Bye!'

Whinge-fest or not, I still think I need that mimosa.

I push open The Wolseley's glass door and step into the hubbub inside, give my name to the man on the desk and . . .

Oh.

Olly is sitting at the table.

305

For a moment, I sort of wonder if he's maybe ended up here by pure coincidence – a nice romantic lunch with Tash, perhaps, before they get the train down to Sussex themselves later this afternoon – but as he gets up to greet me, I realize that it's obviously not a coincidence: he'll have found out from Nora that she and I were due to meet here.

'Libby.' His face is breaking into a huge smile. He looks incredibly handsome, albeit a little more formal than I'm used to seeing him, in a smart shirt and with his usually messy hair tamed for once. 'How fantastic to see you.'

'You, too!' I hug him, tightly, and refuse to inhale his lovely, familiar scent as I do so. We hold onto each other for rather longer than I think either of us intended, though. 'I mean,' I go on, reluctantly pulling myself away, 'it's a bit of a surprise . . .'

'Yeah, sorry about that! Nora mentioned she was meeting you here – oh, she's probably running late, by the way; Mum just called me ten minutes ago and mentioned that she'd only just left theirs . . .'

The closeness of the Walker family never ceases to amaze me, even twenty years after first meeting them all. At times it's made me envious, at times I find it a tad claustrophobic, and then at times like now, when Nora and Olly and their respective partners, *and* Clara, *and* Nora and Olly's mum and dad are all getting the show on the road ready to come down to Sussex for my wedding, I'm just profoundly grateful that I've got them all in my life.

'Well, even better that you're here, then,' I say, sitting down in the booth opposite him. It's such a tonic to see him, such a refreshing gasp of sweet, clean air, that I don't even feel the awkwardness or discomfort of our most recent meetings. 'You can keep me company in a mimosa!'

'I shouldn't. I do have to get back to the restaurant for the end of lunch service.' He looks torn, thinking about this for a moment. 'Though. . . well, I guess if I text Jorge and tell him I'll be late. . .'

'Exactly! You're the boss.'

'That I am.' He grins at me, takes out his phone and sends the text. 'Come on, then, Liberty. Let's drink!'

Him calling me Liberty – something he never ever calls me – sends a bit of a shiver down my spine for some reason. 'Wow,' I say, trying to hide the fact that he's suddenly making me feel all heart-flippy. 'We haven't had the chance to sit across a table from each other since . . . well, if you don't count that awful night at the hospital, I guess it was all the way back at the bistro. When we drank all that champagne, and . . . thought we'd found the Mystery Cheese.'

'God, Lib, that seems ages ago.'

'It does.'

'A different world.'

'Tell me about it,' I say.

'Though it reminds me, by the way – amazing news. I think I might have found a new lead on the Mystery Cheese.'

'Oh?'

'Yeah, I meant to text you about it, but . . . well, you know how busy things get. But a former chef mate of mine has just started trading at Bermondsey Market, importing French cheese and wine . . . I went over there to check it all out a few weeks ago, and we got chatting about cheese, you know, as you do.'

'As you do.'

'And I told him all about the Mystery Cheese – well, I told him a *bit* about it. I didn't actually say that you and I have been trying to hunt the thing down for over a decade, obviously – and he said he has a few ideas about what it might be. Anyway, he called me yesterday and told me he's just had a big delivery and that I ought to go and have a little look some time soon. Obviously you're just about to go away on honeymoon, but – I don't know – maybe when you're back . . .'

'Olly, I'd love to!' I grab his hand. 'I mean, we're only away for a week, until just after Christmas . . . Joel couldn't take any more time. So I'll be around.'

'OK, great.'

'Just promise me you'll ask me, OK?'

'OK.' He doesn't quite meet my eye. 'I promise I'll ask.'

'I mean, please, Ol, don't. . . don't just decide I must be too busy.'

'No, no. I wouldn't do that. But, you know, if you *are* too busy, that's OK, too. I can go and check it out myself.'

'But I won't be. Too busy. No matter what.'

'Well. OK. That's great to hear!'

'Yes. It's a date!'

A slightly strained silence falls between us, during which I grab a passing waiter, order a couple of mimosas, and then go on, non-sequiturially, 'So! How's Tash? Is she on her way down from Glasgow now, or did she come down last night?'

'Oh, she was here late last night.'

'Great! I'm looking forward to seeing her!'

'Yeah . . . about that, Lib. I don't think . . . I don't think we're going to be able to come.'

'Sorry?'

'To the wedding. I don't think Tash and I can make it.'

'You . . . sorry?' I repeat, dumbly. 'I don't get it.'

'I mean, I know it's horribly late notice, and I wouldn't be doing this if we had a choice. Her dad's having emergency hernia surgery tomorrow morning.'

'I . . . I mean, that's obviously bad news . . . But I don't see . . .'

'Well, these things can be a bit touch-and-go.'

'Hernia surgeries? Really?'

'Oh, yes! Not fatal, or anything – at least, we hope not – but he's seventy-two, and he's not been in the best of health for a while, and Tash really wants to be there to support her mum . . .'

'Right. I get that.' I clear my throat. 'But do *you* need to be there, too?'

'I kind of do.' He shifts a little bit in his seat. 'I know it sounds unnecessary, but . . . well, after she was so amazing when Mum and Clara had their accident, I don't want to just leave her and her mum to get on with it alone. I mean, Tash is an only child, and her mum gets a bit stressed out about these things . . .'

'But this is my *wedding*, Olly.' I stare at him. 'Can you not even just dash up to Durham afterwards? The ceremony is at two thirty, so you could miss the reception and probably still get up there by late evening . . . oh! I could even see if Joel would be able to let you use the helicopter . . .'

'Libby, come on!' Olly looks more desperate than ever. 'I'm not going to get your fiancé to fly me around the country.'

'He wouldn't mind!'

'But I would! Look, this is utterly shit timing, I recognize that. But I've looked into all the train times, and even if I only came to the ceremony, I wouldn't be able to get up to Durham until way too late to be any practical use to Tash and her mum. And they need me, Lib, they really do.'

'*I* need you,' I say, helplessly. And then, immediately, feel as if I'm sounding like the worst Bridezilla imaginable. 'Look, I get that Tash's dad is old and unwell, and I get that they're worried, but he'll be in a great hospital, and Tash and her mum can get by together just for a day, surely, and . . .'

'Please!' Olly says. He sounds anguished. 'Please, just . . . it's shit timing. And I'm so, so sorry. But I have to be there. There's nothing else I can do.'

I sit back in my chair. 'OK,' I say. I feel, oddly, completely emotionless. Bleached-out, almost. 'It's OK. It's just shit timing. As you say.'

'Look, is there anyone else you can grab at the last minute, to take our places? I mean, I know you're keeping it small, and I don't want our absence to leave a gaping hole in your seating plan . . .'

'The seating plan? Oh, don't worry, Ol. That's the least of my worries.'

'What do you mean?'

310

'Well, not having you there is a bit of a gaping hole,' I say. 'Irrespective of the seating plan.'

'Oh. I know.' He stares, at the table. 'But I'll be there in spirit! I promise you that. And . . . I don't know, I assume there's going to be a video . . . Mum and Dad are coming armed with their ancient camcorder, I warn you, even if there's not going to be a professional there!'

'That's nice.' I want, I desperately want, to shake off this horrible, flat sensation. 'I'm looking forward to seeing them.'

'Don't be like that,' he croaks. 'Please.'

'I'm not being like anything, Ol! Of course I'm happy your parents are coming. It's just . . . they're not . . . you.'

What I can't say to him – what I can't really even say to myself, actually, given how silly it sounds, and given that I'm getting married to Joel twenty-four hours from now – is that I've sort of had this silly fantasy a few times recently. More than silly. Ridiculous. A fantasy about the moment in the wedding where the vicar asks if anyone knows any lawful impediment that would prevent the couple getting married.

I mean, obviously I haven't *really* been hoping that Olly would get to his feet and cry out, 'Yes! I know an impediment! Stop this wedding at once! I'm hopelessly in love with her!'

I said, already, that I know it's ridiculous.

But obviously the fact that he's not coming, now, turns a ridiculous fantasy into a non-existent one.

Our mimosas are arriving, thank God, to interrupt this awkwardness.

As soon as the waiter puts them on the table and leaves, both of us pick up our glasses and pretty much down the entire lot in one gulp.

'So!' Olly says, after a moment. 'You're all . . . ah . . . excited about tomorrow? Everything going smoothly? No last-minute hiccups?'

I desperately want to get things back on an even keel between us, and he obviously does too, so I try to shake off my sense of disappointment – OK, my sense of crushing despair, and say, chirpily, 'Well, unless you count every single thing my mum and sister are doing . . .'

'Got it.' He finishes the dregs of his mimosa. 'God, Libby,' he suddenly says. 'Who'd have thought, nearly twenty years ago, that one day we'd be sitting here together like this . . . you about to get married, me engaged . . .'

'You're right. I'd never have thought it.' I polish off my own drink. 'But here we are!'

'Here, indeed, we are.'

We both fall silent again.

I think I have to say something. I mean, Say Something.

Because I just can't live with this horrible feeling. This feeling that everything is. . . *wrong*. It's like agitation mixed with frustration mixed with fear. It's like the onset of the worst migraine you've ever had, combined with imminent gastric flu. I feel uncomfortable, and stressed, and more than a little panic-stricken, and it's no way to live. It's no way to live for a day, or a week, let alone for the rest of your days on this planet.

It's why, without yet knowing exactly what the Something I'm going to Say is, I blurt, 'Olly, I just . . . I really, really wish you could come.'

No. No, that wasn't the right Something. I need to go further, be bolder . . .

'I know. Me too.' Olly sounds faintly strangled now, as if there might have been an insect in his drink and he's only just realized he swallowed it. He clears his throat, noisily. 'But I have to do the right thing by Tash, Libby, I know you understand that . . . Should you get that?'

'What?'

'The call. It might be something important . . . wedding-related . . .?'

I glance down at my ringing phone. It's Mum.

'OK, one second,' I sigh, picking up the phone. 'Mum? Is it really important?'

There's no reply. Or rather, there's no *words* of reply. There's just a stifled sob.

'Mum?'

'Yes, it's me . . . oh, Libby, I've done something ever so stupid.'

Given that she's at the hairdresser, my mind boggles for a moment. Has she let them give her a perm? A Hoxton fin? A *mohawk?*

'It was all the shopping this morning that did it,' she goes on. 'I suppose it was a bit silly to go and put all that stuff on my debit card, but I didn't even think about going over the limit . . . and now I'm trying to pay at the hair-dresser's, and it's all added up to more than I thought . . .'

'How much?'

'Seven hundred and thirty.'

'*Pounds?*'

Her silence on the other end of the line confirms this.

'How on earth . . .?'

'Well, I had the colour, obviously, and they gave me a lovely conditioning treatment beforehand, and then the cut itself was two hundred and ten, because it was with the most senior stylist . . . well, apart from Nicky himself, of course . . . Anyway, my card's been rejected,' she goes on, in a very small voice, 'and I'm just hoping, darling, that you might be able to come over and help.'

'Mum, my card's going to get rejected too, if I try and put seven hundred and thirty quid on it!'

'But, darling,' she lowers her voice, 'you're about to marry, well, a very rich man.'

'Yes, and I still have my own bank account,' I say, hotly. 'With not very much in it!'

Except, of course, that I do have one of Joel's credit cards in my wallet right now, for final payment on the Jenny Packham dress.

'I just feel so stupid,' Mum is saying, in a smaller, quieter voice than ever; a smaller, quieter voice than I've ever heard her use before. 'This whole thing was stupid. I got myself into a sort of frenzy, really, because I didn't want your father to see me looking old and worn-out. It's been twenty-five years since I last saw him, and I suppose I just wanted to look like I used to back then. As if he was ever going to realize what a mistake he made, dumping me!'

'It's all right, Mum.' I'm already getting to my feet. 'Stay there, and I'll come and bail you out, OK?'

'Really?' The relief in her voice is palpable. 'You can do that?'

'Yes, I can do that. Temporarily, I mean. You'll still have to pay me – or rather, Joel – back.'

'Of course! Honestly, Libby, what do you take me for? I know I may sometimes come across as a bit bedazzled by all the wealth you're marrying into, but—'

'I'll be there in ten minutes,' I interrupt her. 'Bye.'

I get to my feet, pushing back the chair and pushing aside, as I do so, my moment of madness before the call came from Mum. I mean, obviously I can't Say Something. What the hell was I thinking? The wedding is tomorrow. The time for Saying Something has gone.

'Sorry, Ol,' I mumble, 'I just need to dash . . .'

'Everything OK with your mum?'

'Yes. I mean, if you don't count her being bloody silly.'

Though even as I say this, I realize it's a bit harsh on Mum. For all her maternal crimes – and they're myriad, don't get me wrong – I guess wanting to look and feel her best at my wedding isn't the worst one. And as for looking her best in front of Dad, after a gap of twenty-five years . . . I get that. How you can still need to matter to someone you once loved, even after all that time.

'I'd better go,' I tell him. 'Can you wait here for Nora, and let her know I'll be back in a few minutes?'

'Yes. And then I'll leave you two girls to it,' he says, rather flatly.

'And look . . . if anything changes. With Tash's dad, I mean . . .'

'Of course.'

He leans down and places a soft kiss on my cheek.

And then I go up on tiptoe and kiss his cheek, in return.

And then he puts his arms around me, and I put my arms around him, and despite the fact we're slap in the middle of a busy, bustling restaurant, and that people must be staring, and that my mum is waiting for me to come and bail her out with Joel's credit card, we just hold on to each other.

I'd quite like the world to stop turning right now, please. Anything to make this moment last longer.

But the world won't stop turning and, even if it did, the waiting staff at The Wolseley probably wouldn't stop with it, because one of the waitresses is just asking us if we could possibly just step sideways so we can let her get to the nearby table . . .

'You know,' Olly says, rather thickly, as we pull apart, 'you'll be having such a wonderful day tomorrow, Lib, that you won't notice who's there and who's not! You'll only have eyes for Joel.'

I don't have anything I can say to this and, even if I did, I'm not sure I'd be able to form the words anyway. So I just nod, and give Olly's arm a final squeeze, and head for the doors without looking back again.

Chapter 15

It's been such a roller coaster of a day that I forget, until I'm only about ten minutes away from arriving at Barham Station, that I'm supposed to call the house to let someone know I'm arriving, so they can send one of the cars to meet me.

Assuming it'll be either Sav, Rachael or Rebecca who picks up the phone, I'm pretty taken aback when I don't recognize the voice at the other end of the house line.

'Hello, can I help you?'

'Oh, er . . . this is Libby . . . sorry, who am I talking to?'

'Barbara.' There's the briefest of pauses before she goes on. 'Your future mother-in-law.'

'Oh, God!' Oh, *God*. 'Barbara, I'm so sorry, I didn't recognize your voice . . .'

'That's all right. I'm probably not even supposed to be picking up this phone, but I like to be useful.'

'OK, but . . . well, I'll probably just try one of the assistant's mobiles, instead . . . I just need to get one of them to send a car out to the station to pick me up.'

'Oh, I can do that.'

'No, no, Barbara, I don't want to trouble you. You've better things to do, I'm sure, than tracking down one of the assistants.'

'No, I meant I'll come and pick you up. What time train are you on?'

What? No. *No.*

'No!' I actually yelp, out loud, before realizing that this is truly one of the rudest things I could possibly have said to Barbara. Who, after all, won't realize that I'm a bundle of nerves about meeting her, and that my plan — to get myself groomed to the hilt and then knock back at least one double vodka before this evening's big face-to-face meeting — is going to be completely stymied by having to meet her as I get off a train, sober, in ten minutes' time. 'What I mean to say, Barbara is—'

'Just tell me your train time, and I'll be there.'

'I get in about ten minutes from now, but—'

She lets out a brisk *tut*. 'You do like to swing by the seat of your pants, don't you? All right, I'll be there then.'

And she hangs up.

For at least seven of those eight minutes, I just sit frozen in my hard, slightly grimy seat, staring at the Sussex countryside passing by, unable to think clearly for sheer panic.

With less than three minutes to go, the 'fight' part of my flight or fight response finally kicks in, and I have the wherewithal to drag a comb through my hair, scrabble through my bag to find a slightly stubby lipstick, and then dart to the horrible train loo to check out my reflection in the mirror there.

For someone who's getting married a little less than twenty-four hours from now, I could look better. I look tired, mostly, and a bit gaunt, and combing my hair hasn't helped much (maybe Joel was right about the longer hair not suiting me) and then there's the fact that I've spent quite a bit of the journey from Victoria crying. . .

I know it's not as if I've said goodbye to Olly for ever, or anything. But I can't seem to help the fact that it feels that way.

Not the time to think about that now, though, when the train is slowing down for Barham Station and, any moment now, I'll be stepping off the train to meet Barbara in person for the very first time.

And I can see her, actually, before the train has even ground to a complete halt: the tall, incredibly striking woman standing perilously close to the edge of the plat-form, talking on her mobile.

I gather my things – handbag, Jenny Packham garment bag, courage – and step off the train.

She gets off her phone as soon as she sees me, and strides purposefully towards me.

'Libby.' She kisses me on both cheeks. 'Good to finally meet you. Come on,' she adds, already striding off in the direction of the car park. 'It's freezing, and the car will be warm.'

It's a bit of a struggle to keep up, what with the fact that she's so tall and long-legged, and I'm carrying all my stuff, but I do. Mostly so that I can sneak glances at her as we hurry along. Though dusk is already gathering, it's easy to see how beautiful she is in person: raven hair pulled back in a sleek ponytail, Joel's blue eyes and cheekbones, which are even more razor-sharp this close up than they were on the Skype call when I first 'met' her. She's wearing what looks like Joel's waxed jacket over jeans and expensive-looking black knee boots, and she looks a good decade or so younger than (I think) she really is, which is in her mid-sixties.

'It's so good of you to come all the way out to collect me, Barbara,' I say. 'Especially when you must have only just got to Aldingbourne yourself.'

'Oh, we got in about two hours ago. My mother is having a nap back at the house, but I was already climbing the walls with boredom, waiting for everything to get going. Joel has gone to collect Julia from Gatwick, as I'm sure you know, so I haven't even had the chance to have a proper catch-up with my son. And frankly,' she adds, in a voice that – despite its light Slovakian accent – somehow reminds me of Grace Kelly's – 'I couldn't spend another minute being fussed and faffed over by any of those assistants. Lovely girls, but *really*, they're just too much. Here we are. Hop in.'

OK, well, admittedly it's only been about forty-five seconds since we met, but it's going better than I thought so far, if only because I'm secretly gladdened to hear that Barbara finds Sav, Rachael and Rebecca as overwhelming as I do. So I put my garment bag on the back seat and then jump into the black Range Rover with a little more of a spring in my step than I'd imagined I might have, fastening my seatbelt before Barbara pulls off.

'So!' she says, with the air of someone starting an Important Conversation. 'I finally get to meet my new daughter-in-law!'

'Yes, it's wonderful. Sorry it's been so hard to meet up before now, but you know what Joel's schedule is like, and—'

'Oh, don't worry. I know my son! And I have a hectic schedule myself.' She snaps her fingers a few times, as if to demonstrate the speed with which she gads about the world. 'Here, there and everywhere, recently. But it's an exciting time for the foundation. We're taking on several new projects next year. You and I must sit down together, in fact, after the honeymoon, and earmark the things you're really interested in. You're a gemologist, right?'

'Er – no, I'm a jewellery designer. I mean, I do work with gemstones, obviously, but I couldn't say I know all that much about—'

'Perfect! You can come out to Afghanistan with me in February to take a look at the project we're starting up out there. I don't know if you've ever worked with lapis lazuli, but there are a great deal of human rights concerns about the workers in the mines, and we're very keen to shine the spotlight on child labour in the—'

'Afghanistan?'

'Yes.' She glances over at me, taking her bright blue eyes off the road for rather longer than feels comfortable. 'What's the problem with that?'

'Er . . . well, I'm not all that up to date on *very* recent events over there, but isn't it a bit . . . um . . .' I quail, rather, under her intent gaze. 'Unsafe?'

She frowns. 'Badakhshan is one of the most stable regions in Afghanistan.'

'I'm sure, but . . .' I let out a brief, nervous laugh. (And wonder how it is that we're planning an itinerary for a trip to Afghanistan, only moments after meeting, rather than discussing, oh, I don't know, the usual sorts of things daughter-in-laws might discuss with their mothers-in-law the day before their wedding. I mean, I'm no bridezilla, but wouldn't most people be engaging in chit-chat about the flowers and the canapés instead?) '. . . it's still . . . er . . . Afghanistan.'

'I don't understand. Are you planning on being pregnant already by then, or something?'

'What? No, no, God, no . . .' I can feel my cheeks flame. (Actually, *this* might be a more normal mother-in-law conversation, and I'm not sure I like it.) 'That's not the reason I'd be concerned about safety.'

Her frown deepens. She seems to be able to drive, along the twisty Sussex B-road, without needing to glance at the road more than once every few seconds. A lifetime, I don't doubt, of driving aid trucks along dirt tracks in Central Africa.

'Safety is an illusion, Libby. You could get hit by a bus while running errands in Chichester.'

'Well, yes, I *could*.' I laugh again, in a fruitless attempt to lighten the mood. 'But statistically, surely, that's quite a lot less likely than . . . well, you know— ' *getting kidnapped by the Taliban and ending up publicly stoned to death in the streets of Kandahar?* – 'the sorts of things you read about that happen in, er, that part of the world.'

'Ah, well, that's the trouble, really, isn't it?' Barbara takes a corner with impressive control, given that she's driving fast and not really looking at the road as she does so. 'Reading about these things rather than being on the ground, *experiencing* them. I mean, no offence, Libby, but how are you ever going to be able to speak about your work with real knowledge, with real *passion*, if you're just regurgitating something that someone has sent you in a memo?'

'Speak?'

'Mm-hm.' She reaches up and pulls down the visor, to shield her eyes from the glow of the winter sun that's just starting to set over the field ahead of us. 'I've always felt Joel's wife should be a real figurehead for the Perreira Foundation, someone who can stand up in front of an audience and tell them the things they need to hear. Joel's superb at that, obviously, but, let's be realistic, it never hurts to hear the same message from a young, attractive female . . .' Another rather lingering glance in my direction, as she openly assesses whether or not she's been strictly accurate in calling me *attractive*. She seems to be having a couple of doubts because, after a moment, she goes on, 'I assume you've been growing your hair that long so you can put it up for the wedding? I think a slightly shorter style would look more chic on you, actually, Libby. And has anyone ever taught you how to do your own makeup? It's a great confidence booster,' she goes on, before I can reply, 'and vital if you're ever going to be meeting big donors or talking to reporters in an area where we haven't been able to take our own professional hair and makeup people. And, of course, that'll be the case in Afghanistan. Now, I'll speak to my assistant Elena and make sure she coordinates with *your* assistant for the travel plans . . . I'm heading out to Peshawar on the eighteenth of February, and then due to fly from there to Kabul on the twenty-first, I think, so it'll probably make the most sense for you to fly on the—'

'Barbara!' I yelp. 'I didn't think we'd actually agreed the trip yet, had we?'

'Well, all right, I guess you'll want to discuss it with Joel first. I suppose he might be keen for you to take one of his security people with you, although *I've* always managed perfectly fine without them . . . mind you, there was that incident last year in Angola when I'd probably have appreciated Esti and her martial arts expertise . . .'

'Look, can we just . . . put all this on the back burner, Barbara, please?' I stare at her. 'I'm getting married tomorrow, after all, and I haven't even finished packing for the honeymoon yet! Making travel plans for *Afghanistan* just seems a bit . . . previous. And besides,' I go on, my voice strengthening a bit, because I just *have* to say this, don't I? 'I've already started explaining to Joel that I'm honestly not sure I'm the person you want to take on a full-time job with the foundation.'

Barbara slams on the brakes, though this is to avoid a rabbit streaking across the road in front of us, rather than an act of anger. She doesn't, in fact, look angry at all, as she turns her stunning face towards me again; merely surprised. No: astonished.

'Why on earth not?'

'Well, I do have a job already, for one thing! One I really enjoy, and that I'm pretty good at. And I don't think I'd be – at all – good at the sort of thing you do. You've been a professional aid worker for thirty years! You probably speak five languages—'

'Eight. Nine, if you count my conversational Mboshi.'

'. . . and you're trained for disaster relief, and accustomed to dealing with NGOs, and know how to negotiate with governments and tribespeople . . . I'm a jewellery designer,' I go on, somewhat desperately. 'It's not that I don't want to help people far less fortunate than myself, I just don't think I'm remotely equipped to do the sorts of things you need to do to actually help them! I mean, I once accidentally set my own head on fire on a location shoot for a TV show. In King's Cross. Am I really the sort of person you want by your side as we set off into a remote region of Afghanistan?'

Barbara doesn't laugh at the head-on-fire story. Nor does she express any particular interest in hearing any more about it. (But then I'm rapidly suspecting that Barbara might not have that much of a sense of humour. Or, in fact, that much interest in anything that doesn't involve her work.)

'Then what sort of thing did *you* have in mind?' she asks, rather peevishly. We've just turned the corner into the private road that leads towards Aldingbourne, so I guess the silver lining is that this conversation is going to be over pretty soon. 'Because Lillian, my previous daughter-in-law, never really committed herself to any of the wonderful work we do, and that made it difficult for her and me to get along. That's not a threat, by the way. I never have any major issues with any of the women my son has dated, as long as they aren't shallow gold-diggers. Which I don't get the impression you are. A gold-digger, that is.' She doesn't, I notice, comment on the *shallow* side of things. 'But I think everyone – Joel included – will feel rather let down if you don't at least *try* to step up to the plate. You're about to be in an astonishingly privileged position, you know, Libby. Wife to a very, very wealthy man. Don't you want to give anything back?'

Right about now, I'm ashamed to say, the only thing I can think of that I want to give back is my engagement ring.

'No, I really would like to give something back! And I know how privileged I am, Barbara, honestly. But wouldn't it be better for me to take my time working out what sort of thing I'd actually be good at? For the foundation, I mean. And leave the really serious stuff to the people who actually know what they're doing, and can do it properly?'

'Hmm.' She actually makes a mulling-it-over sound as we pull into the driveway. 'I suppose you know best, what your limitations are.'

I clear my throat. 'I'm not sure they're *limitations*, as such. I'm just trying to be realistic.'

'Of course. Well, as I say, you know best.' She says this in a voice that implies the exact opposite, and pulls the Range Rover into a space right outside the house. 'And you have a lot on your plate, with the wedding, and . . . all that kind of thing.'

She says *this* in a voice that implies I'm the worst kind of airhead for not spending my every waking moment thinking about ways to alleviate poverty and suffering in the world.

'I guess maybe I just find it hard to imagine how anyone can sit on the sidelines when they're in a position to help. From my own personal experience, that is. I'm sure Joel's told you that my mother's a Holocaust survivor, and then of course I grew up behind the Iron Curtain . . . it's given my son a real drive to succeed, and help people along the way. I mean, that's absolutely integral to his character. I don't know if he's ever going to be truly happy with someone who . . . oh! Speak of the devil!' she finished, as the door on my side opens, and Joel is on the other side of it. 'Ahoj, miláčku!'

'Mamicka?' he says, looking surprised to see her. 'I didn't know you were driving! Actually, I didn't even know you were *here* . . .'

'Oh, you were busy, *srdiecko*, I didn't want to disturb you. And then Libby called and said she was at the station . . . what a perfect opportunity to get to know my new daughter-in-law a little! We've had a good talk, haven't we, Libby?'

'Yes,' I say. 'A great talk.'

'And now why don't I leave you two to it for a few minutes while I go and wake up Babicka?' Barbara says, sliding out of her seat with a deliberately nonchalant air that bears little relation to the intensity she's just shown with me for the duration of our drive. 'We'll all have some tea together in the sitting room, I hope? I'm assuming Julia is here?'

'Yes, she's just upstairs with the nanny, settling into her bedroom. Go and knock and tell her you've brought presents – I'm assuming you've brought presents? – and she'll be downstairs quicker than you can say *Snow White*.'

'Of course, but I didn't buy her that Disney Princess doll you suggested, *miláčku*. I bought her a lovely folk doll from my trip to Burkina Faso instead . . .'

'Lovely, *Mamicka*,' Joel says, though somewhat distractedly. 'I'm sure she'll appreciate it.'

I'm sure of nothing of the sort, but I'm just rather relieved to see Barbara close her car door and head for the house.

I mean, obviously I've never met a prospective mother-in-law before, so I've no idea what sort of criteria to judge these things on . . . and at least, I guess, she wasn't openly hostile about the idea of me marrying her darling boy, or anything. In fact, she seemed to be more . . . confused by my presence in Joel's life than anything. And, to be fair, if she was expecting me to be some sort of gorgeous Amazonian adventurer, with a PhD in International Relations and the ability to leap tall buildings in a single bound—

'Libby.' Joel sounds tense. 'Did you spend seven hundred pounds on my credit card this afternoon?'

'Yes, I did. Or rather, I *put* it on your credit card, because

I knew for sure that would cover it. Mum's going to pay you back, obviously. It was for her haircut, she went a bit overboard . . .' Something suddenly occurs to me. 'How do you even know about the credit card charge, anyway?'

'American Express called me. That card is hardly ever used, and then suddenly there was a seven hundred quid charge from a hairdresser's salon, out of the blue. It triggered a security alert. I was with my lawyers when they called, actually . . .' His face is set in rather grim lines, to match his tense voice. 'Libby, look, we might need to revisit this pre-nup thing, OK? That call really spooked the lawyers, and they're not at all happy that we don't have anything in place. So look, they're drawing up some documents right now, and we should have something to look at some time this evening . . .'

'Joel.' I stare at him. 'I don't want to spend the night before my wedding looking at a pre-nup.'

'Well, nobody does, and I feel foolish that I didn't insist on it before. I just didn't think you were . . . well, I'm quite sure your mother didn't *plan* to overspend on her hair, but you have to look at it from the lawyers' point of view – the day before the wedding, and the fiancée suddenly starts splashing the cash . . .'

'I wasn't splashing the cash! I was bailing out my mother! Who is going to pay you back every single penny, I absolutely assure you!'

'OK, calm down . . . Look, the pre-nup is to protect you as much as it is to protect me. I've told the lawyers to make absolutely certain that you're well provided for.'

I slam the Range Rover door behind me. 'I don't want to be well provided for! I don't want a penny of your money, Joel. Have you stopped believing that?'

'Oh, come on, Libby, you can't tell me you haven't got used to my way of life by now! And I haven't seen you *objecting* to any of it, exactly.'

'That's not true. I objected to you spending eleven grand on a suit.'

'Oh.' His eyes go rather cold. 'The suit again. If I recall, you didn't *object* so much as mock me . . .'

'I didn't mock you! I just queried whether it was really necessary to spend that much on a suit for a kids' party!' I take a deep breath, because we're heading into dangerous territory here: I don't want a re-run of the Suit Row the night before the wedding. Not when it made Joel sulk for days last time. 'Look. Please, tell your lawyers I'll happily sign a piece of paper waiving all rights to a single fiver of your fortune — I think it's an insult, but I'll sign it — as long as I don't have to sit and pore over endless documents this evening, when my family and friends are arriving, OK?'

'Well, I think that's foolish. And I think it would behove you to be a little more sensible about these matters, actually, Libby. I'm quite happy to pay for you to find a lawyer of your own, who I'm sure will be happy to read any documents on your behalf, tonight, if you feel you won't understand them . . .'

'Hey! I'm not stupid!'

'No, Libby, I know that. But this is serious stuff.'

'I can be serious, too, you know! In my own way! And

nobody's even giving me a chance to find my own way into your world, Joel. Just because I'm not forever jetting off to typhoon zones and negotiating fair-trade deals with Rwandan warlords . . .'

'Are you mocking my mother?' he snaps.

'No, I'm not mocking her! She's obviously an absolutely amazing woman, Joel. Nobody needs to tell either of you that. But nevertheless, both you and she seem to think it's OK to tell *me* what to do with the rest of my life.'

'The foundation, you mean? Oh, come on, Libby, she's just passionate about her work! And, honestly, would it kill you to take a fraction more interest? I mean, you seem pretty passionate yourself about bailing your dear old mum out of an apparent crisis . . . I'm just surprised you don't seem to feel the same way about displaced children in need of emergency aid!'

'Joel, I have every interest in the foundation. But right at this very moment in time, for me, charity begins at home. Any minute now, I'm supposed to be meeting my future stepdaughter for the first time. I'd like to concentrate on that one particular child until after that, if that's OK with you?'

'Fine.' He glares at me. 'And if you're going to insist you're far too busy to read a pre-nup or talk to a lawyer yourself tonight, then we'll just have to do it after the wedding.'

'A post-nup?'

'Yes. That can be done.'

'But I don't want any kind of . . . nup! Isn't marriage supposed to be about romance? Even a little bit? And trust, and companionship, and—'

'Have you been drinking?' he interrupts me to ask, brusquely.

'Because I'm talking about romance?'

'No. Because you look a bit pissed!'

'I had one mimosa with lunch! And a glass of champagne at the wedding dress shop! Hours ago.'

'Great!' He throws his hands up in the air. It's such a melodramatic gesture, for someone who usually remains pretty cool, that I can't help but feel it's a rather put-on way to bring an end to our row, with me placed very firmly in the wrong. 'Congratulations, Libby. The first moment you meet my daughter, my mother and grandmother, and you're drunk.'

'I'm not drunk! I had a couple of drinks! Don't be ridiculous . . .'

'And you wonder,' he snaps, turning sharply and starting to stalk back towards the house, 'why people occasionally think you're anything other than a hundred per cent serious!'

'Joel—'

'Can I suggest you get one of the girls to bring you some strong coffee,' he throws over his departing shoulder, 'before you come down to tea with my family?'

The front door doesn't slam behind him, because there's a staff member (of course, and a witness to our row; how wonderful) holding it open for him. But it might as well do.

Chapter 16

I've gone through the evening on autopilot, to be honest with you.

I mean, I know what you *think* you'd do in this scenario – the one where you and your fiancé have a bitter row the night before your wedding. The one where his mother subtly lets you know that you're not really good enough for him, and that she's pretty sure your relationship is doomed to failure. The one where he starts insisting on a pre-nup, or a post-nup, or any kind of miserable financial arrangement, despite the fact he ought to know by now you couldn't give two hoots about his bloody money. You think you're going to summon the guy who can drive you back to the station and zoom off in his Land Rover to catch the first train back to London, never to return.

But the reality is a bit different. The reality is that you can't put two coherent thoughts together to come up with something – anything – like a strategy for dealing with all these curveballs. The reality is that you have to go into the house even if you want to find the Land Rover driver, let alone because that's where all your stuff is. And the reality is that once you're in the house, you're suddenly faced with introductions to his grandmother, who's just flown all the way in from Florida to attend your wedding. And then, of course, his daughter appears, and she's – there's really no other word for it – heavenly, with her big, solemn blue eyes, and her downy skin, and her golden curls. And she sits very sweetly right beside you on the sofa, drinking a glass of juice with one hand and then, after a while, squirming the other hand into yours, to hold.

Follow this up with a hasty shower and change into your rehearsal-dinner dress, and then back downstairs to greet all the other guests, including your mum and sister and best friend and her family . . .

All I'm saying is, that the reality is that even if you might want to call a sensible halt to the proceedings, while you take some time to get your thoughts together, it's actually nowhere near that simple.

The rehearsal dinner, too, has sort of taken on a life of its own. The dozen or so dinner guests have feasted on marinated salmon, roast poussins, and have just finished some (probably, nothing seems to taste of anything to me) delicious lavender and honey ice-cream, made from lavender grown in the biodynamic garden. The wine has flowed – though not for me, as I haven't felt comfortable drinking any of it, to be honest – and there have been speeches: not from Joel, obviously, who's saving his up until tomorrow, but from his mother, who has (actually quite kindly, albeit still with that air of mild surprise) welcomed me to the family, and from Nora's dad, who got a bit overcome and actually shed a tear or two when he talked about what great friends Nora and I had been to each other over the years.

Though I'm avoiding Nora ever so slightly right now, I have to admit, as everyone starts to leave the dining room and filter through to the library for coffee and petits fours (made by Bogdan's hot pastry chef). She's been giving me The Big Eyebrows all night, across the room, presumably because she's noticed I'm looking a bit wan, though I expect she thinks it's about Olly not making it tomorrow.

I've never been very good at lying to Nora – in fact, I'm bloody awful at it – and seeing as the last thing this rehearsal dinner needs is a hormonal pregnant woman tapping her glass and announcing to the room that she thinks the wedding tomorrow should be on temporary hiatus because the bride is having some *serious* doubts, I think avoiding her is the best course of action.

Besides, Julia is flagging, yawning huge jet-lagged five-year-old yawns, so when she says she wants me to go upstairs with her to read her a story, I seize the opportunity: for bonding with my soon-to-be-stepdaughter, yes, but also, less selflessly, a chance to get away from it all for half an hour.

'You're going upstairs with Libby for a bit, are you?' Joel asks her, tenderly, as I go to tell him where we're off to. 'That's nice, darling. Be on your best behaviour!'

It's not the time, is it, to ask if he's talking to me or to her?

I mean, I know marriage isn't all Happy Ever After. But

still, if you're starting to have genuine doubts that you're not even Happy Right Beforehand . . .

'Libby?' Julia is asking me, now, as we walk up the stairs together. 'Can I come and see your room, please?'

'Oh . . . I thought you wanted me to read you a story?'

'Oh, yes, I do. But I really want to see your room, first. And your dress,' she adds, after a moment's thought. 'Will you show me your princess dress?'

'Er, you mean my wedding dress?'

'That's right.' She gazes up at me, those blue eyes, so like Joel's, wide and friendly. 'The one you're going to wear tomorrow.'

'I suppose that should be OK . . . but are you sure you don't want to wait for tomorrow, and have the surprise?'

Julia thinks about this for a moment, wrinkling her nose. 'I don't think,' she says, eventually, 'I like surprises very much.'

'You know what, Julia,' I say, leading her down the corridor towards the bedroom I'm sleeping in for the night, 'neither do I.'

I moved all my stuff over here earlier this morning – seems like a lifetime ago, now – so that Joel and I wouldn't end up sharing a bedroom together the night before the wedding. It's a lovely room – all the rooms at Aldingbourne are lovely, let's face it – and it's made, technically, even lovelier by the fact that my stunning wedding dress is hanging on the back of the wardrobe.

'*Wow*,' says Julia, stopping dead, as we walk into the room, and staring. 'Is that it?'

'Yes, that's it!'

'That's the princess dress you're going to wear tomorrow? To marry my daddy in?'

'Mm-hmm.' I clear my throat. 'Do you like it, then?'

'I *love* it.' She gazes up at me, her solemn little eyes shining. 'Will you put it on?'

'What, now?'

'Yes!'

'Oh, I don't know, Julia . . . I think it's supposed to be bad luck to put on your wedding dress the night before your wedding.'

Actually, I'm not at all sure that this is the case. Bad luck for your husband-to-be to see you in your dress before your wedding: yes. But bad luck to try it on, to curry a bit more favour with your adorable five-year-old stepdaughter-to-be . . . no. I don't think so.

'Please?' she asks. 'I'll go and put on my bridesmaid dress too, and we can have a rehearsal!'

'Oh, well, let's not risk getting your lovely bridesmaid's dress wrinkled or stained,' I say, because I don't want to get the blame if this turns out to be the case. To distract her, I add, 'All right, I'll try my dress on, then, Julia, but only for a couple of minutes, OK?'

'OK! We can play princesses!' she says, happily, possibly not *quite* accepting that I really am only going to put it on for a couple of minutes.

As I unzip the Jenny Packham dress-carrier, there's a quick tap at the door, and – without waiting for an answer – Cass suddenly sticks her head around it.

'Lib,' she hisses, 'I need to . . . oh.' She looks at Julia. '*She's* here.'

'Who's this?' Julia asks.

'This is my sister, Cass . . . your sort-of-auntie, as of tomorrow, I guess.'

'Oh.' Julia stares at Cass for a long moment. 'I don't think I like the idea of that.'

Cass snorts. 'You and me both, kid. Now, look, Libby . . ..' she adds, teetering into the room on some eight-inch heels that give me vertigo just looking at them. (She's looking, I have to say, sensational tonight, in the body-con, plunge-front dress she settled on when she found out it was a sit-down do – and, trust me, when my sister does plunge-front, she *really* does plunge-front.) 'You have to tell me what the deal is with this Nick guy.'

'Joel's best man?'

'Yes. Is he gay, or what?'

'Cass!' I jerk my head in Julia's direction.

'Oh, actually, you're right . . . Juliet, is it?' Cass asks, leaning down, suddenly, to Julia, creating a pretty perilous situation for the already straining fabric of the plunge-front dress.

'Julia.'

'Sure. Whatever. So, look, Julia, this Nick guy who's your dad's best friend . . . is he gay, or what?'

'That's not what I meant!' I yelp at Cass. 'You can't ask her that!'

'Why not? She's known the guy longer than you have.'

'Yes, but she's five!'

'Almost six,' Julia tells me, earnestly. 'Besides, I know what gay means. It means men who like men better than they like ladies, right?'

'Right!' Cass looks pleasantly surprised, and gives Julia an approving high-five. 'So, *is* he gay? Your dad's friend Nick, I mean.'

'Hmmm . . .' Julia screws up her nose, thinking about this. 'I don't *think* so . . . I mean, Mummy never really liked Uncle Nick all that much, is all I really know about him. She said he's . . . got a tight wand?'

We both stare at her for a moment, unsure how to translate this. Unsure, to be honest, how to *react* to this . . .

'Oh! He's a tightwad?' Cass, showing once again that, when it really matters, she's no dumb blonde. 'Is that what your mum said?'

'Yes, that's it!' Julia beams at us. 'I think maybe he has quite a lot of money, but he's really mean about spending it. Mummy's still friends with the lady who used to be married to Uncle Nick, so she knows that sort of thing. Well, I think Uncle Nick has been married to quite a lot of ladies, actually . . .'

'Good stuff, kid, good stuff . . . so, that takes us all the way back to the question of whether or not he's maybe *secretly* gay . . .'

'For God's sake, Cass!' I have to call a halt to this, as Julia's soon-to-be-stepmother. As a responsible adult. As a *human being*. 'Is there the slightest possibility you could think about something other than yourself, do you think, during the course of this weekend?'

'Hey, I *am* thinking of someone other than myself! I'm thinking of *you*, Lib. I mean, your life's going to be *so* much better if I manage to shack up with Nick. You'll have someone fun to hang around with! I mean, Joel and his family are pretty *serious*, aren't they? No offence, Jules,' she adds, to Julia. 'Anyway, you seem really great yourself. God, if only the stepkids I had for a while had been as cool as you! I might still be with Zoltan now . . .'

'Instead of trying to hook up with the best man the night before my wedding,' I say, irritably. 'Then I think we *all* wish they'd been as cool as Julia.'

Cass regards me with annoyance. 'Well, you're being no help at all, Libby, I have to say. And what the fuck are you doing, squirrelling yourself away up here like this? I think there's about to be some slideshow downstairs, or something. Pictures of Joel's childhood, or some such snooze-fest.'

'Oh, God . . . Julia, shall we pop downstairs now, for the slideshow, and come back up and I'll try the dress on later?'

'But you said you were going to show me *now*,' says Julia, her angelic little face crumpling.

'OK, OK, I'll show you now, but very quickly,' I say, as firmly as I feel able. 'Cass, if Joel wants to know where I am, can you just tell him I'll be down in a minute?'

'Fine.' Cass teeters back towards the door. 'But I can't guarantee I'm going to be able to stick out this bloody slideshow myself, you know. If Nick expresses the remotest interest, I'm going to try to get him outside for a cigarette, and then I'll see what happens when I make my move.'

340

She glances down at her plunge-front, and jiggles her boobs for a moment, either to readjust them to their most pert level, or just to remind herself how fabulous they are. 'Thanks again, kid,' she adds, to Julia, before she closes the door behind her. 'You and I are going to get along swimmingly, I can tell.'

Even though she's only five, I'm pretty uncomfortable about the idea of changing in front of her, so I take the dress down from its hanger and head towards the bathroom.

'Will you be OK here for a moment, Julia?'

'Oh, yes, that's no problem, Libby.' She perches on the edge of the bed. 'Oh, I had one question for you. Have you had your call from Grace yet?'

A jolt runs through me.

'What did you just say?'

'Your call from Grace,' she repeats. 'Have you had it yet?'

'I . . . do you mean . . . sorry, Julia, are you talking about . . . Grace *Kelly?*' I crouch down beside her for a moment. 'Were you playing in the attic today? Did you . . . meet anyone up there? A blonde lady? Sitting on the old sofa?'

Now she's staring at me like I'm the crazy one.

'I haven't been up in the attic at all. I was just wondering if you'd had your call yet. Because Mummy's been saying it's only a matter of time until you get your call from Grace.'

Based on her *tightwad* confusion a couple of minutes ago, I'm starting to realize that there could be a translation element to this. And, let's face it, with Bogdan in my life, I'm pretty adept at translation these days.

'Julia, is your Mummy saying . . . *fall* from grace?'

'Yep, that's it.' She nods. 'Mummy had one while she was married to Daddy, she says. And I heard her telling Grandpa that it was only a matter of time before you had one, too. On account of the fact,' she goes on, in an oddly adult way that makes it plain she's simply parroting grown-up phrases she's overheard, without necessarily understanding what any of them really mean, 'that Daddy has a hard time dealing with imperfection. Because, you know, he puts people up on a pedant's stall—'

'Pedestal?'

'. . . and then can't handle it when they start to seem a bit more human.'

I'm feeling a sudden chill in the room, and it's not merely because I'm only wearing a layer of thin lace.

I quickly straighten up, because it's absolutely not right of me to be continuing this conversation with Joel's child. If I want to talk about this with him – and I think, terrifying though it feels with the wedding approaching like a speeding juggernaut – that I have to, I need to talk with *him*. Find out if he'll concede that there's any truth in what his ex-wife is saying.

I mean, let's be honest, it's all pretty familiar-sounding stuff, given the way things have gone between us in the last couple of days. Given the way he worshipped the very ground I trod on from the moment we met. Given the fact that his mother seems pretty clear that I'd have to be Mahatma Gandhi crossed with Mother Teresa (but still able to look decent in a frock and heels) in order to live up to Joel's astonishing standards.

'I'll just go and put my dress on,' I say, 'and then we really do need to go downstairs to watch Daddy's slideshow.'

She nods, and I step into the bathroom.

I don't actually lock the door, just push it to, then step out my of shift dress. Then I step into my wedding dress and – with shaking hands – pull it up.

I gaze at myself in the full-length bathroom mirror.

I look like a total stranger.

Don't get me wrong: the dress is exquisite. It really does flatter my figure, with its bias cut and drapey sleeves, and it is hand embroidered with thousands and thousands of tiny crystal beads that catch the light and cast an almost ethereal glow about me. If it's this effective in the artificial light of the bathroom, I can only imagine how incredible it's going to look by candlelight in an early Victorian chapel, at dusk on a crisp winter's afternoon.

If I actually end up there, that is.

I draw a deep, shuddering breath.

Oh God, oh God, oh God.

Do I tell Joel I need more time? Do I call it off, out-and-out? Do I go ahead with it all, just to save the sheer mortification for both of us, and then tough it out until I can find a dignified exit strategy? Do I go ahead with it and throw my whole weight behind it, and hope that Joel will learn to just accept me as I am . . .?

I mean, I do love him. At least, I think I love him. I love *aspects* of him. I love things about him despite certain other things . . .

At a noise behind me, I turn round.

Julia, swift and almost-silent as a little mouse, has just darted in behind me, picked up my shift dress, and darted back out again.

Then she shuts the door.

A moment later, I hear a key turn, on the outside of the door, in the lock.

I gaze at it for a moment.

'Um . . . Julia?'

'Yes?' Her voice, on the other side of the door, isn't hostile.

'I . . . er . . . you seem to have locked me in?'

'Yes.'

'Right. I mean, could you . . . unlock it, maybe?'

'No,' she says, decisively. 'I can't. Because I really don't want you to marry my daddy, you see. I don't want a step-mummy. Step-mummies are *bad*. They always try to harm the princess, and give her poisoned apples, and things.'

Oh, for fuck's *sake*.

'Julia . . .'

'If you don't come down for the rest of the night, he's going to be really cross with you. It'll be your call from Grace, the one Mummy was talking about. So he won't want to marry you after that. And even if he does come up and find you, that's OK too, because he'll see you in your dress before the wedding, and then he *can't* marry you. That's the law, right?'

'No!' I rattle the door-handle. I'm in no mood just now to be entranced by her whimsical views. 'Julia, just open the door. You're going to get in big trouble . . .'

'*If* anyone actually hears you. I'm going to lock your

344

bedroom door, too,' she adds, almost conversationally, 'and hide the key so nobody can find it.'

Her five-year-old logic isn't quite impeccable, but she's thought it through pretty effectively, nonetheless. Nobody will hear me yelling if the bedroom door is shut, too and, even if they do realize I'm up here, they've still got to get in somehow. And I will miss the slideshow. And Joel will be pissed off with me. And he will see me in my wedding dress . . .

Oh! My one saving grace (no pun intended) – Cass. She knows I'm up here. She'll send up a posse, when I don't come down . . .

'In fact,' Julia goes on, almost as if she can read my mind through a heavy bathroom door, 'I might just say I think you've run away, or something. That way nobody will come and look for you. Oh, but don't worry,' she adds, 'I'll come up in a couple of days' time and push some biscuits under the door. I may not want a new step-mummy, but I don't want you to starve, or anything. You can drink the water from the bath tap.'

And that's that. Silence. She's obviously gone, presumably locking the bedroom door behind her.

The major flaw in her half-cooked plan becomes apparent to me a moment later: the bathroom has a huge, almost floor-to-ceiling double window that leads out on to the narrow, balustraded balcony that runs pretty much all the way around the second floor of the house.

I hurry to open the double window, lean out and see, right away, that another window, in the room the next but one along from mine, is also open. I think it's the room Barbara has been put in, actually, because there was a bit of very last-minute touching-up of paintwork going on in there this morning, and the window has presumably been left wide like that to air the fumes before bedtime.

I can easily climb out, walk quickly along the balustrade bit, and get in that window, then nip downstairs and try to get someone's attention before Joel does, in fact, see me in my wedding dress.

Not that it matters, probably, any more, to stick to the superstitious tradition. Because that's only if the wedding is actually going ahead. And, let's face it, that's seeming less likely with each passing minute of this day.

Still, the wedding dress is the only thing that might cause any problems on this little journey: even if I'm not actually going to wear it down an aisle any time soon, it's still a stunning item that I can't possibly damage in any way. So I'm going to have to be r-e-a-l-l-y careful, as I step out of the window and up on to the little balcony, that I don't catch it on anything, or get the hem grubby at all. But actually, if I hold the skirt a couple of inches off the floor, and keep the swooshy bias-cut fabric pulled fairly close to my legs, I think I'm going to be OK.

I'm almost at the other open window, and just congratulating myself on my good sense in not picking out some truly impractical, Cinderella's ballgown-style meringue when, quite suddenly, the floor opens up beneath me.

I mean, my foot actually goes straight through what I'm walking on.

Somehow I have quick enough reactions *not* to just blindly put my other foot right down in front of me, which would be a bad, bad idea, seeing as the balcony floor – presumably badly affected by my weight after not having been stepped on in . . . years? decades? *centuries?* – has literally begun to collapse all around me. It's like an avalanche of shale and weak concrete, with me right in the middle of it.

I do the only thing I can do, which is to throw myself sideways – *not* in the balustrade direction, but towards the wall – and put one foot, and then the other, on to the wide windowsill closest to me. It's not the room I was aiming for, the one with the window wide open, but it's the only surface I can see that looks as if it's going to hold up. I put my hands on to the jutting-out brickwork around the window-frame, and grip as tightly as I can.

This is not good.

I mean, sure, the window-ledge is wide – just wide enough for my entire foot. But I'm wearing heels. With leather soles that don't grip all that well at the best of times, let alone on a chilly, slightly rain-spattered window-ledge.

And, more to the point, I'm two storeys up. Two extremely tall storeys, thanks to the Georgian architects of this place, and their fondness for a high ceiling.

And the balcony that, only five seconds ago, was beneath my feet, is now little more than a crumbling ruin. There's at least an eight-foot clear gap through which I can see down to the gravel driveway a good – oh, *shit* – thirty feet below.

This must be the dodgy masonry that Joel's planning to repair this coming spring, under my aegis. Masonry that's chosen a really bad time to throw in the towel, several months too early.

What am I going to do? I can't, I absolutely cannot, grip on to the brickwork for ever. I mean, there's nothing to really *hold*, if you see what I mean, just two right-angles that my hands are holding like a crab's pincers.

'Help!' I call out. 'Anyone? Help!'

But it's pretty windy up here, and I'm a long, long way up and, as far as I know, Joel has started his slideshow way down below anyway, so the chances of anyone hearing my plaintive cries are . . . let's be realistic. They're zero. I mean, even the noise that mini-avalanche of concrete must have caused, smashing down to the gravel drive below, won't have been audible. It's fallen down at the back of the house, and everyone is in the library, in the front corner.

I'm trying very, very hard not to panic, but it's getting harder with each passing second. There's nothing else for me to hold on to. Nothing at all. I look, frantically, left and right, below my feet and above my head . . . the only thing sticking out at all amid the vast expanse of smooth wall is the ledge from the small window right above me. An attic window, presumably. Even if I could reach up and grip it, which would be a stretch, it wouldn't give me anywhere to put my feet. I'd just have to sort of dangle off the side of the house. Instead of clinging to the side of it, as I'm doing now.

It's a kind of Sophie's Choice, really, of catastrophes.

I really think I'm a bit fucked.

I don't know how long I can stay on this ledge for. My feet are already slipping, and I think I just heard a faintly sinister cracking sound that is probably the wood giving way beneath my weight. If the ledge breaks off, I'm done for. That's it. I'll be straight down through the hole to land on the driveway below.

I guess I've had a good enough life.

I mean, my childhood was pretty crap, admittedly, and I definitely got dealt a bit of a short straw in the parents department. But hey, it could have been a hell of a lot worse. And I've gone on to make a decent success of myself since then, right? I leave a bit of a legacy behind me, with my jewellery, even if I've not managed to have a child yet, or anything. And all right, I've made an absolute pig's ear of my love life, but at least I can plummet to my certain death knowing that the people I love are happy. Nora, in her idyll of Mark and Clara and the new baby. Cass, who'll probably turn my messy demise to her advantage and use Joel's best man as a (rich, albeit penny-pinching) shoulder to cry on. Olly, who . . .

Olly.

Oh, *Olly*.

If I'm going to die, in this terrible, undignified way, crumpled in a gory heap in my never-used wedding dress, I want Olly to be the last thing I think of. Not Joel. Joel, whose standards of perfection, both for himself and others, I could never, ever live up to. But Olly, who has always taken me the way I am. Flawed. Limited. *Imbecilic*, frankly, ever to have meandered out on to a two-hundred-year-old flat roof in the first place—

'Oh, my God!'

I can hear, faintly, a sudden scream from below.

It's Cass. I can just see that it's Cass, appearing in the floodlit garden. She must have persuaded Nick to accompany her outside for a cigarette and a snog after all!

'Cass!' I bleat, even though I know she'll be hard pressed to hear me back. 'Get someone!'

'She's going to jump!' Cass shrieks, to an accompanying bark of alarm from Nick, suddenly appearing from around the side of the house to join her. 'Everyone! Come quick! Libby's suicidal!'

What? *No* . . .

'I'm not bloody suicidal!' I call back, but obviously I can't yell anywhere near as loudly as Cass, because it'll make me wobble too much on my ledge. (A ledge that, even as I say this, makes another alarming cracking sound beneath my feet.) 'In fact, I really, really don't want to die!'

Now Nick has vanished, presumably to tell the assembled wedding guests that the bride-to-be has put on her white frock and is threatening to leap from the second storey and End It All.

'Libby, don't do it!' Cass howls. 'I know maybe I've never really been there for you, I know maybe I've always been too wrapped up in myself, but that's only because my life always seemed so much more interesting than yours!'

As suicide-prevention speeches go, I have to be honest, it's not the greatest.

'If you want to back out,' she's going on, 'and not marry Joel, then all you have to do is say so! He'll get over it! To be honest with you, he's seemed pretty distant all night, so I'm not sure he'll be all that bothered anyway . . .'

But now there are more shouts, and more people are coming running. I can just make out Joel, and Barbara, and Bogdan, and – shrieking loudly enough to cause another avalanche – Mum.

'Libby?' Joel shouts up, through cupped hands. 'Just stay where you are! Don't jump! Don't do it!'

'I'm not bloody jumping!' I croak. The ledge cracks once more; I can feel, now, that it's really starting to come away from the wall. 'Help me!'

'Nick's going to come up and try to open that window!' Joel yells, sounding as cool and calm in this crisis as he did with Nora and the helicopter all those months ago. 'Just hang on, Libby!'

'No, he can't . . . if he opens the window, there's nowhere for me to go.' Another, horrifying crack, and the ledge actually comes away beneath my left foot. 'A ladder . . . quick . . . bring a ladder . . '

'Libby, am imploring you!' This is Bogdan, now, his voice booming out of the darkness. 'Do not be doing this. Yes, you are not truly loving Joel. Yes, you are still grieving for the fact that Olly is not loving you as you love him. But death is no solution. Certainly not this horrible, messy death. Could you at least not consider possible option that is not leaving you looking diabolical at funeral?'

Oh, for the love of God.

And I really mean that right in this instant, actually, because just as Bogdan finishes speaking, I feel the other side of the window-ledge crack beneath me.

So this is it.

I hear screams from below, I feel my feet hang free, and I feel the searing pain in my hands as I try, fruitlessly, to grip on to the brickwork for a moment or two longer, for as long as I can take my own weight, at this precarious angle, before I drop.

And then, out of nowhere, I feel a hand grip my wrist. Really grip it, like a vice.

And then another hand grips the other one.

Shocked, I release my fingers from their futile hold on the wall, and just let myself be lifted up. I can hear astonished shouts, now, from the garden, as I instinctively use my feet, only one of them still clad in its shoe, to push against the wall and take some of my weight out of the hands of whoever it is who's pulling me up.

When I glance upwards, just for a moment, I can see that it's Grace Kelly.

And Marilyn Monroe. And Audrey Hepburn.

The shock almost sends me tumbling backwards, despite Grace's – and Marilyn's – impressively strong grip, so I focus for a couple of seconds more and use my elbows, as the three of them haul me through the small attic window, to hook myself safely over it. Audrey's skinny arms are around Grace's waist, anchoring her to the floor as she takes half my weight from her hold on my left wrist, and Marilyn, a sturdier presence, is pulling me by my right. As soon as the majority of me is safely over the window-ledge, they're reaching out to pull the rest of me in, too, in a heap of slippery beaded silk, my other shoe falling off as they do so, and tumbling thirty feet through the hole in the balcony to the ground below.

I lie, face-down, on the attic floor for a moment, unable to speak.

'Well!' Grace Kelly sounds pretty out of puff herself. 'I certainly never thought I'd see *you* again!'

I look up at her. At the three of them.

Grace is far older than the last time I saw her – early fifties, perhaps? – and she's no longer wearing her wedding dress. Instead she's in a rather stiff, pale tweed suit over a silk blouse, pristine white gloves on her hands. She still looks ravishing, and her skin still has that incredible pearlescent glow, but she's fuller-faced, softer-figured, with faint lines etched around her eyes, and her hair looks as if it's been lacquered into place with Superglue. Marilyn, by contrast, is pretty much exactly the age she was when I last saw her. She's wearing her nude spangles from *Some Like It Hot*, candyfloss hair somewhat askew from all her efforts at hauling me from my certain doom. Audrey, her big eyes fixed on me with surprising calmness, is ageless as ever, and wearing exactly what she wore the last time I saw her: her little black Givenchy dress from the opening scene of *Tiffany's*, with her hair in a beehive and her hands in elbow-length black gloves.

'Me either!' Marilyn, sounding more than a little breathless, leans down to put her arms under my armpits and haul me towards the sofa. 'Here, honey, you need to sit down . . . a terrible shock like you've just had is enough to knock the wind out of anybody!'

'I'm . . . I'm OK,' I fib, as I feel the Chesterfield take my weight. 'Thank you – thank you *all* – so much for saving my life.'

'Oh, honey, it was nothing!' Marilyn sits her warm, curvaceous body down right beside me and reaches for a martini glass that's balanced on the arm of the sofa. 'Have a sip of this, it'll help.'

'I'm . . . I'm all right,' I croak, because I'm wise to the fact that whatever cocktail she's got in there, it's going to taste absolutely undrinkable. 'Thank you.'

'Oh, come on, honey, you look like you need it. I'm only sorry I don't have any rye whisky, or whatever it is you drink in Canada . . .'

It might have been eighteen months since I last saw her, but I see that her delusion that I'm Canadian remains as strong as ever.

'Oh, Marilyn, dear, she's not Canadian.' Grace Kelly's accent sounds more Anglo than American now, or perhaps that's just in contrast to Marilyn's all-American burr. 'She's British. Or, rather, as British as a person can be when they only exist in my subconscious . . . Golly,' she adds, gazing at me for a moment, before coming to sit on the Chesterfield herself, although at a rather more regal distance, down the other end. 'It's been a long, *long* time since I dreamed about you. And I never thought I'd see you in a dream with these two.' She subjects Marilyn to

354

one of her penetrating stares, and then – less beadily – Audrey, too.

'Hey! Now just hold on one minute,' Marilyn says, breathily. 'You're trying to say . . . what? I'm just someone in your dream?'

'Well, of course, Marilyn!' Grace looks rather shocked that Marilyn is even asking this. 'You can't possibly be here, you've been—'

Somehow, despite everything that's just happened, I have the presence of mind to jab Grace Kelly in the thigh with one of my fingers. And she, somehow, has the presence of mind to realize that I'm warning her not to say the words *dead for the last twenty years*. She glances at me, along the Chesterfield, with a certain degree of understanding, and nods her graceful head, almost imperceptibly. I don't think she's any less certain that we're all playing parts in her subconscious, but at least she's sensitive enough to realize that she'd better not blurt out anything about Marilyn's untimely death to her face.

'I've been what, honey?' Marilyn asks though, before anyone can answer, she suddenly gives a little shiver. 'Gee, it's awful chilly up here, wherever we are. Is this your new apartment, sweetie?'

'No, it isn't her new apartment,' Grace says. 'And honestly, Marilyn, dear, if you're chilly here in my head, don't you think it might behove you to put on a few more clothes? It would hardly be surprising if you caught your death of cold in that skimpy . . . well, can one actually call that a frock? It looks as if you might have come out in your negligee by mistake.'

355

'Well, I sure do appreciate the advice, Your Most Royalness,' Marilyn says, raising a slightly wobbly Martini glass to Grace before pressing her bosom up right next to my arm as she whispers into my ear, 'Say, if she was anybody other than Princess Grace, I'd have a thing or two to say about *her* style. She only got married a couple of years ago, and here she is looking like a fifty-year-old woman! Makes a girl kinda glad she's never managed to meet a prince herself, right?'

Before I can reply, Audrey has come and sat down in the space between Grace and me, and placed a cool, gloved hand on my shoulder. (The other hand is, naturally, holding on to a cigarette in a long holder, on which she takes an elegant drag before she speaks.)

'Are you feeling all right, darling?' she asks, gently. 'That must have been one heck of a shock for you, back there.'

'It was . . . not quite so much as a shock as this, though. I mean, don't get me wrong, it's . . . amazing to see you again, Audrey . . .'

'Wonderful to see you, too.' She squeezes my shoulder and takes another elegant drag on her cigarette. 'And it looks like congratulations are in order!'

'Huh?'

'The dress.' Her hand moves down to the fabric of my dress, which she examines, for a moment, in an expert fashion. 'It's beautiful. Is this hand-stitched lace? And I just adore this ivory on you. So much more flattering than white.'

'Hey, Audrey's right! I didn't even notice!' Marilyn gasps,

excitedly, as some Martini sloshes out of her glass and lands perilously close to the lace fabric that Audrey is so interested in. 'Honey, this is terrific news! You gotta tell us all about it! Who's the guy? Ooooh, is it that one you were always crazy about?'

'Olly,' Grace interjects, with a raised eyebrow in my direction. 'That was the fellow's name, if I remember correctly? It's all such an awfully long time ago . . .'

'No. I'm not marrying Olly.' I meet Grace's eye. 'It's the other one. Joel. Remember: the billionaire?'

'*Honey!* You bagged yourself a billionaire? Now, this really *does* call for a celebration! Is he cute? Smart?' Marilyn flings herself backwards on the Chesterfield, displaying her sumptuous, sequin-covered body to impressive advantage. 'I always knew you'd end up with a good one, honey, even if it isn't exactly the one you always wanted . . .'

'Honestly, darling, we'd love to hear all about him,' Audrey tells me. She clears her throat. 'Though, I'll admit, it probably isn't the *greatest* sign that you ended up on a roof in your wedding gown . . .'

'No, no, that was just because Joel's daughter tried to lock me in a bathroom . . . which, to be fair, I guess isn't the greatest sign, either.' I take a deep, slightly ragged breath. 'Look, I really don't have long, guys, because they'll all be up here in a minute looking for me.' (In fact, I'm pretty surprised, now I think about it, that they're not up here already.) 'So I just need to ask – what the bloody hell do you think I should do?'

'Do?' All three of them echo.

'Yes. Should I get married tomorrow, or shouldn't I . . .? I mean, you know what it's like,' I go on, turning to look at Grace, on the other side of Audrey. 'You remember the night before your own wedding, right, and how all those questions were running through your head. About Clark Gable, and whether you'd made a mistake letting that run its course—'

'Oh, I just adore Clark Gable!' Marilyn gasps, not terribly helpfully. 'You know, when I was a little girl, I used to imagine that he was my father.'

'And I know you were having a few doubts,' I go on, to Grace, 'about whether marrying Prince Rainier was going to make you truly happy—'

'Oh, goodness, no, I wouldn't go so far as to call them doubts,' Grace replies, though there's an edge to her voice that suggests even she knows this is a bit of a fib. 'I was merely taking the opportunity, given that I'd never had a dream like that before, to ask a few searching questions of myself. And, come to think of it, I've never had a dream like that *since* the night before my wedding . . . and now here you are, all over again, in a wedding dress of your own this time.' She puts a rather weary hand to her cheek. 'Is this because I've been so worried about Caroline? She's been so terribly unlucky in love herself, bless her heart, though she does rather compound the problem by making some dreadful choices.'

'No, look . . . it's not about Caroline. It's not about you, Princess Grace, really it's not. Not this time,' I add, because I can see that she's going to put up a time-consuming fight if I insist it wasn't about her the previous times, either. 'I just really need to know what you think. Marry a man I'm not absolutely certain I'm in love with, to stop myself forever hankering after a life with my soulmate? Or go it alone and take the risk that I never get over losing Olly?'

There's silence for a moment.

Then Marilyn and Audrey start to speak at exactly the same time.

'Honey, if I were you . . .'

'Well, darling, if it were me . . .'

'Oh, sorry, Audrey, honey!' Marilyn reaches over me with her Martini-holding hand (*millimetres* away from my Jenny Packham, this time, are the drops of very real-looking cocktail that slosh over the edges of the glass) to give Audrey a little pat on the arm. 'You go right ahead. What you'll have to say is bound to be a hell of a lot smarter than anything I have to say.'

'Don't be ridiculous, Marilyn,' Audrey says, in her gentle, unique voice. 'Your advice is just as valid as mine. More, probably, for someone who falls in love as easily as you do.'

'*Falls in love* is certainly *one* way of putting it,' Grace murmurs, not quite quietly enough for Marilyn not to hear.

'Hey, now, Your Worshipfulness!' Marilyn sounds indignant as she rounds on Grace. 'We can't all be lucky enough to bag ourselves a prince, you know, to get an escape route out of Hollywood!'

'What on earth are you talking about?' Grace snaps back. 'I wasn't looking for an escape route out of Hollywood!'

'Oh, no? Because I sure as hell could use a handsome prince to come and rescue me right about now!'

'Marilyn, that's entirely your affair.' Grace's voice is crisp as ever, but she sounds more upset than I've ever heard before. 'I didn't want Rainier to rescue me from anything, least of all Hollywood! Frankly, I'm still . . . well, I'm rather peeved that I've never been able to go back!'

I can hear, down in the distant regions of the ground floor, raised and concerned-sounding voices.

'Please,' I beg, 'just tell me what you were about to say, Audrey. Tell me what I should do.'

'Oh, darling. I'm never going to tell you what you should do.' Audrey's huge, catlike eyes are fixed on mine. 'All I can tell you is what I'd do. And I'd follow my heart. And never look back.'

And with that, she vanishes. Literally. She just melts into the air around her, as if she's never been there in the first place.

'Hey!' Marilyn sounds even more astonished than I feel. 'What the . . . where the hell did Audrey go?'

'Oh, for heaven's sake, Marilyn, how are you finding this quite so hard to grasp? You're all in my dream, and—'

'Marilyn,' I interrupt Grace, because the voices are getting louder, now, as people head up the first flight of stairs towards us. 'No time for all that. What would you do?'

'Honey, you know what I'd do! I'd marry the guy. I always marry the guy. Sure, marriages have their ups and downs, but at the end of the day, a husband is family. And family's the thing we all want most in the world, right?'

And now it's her turn to vanish. One moment she's there, in all her spangly, lustrous *Marilyn-ness* . . . the next moment, just like Audrey, it's as if she's never been.

'Well!' Grace Kelly says, with a note of impatience in her voice. 'Terribly helpful from both of them, I don't think! Follow your heart; have a family . . . I'm sure they were both trying to help, but this is no time for wishy-washy sentiment. You need clarity. A firm opinion. Is that correct?'

I nod, wordlessly, hearing Joel's voice calling, now, from the floor immediately below the attic.

Grace pulls off one of her pristine gloves and places a cool, slightly powdery hand on top of mine. 'Marrying a man you don't really love,' she says, her bright blue eyes fixed on mine, 'is never going to lessen the ache in your heart for the one that got away. Now, in my particular case, it had its compensations. If I had to go back and live *my* life over again, I'd still do exactly the same thing. At least – ' those eyes waver, for just a second – 'that's how I feel about it most days. I might have the occasional moment of hesitation if you asked me right in the middle of watching somebody else act their little heart out in one of Hitch's movies.'

'Libby?' Joel's voice is at the bottom of the attic stairs, now. 'Are you up there? I'm coming . . .'

'But to anyone else who ever asked,' Grace goes on, hurriedly, 'to you, in fact, my dear dream-girl . . . well, there's only one course of action I can suggest. Don't marry him. Find another way to make your own Happy Ever After.'

Then she, too, vanishes. Gone. In a flicker of an eye.

Her immaculate white glove is, however, still sitting on my lap where she left it.

And now the door is opening, and Joel is standing in the doorway.

'Libby,' he says. 'Oh my God . . .'

He hurries through the storage boxes to reach me, on the Chesterfield.

'The rubble blocked the main entrance,' he says. 'And the kitchen door was locked from the inside. It took five minutes to get one of the chefs to hear us banging on it . . .' He collapses on to the sofa beside me. 'What the fuck?' he goes on, staring at me with wide, shocked eyes. 'How did you manage to pull yourself up like that? We all thought you were . . . well, I thought I saw you begin to fall.'

'I know. I . . . don't know how that happened.'

'No. I mean, I've never believed in miracles before, but that sure as hell looked like one.'

I don't reply to this. I take a deep, deep breath instead.

'Joel,' I say, because I know if I don't get it out straight away, the moment will pass. 'We can't do this.'

He opens his mouth, I think about to ask *what do you mean*. But then he just closes it again.

After a moment, he says, 'Sorry, Libby, but . . . have you been *smoking* up here?'

'No,' I say, truthfully. I scrunch Grace's glove up in my hand, so that he can't see it, and hope that he doesn't notice – as I've just done – that Marilyn's half-empty Martini

362

glass is sitting precariously on the arm of the sofa right next to him. 'I haven't been smoking. It must have been someone else.'

'Right.' He stares at his hands for a moment. 'It's going to be pretty embarrassing,' he goes on, non-sequiturially, 'to send everyone away without a wedding.'

'Yes. Horribly. But that isn't a good enough reason to do it.'

'No, I guess not.' He thinks about this. 'I mean, we could just go ahead tomorrow, give them all what they came for, and then annul it as fast as possible?'

'Do you think that's a good idea?'

'No, I think it's a terrible idea.' He grins at me, ruefully. 'Julia's going to be devastated, you know.'

'Oh, I think she'll be OK.' We sit in silence for another moment. 'I'm sorry,' I add, quietly.

'It's OK. I'm sorry, too. I mean, if I drove you to want to *kill* yourself . . .'

'God, no, that wasn't what . . . it was just a silly accident,' I say, because there's nothing to be gained from getting Julia into any trouble. 'You haven't driven me to anything of the sort. I just don't think either of us is the right person for the other, do you?'

'Oh, I don't know . . .' He can't actually continue this. 'Well, all right,' he concedes. 'I suppose it's possible that I might have gone with my heart on this thing between us, when I should have gone with my head. I mean, I always go with my head. My entire life. It's just the way I am. And I'm pretty sure you always go with your heart.'

363

'I do. For what good it does me. Yes, I do.'

'And I have to ask, just because of what Bogdan just said . . . uh, about this Olly guy . . .'

'Don't worry about what Bogdan said. Olly's . . . out of the equation.'

'The equation being Libby plus Joel equals zero?' But he smiles, again. 'We'll explain it somehow. I'll get the assistants to tell them or something, right? That way we can hide ourselves away and not actually have to face anyone.'

'Well, they are *very* good assistants,' I say.

'They are.' Joel gets to his feet. 'The dress is gorgeous, by the way.'

'Thank you.'

'I would have liked to have married you, in it.'

'Me too. In another life.'

'In another life.' He leans down and gives me a quick kiss on the cheek. 'You should come down and have a strong drink, or something. I can have it sent up to you in your room, if you'd rather not run the gauntlet of . . . well, of my mother? And yours, for that matter.'

'Actually, could you get someone to send something up here, if that's all right? I'd just like . . . to stay here in the quiet for a few more moments.'

'Yeah, sure. Can I bring you anything myself? Blankets?'

'I'm OK, Joel. Thank you.'

I watch him head out through the door, pulling it half closed behind him.

I sit very, very still for a few moments.

But there's no sign – no sign whatsoever – of Grace Kelly, or Marilyn Monroe, or Audrey Hepburn rematerializing on the Chesterfield beside me.

There's just Marilyn's Martini, the smell of Audrey's cigarette, and Grace's white glove, clutched tightly in my right hand.

Chapter 17

So I'm on the early train back to London this morning. And when I say early, I mean early: it's only eight fifteen, and we're already pulling out of the station on our way.

Joel offered – impeccably mannered as ever – to drive me back home himself, but I declined. Things might be OK between us, but that doesn't mean a two-hour car journey would be advisable. Besides, he's got his mum, grandmother and of course Julia to entertain, back at Aldingbourne: all of them (except perhaps Julia) fully expecting, until about eleven o'clock last night, a wedding to take place today.

And I've left this early precisely to avoid the inevitable long, torturous conversations with Mum and Cass that I know for a fact would take place. Mum, as she did late last night, trying to convince me to go ahead with it all 'even if you *don't* really love him, darling! After all, marrying for love is a luxury, really, that I don't think you can honestly afford!' and Cass bending my ear about Nick who – I have to admit – does sound as if he's pretty firmly lodged on her hook, after whatever it was she was doing with him in the garden before she saw me on the roof last night.

In the end, I have to admit, I took refuge in Nora and Mark's cottage for most of the night, because I knew that otherwise I'd be plagued by middle-of-the-night visits from Mum, accompanied by weeping and wailing and gnashing of teeth, in an attempt to wear me down and make me change my mind.

I still didn't get much sleep, though – Nora and I stayed up half the night talking everything over – and the train left the station too early for there to have been any sort of coffee facilities available on a Saturday morning, so I'm feeling thoroughly wiped out. But even though I'd just like to close my eyes and sleep, I should give Nora a quick call now, to let her know I've made it to the train.

I make it a FaceTime call, because I feel the need to actually see her in (sort of) person, to stop my resolve from wavering. And Nora answers, in typical fashion, after only a couple of rings.

'Lib. You're on the train.'

'I'm on the train.'

It's weird, after all the drama of the last twenty-four hours, that here I am having one of those mundane *I'm on the train* conversations. But that feels like about all I'm capable of, as another wave of tiredness swashes over me.

Nora, still in Mark's pyjama top (and looking way better than you'd think possible for a newly pregnant mum of a one-year-old who was up talking to her best friend most of the night) gives me a thumbs up.

'Good,' she says. 'So. You're still in the same place you were last night. You're still comfortable that you're doing the right thing?'

'Leaving Joel? Well, I don't know if I'd go as far as *comfortable*, Nor. I mean, I can't stop thinking about all the people I've let down, and the embarrassment of the last-minute cancellation . . . But yes. I do know I'm doing the right thing.'

'Well, like I said last night, Lib, I know you're doing the right thing too.' Nora glances away for a second, checking on Clara sleeping somewhere out of sight, then says, 'And then there's the other thing.'

'Yes.'

'My stupid brother.'

'Your stupid brother.'

'Look, I'll say it again. You're never going to be able to live with yourself if . . .'

But I don't hear the end of Nora's sentence.

Because Dillon has just sat down in the seat opposite me.

Yes. *Dillon* has just sat down in the seat opposite me.

'Hi, gorgeous,' he says, in a soft voice. 'How are you doing?'

'Who's that?' Nora demands. 'I can hear someone talking to you.'

'Yes. It's Dillon.'

'*Dillon?* Libby Lomax, if you end up . . .'

'I'll call you back later, Nor, OK?' I say. 'I love you, but everything's fine, and you should get some sleep.' I just

368

have time to see her wave a fist at me before I end the call, put my phone down on the table and look directly at Dillon.

'What in the name of God are you doing here?'

'Travelling back to London,' he says, 'same as you.'

'That's not what I meant! Did you get on the train at Barham?'

'No, no, I've been on since Rye. A lovely couple of nights I've spent there, as a matter of fact. Taking in the sea air. Pottering around the antiques stores. Popping into the teashops for a nice scone and a proper cuppa . . .'

'I'm lost. You spent a couple of nights in Rye . . . *why?*'

'Well, I don't know if you've noticed, sweetheart, but there isn't much in the way of luxury hotels in this part of the world. Boltholes suitable for a star of my magnitude. So it was either Rye or Brighton and – if I can be honest – Brighton has rather too many, shall we say, *temptations* for a man such as myself. Bars, nightclubs, scruffy-looking dudes openly dealing drugs on the seafront . . .'

'Dillon.' I lean across the table and fix him with a very firm look indeed. 'I'm not interested in why you chose Rye over Brighton. I'm asking why you were staying down here at all.'

He shrugs. 'To be near the wedding, of course. So that when it all went tits-up at the last minute, I could be nearby to help you.'

'What do you mean, when it all went tits-up?' I croak.

'Oh, Libby, love, it was a disaster waiting to happen, you and that . . . sorry, I've already forgotten his name.'

'Joel.'

'Yeah. Him. It was a disaster waiting to happen. Anyone could see you weren't really in love with him, and that he wasn't really in love with you. Now, obviously it would have been better for you to have properly recognized this before you tried to jump off a roof last night—'

'Bogdan,' I say. 'Bogdan told you.'

'He did. Oh, and he told me you'd be on this train this morning, by the way, in case you were starting to wonder if I was secretly psychic, or something. I mean, I know you realize I'm a pretty multi-talented guy, and you're quite accustomed to me working my magic in the bedroom, but—'

'I wasn't,' I interrupt him, 'trying to jump off a roof. Just FYI.'

'Oh, well, *I* know *that*, Libby.' He rolls his eyes. 'I've never met anyone more committed to, well, *life* than you are.'

'Really?' I swallow, rather hard. 'Even though I keep on screwing my life up?'

'Sweetheart, precisely *because* you keep screwing your life up! I mean, look at you. You had the crappiest career in the world before you turned everything around and became this shit-hot jewellery designer. You set your head on fire with a cigarette and ended up being utterly adored by the guy who had to put you out . . . and I do adore you, by the way,' he adds, in a nonchalant sort of way, 'in case you ever had occasion to wonder. Oh, and then there's your love life. Loads of girls would have just sunk into a pit of despair when they realized they'd have to watch their one true love waltz off into the sunset with someone else . . . but not my Fire Girl. You picked yourself up, dusted yourself down, and bagged yourself a billionaire!'

'Don't take the piss,' I say, quietly.

'I'm not. I admire you so much, Libby, for trying so damn hard to move on. And so what if it all went wrong? You tried, didn't you? Isn't that always the main thing?'

'Theoretically, yes, but in this particular case, me *trying so damn hard to move on* has just led to major embarrassment and all the expense of a cancelled wedding. And it still hasn't worked.' I can feel a little sob rising in the back of my throat, the same sob I managed to swallow down a moment ago. 'I still can't shake off the feelings I have for Olly. I mean, I'm just about managing to keep at bay the feelings of bitterness and regret, because, well, that way madness lies. But, right now, I don't know if I'll ever manage to get over him.'

'Well. Do you have to?'

'What do you mean?'

He doesn't say anything for a moment. Then he reaches into his coat pocket, pulls out a napkin wrapped around something, opens up the napkin and puts its contents – a chocolate croissant and a Danish pastry – on the table between us.

'Hotel breakfast,' he says. 'I took some with me.'

He breaks off a piece of the Danish and hands it to me.

'Look, Libby,' he goes on. 'I know you're never going to be the type of girl to muscle in on somebody else's boyfriend . . .'

371

'Don't,' I say (or more accurately, spray, through a mouthful of Danish: I realize that I am – not surprisingly, I suppose – absolutely starving). 'Honestly, Dillon, I've already had this from Nora last night. Please, don't even go there.'

'Go where?'

'You know what I mean. I'm not that person, Dillon. If things aren't meant to be, with Olly, then I'm not going to scheme and plot to make them the way I'd like them to be.'

Dillon makes a kind of *pshaw* noise with his teeth and his tongue. 'Don't give me any of this bollocks about Meant To Be. I'm Meant To Be dead as a doornail right at this very moment, you do realize? The amount of toxic crap I've shoved into my body over the past ten years, I'm cheating Fate just by sitting here! And what's the better outcome, would you say? Me cold in a grave, just because I accepted my just deserts, or me sitting here right now, dazzling you with my charm and good looks, because I dared to say *I'm not done yet?'*

I don't say anything. I just gaze out of the window for a moment, watching the frosty Sussex countryside racing past.

'So,' I say, through sandpaper lips, 'you'd tell him, then, would you? You'd tell Olly how you felt about him?'

'Oh, sweetheart, I'll *happily* tell Olly how I feel about him. You'd never have to twist my arm to get me to do that! In fact, I'd relish the prospect. *You're an idiot,* I'd tell him, *you're a wanker, you're—'*

'Dillon.'

'All right, all right, I know what you were asking. Yes.'

'Yes?'

'Yes, is the answer to your question. If I were you, I'd tell Olly how I felt about him. No shadow of a doubt. I mean, come on, Libby. He loved you all those years. He put in the time. He paid his dues. So now, don't you think it's time to let him know that none of that time was wasted?'

'But I'm letting him move on—'

'Yeah, and what if he doesn't want to move on? What if he's only moving on as a last resort? Jesus, Libby, wouldn't *you* want to know? I mean, you've only been helplessly in love with him for a year, right? And if your wedding was going ahead this morning, but he'd turned up at the altar, all dramatic and windswept and rain-drenched, and announced that he loved you still, you'd want to know that before you made your decision to marry Joel or not. I know you would. And if you're about to tell me that you couldn't do it to the poor, innocent girl Olly's got himself involved with . . .' He shrugs. 'Bloody hell, Libby, I'd rather rip off somebody else's Band Aid fast, rather than peel it off millimetre by painful millimetre. She doesn't deserve to end up with someone who'd rather be with someone else.'

'But, Dillon, that's all assuming Olly *does* still have feelings for me!'

'So? If he doesn't, he doesn't. Then you can let him marry this other girl with a clear conscience. And – I don't know – head off to the desert yourself and join the Foreign

Legion, or whatever bonkers thing you want to do to get over living the rest of your life without him.' Dillon bangs the palm of his hand on the table, making the pastries jump. 'Challenge Fate at its own game, Libby. Take your own destiny into your own hands. Didn't you ever think that might be the thing to do?'

'Yes. Someone else told me that, too.'

'A person with a history of making good decisions?'

'A person with a history of making . . . the right decisions for herself. And never regretting. And never looking back.'

'Sounds like my kind of gal.'

'Oh, Dillon. You have no idea.'

'Then listen to them, whoever they are! Nobody's suggesting you have to forge your own happiness out of the ashes of someone else's misery. You just need to tell Olly the truth. Let him know your feelings. Then, if things don't shake themselves down to where they're meant to be . . . well, then Fate really *has* won. Until then – and as I like to say to myself every single morning, incidentally, when I open my eyes sober as a nun and ready to start a brand-new day – it ain't over until the fat lady sings.'

I take a deep breath. Inhaling, as I do so, some Danish pastry crumbs, and starting to cough and splutter until my eyes water. Dillon produces a bottle of spring water from another pocket of his coat and passes it to me, watching me rather fondly as I glug most of the contents to wash the crumbs away.

'Better?'

'Better,' I say, putting the bottle down. 'And,' I add, 'I

suppose you're right. It's time, probably, to put my big-girl pants on and think about coming clean to Olly.'

'It is. I mean, obviously I'd *far* rather you were thinking about taking your big-girl pants *off* . . .'

'Bad choice of phrase.'

'No, no, it was an excellent choice of phrase.' He settles back in his seat and half closes his eyes. 'Gives me plenty of food for thought, my gorgeous girl, for the rest of this endless fucking journey back to civilization. I mean, you've no idea how tedious it was in Rye, or wherever the fuck it is I've been hanging about for the last two days. I've even ended up spending three grand on antiques that are being shipped to my flat any day now, just to get through the days. And if I ever have to see another scone again . . .'

'At least you stayed sober.'

'Yeah.' He grins at me. 'At least I stayed sober.' He closes his eyes again, then opens them for a moment to add, 'Oh, and for what it's worth, if you're worrying that it might turn out that Olly *isn't* still head over heels in love with you, I wouldn't. When someone falls in love with you, Libby, those feelings never go away. Trust me, darling, I know.'

This time, when he shuts his eyes, he keeps them closed.

*

I part ways with Dillon at Victoria, a few minutes after our train gets in. He gives me a huge hug, extends an invitation to come and join him at his parents' house in

Ireland for Christmas next week ('Let's face it, Libby, you've just dumped a billionaire. Your mum and your sister aren't going to want to sit across a turkey opposite you without wanting to rip the legs off and beat you to death with them') and tells me to call him after I've had the chance to talk to Olly.

Which, I guess, is what I know now that I have to do.

When he gets back from Durham, that is. I'm queasy enough about the prospect of possibly throwing a hand grenade into Tash's life to begin with; I'm certainly not going to do anything of the sort until after her dad's emergency hernia operation.

Anyway, right now, what's far more important is to think about practicalities. I've got to move my stuff out of Joel's Holland Park house and into . . . where? Dillon – of course – has offered me his place for as long as I need it, and I've already had a few garbled texts this morning from Bogdan telling me that he'll ask his father if my old Colliers Wood flat is tenant-free at the moment . . . I can't tell, with my head so muddled, whether going back there would be a backwards step or whether it might feel like *home*. And maybe none of that matters, and maybe I just need four walls (actually three, if I move back to Colliers Wood) and a roof over my head, and then I can take bigger decisions about—

Hang on, my phone is ringing.

It's a mobile number I don't recognize.

I'd better answer, in case it's someone I've forgotten from the wedding guest-list, calling to ask me some detail about the day. Joel's trio of assistants were all set up to make the cancellation calls, early this morning, to the twenty-odd guests who weren't at Aldingbourne to witness my rooftop theatrics last night, but it's possible that one or two of them might have slipped through the net . . . actually, what am I saying? If Joel's assistants were on the case, none of them will have slipped through the net. Still, I do owe some people an explanation, and the conversation isn't going to get any less embarrassing the longer I leave it.

'Hello?' I say, answering the phone. 'Libby speaking.'

'Libby. It's Tash. I can see you.'

I practically drop the phone in horror.

Does she *know*, already, about my evil plans to speak to Olly? Has she had me followed?

'Relax!' she goes on, in a faintly irritable tone. 'I haven't been stalking you. Nora told me you'd be getting into Victoria around now. I'm in Starbucks. Turn around, I'll wave at you.'

I turn around, on shaky legs, and can indeed see that Tash is sitting just inside the doors of the station branch of Starbucks, a hundred yards away. She waves at me.

'Come over here,' she says. 'I've already bought you a coffee. Cappuccino, right?'

'Er . . . yes . . . a cappuccino . . . but, Tash—'

'Just come over,' she says, abruptly. And puts her phone down.

Well, I suppose this is another big-girl pants moment right here, right now.

When I reach her, half a minute later, she isn't exactly smiling, but she isn't looking massively hostile, either.

'Hi,' she says.

'Hi,' I say.

I wonder if I ought to give her a quick hug, or a kiss on either cheek but, given the tenor of our last meeting, all those months ago at Elvira's flat, I don't know if that's wise.

'This is . . . um . . . thanks for the coffee.'

'That's OK. Sit down, and drink it.' She reaches for a paper bag. 'I bought a couple of muffins, too . . .'

'Oh, that's OK. I mean, I ate something on the train. But thanks, anyway, for . . . Tash, sorry, but . . . aren't you meant to be in Durham right now? I mean, if your dad's having the op today?'

'He's not. Having an op.' She looks at me across the table; she looks tired, with faint rings beneath her eyes; but, other than this, she looks, of course, as fabulous and healthy as ever. 'It's not happening.'

'Sorry – he's *not* got a hernia?'

'No. Well, yes, he has, as a matter of fact, but not one that needs an emergency operation. He's booked in for routine surgery shortly before Easter.'

'Right . . . um . . . then why did you tell Olly . . .?'

'Well, he knows, now, that it wasn't true. That it was sort of a test, I suppose.'

'Sorry – you told Olly your dad was having an emergency op to see how he'd react to the news?'

'No. I told him my dad was having an emergency op so that he'd have a reason not to come to your wedding. I

378

wanted to see how quickly he took me up on it. And I got my answer.'

'What do you mean?'

'Libby, look.' She runs a distracted hand through her blonde hair. 'I barely had to even finish my sentence and he was already telling me we shouldn't come to the wedding. He was seizing the slightest excuse to avoid coming. Anything so that he didn't have to see you walk down the aisle. You know, on account of the fact that he's still in love with you.'

My hand freezes around my cardboard coffee cup.

'Seriously, Libby,' she goes on, with a short laugh, 'I could probably have mentioned that my dad had an ingrowing toenail, or a slightly sore cuticle, and he'd still have been telling you we had to cancel. But, either way, I got the proof I wanted. Which is why, incidentally, I've just broken up with him.'

'You've . . . *what?*'

'Broken up with him. Last night. Well, come on, Libby!' She laughs again, not unpleasantly. 'What would you expect me to do? I'm not going to stay with someone who, deep down, wants to be with somebody else! I'm not going to be anyone's second best! I'm way too good,' she adds, matter-of-factly, 'for that.'

'Yes,' I croak. 'You are.'

'Thank you. So anyway, I called Nora first thing this morning, just to let her know that Olly might need her support, and she told me your news. The wedding being off. Which, sorry about, by the way.'

'No, it's OK. It was . . . the right thing to do.'

'Well, obviously it was the right thing to do,' she says, brusquely. 'You should no more be with Joel Perreira than I should be with Olly Walker. It's all wrong. Right?'

'Yes, it's all wrong . . . but, Tash, I just . . . are you sure? Sure that Olly still feels that way about me?'

'Oh, God, Libby!' Tash takes an impatient swig of her own coffee. 'Didn't you just hear what I said? He couldn't face watching you marry someone else! Isn't that enough? I mean, I didn't sit up with him late into the night holding his hand and drawing out every last morsel of the bloody truth about his feelings, no, but I hardly think that's my job, is it?'

'No. No, it's not.'

'And then there's your bloody cheese thing.'

'Sorry?'

'Well, that's how it all started. When he came to pick me up from the airport the other night. He was all starry-eyed and Love's Young Dream, and going on and on about having found that cheese you and he keep searching the globe for . . . or *maybe* having found it . . . I honestly didn't pay much attention to the details. It's your thing. Yours and Olly's thing. I mean,' she adds, wryly, 'if a girl can't even compete with an ash-covered goat's cheese, she knows she's on a hiding to nothing. You and Olly are so obviously meant to be. And I'm not fool enough to stand in the way of Fate.'

OK, I've always found Tash about as warm and cuddly as a granite rock-face, but now I want to throw my arms around her and squeeze her tight.

'Oh, God,' she says, already shoving her chair backwards as I get up from mine and move towards her, 'no, no. There's no need for all that. There's only one thing I actually want you to do, Libby, and it's certainly not to smother me in gratitude. That isn't why I've done this. All I want is for you to make this thing with Olly happen. Make it work. Because I've not set back all my own plans, trust me, for you two to faff about with each other and never get the deal done. All right?'

'Yes,' I tell her. 'All right.'

'Oh,' she adds, with a more genuine smile than I've ever seen her give me in all the time we've known each other, 'and if you really want to show me any gratitude, you can introduce me to the gorgeous, available billionaire you've just unceremoniously ditched at the altar. I mean, after an appropriate interval, obviously.'

'God, Tash, absolutely, I'll—'

'I'm joking,' she says, though her tone of voice suggests that she wasn't, in fact, joking at all, and that actually she's already got the seeds of Another Plan sprouting in her mind.

Which is, to be fair, good for her. And actually, she and Joel would be a pretty damn perfect couple, now I think about it. His mother would certainly approve of a tall, blonde neonatologist spreading her largesse over the foundation, and Joel needn't have any of his usual worries with women, about Tash being in it for his money – his status, yes, maybe, and definitely his irreproachable sperm, but certainly not his money . . .

381

'Just sort your own life out, Libby, first, OK? You can get around to matchmaking somebody else when you've finally managed to do what you should have done almost twenty years ago.' Tash gets to her feet. 'All right,' she says, reaching down to pick up a Longchamp holdall beside the table. 'Well, I've got to get to Gatwick for a flight back to Scotland. I'd wish you good luck, but I don't actually think you'll need it. So . . . I don't know. Happy Christmas, I guess. And please, make him happy.'

Then, with a brisk, unsentimental wave, she's off through Victoria Station, the milling crowds of pre-Christmas travellers parting before her as she strides, impressively, onwards.

Chapter 18

Yes, obviously I should be in Holland Park right now, packing my worldly goods. Obviously I should be calling Bogdan and seeing where we've landed with his dad and the Colliers Wood flat.

But instead I'm here, at freezing cold Bermondsey Market, looking for the cheesemonger that Olly told me about.

Except that there appear to be at least four cheese concessions here, and the market is vast and appears to be on at least two different sites, and on the last Saturday before Christmas next week, it's pretty packed with people. So finding the correct cheesemonger is proving more difficult than I thought. I queued for almost twenty minutes at the first one before I could manage to ask someone behind the counter to pop and ask the owner if he's a friend of Olly Walker's (no, was the answer, and I wasn't popular for asking the question) and it looks as if I'm going to have to do the same at the second one, where I've already queued for five minutes, watching a very earnest woman being given subtly different Bries to taste by an even more earnest woman, and wondering if this was a good plan in the first place.

I just kind of wanted to turn up to Olly's with the Mystery Cheese, that's all. When I go round there later tonight. I haven't really thought beyond that – Tash would *not* be impressed with my strategizing skills; nor Grace Kelly, for that matter – but part of me just feels that if we have the cheese there with us, the rest of That Conversation, after so many missed opportunities and un-seized moments will just . . . flow?

I don't know.

I don't know about anything any more, to be honest, apart from how slowly the hours are going to go until Olly gets off work this evening. I'm just trying to break the rest of the day down into manageable chunks, so that I don't go out of my mind: first, locate correct cheesemonger. Second, (hopefully) buy Mystery Cheese. Third, go to Holland Park, pack as much as possible. Fourth, have shower. Fifth . . .

I can hear my phone ping with a message. I grab it out of my bag, half expecting to see a text from Tash asking, in capital letters, *WHY ARE YOU FAFFING AROUND AT FOOD MARKET WHEN YOU SHOULD BE TALKING TO OLLY ALREADY???? I CAN SEE YOU, YOU KNOW!!!*

But it's not from Tash (although, I'll be honest, I still wouldn't put it absolutely past her to be lurking somewhere here at Bermondsey, keeping tabs on my progress), it's a WhatsApp from Mum.

384

I suppose, it reads, ever-so-slightly snittily, *you'll be wanting to have Christmas with me and Cass, then?*

I'm not quite sure what to reply to this – or, indeed, whether to reply at all – when a second message comes up.

You probably did right thing, it says. *Even if he was a billionaire. Please never feel need to jump off roof again. Wouldn't know what to do without you. Mum x*

My eyes are suddenly so full of hot tears that I think I'd better leave my place in the cheese queue. Not that the women having their in-depth discussion about Brie would notice, but there's quite a few people behind me by now, and I'd rather go around the corner, collect myself, and then come back and join the end of the queue without anyone staring.

'Oh, God, sorry!' I gulp, to the person I've just bumped into, on their way into the cheesemonger's just as I'm on my way out. 'I didn't see you . . .'

'Libby?'

Through the blur of tears, I can see, now, that it's Olly.

OK, I may not have had a perfectly thought-out plan, but this definitely wasn't part of it. I haven't slept, I never took my makeup off last night, I'm still wearing the leggings I borrowed from Nora and the too-big sweater I borrowed from Mark, and my eyes are red from crying.

'Olly,' I say, in a voice that sounds absolutely nothing like my own. 'I was just . . . I was here for the Mystery Cheese.'

'Me too.' He gazes down at me; he looks pretty short

on sleep himself. 'Hang on, though. Aren't you supposed to be getting married in about two hours' time?'

'Yes. Or rather, no. Hasn't Nora called you yet? Or your parents?'

'No . . . though, Nora has been trying me, but I've not actually had the chance to get back to her yet. I don't understand.' He puts a hand on my shoulder. 'Is the wedding *off*?'

'Yes, it's off. It's really embarrassing. But it's off. Everything's off.'

'And that's what you're crying about?'

'No, I'm crying because I just got . . . well, a bizarrely nice message from my mum. I mean, I assumed she'd be furious about the wedding, but it looks like she gets it. Or, at least, even if she doesn't get it, she's prepared to accept that I've done the right thing.' I blink back a couple more stray tears. 'Sorry, Ol, but you know what my mum's like. This is pretty much a first.'

'I know.' He squeezes the hand on my shoulder ever so slightly. 'You're freezing,' he adds.

'Yes. You too.'

'Yeah, I am pretty cold. Shall we walk?'

'But I was just queuing at this place, to ask them about—'

'The Mystery Cheese? No, this isn't the place that my mate runs. I was just popping in here because they do amazing sourdough bread, and then I was on my way over to my friend's. It's the other side of the market, across Old Jamaica Road . . . shall we head over there now?'

'Yes.' I wipe my remaining tears off my face with my coat sleeve. 'Let's do that.'

'Great.' Olly takes his hand off my shoulder, and we start walking in the opposite direction he's just come from. 'I have, um, a bit of news myself, actually, Libby. Me and Tash have . . . we've split up.'

'I know.'

'You know?'

'Yes. We met up at Victoria this morning.'

I'm not sure, the moment I've said this, whether it was the right thing to say or not. Because now Olly is going to ask why Tash met me this morning, isn't he? And I'm still no closer to formulating what I actually want to say than I was several hours ago.

But there's never going to be a right thing to say, and there's never going to be a right time to say it. After almost twenty years of us never managing to say *anything* to each other, let's face it, it doesn't matter what, where or how it's said. It just needs to be out there.

I shove my hands into my coat pockets, so that I have something to do with them while I start saying whatever it is I'm going to say, rather than waving them around like some sort of lunatic . . . and feel something soft, scrunched up in a ball, inside one of them.

It's Grace's glove.

I wrap my hand tightly around it, for some of her strength, as I start talking.

'Tash told me,' I say, 'why you've split up.'

Olly just blinks at me. He doesn't say anything.

'It's why I'm here,' I go on, my words starting to tumble out, now. 'Trying to find the Mystery Cheese. I had this plan that I was going to turn up at your door late tonight, after you got home from work, and just . . . I don't know . . . wordlessly present you with the cheese. And then you'd look at it, and look back up at me, and this expression of wonderment would begin to grow over your face, and then you'd draw me in through your front door, and. . . the cheese would have to have sort of melted into the background by this point, I guess. I mean, not *literally* melted, like an over-ripe Camembert, or anything, but just seamlessly disappeared somewhere, you know, the way these things happen in . . .'

And I stop. Because this just sounds ridiculous, now. I mean, I know only a moment ago I thought it didn't matter what was said, that it was just important to Get It Out There. But that was before I managed to utter the phrase *an overripe Camembert*. I may not be Shakespeare, or Billy Wilder, but even I know that no grand declaration of true love has ever, *ever* contained a reference to stinky cheese before now.

'In the movies?'

I stare at Olly, who's just spoken. 'Sorry?'

'You were just about to say, *in the movies*, right?'

'Oh. Oh, yes. Yes, I was.'

There's a moment of silence, while we carry on walking. Then, quite suddenly, Olly stops. 'Hang on a sec,' he says.

And he pops through the open front of the unit we've just arrived at.

388

Leaving me standing outside, my mouth open wide from all the silly things I've just thoughtlessly blurted, and my entire body consumed by this agitated, uncomfortable, pricklish feeling, the way I imagine it feels if you don't make it to Heaven and you don't make it to Hell and you're just left in whatever that celestial limbo is called, for the rest of your life.

Purgatory.

Epilogue

Three months later

'Heaven.'

I look at Bogdan; or rather, I look at his reflection in the mirror.

'Really?' I ask.

'Really truly. Heaven,' he repeats. 'Would not be saying this if was not true, Libby, am assuring you of that.'

'OK!' My face breaks out into a smile. A huge smile. 'Well, then, if we're happy with my hair, I can. . .'

'Is just really beggaring question,' Bogdan goes on, with the air of a man considering the really Big Things in life, 'why you are not agreeing to me giving you proper fringe shape months before now. Is taking the years off you, Libby. Is making you look less haggard. Is finally giving you the bones of the cheeks. Is making you look . . .' Touchingly, there's a sudden tremor in his voice, and his places both his huge hands, gently, on top of my dressing-gown-clad shoulders. '. . . Is making you look beautiful, Libby,' he finishes. 'Is making you look like most beautiful bride in all of world.'

Oh, I should say: that's what I am, today. A bride.

A proper one this time. Not one who calls off her wedding at the eleventh hour. Not one who's about to marry the wrong man. A bride, instead, who – at long last – is about to marry the right one. The only one.

Olly.

He's just sent me a text, actually; I can see it's just pinged up on my phone on the dressing table in front of me.

Can't wait to see you. Let's do this. Xxxxxx

There's a very recent text from Dillon on my phone, too, that I've only just seen: *I bet you make a fucking hot bride, Fire Girl. Have a wonderful day, sweetheart x*

I'm about to reply (to Olly; I'll message Dillon another, more appropriate day), just to let him know that I won't be late, or anything, when there's an almighty howl from the back room.

We're at Starz In They're Eye'z (yes, that's how it's written), Bogdan's brand-new salon, a tiny jewel of phenomenal kitsch-ness at the Clapham end of Balham High Street. He only opened a couple of weeks ago, but he's kept this Saturday morning completely free of other customers so that me, Cass, Nora and Mum can have our hair and makeup done here and get into our dresses before taking a smart white taxi-cab along to the wedding venue, a secret garden tucked away near Olly's restaurant in Clapham. The smell of (hot pink) paint is still fresh here at *Starz*, and (hot pink) feathers are still moulting from the brand-new feather boas that Bogdan has artfully draped around all the bulb-lit mirrors, but the place is gorgeous.

Not to mention a testimony to the Moldovan work ethic: Bogdan only 'came out' to his parents about his secret hairdressing career six weeks ago (he's still not come out in any other sense, but I think we're all assuming the hot pink and the feather boas will pretty much take care of that) and after all the shouting and wailing and threats of ignominious return to Chişinău had died down, Bogdan Snr was throwing out the tenant of the tiny corner newsagent that occupied this site and converting it into this salon for his beloved boy. Half a dozen Moldovans hammered and chiselled for three feverish weeks, and now you'd never know this place had ever been anything *other* than a supremely camp boutique hairdresser's, with a nail bar in the back for pamper parties.

The nail bar – currently being used as a dressing room – is where the howl has just emerged from, in fact, and a moment later, the door is thrown open to reveal Cass standing in the doorway.

'Look at me!' she shrieks. 'It's a fucking *disaster!*'

We look at her. She's bursting rather exuberantly out of a flesh pink bustier top, and pleasingly filling the matching ra-ra mini-skirt she's wearing on the bottom. Her hair, piled into a gravity-defying up-do over the last two hours by an exhausted Bogdan, is looking lush and verdant, and unless you count the fact that I, personally, would have left off about six layers of that mascara and most of that ocean of lipgloss, I'm not seeing a disaster.

'Cass,' I say, 'you look terrific. I mean, OK, it's not the

most traditional bridesmaid's look, but I didn't think traditional bridesmaid was what you were going for.'

'You have to be fucking kidding me! Of course it's a
disaster! I've starved myself for almost three whole months,
Libby, ever since you first announced this wedding, and
I've *still* not got a proper thigh gap!' She hoists her tiny
skirt up far enough that we can see the lower slopes of
her nude G-string, and flaps the hem around frantically.
'What should I do? We've got half an hour until the ceremony, right? Should I see if I can fit in a couple of hundred
squats before then? They'll probably be more effective if
I'm doing them in heels, too, so I'm in with a chance. . .'

'Cass, for God's sake. You don't need to do two hundred
squats.'

'Lunges,' suggests Bogdan, helpfully, 'are more effective
on deep inner thigh muscle that am suspicious you are
wanting to be targeting.'

'You know, Bogdan, I think you might be right about
that.'

'Am right. If you are hoping for lean look of Sarah Jessica
Parker rather than hefty bulk of Fedor Kassapu.'

'Who's Fedor Kassapu?'

'Is famous Moldovan wrestler. Is winning gold medal in
Barcelona Olympics. Is my childhood hero. Is proving to
me, in boyhood days, that is OK to be big of the bones,
and that is OK to have the unusual amounts of body
hair. . .'

'Fucking hell!' Cass shrieks. 'No, I don't want to look

like some huge, hairy wrestler! Lunges! I need to do lunges!'

'Look,' I say, 'nobody's even going to *see* your thigh gap . . .'

'Well, of course they're not, because I *don't even have one!*'

'. . . unless you're planning on performing some sort of exotic dance at the end of the ceremony, or something,' I finish – a tiny bit nervously, because it's always possible that Cass *is* in fact planning an exotic dance at the end of the ceremony. Having recently dumped Joel's best man, Nick (who *didn't* turn out to be remotely gay but *did* turn out, unfortunately, to be a tightwad) she's on the prowl for a new man. Olly's friends – unsuspecting souls that they are – won't have the slightest idea what's hit them. 'Come on, Mum,' I add, as Mum emerges from the dressing-room, radiant in the crimson Oscar de la Renta number she maxed-out her credit card on for my *previous* wedding. 'Tell Cass she looks stunning, and to stop worrying about some silly thigh gap.'

'Darling, Libby's right. You do look absolutely stunning. All eyes will be on you, Cass, I absolutely guarantee it.'

'Good to hear,' I say, drily. 'Just what a bride wants to hear on her wedding day.'

'Oh, come on, Libby, you know what I meant!' Mum looks over at Cass, (who's started a routine of deep lunges, using Bogdan's tree-trunk of an arm to help her balance in her teetering heels) to get her support. 'Honestly, Libby, there's no need to turn into a bridezilla. This day's not *only* about you, you know. And it's all very well for you, finally marrying the man of your dreams, but your poor sister is getting absolutely desperate to meet a man worth settling down with. . .'

'I'm not *desperate*, Mum!' Cass hisses at her. 'And if you tell any of the men at the wedding anything of the sort, I swear to God, I'll kill you.'

'Honestly, the pair of you!' Mum throws up her hands in despair at her daughters. 'Where's all this stress and aggression coming from, on a day that's supposed to be filled with joy, and love, and excitement?'

'I'm not stressed, Mum, I promise you.' Because nothing is going to rile me on this longed-for day; absolutely nothing. 'And trust me, I'm brimming with more than enough joy and love for all of us.'

'Yes, yes,' Mum says, distracted already. 'But look, can we just have a quick moment to discuss how green and sick your father's going to feel when he sees how amazing I'm looking these days?' She gives a little scarlet twirl. 'I mean, this is *so* flattering on me, isn't it? I've no idea what his new wife is going to be wearing, but I can't imagine she'll hold a candle to me.'

Which isn't *exactly* the sort of joy or love I thought we were just talking about.

But thank God, it really is time for me to head into the back room myself and get Nora to help me put my own dress on, so I can leave Mum to her gleeful twirling and Cass to her frantic lunges, and go and have a properly bridal moment of my own.

Nora, in the back room, has just finished pulling on her own far more appropriate bridesmaid's dress, a pretty pale grey prom dress that skims her burgeoning bump, and is already heading for my dress, draped over the back of the Chesterfield sofa.

Yes, Bogdan's taken charge of the Chesterfield. Just for now, just until Olly and I find ourselves a new flat together, one with a living room big enough to house it plus all our other combined furniture. Or maybe, just maybe, I'll decide to let Bogdan keep it here instead even when we do find a new flat. After all, thrilled as I'd be to see any of my Hollywood goddesses emerge from its refurbished interior again, it's not as if I actually need any of them now. Marrying the love of your life pretty much puts paid to all that.

'Come on, Lib!' Nora chivvies me. 'It's already half past one, and we don't want to be on the way a minute later than quarter to two! Now, let's get you into your dress. Ohhhhh,' she adds, unable to prevent a little sigh escaping her as she lifts it off the sofa. 'I still can't get over how gorgeous this is, Libby. It's going to make you look like a movie star!'

'Well, I'm not sure about that,' I say. 'But you're right about the dress.'

It's a stunner, all right. I've been incredibly chilled-out about this entire wedding from the moment we decided to do it (the morning after we woke up in Olly's bed together after the day of the discovery of the Mystery Cheese, just FYI) but the one thing I was pretty adamant about was the style of the dress. And this is what, after some serious vintage-store trawling and several visits to a clever seamstress, I've ended up with: a 1950s full-skirted, princess-length number in pure white lace, all the better to set off Grace Kelly's gloves that I'll also be wearing.

Oh, and I've spritzed myself with some of Marilyn's vial of Chanel No 5, and Audrey's tortoise-shell sunglasses are all nestled in my white lace wrist-held bag, just so I can feel as if they're with me today in (no pun intended) spirit.

My grandmother's cathedral-length vintage-lace veil, the one that led to my nasty accident almost two years ago, has been expertly re-fashioned, by the same clever seamstress, into the fly-away veil that I'm already wearing, cleverly pinned into my hair by Bogdan before he put the finishing touches to his Dream Fringe.

'Come on, Nor,' I say, with a smile, as I hear her start to gulp with sobs the moment I step into my dress, and she starts buttoning me up at the back. 'We've got a whole ceremony and reception to get through!'

'Then you should have thought of that before you decided to make me the happiest woman on the planet by marrying my brother!'

'Second happiest,' I point out.

'Oh, God, what are you doing to me?' she howls. 'Besides, I'm *pregnant*, Lib! I won't be held responsible for my hormones.'

'Well, I'm glad I'm making you happy.' I squeeze her hand as I turn round, which only sends her off into a fresh round of sobs, huge choking ones this time that actually send me dashing back into the main salon to find her a glass of water.

At the sight of me in my dress, there are a couple of gratifying sighs of admiration from Mum and Bogdan, and an enraged shriek of jealousy from Cass (which is pretty much the same thing as a sigh of admiration) but there really isn't any time for much more than that. After Nora's sipped her water and blown her nose roughly a dozen times, it's out to the waiting white taxi with all five of us, Cass still lunging every step of the way for maximum toning effect.

Generously by Mum and Cass's standards, I'm even allowed the most comfortable position in the taxi, with Cass and Nora either side of me and Mum and Bogdan opposite. And it's only now that we're actually on our way that I start to get butterflies in my stomach. Because these last three months have been such sheer bliss that I've not had the slightest fraction of a soupçon of a hint of nerves about the Big Day. But, right now, knowing that people are waiting for me to arrive at the Metro Gardens . . . that my dad will be there, that all eyes will be on me, that Olly will get his first look at me in my wedding get-up . . . it's more butterfly-inducing than I'd have thought. I'm just glad, now, that the traffic is pretty light, so there's no stress about Saturday afternoon snarl-ups making us late, and we can whizz easily along Clapham Common Southside towards our destination. We're almost there when Mum starts to get all teary-eyed, too (though I can't help but suspect there's just a *teeny* part of her that's competing with Nora's rivers of emotional tears and – bless him – with

Bogdan's thinly disguised sniffles) and I'm just wondering if there's any chance at all if Cass is going to up the ante and fling herself to the taxi floor in keening hysterics when something out of the window catches my eye.

We're passing *Nibbles*, Olly's restaurant, and Olly himself is at the top of a very precarious-looking step-ladder, a paintbrush in hand, right outside.

So precarious, in fact, that as the taxi pulls to a halt at the nearby lights, I can see that the ladder is wobbling beneath his weight, and looking dangerously close to . . .

'He's going to tip over!' I shriek, and before any of my weeping bridal party can stop me, I've pulled open the taxi door and am leaping out, pretty precariously myself, through a lane of traffic, to his side.

I'm too late, though, because the ladder has in fact tipped, and he's fallen eight feet down to the pavement, landing hard on his backside, before I can reach him.

'Ow!' he yelps, followed by an astonished, 'Libby?'

'God, Olly! Are you all right?'

'Yes. . . I think so. . . my bum hurts,' he says, before glancing down at his beautiful white shirt. 'Oh, bloody hell,' he says, because there's a huge black paint stain smack in the middle of it now, from the paintbrush he was holding – and which is now on the pavement beside him – when he fell. 'This is all Bogdan's fault.'

'Libby!' comes the voice of Bogdan himself, from the taxi. 'What are you doing? Is the terrible luck for the grooming man to be seeing the bridal lady before the wedding!'

'You know what, Bogdan?' Olly says, crossly, getting to his feet. 'It's actually pretty terrible luck for the grooming man to be hiring you the night before his wedding to change the sign above his restaurant! *That's* what's bad luck!'

He points up to where the word *Nibbles* is usually painted above the plate-glass windows.

It says, now, *Libby's* instead.

Or, to be more accurate, it says *Libby'z*.

'Is problem with this?' Bogdan asks, indignantly.

'Yes! I spotted the *z* just as I was leaving the place five minutes ago after checking that things were all set here for us to come back to the reception,' Olly says, with an exasperated glare in Bogdan's direction. 'Bloody hell, Bogdan! It was all meant to be perfect for . . . for *you*,' he adds, suddenly looking down at me instead.

All the exasperation vanishes from his face, to be replaced with an expression of open-mouthed awe.

'My God, Libby,' he utters, after a moment. 'You look . . . Wow.'

'You don't look exactly shabby yourself,' I say.

This is an understated way of saying what I really want to say (but which I feel isn't exactly bridal) which is that he looks, as Dillon might put it if he weren't talking about his arch-nemesis Olly, extremely fucking hot. The paint-spattered white shirt fits his muscular body to a tee, and I can tell it's only going to look even better when he puts his smart charcoal-coloured suit jacket back on over the top. His usually-scruffy hair is . . . well, it's still fighting its natural scruffiness, to be honest, but it looks eminently touchable, and his gorgeous, open face is looking lightly tanned after all this unseasonably warm mid-March weather we've been having.

Olly. My Olly. My very, *very* soon-to-be husband.

'You didn't need to start re-painting signs and re-naming places just for me,' I go on, suddenly feeling slightly shy.

'Oh, Libby. Darling. I just wanted you to have the surprise when we arrived here later on.' He reaches down for my hands and interlaces his fingers through mine. 'This place was always meant to be named after you, so what better time to put it all right than the moment we get back here together as husband and wife? God,' he adds, with a sudden laugh. 'That sounds a bit grown-up, doesn't it?'

Before I can reply, there's a fresh call from the still-waiting taxi.

'Darling, honestly, it really is the most terrible luck for Olly to be seeing you before the ceremony,' Mum yells across the pavement. 'I saw both your father and Cass's father before my weddings, and those marriages turned out to be utter disasters! Of course, you do have to take into account the fact that your father was a complete shit, and Cass's father ...'

'Hi, Marilyn,' Olly calls back to her, manfully taking control of the situation in the way he always seems to manage to do with my complicated family. He even pulls me a little closer towards him, perhaps instinctively signalling to her that he's not about to let me take any crap from her today, of all days. 'You all look great, by the way! But you know what – if Libby's OK with it, maybe she and I will just walk the last little way to the ceremony by ourselves, and see you all there?' He glances down at me. 'I mean, I don't know what you think, Lib, but in my opinion we've already weathered enough bad luck to withstand that kind of superstition.' His hands squeeze mine, gently. 'I'm pretty sure you and I are going to be able to tough anything out, right?'

I smile up at him. 'Right.'

'Oh!' He suddenly looks concerned. 'Unless there are any issues with unsuitable shoes . . .?'

This is why you marry a man like Olly. He thinks about those kinds of details. He thinks, as it turns out, about *me*, before he thinks of anything else.

I go up on tiptoes (not that far, actually, because I am wearing pretty unsuitable heels; heels that I know Audrey and Grace would disapprove of as much as I know that Marilyn would love them) and place a soft kiss on his even softer lips.

'I'd love to walk there with you,' I tell him. 'Let's do it.'

The grumbles from most of the occupants of the taxi (not Nora, who's just started sobbing again) are brought to an end, fortunately, by the fact that the taxi driver takes matters into his own hands and pulls out into the traffic again to drive the last few hundred yards to the venue.

But for now, we're alone.

Olly glances down at his spattered shirt. 'Oh, God . . . should I go in and get one of the waiters to swap shirts with me?'

'No. You look perfect, Olly, just the way you are.'

'Ditto.' He gazes at me, again, with awe. 'Jesus, Libby, am I the luckiest man in the world right now, or what?'

'Oh, I don't know about that. You might be the luckiest man in *Clapham* . . .'

'Better than *that*, Lib! Let's agree that I'm at least the luckiest man in London, OK?'

'Eight million people in London . . . half of them men . . . all right,' I tell him. 'I'll give you that. You're the luckiest man in London.'

'That I am.'

'And I'm the luckiest woman.'

He grins, his handsome face more alive than I've ever seen it in all these years. 'Shall we just agree,' he says, 'that despite everything, somehow you and I have ended up the luckiest *couple*? Because honestly, Lib, I was just thinking this morning about all the ways this nearly went so wrong . . .' He gives a little shudder. 'You know I'm not a religious person, but sometimes I think there must have been *someone* out there rooting for us, somewhere. Don't you think?'

I think of the Chesterfield, tucked away in Bogdan's new nail bar, and I nod, emphatically.

'I absolutely think so, Ol, yes. There was someone rooting for us. Maybe even more than one person.'

'But we got there in the end.' He pulls me a little closer still, and wraps his hands around my waist. 'Better late than never.'

I do likewise, slotting my hands together in the small of his back and feeling my whole body simultaneously

403

explode with desire and relax with contentment as I do so. I'm dimly aware that a middle-aged woman passing us has just let out an audible 'Awwwwwww' at the sight of a fully dressed bride and a smart, if paint covered, groom, snuggling up together in the middle of Clapham High Street.

'*Much* better late,' I agree, 'than never. And you know what,' I go on, 'the more I've thought about it, the more I think it was always meant to be this way. I mean, sure, we could have been together all those years . . .'

'. . . if I hadn't bottled it every time I thought about saying something. . .'

'. . . if I hadn't been incapable of seeing what was staring me right in the face . . .'

'. . . if I hadn't talked myself out of it all the times I thought about just grabbing you and kissing you. . .'

'. . . if I'd just stopped running around in circles trying to fake a big, romantic Hollywood happy ending with the wrong people,' I finish, 'well, then things wouldn't have finished as perfectly as this. Because you never really know what you've got until you've nearly lost it for ever.'

Olly nods. 'Though trust me,' he says, softly, leaning closer to place his forehead against mine. 'I always knew what I had in you, Libby. My best friend. My true love. My soulmate.'

The moment only gets better when he moves his lips to mine, and starts to kiss me.

And better still when a few moments later we break apart and, holding hands, start to stroll along the sunny street towards the wedding venue, where – after all these years – we're finally about to become husband and wife.

As big, romantic Hollywood happy endings go, I don't think it can possibly get any better.

Wherever they are, wherever they came from, I hope that three big, romantic Hollywood heroines are very proud of me.

A Q&A WITH
Lucy Holliday

Hi Lucy, we can't believe your brilliant series has come to an end *sob*! Are you going to miss Libby and the gang?

I'm going to miss them terribly! Stupidly, I don't think I'd realized quite how much until I typed the final word of the final chapter of the final book. It had been a pretty intense experience meeting the deadline, so I assumed I'd be relieved when I made it over the finish line. The moment I finished I drooped miserably downstairs to find my husband, who was expecting me to be ecstatic and had a nice celebratory supper waiting. Suffice it to say he was pretty bemused when I spent the whole meal lamenting the fact it was all over, and that I'd never get to write about Libby or Dillon or Bogdan again.

How did the idea to conjure Hollywood's most fabulous starlets in Libby's hour of need come about?

I just really liked the idea of a kind of modern-day fairy godmother and have always worshipped Audrey Hepburn in particular. I'm not sure I had ever wondered before what it would be like to be friends with her, but I started thinking about some ideas for these books only a few months after my daughter was born and I was VERY sleep-deprived. From sleep deprivation (apparently) comes inspiration! I sort of began to put a few unconnected thoughts together in my muddled mind, and *A Night in with Audrey Hepburn* is what came out of it.

If you could have your own Hollywood fairy godmother, who would it be?

I think it would have to be Audrey, actually. Sorry, I know that's a boring answer, but... well, wouldn't everyone want her as a fairy godmother if they could?

Libby isn't stranger to the odd cock-up or misdemeanour. Do you think we can learn a lot from her? Do the mistakes help to shape her in the end?

Yes, I think that the mistakes we make in our twenties and early thirties (or even longer, for some of us, come to think of it...) are the things that end up shaping us. One thing I very much enjoyed about Libby, as she came out on the page, was that she struck me as a person who, no matter what her mistakes, didn't seem to live a life feeling embittered or full of regrets. Yes, she keeps messing up. Yes, her sister is the golden child who can do no wrong. Yes, she's hopeless at relationships. But still nothing really seems to daunt her. She doesn't shout it from the rooftops, but in her own way she's pretty steely, and I think the dreadful mistakes and cock-ups she does make are really just things that make her stronger still.

Tell us a little bit about your writing process. Do you have a particular place you like to work? Do you like to stick to a set routine?

Yes. I get up at a leisurely hour, take a long bath with oodles of Laura Mercier bath products, waft down to the kitchen where I make myself a perfect single espresso, before taking a gorgeous fruit plate up to my pristine study, where I spend a productive few hours tinkering with what I wrote the day before and then... oh, hang on, I have a three-year-old daughter, so my routine looks absolutely nothing like that. I basically hurl her in the direction of afternoon pre-school, or doting grandparents, or (more often than not) her bed in the evenings, before sprinting to the computer and writing like a demon until I feel less panicked and guilty about not meeting my word count for the day. I'd love a more sedate pace, and I'd REALLY LIKE MORE HOURS IN THE DAY, PLEASE, but on the positive side, my daughter is actually a huge source of inspiration and I actually don't think I'd have written these three books without her around. I started when she was a tiny baby and now she's a diva to rival any Hollywood goddess herself, so I feel like she has grown up with this trilogy.

What kind of books do you like to read yourself? Any favourite authors?

Currently, most of the books I'm actually managing to read are children's books (!), so may I just thoroughly recommend Dr Seuss and anything illustrated by Nick Sharratt... When I have more time, I read anything and everything. I do actually love some amazing YA stuff – Patrick Ness and David Levithan spring to mind. I always, always adore Marian Keyes and would read the telephone directory if she decided to re-write it one day. I love Sophie Kinsella (who doesn't?) and Jojo Moyes. And if I'm in the mood for something a bit weightier, I'm never anything other than gripped by the novels of Hilary Mantel.

You've created some fantastic, memorable characters – the slightly hapless but lovable Libby; the eccentric Bogdan; Dillon the lothario... who was the most fun to write? And do you see yourself in any of the characters?

Bogdan, Bogdan, Bogdan. He was the most fun to write. If ever I got bogged down with difficult parts of the book, I'd set off on a Bogdan tangent just to cheer myself up. There are dozens of scenes featuring him that never even made it to Draft 2 or 3, let alone the final version, because he was just a blast to write. Dillon was a pretty close second (also partly because I have a bit of a crush on him) and Cass was always enjoyable to write too. In a different way, I really loved writing Nora, because I loved thinking about the history she and Libby had together. Olly was very, very hard to write, because their relationship is so complicated, and he got more difficult as the series went on. He was enjoyable, but in a different way.

As for whether or not I see myself in the characters... I can be quite a lot like Libby, because I've always been a hopeless dreamer and romantic. But she's very much a mix of me and friends of mine (no names!), and of course a huge amount of her just exists only in my head.

And finally, we have to ask, if you could ask four celebrity guests (past or present) to a dinner party, who would they be?

I love this question. We tried this out one family Christmas, asking everyone at the table their dream dinner guests, and I think my poor husband was rather disheartened to hear my list, which was something along the lines of Daniel Craig; Christian Bale; Brad Pitt; Idris Elba... But with my sober hat on, and thinking about it FAR more seriously (obv) I'd have to say... Ava Gardner (not one of the goddesses I wrote about, but I think she'd be a hoot); Jennifer Lawrence; Michelle Obama and Angela Lansbury. I think that could make for quite an extraordinary girl's night in. And Angela Lansbury could sing the *Beauty and the Beast* soundtrack to us all after we'd all had too much to drink and started to wallow. I wouldn't say my three Hollywood icons of Audrey, Grace and Marilyn because I feel like I already know my own versions of them now from these books, and I'm happy leaving them where they are.

Thanks so, so much to everyone who's read and enjoyed them! xxx